Rosalind Miles is a writer and lecturer who lives in Warwickshire with her husband and two children.

D1147338

Also by Rosalind Miles

ROSALIND MILES

Return to Eden

Futura

A *Futura* Book

Copyright © Eden Productions Pty Ltd 1984

First published in Great Britain in 1985 by
Futura Publications, a Division of
Macdonald & Co (Publishers) Ltd
London & Sydney

RETURN TO EDEN
Taft Hardie Group Pty Ltd presents a McElroy & McElroy Production
Produced by Hal McElroy
Directed by Karen Arthur
Starring Rebecca Gilling, James Raine, Wendy Hughes and
James Smillie
Adapted from the mini-series RETURN TO EDEN created by
Michael Laurence

ISBN 0 7088 2925 2

Typeset, printed and bound in Great Britain by
Hazell Watson & Viney Limited,
Member of the BPCC Group,
Aylesbury, Bucks

Futura Publications
A Division of
Macdonald & Co (Publishers) Ltd
Maxwell House
74 Worship Street
London EC2A 2EN
A BPCC plc Company

Alas! the love of women! It is known
    To be a lovely and a fearful thing,
For all of theirs upon that die is thrown,
    And if 'tis lost, life hath no more to bring
To them, but mockeries of the past alone,
    And their revenge is as the tiger's spring,
Deadly and quick and crushing – yet as real
    Torture is theirs: what they inflict, they feel.

Lord Byron – *Don Juan*

Chapter One

As dawn broke like fire over Eden, the old man lay dreaming his last dream. In the great oak bed of his forefathers he dreamed a dream of triumph, for he strove all night, then at last grunted with satisfaction, smiled to himself, and wrung the hand that held his as if to seal a bargain. For Max Harper, veteran of a thousand victorious struggles against nature and her elements, men and machines, it was a fitting way of taking leave of a crowded life. Afterwards he breathed lightly but easily. He became quiet and serene, his features soft and relaxed as they had never been in life.

For the girl at his bedside the nightmare was only just beginning. The long velvety scented hours of darkness passed by bringing in their wake a rising tide of dread. Panic broke over her like a great wave. 'Don't go,' she prayed, 'don't leave me, please don't go . . .' At first the tears had come so freely that she thought she would never be able to stop weeping. But after the dragging hours of the night vigil, she had cried herself out and now her whole being was reduced to a twisted knot of pain around her heart. Feverishly she sought relief in low muttered questions, demands and expressions of hopeless love for the still figure: 'How can I manage without you . . .

'Without you there's nothing. You've been everything to me. It was your smile, your hand I reached for, not Katie's; your coldness, your absence I dreaded; your face I knew better than my own. But I never knew *you* – don't go before I have a chance to, when I need you so much . . .'

The doctor looked at his watch and nodded to the nurse. Unobtrusively she slipped from the room to give the signal for the last act of the ritual. From all over the vastness of Australia's Northern Territory, by car, landrover, heli-

7

copter and light airplane, the friends, acquaintances, and business associates of the dying magnate converged on Eden. They gathered in the dark-panelled library of the great stone house, excited as men are by the approach of death, and hovered there under the portrait of the man whose life and work first brought them together, and whose passing united them once more. They were tense but not afraid. Max Harper had secured the future as he had always controlled the past.

Outside in the gathering heat of the dusty forenoon a group of Aboriginals from all over the station kept a patient watch. Yowi, the spirit who warns of the nearness of death, had breathed into the ear of the one in their tribe wise enough to hear such whispers. So they had drifted in for the final hours, to honour an old man's last dreaming. Now in the hot still day they stared unblinking at the magnificent old homestead, at the planes, the two helicopters, and the unusual number of parked cars, all covered with a thick layer of dust.

Silence blanketed the landscape. The burning sun beat down relentlessly. But even the two youngest members of the group, the brothers Chris and Sam remained motionless. They waited with fatalistic resignation, for they knew what was going on inside the house and their souls were ready to accept the inevitable. By their age-old communion with all living things, they knew the moment when Max Harper slid out of this life into the limitless regions of space, the home of the All-Father himself, to find beyond death the new creation.

Inside the darkened bedroom the oppressive stillness was broken only by the shallow breathing of the big man in the bed. Suddenly he gave a deep sigh that ended in a gasp as his last breath left his body. The doctor quickly stepped forward and released the old man's heavy hand from the girl's grasp. With professional detachment he checked the pulse, felt it gone, and laid the arm down on the bed. His eyes met the wild questioning in the girl's, and he nodded slowly, just once.

8

As if in a dream the girl moved forward, and without a sound knelt down beside the bed. She took the dead man's hand in hers, kissed it and brushed it lightly against her cheek, holding it there for a moment. At the familiar touch of the warm rough muscular hand the tears began again, slowly and painfully. But her face was set and still. She would not now allow herself to weep.

After a while she rose, brushing the tears from her cheeks. With a final long glance back at the man in the bed, she moved to the door and walked stiffly down the hallway. Through the window she dimly noticed the mourners outside. Squatting in the dust one of the Aboriginal women cried out, her hand clutching her head. In a liquid guttural she began a chant, and the others took it up.

'Ninnana combea, innara inguna karkania . . . O Great Spirit, All-Father, the swamp oaks sigh and weep, the gum trees shed tears of blood, for darkness has come upon one of your creation . . .'

Soothed by the chant, she brought her emotions under control and entered the library. Her presence gave the signal they had been expecting to the men waiting there, and at once the conversation died. All faces turned towards her. Each one of these men possessed the quality of assertive individualism that would make him stand out in a crowd. But first among equals was Bill McMaster, managing director of Harper Mining and its subsidiary companies. Immediately he detached himself from the company and came towards the forlorn girlish figure in the doorway. His craggy face puckered with compassion, he took her arm inside his and making small unintelligible sounds of comfort drew her gently into the group.

From the back of the room Katie, Eden's house-keeper, came up with a silver tray holding glasses of foaming champagne. Her normal cheerfulness quite suspended, she could not look at the girl she had known from babyhood, but contented herself with silently dispensing the drinks

9

without a word. Taking a deep breath, the girl confronted the men with outward calm, raising her glass in a toast.

'To Max Harper. My father. May he rest in peace.'

As they drank, Bill McMaster stepped forward. Centre stage, he lifted his glass to the huge portrait of Max that dominated the room and all the men in it as they stood there with the girl.

'To Max Harper!' he began. 'He was a bloody good boss, a bloody old tyrant and a beaut bloke. He was one in a million. What he didn't know about mining wasn't worth knowing. We all owed him everything. We still do. Whatever we did for him we'll do for you, girlie. We're right behind you. As long as there's a Harper at the head of Harper Mining, we'll all be doing OK. So raise your glasses again please boys – this time to Stephanie Harper. May she prove to be a chip off the old block, and may Harper Mining continue to prosper and flourish with *her* at the helm!'

'Stephanie Harper' – 'to Steph' - 'Stephanie' –

The toast went round. Numb and aching, Stephanie only half heard the words. But the message spread through her consciousness like ripples on a clouded pool. The King is dead – long live the queen. Here? Here in Eden where my father was king? She threw back her head in fear. Above her the portrait of her father glowered in vivid oils. Stephanie caught his eye, that well-known hawk-like stare, and was lost.

'No!'

The scream ripped from her, shocking the bystanders, terrifying herself.

'I can't! I can't! I can't!'

Trembling uncontrollably, brushing aside the outstretched helping hands she backed away, turned and raced out of the house. Blindly, like a thing possessed, she made for the stables. The Aboriginals watched impassively as she flew down the long drive at a dangerous gallop, out through the gates of Eden and into the sanctuary of the measureless wastes of rolling scrubland beyond. Only there could she be herself. Only there could she vent her grief. Onward and onward powered the mighty black stallion, the pounding of his hooves in tune with the rhythm of her throbbing heart. Rider and horse were near exhaustion when she finally paused in the great emptiness to hurl her reproaches at the wide uncaring sky. The brown sun-burned landscape stretched from horizon to horizon, dwarfing the wild-eyed sweating stallion and the tousled dust-covered girl, standing in her stirrups on the rearing horse to sob and scream, 'Daddy, daddy, how could you – I need you so, how could you do this to me, how could you leave me so alone –'

'Stephanie? Steph, where are you?'

With a start Stephanie came to. She could hear a light footstep on the stair and in a second Jilly entered the bedroom.

'Where were you, Steph? You were miles away.'

'Yes – literally miles – I was thinking about Eden.'

'Eden?' Jilly glanced round the luxurious bedroom and playfully assumed an affected British butler voice. 'This is the Harper Mansion, modom, in Sydney, not the country seat of the family.'

'Oh Jilly, it's so good to see you.' And feeling uncomfortably close to tears, Stephanie threw her arms round her friend.

Jilly was the first to disengage from the embrace, holding Stephanie at arm's length and regarding her shrewdly.

'Looks as if you could do with a bit of cheering up,' she said gently. 'What's up, kid?'

'Oh, nothing.' Stephanie blushed with painful self-consciousness. 'It's just that I was thinking about –'

Jilly followed her gaze to the oversize photograph of Max in its elaborate silver frame on the bedside table. She laughed in affectionate mockery.

'Stephanie Harper, I'm ashamed of you! You're not supposed to be thinking of your father on your wedding day!'

'I think of him every day,' replied Stephanie simply.

It was true. Max's presence, his hold over her life, seemed almost as powerful now as it had been seventeen years ago when he died. Jilly nodded.

'He ran your life for you, that was it. Sometimes I think he didn't let you have enough room to grow by yourself. There's a lot more to you than you've ever had the chance to let out – a lot more, kiddo. Maybe now's your chance!' And with an impish grin Jilly raised her glass of champagne.

She was rewarded with an answering smile on Stephanie's face. That's better, she thought. If only you knew how lovely you can look when you smile, you'd wear a permanent grin like the Cheshire cat. But she knew better than to make the shy Stephanie conscious of her looks or behaviour. She knew too the subject calculated to make Stephanie radiant with joy.

'So tell me about the lucky man,' she began. 'Is he like Max? Is that the source of the fatal attraction? He must be a bit special, for a whirlwind romance like this.'

Stephanie glowed. 'Oh Jilly, he *is*. He's absolutely wonderful. I suppose he is a bit like Dad – he's strong and determined. But he's kind, too, and considerate – and he makes me so happy . . .'

Jilly looked at her carefully. There was no doubting the truth of what Stephanie said. She was brimming over with love and happiness. Her face, which normally wore such an anxious and self-deprecating look so that casual observers thought her plain, was transfigured. Her eyes were shining and her mouth, often sad and pinched, was full, open and smiling, revealing her perfect white teeth. My God, you could be beautiful! thought Jilly with a deep sense of shock.

At that instant a worm of jealousy began to stir within her. Confused and obscurely distressed, Jilly forced a bright smile and tried to concentrate.

'Well, if you don't finish getting dressed, you won't be

12

ready for him till next Wednesday week! Let me help you.'
And taking her friend by the arm, Jilly led her to her
dressing table and sat her down before the mirror.

Stephanie flushed again, this time with pleasure. She
took Jilly's hand and squeezed it warmly. Jilly had always
been so good to her, ever since they were little girls
together. She was so lucky to have one good friend.
Suddenly a thought struck her.

'Jilly, how terrible! I haven't even said hello to you
properly yet. How are you? How was your trip?'

'Plenty of time for all that when we've caught up on
you,' replied Jilly briskly. She crossed the room to the bed
and picked up a jacket lying there. Chanel-style, in heavy
hyacinth blue silk, it echoed the colour of Stephanie's eyes
and would certainly flatter her figure. She turned back to
the dressing table and helped Stephanie on with it.

'Now put me in the picture, will you, Steph?'

Stephanie gave a happy laugh.

'What do you want to know?'

'Everything!' cried Jilly dramatically. 'My God, when I
got your telegram I nearly fainted. I pop off on vacation
for a few weeks, and as soon as my back is turned, bingo!
You're in love and about to get married again.'

'Six weeks,' corrected Stephanie. 'I've known him for
six weeks.'

'Well, let's face it, it's still happened very fast. Steph –
are you absolutely certain you're doing the right thing?'

Stephanie let out a peal of joy.

'I've never been more certain of anything in my life!'

'How did you meet him?'

'On a tennis court, of course.'

Jilly gave an ironic grin.

'Where else would you meet a tennis champion? Ask a
silly question . . .'

'It was a charity match,' Stephanie went on, her
enthusiasm kindling again. 'I was there because Harper
Mining was one of the sponsors. Afterwards he asked me

to play a game to relax him – and would you believe it? He let me beat him! Wasn't that terrific?'

'Sounds as if you were a dead duck from the word go,' said Jilly, trying to keep the caustic out of her voice. 'Why didn't the pair of you just run away to the woods? You don't need this big wedding. You don't need me or anyone.'

Stephanie looked up from her mirror, where she was carefully applying a neutral foundation makeup, shock and hurt in her eyes.

'Oh Jilly! I needed you here today, *you* more than anyone. For once in my life I've got something good, and I've got to get it right. And I need your help. I really do.'

'Wild horses wouldn't have kept me away,' Jilly reassured her. 'Least of all that last-minute airline strike. New York was boring anyway. Wrong time of the year. I only went along for the ride, because Phillip had to be there. Should've known better.'

'Did Phillip mind coming home early?' Stephanie was delicately tracing just a hint of blue eyeshadow on her lids.

Jilly's expression hardened, and a shadow of derision passed across her face.

'My dear, you know Phillip never argues! That's far too undignified for him. Anyway, he'd finished all his business. We were about to fly down to Acapulco for our last week and try to find some life mingling with the jet set. Between that and the wedding of the year, as the papers seem to have dubbed it – no contest!'

Stephanie smiled nervously, and again sought her friend's reassurance.

'Yeah – I've read the papers. I know what they're saying –' she paused, and holding up her left hand checked the charges off one by one on her fingers – 'that Greg is marrying me for my money, *of course* we expected that from the start, that's an old one by now – that he's years younger than I am – that he's finished in tennis anyway and I'm his retirement insurance – that he has a terrible reputation where women are concerned –'

14

'He has indeed,' said Jilly quietly.

'But Jilly, I don't care,' Stephanie burst out. 'It's amazing. Here's me, a woman who has always worried so much about what other people think. This time, I'm so crazy about him, I don't mind.' She turned back to the mirror and continued to make up her face with renewed firmness, speaking in a passionate rush.

'I just can't get over my luck, Jilly. He loves me, he really does. There are some things a man can't fake.' She paused to blot her unobtrusive pink lipstick on a tissue. 'And after all, who am I to judge him? With two broken marriages behind me, I'm in no position to criticize. I died the death over those two, you remember. As if it matters now to anyone but me. I'm not a kid anymore, either – with forty on the horizon, how much longer have we got?'

Through the mirror Stephanie noticed Jilly bridle and move across to the side table to refill her glass of champagne.

'Oh, I don't mean you,' she added hastily. 'You're younger than I am, and besides, you've got Phillip. And you've always been so much more attractive than me, more poised, slimmer –' Stephanie faltered, and unconsciously started to smooth down her jacket, as if to flatten the heavy breasts she had always been sensitive about. Then, gathering courage, she plunged on.

'Anyway, you've always been lovely and you always will be. For myself, I doubt very much if I'm one of those women whose looks will improve with age. Whatever his reasons for marrying me, I'm just grateful that he wants to, that's all.'

Stephanie's eyes were clouded with anxiety now, and her mouth set in that sad little line Jilly knew so well. She crossed over and put an affectionate arm around the drooping shoulders.

'Hey, come on,' she said softly, 'where's the famous fighting Harper spirit? You've had your lousy luck. You were due a lucky break, that's all.'

Stephanie's smile broke like sunshine after rain.

'D'you remember when we were little girls how we used to dream of marrying a handsome prince when we grew up? Well, Greg is mine. It took a while, but he finally showed up. And he's been worth waiting for.' She turned to Jilly with determination. 'I want him – more than anything in my life. And I happen to believe that he cares for me, too.'

Jilly regarded her seriously for a moment, then gave her an understanding smile.

'Well, he's certainly very different from your other two,' she said lightly. 'First a Pommie aristocrat, then an American research scientist – you do pick 'em! D'you realize, Steph Harper, that this is the first authentic, genuine, all-the-way-through dinki-di Aussie you've chosen? Not that I didn't love the Honourable Whatsis-name – but he had no staying power. And then your Yankee boffin – you have to admit, it's been a chequered career, my dear.'

Stephanie frowned uneasily, but concentrated on trying to fix her earrings in place. Large, high-quality sapphires surrounded by diamonds, they had always been favourites, but now she was racked by doubt. Were they the right blue to go with the suit? She was longing to ask Jilly. But Jilly was holding forth quite regardless.

'For a much-married woman, you're a dark horse, you know. Let me see. First you departed to England in a puff of smoke, when you'd hardly ever before been away from Eden, and came back with a Pommie husband and a baby daughter. Then, before I'd had even the first of my seven-year itches with Phil, it was off with the old and on with the new – how long did Dennis's father last?'

'*Don't*, Jilly, please don't.' Stephanie was fiddling furiously with the catch of her pearl necklace, obviously unhappy. 'This is a new start for me, OK?'

Regretfully Jilly abandoned the fascinating topic of Stephanie's past. Setting down her glass, she gave a hand to fasten the necklace, then gently straightened the attractive puritan-style lace collar of Stephanie's blouse.

'So it's third time lucky, eh?' She looked at her watch. 'When he comes.'

'Yes, it is, Jilly, it is!' Stephanie glowed. 'Greg's a good man, believe me. You'll like him, you'll *love* him, you really will.'

As the white Rolls-Royce Corniche convertible snaked up the winding streets and avenues making towards Sydney's Darling Point, its driver was raging with cold fire.

'What kind of a dick-head is late for his own wedding?' he muttered furiously.

'Your kind, Greg,' replied his best man equably. He had been cooling his heels in the bridegroom's flat for an hour and a half, and saw no reason to pull his punches.

'You wanted to make an entrance – keep 'em all waiting – tease her a little, am I right? Go on, admit it. You didn't want to feel like Stephanie Harper's lap dog, with a bow around your neck, up there begging to be married to her just because she can buy and sell us all ten times over.'

'Will you shut up!' hissed Greg between clenched teeth, gripping the wheel tensely as he threw the Rolls round a dangerous bend in the road. 'I don't believe this – it's my wedding day, and I'm getting all this hassle from a no-good tennis bum –'

'I beat you last week!'

'For the first time.'

'But maybe not the last, mate – not the last.'

Greg fell silent, brooding. It was true, and it had been an unpleasant shock. He had never had any problem holding Lew Jackson, his junior by five years, at bay before. It was one thing to go down to the big brats like McEnroe. But to a kid he could remember when he couldn't even hold a racquet straight . . . Greg shivered imperceptibly in the humid air. They were moving up on him all right. Wise move to get out now – in style –

His train of thought was interrupted by Lew, obviously feeling that to triumph over a groom on his wedding day was not in the best of taste.

'It was your leg beat you, not me,' he asserted off-handedly. 'You've had bloody bad luck with that knee, Greg.'

Or good luck, thought Greg with secret amusement, to have something to blame every defeat on, yet which also added lustre to every victory, as wincing with simulated pain he smashed the final ball past his defeated opponent . . .

'No whingeing, mate,' he said out loud, magnanimously. 'Let's leave that to the Poms. Fair and square victory. You're a rising star. Why else would I pick you for my best man? Can't have any tired old has-beens at the wedding of the year, can we? There'll be enough of those on Stephanie's side – the board of Harper Mining for a start!'

Lew laughed delightedly, and punched Greg on the shoulder. You couldn't help liking the bloke – always had something to say for himself, never stuck for any easy pleasant answer. Covertly he studied the classically regular profile, the thick fair hair springing away from the brow, the strong golden-brown hands on the wheel. God, if you were a girl, you could really fancy Greg Marsden, he decided. No wonder all the tennis groupies were crazy for him. That little French girl had had ants in her pants for him so bad that she'd moved heaven and earth to get at him. Hot stuff, too, so the word went – kept it up all night and most of the next day. No wonder he'd lost the Classic the following evening . . . Lew smiled to himself. Well, just as well Greg'd sown his wild oats. There wouldn't be much of that ahead for him with Stephanie Harper. Oh, she was a nice woman all right. But as a partner for a man who'd be a gold medallist in the Sex Olympics any day – sooner you than me, Greg.

Through a combination of brilliantly dangerous driving and an intimate knowledge of the street map of Sydney, Greg had caught up on some of the lost time. He was feeling more cheerful as he covered the last couple of miles, and hurled the great motor up the tree-lined avenue towards the Harper mansion. Set on a prime site above Sydney harbour, this had been a triumphant expression of Max Harper's might and magnificence. He had built the huge white house as his Sydney home when his business and its subsidiaries had expanded eastwards out of the Northern Territory and become more and more focused on Australia's business capital.

Now, the grand waterfront home was one of the principal private residences of Sydney. With mature trees providing shade from the noonday heat, well-tended lawns sweeping down to the waterside, and elegant, well-appointed rooms, it was the epitome of gracious living. Greg thought ahead to the vivid sun-drenched garden, the ranging verandahs and cool interiors, the glass of chilled champagne and the respectful welcome awaiting him. That was the life. That was what he was entitled to, that and plenty more like it. And it was all within his grasp. His spirits soared.

But Greg's good humour vanished in an instant as he rounded the corner of the road that led up to the mansion. Outside the gates, between the parked Mercedes and Ferraris of the guests, a large crowd of reporters and newsmen blocked the pavement and spilled out into the road. All the instantly recognizable hacks he was familiar with from the tennis circuit were there, plus a bevy of hackettes and harpies from the glossy magazines. In addition there were a number he had never seen before who must be from the news agencies or overseas publications – and a gaggle of lissom, sun-bronzed groupie girls come to give their hero a send off, among them –

'Sweet Jesus fucking Christ!' – that wasn't the French girl in the red dress at the back? Greg broke into a cold sweat and the rage awoke again deep inside him.

'Steady on, Greg.' Lew was taken aback by the vicious oath and threw him a warning stare. 'Remember the old Aussie definition of foreplay, mate, "brace y'self"? Y'don't piss on the press, remember.'

With an effort Greg swallowed the advice and nodded. By the time they had covered the distance he had mastered himself and, as they came into view of the crowd, a pleasant relaxed smile played over his features. The Rolls slid to a halt, blocked by the bodies at the gates, and the vultures descended.

'Here he comes,' called a female reporter, forcing her way to the forefront of the jostling mob, tape-recorder at the ready. 'Now Greg, how does it feel to be marrying Australia's wealthiest woman?'

Greg treated her to his special smile.

'Fan-tastic!' he drawled.

'We were beginning to think you wouldn't make it, Greg.'

'Blame the traffic. And my best man here – he kept me waiting.'

'How come the press have been barred from the wedding?' This was the truculent demand of a disgruntled newshound from an international agency. Greg shrugged disarmingly.

'Sorry about that. I appreciate it's bound to be disappointing for you boys and girls. Fact is, Stephanie wanted it to be kept to family and friends. She's not used to the press like I am. And I hope she's marrying me, not my fans.' He smiled apologetically. Keep 'em sweet, he thought, just keep 'em sweet. It's so easy when you know how.

A photographer was busying himself taking shots of the gleaming white Rolls with its distinctive 'TENNIS' numberplate.

'Nice car,' he said admiringly. 'Wedding present?'

'Yep', replied Greg coolly, 'that's right.'

Out of the corner of his eye he could see one of the queen harpies shoving her way through to the car door. For the first time he regretted that the open top of the convertible left him so vulnerable to the outside world and wished he could just buzz up an electric windscreen to close in her face. Here she came.

'For the benefit of my readers worldwide,' she demanded, 'what's your response to critics who say you're marrying Stephanie for her money?'

This was an old one already, and Greg handled it without a flicker.

'Doesn't worry us. They can say what they like. As long as I can make Stephanie happy.'

'So it really is a love match then?'

'Absolutely. And I can recommend it to anyone.'

Nice one, Greg, thought Lew admiringly. He really could turn on the charm when he wanted. Not much more to put up with now.

'What about your career, Greg?' This was the voice of one of the leading tennis journalists, a man who had followed Greg's progress since he'd been a raw and lanky kid fresh out of nowhere with a stunning combination of power and grace and a ferocious frenzy to win at all costs. 'Does this mean the end of tennis for you?'

Greg looked hurt. 'No way, mate, no way.'

'But you've got to admit you've been having problems with your form over the last year. Bluntly, it hasn't been up to scratch, has it? Too much of . . . the good life, maybe, Greg, know what I mean?'

Greg's fingers burned on the driving wheel with the impulse to smash the leering journalist in the mouth. He forced himself to remain calm, and fought off the powerful impulse to look back over his shoulder at the tennis groupies to see if that was the French tart after all. He smiled lazily.

'You don't want to believe everything you read in the papers. You should know that, mate.'

'So what about a comeback, then?'

Greg opened his eyes wide in mock amazement. 'I've never been away!'

'So it'll be the international tennis circuit again for you next year? Maybe Wimbledon again?'

'That depends on Stephanie,' Greg replied. 'It all depends on how she'd feel about undertaking a tour. She's my top priority now.'

'Is this your first marriage, Greg?' The female reporter was here again. Greg appraised her swiftly in passing.

'Yep,' he said crisply, 'and I'll miss it if I hang around out here with you guys much longer. Gotta go. See you.' He let in the clutch of the car, but as it moved off, was unable to resist the impulse to flirt with the young woman taking down his every word in her recording machine. 'That's a nice body you've got there,' he told her with a grin. 'Mind what you do with it. Behave yourself.' And well satisfied with the blush of gratification he had produced, he sped off up the long winding drive.

Up at the house, a thirteen-year-old boy with an expensive movie camera was recording the arrival of the wedding guests who had been pouring into the grounds for the last hour. From the balcony above, which gave out onto the master bedroom, Jilly watched him bustling about, shooting this and that with more enthusiasm than accuracy. Turning, she re-entered the bedroom, where Stephanie had completed her preparations and was just making final adjustments to her thick brown hair. He's late, she thought. Is Steph worried?

'What about the children?' she asked Stephanie's back. 'How do they feel about all this?'

Stephanie frowned anxiously. 'Dennis is OK,' she said thoughtfully. 'In fact, he's quite thrilled at the thought of having a Wimbledon champion for his new dad. And Greg's bought him a fantastic movie camera for a present – he's so thoughtful like that, Jilly – so Dennis is in his element today, loving it.'

'But Sarah –?' Jilly prompted the unspoken worry. Stephanie sighed.

'Well, she's at a more difficult stage. Fifteen must be an awful age to have your mum fall desperately in love with someone.' Stephanie coloured faintly with self-consciousness. 'Especially a younger man.'

Jilly raised her eye-brows in enquiry.

'I don't think she's forgiven the difference in age between me and Greg.'

'It's not so great,' said Jilly soothingly. 'That's nothing these days.'

'But these things seem huge to a fifteen-year-old. Besides, I haven't handled it all too well. I just went head over heels when I met him. I was so absorbed in Greg I even forgot Sarah's school concert, and she had an important solo. I haven't played the piano with her or heard her practice for ages – result, she's terribly jealous, resents him, hates me.'

Stephanie buried her face in her hands, and Jilly could sense the pain coming to the surface. Briskly she took charge.

'You'll ruin your makeup if you do that, kid. Come on now. Think positive. It'll all fall into place. You've landed one of the most eligible bachelors in the southern hemisphere now that Prince Charles is spoken for, so don't worry. Enjoy, enjoy! After all, you're not marrying him to please them, are you? Please yourself, for once in your life, Stephanie Harper, please yourself!'

With a deep indrawn breath, Stephanie lifted her chin, squared her shoulders and stood up. She turned to face Jilly with a smile.

'You're right. I'm being so silly. I'll be just fine as soon as Greg gets here. I know he's a bit late. But he won't let me down.'

'Atta girl!'

Jilly crossed to her friend, took her hand, and led her towards the wide floor-length mirror on the other side of the room. Together the women stood in silence looking at their reflections. Stephanie, tall and shy, with a tendency to be nervous and ungainly, had nevertheless a coltish grace that belied her age, and her girlish gestures placed her nearer to twenty than forty. Now, in her exquisite misty blue two-piece, which made her eyes look like bluebells in springtime, she was lovelier than she had ever been in her life before.

But if only she could follow it through, thought Jilly with rising irritation. She's not colour blind. She ought to

23

know that those sapphire earrings don't go, they're the wrong blue. And though she's tall, she ought to have given up on her sensible shoes for this day of all days. And why doesn't she do something with her hair, instead of just looping it up into those unbecoming bangs held back by stupid slides . . . God, if I had her money . . .

Suddenly Jilly met Stephanie's eye in the mirror. The warm, loving smile of her friend beamed at her joyfully.

'You look wonderful, Jilly! I love your outfit – Fifth Avenue?' Immediately Jilly felt a pang of guilt. Why am I such a bitch, she asked herself miserably. What's wrong with me? Rather too hastily she said, 'So do you. Look wonderful. You look very nice.'

'Honestly?'

'Honestly.'

With a strange little grimace, unconvinced, Stephanie turned aside and sank down on the bed.

'Oh, Jilly, it's not only the kids that are wrong – it's me. I'm so afraid I won't hold him, won't be able to keep his love. He's such a star, and I'm so ordinary – he's a tennis champion and I'm such a rabbit at anything athletic, I can't even swim –'

'Just get him on a horse, my dear,' advised Jilly sagely. 'You'll whack the pants off him.' She held a meaningful pause and gave Stephanie a wicked look. 'Which, as I take it, must be the general idea . . .?'

Stephanie blushed hotly, but was very obviously not displeased by this turn in the conversation. She dimpled, looked down, then jumped up and ran into the dressing room off the bedroom. Reappearing with a large and elegant box, she opened it to reveal among the sheaves of silver tissue, an entire trousseau in black satin, foaming with silk ribbons and lace. Jilly bent down in wonderment to inspect the contents. Each item was distinct and exquisite,and each bore on its label a very famous French name.

Giggling and flushed with delight, Stephanie plucked

24

the negligée from among the set, and held it up against herself. The fabric was breathtakingly sheer, the neckline low and inviting. She pirouetted round the room in girlish glee, singing out in a crazy rhythm, 'Jilly-o-Jilly-o-I-love-him-sooooo-much –'

'*He* gave you that?'

'Ah-hah.' Stephanie giggled an affirmative. 'Well, have I ever worn anything like that before? It makes me feel sexy just to think about it!'

Jilly nodded, and handling the smooth sensual satin felt a stir of sexual interest deep inside her.

'He *must* be quite a guy. And you're a fast worker, Miss Harper. Didn't take you long to get on to . . . intimate relations with him, did it? And just what have you done to deserve this tribute?' Stephanie's colour rose again, but she did not evade the question.

'Nothing,' she said defiantly.

'Nothing? D'you mean that you haven't—'

'Yeah,' said Stephanie, flushed but firm. 'I mean that we haven't. Partly because there hasn't been that much time to ourselves, when we could be sure of not being spied on and caught out by the press. Partly because if it's "your place or mine", neither was right, and I'm not the type for the back of a car, even if it's the Harper Mining limo. But mostly because – after the last two – I've got to get it right. I've got to, Jilly, and I'm going to. I'm a woman now, I'm not an ignorant girl any more – and I reckon I've found the man for the woman in me.'

Stephanie fell silent, and the two women looked at one another with no pretence between them. Jilly knew just what Stephanie meant. Stephanie was that common paradox, a much-married woman who was yet sexually unawakened. Brought up cut off from the mainstream of any society in the isolation of Eden, the only man she had ever known was her father. But as a mining mogul travelling the world, he had left her too often all alone and hungering for love, while at the same time his dominant personality made all others seem weak and insignificant.

Small wonder then, that she had fallen for the first man to show any interest at all in her, an effete offspring of the minor British aristocracy encountered on a visit to London. Their love-making had been a disaster. All the groom's previous experience, indeed his sole interest, lay in boys, which accounted for his attempt to persuade the baffled girl into certain manoeuvres that happily for her peace of mind she completely failed to understand.

Nevertheless, protected in equal measure by her innocence and her ignorance, Stephanie had continued to think well of her tall, good-looking, well-spoken lordling for just as long as she could. The marriage had lasted long enough in England for the arrival of a daughter, when Stephanie's failure to produce the obligatory son, together with the realization that old Max was not intending that his fortune should go to prop up an ailing ducal house, combined to disillusion the English in-laws with the gawky colonial girl. Stephanie for her part had reached an almost terminal stage of homesickness in England's grey and grubby land. Her very soul was pining for the clean and sparkling air of home, for the freedom of the outback, and above all, for Eden. So the brief union was painlessly dissolved and Stephanie returned, with a whole heap of knowledge and experience at her back, but not of the sexual kind.

Understandably, she had wasted no time into bouncing straight into another *mésalliance*, being too unworldly to follow Jilly's advice to shop around now, without feeling compelled to buy. Within three months she was married to an American scientist taking part in a United Nations international research programme on mineral resources who was attached to Harper Mining for the duration. He was safe, kind and middle-aged – he was Max, without the power, drive or sting of Stephanie's dead father – and sex was about as important to him a his once-a-month bath when he came in from some remote outpost where the slightest trace of mineral deposit, however small, engrossed his attention more than his young wife. Jilly privately considered him revolting and could not understand how

26

Stephanie could let him touch her. But with an absent husband repeating the pattern of the absentee father, it was not a problem that arose too often. In a fit of absentmindedness the professor had fathered on Stephanie the baby boy that had eluded her in England. But when his research programme came to an end and withdrew back to the US, so did he. Leaving Stephanie older, but as she freely confessed to Jilly, very little the wiser.

Since then Stephanie had lived quietly, dividing her life between her children and Harper Mining. She seemed to have no trouble doing without men, a fact which baffled Jilly, who had for the last ten years looked outside her marriage in a number of directions for the satisfaction that she needed as a woman. Now, in her thirties, Jilly knew that her sexual need was stronger, more insistent than ever before, her skills greater, her excitement more intense. Had Stephanie started to hear at last the music of the great primal dance? Was she resolved now to join in, before it was too late? Jilly stared at the girl who had been known as 'little Miss Prim' in school with frank amazement. Something about the fearless open gaze, the set of the head, the warm smile playing round Stephanie's lips, gave her her answer.

'Well, good on yer, kid,' she murmured. 'Welcome to the club.'

'Wish me good luck, too, Jilly,' said Stephanie impulsively. 'I know I'm going to need it. Greg is . . . well, he's got kind of a head start on me.'

'From the look of the trousseau, he's ready to give instruction, though,' laughed Jilly mischievously. 'I'd watch out if I were you, Steph. I think he's trying to tell you something.'

'Roll on tonight,' cried Stephanie recklessly. 'Oh, where *is* he?' The unmistakable growl of the Corniche was heard outside pulling up at the front door.

'Talk of the devil,' said Jilly. 'I think the groom's arrived.'

·Chapter Two

In the cool whitewashed hall of the Harper Mansion, Bill McMaster waited with the patience of a man who had waited out greater events than this. But he was not accustomed to waiting, and it did not agree with him. As managing director of Harper Mining, and as Stephanie's surrogate father since Max's death, Bill was on duty today in both his private and professional capacities. He had been among the earliest to arrive at the house, in order to make sure that everything was running smoothly on Stephanie's day of days. But the one thing he had not anticipated was the non-arrival of the groom. His deeply-lined and rugged face, the legacy of the early outback years with Max, bore a sociable expression as he chatted with wedding guests, staff and colleagues. But inside he was cursing himself fruitily and inventively for not having thought to send the Harper limo, with a couple of Harper's heftiest lads, to pick up the errant groom and make sure he'd be delivered on time.

Beforehand everything had been going like a charm. Bill had arrived to find the preparations for the wedding breakfast, the reception of presents and guests, the organization of both the regular and the extra staff, all running like clockwork under the unwavering eye of Matey, the head of the Harper household since time immemorial. One rumour had it that Max had poached him from the yacht of a titled family temporarily moored in Sydney harbour, another that he had been major-domo in a grand European family, for he was not Australian born. But who and what he was had been lost in the mists of time since Max had installed him in the mansion, christened him Matey, and given him *carte blanche* to run a great house in great style. As usual, Max had not been mistaken in his judgment.

28

Matey had played his part in the creation of the Harper legend and had become a cornerstone of it himself.

'Morning, Matey.' Bill wrung the old man's hand with real affection. In his huge wedding tie and oversize carnation Matey was trembling on the brink of absurdity. But his bearing was as erect as ever, and his lofty demeanour and eagle eye saved him from toppling over.

'Oh, Mr McMaster. Morning, sir. How are you? How are things . . . out there?'

Matey always referred to the other Harper homestead at Eden in this way, having never been there, and having no desire to. Bill grinned.

'Fine, thank you, Matey – last time I was there anyway. Big day today.'

'Oh yes, sir, my word *yes*. We've followed all your instructions, sir, and all Miss Stephanie's, and perhaps I may take the liberty of mentioning a few additions of my own. I've taken the precaution of ordering double the quantity of champagne that the catering company thought we needed – we don't want to be *meagre* – and I've moved the exact location of the wedding ceremony farther back into the garden, to provide more shade for the bridal couple and the guests when the sun gets right up at midday. I think you'll find that everything else is under control.'

'As always with you, Matey. You're a marvel, you really are.'

'Thank you, sir. Well, we haven't had anything like this in a long time, have we? Must do justice to the traditions of the house of Harper. If you'll excuse me, sir . . .'

As the old man bustled off, Bill's mind roamed back to the last great Harper ceremonial. Not Stephanie's weddings – the first had taken place out of their ken in England, the second had been a quick and quiet civil occasion in Alice Springs, where the research scientist just happened to find himself at the time. No, it had been Max's funeral – when

29

the whole of the Northern Territory had gathered for a stupendous wake that had gone on for days.

Seventeen years ago ... Bill could still recall Max's death as if it were yesterday. The hours of waiting in the panelled library at Eden, sweating it out, conversing in muted voices just to pass the time. Stephanie's appearance like a ghost in the doorway, her brave but faltering toast to her father, followed by her crack-up, her screaming exit and her headlong flight from the house. Hours had succeeded hours, and still she had not returned. Jim Gulley, the local police chief who had been among the attendant mourners, grew anxious and wanted to send out a search party. He had been talking to the station Aboriginals, and discovered that Stephanie's horse, far from being the usual young lady's tame gelding, was an uncut stallion nearly seventeen hands high and of an imperious and uncertain temper. If he'd thrown her out there in the uncharted wilderness, there'd be precious little hope of finding her alive.

But Katie, Eden's housekeeper, scoffed at Gulley's fears and dismissed them with derision.

'King? Throw Effie? You don't know them like I do. Effie's the only creature, man, woman or child, could get a leg over that brute. Broke him herself, she did, from a foal. He's still only a young'un and he's never known anyone else. He'll come to her hand when he'd kick the daylights out of you,' she added with a scornful glance at Gulley's sweltering bulk. As the long day wore on, Bill had had more than a twinge of fear himself. But he knew Katie of old, knew that she had reared Stephanie, or Effie as she insisted on calling her, from birth, when a terribly protracted and eventually tragic childbirth had robbed Max of the only person he had ever truly loved. The unwanted infant had been handed over to Katie, who had lavished on her all the possessive affection of a love-starved spinster. Katie knew Stephanie better than anyone else in the world. Bill could only hope she was right.

And she was. As dusk descended with its terrifying

tropical suddenness over Eden, Stephanie walked in as calmly as if she had only just left the room to fetch herself a handkerchief. She never again made any reference to what had made her run off screaming, and Bill never asked. She re-entered the library head aloft, chin up, every inch her father's daughter. Bill was not an emotional man, then or ever. But he could have cried with relief, not only at Stephanie's safe return, but at the knowledge that once again there would be a Harper at the helm of Harper Mining. Stephanie. A mini-Max.

It had not all been plain sailing, of course. Stephanie had been inexperienced, green and terrified. For although Max had destined her to succeed him, he had not trained her for the succession. So it had been a laboured slog through books, figures, balance sheets, profit and loss – till young Stephanie had been grey with fatigue, and huge-eyed at the enormity of what she was undertaking. But at her side always, patient and strong, was Bill. He glowed with quiet pride as he recalled the progress of his protégée – how she had repaid his hours, days, weeks and months of effort. She proved herself to have inherited her father's flair for business, a thousand times over.

She had something more, too, a sixth sense that Bill at first found very hard to accept, and even harder to explain. She had an uncanny instinct that would give forewarning of a fall in the stock market or a bad deal, and when Bill pressed her on it all she could say was that she 'just knew'. Where this came from, she couldn't say. Bill called it her 'female intuition'. But privately he attributed it to her growing up at Eden. There, in the wide open spaces, Stephanie had learned the art of being entirely alone, which is the only time you will ever hear that still small voice which can whisper the secrets of life. There too she had spent much time with the Aboriginals, grown close to them, and shared their mystical communion with nature and all living things. So she had a way all of her own with animals and was at one with the whole of creation and the air she breathed. And some of these gifts she brought with her to the city, although to the unperceptive she appeared not simply ordinary, but clumsy, plain, gawky or shy.

She had only one blind spot. Bill sighed heavily at the recollection for it was a central weakness. Stephanie was no judge of men. He shuddered to remember her first two ill-fated marriage ventures, and ran a finger round the inside of his collar as he reflected what a mess either of them might have been. For Harper Mining had got off remarkably lightly on both occasions. The ducal family of the young English scion of the aristocracy were so ready to be rid of her, and so indecently grateful that she was not proposing to sue him for maintenance, that it never occurred to them to hit back. And the Prof, with all his short-comings, was a genuine boffin from his horn-rimmed spectacles to his dried-up fingertips. He disdained all worldly things, especially wealth, and was horrified to discover that he had married into Australia's largest private fortune. But either of them, thought Bill, with just a teaspoonful more nous, could have held Harper Mining to ransom for as much as they could think of.

Could this be about to happen now? Bill had been shocked to the marrow to hear of Stephanie's lightning romance and decision to remarry. Instantly his suspicions were aroused. As a man of the world, he saw Stephanie as a woman approaching forty, sexually unsophisticated, more than a little overweight, and desperately insecure in any dealings with men outside a business context. What was in that for this playboy? Confidentially he unburdened his concern to his wife, Rina, a motherly and understanding woman whose opinion he relied on implicitly.

'You may be misjudging him, love,' urged Rina. 'Give him a chance. You know she's loving, strong, honest and loyal – how do you know he doesn't see that in her too?' Bill didn't know. But he had a bad feeling . . . a terrible pricking of his thumbs . . .

Now, as he heard the engine of the Rolls-Royce coming up the drive, he was torn between relief and irritation. Matey sprang forward to the door to welcome the man who would soon be his new master and conduct him to the chosen spot in the garden where the priest was waiting to perform the ceremony. Bill crossed the wide hall to the foot of the stairway, where Kaiser, Stephanie's devoted Alsatian, lay on guard, protecting his mistress.

'Hello, boy,' said Bill. 'Stephanie coming down, is she?' Kaiser gave a soft answering bark, then pricked his ears and was on his feet in an instant as he heard the tread of feet upstairs. Stephanie and Jilly came together down the stairs to meet Bill at the foot.

'Stephanie – my dear – you do look lovely. What a picture you are.'

'Thank you, Bill.' For once Stephanie received a compliment without self-consciousness.

'And you, Jilly. Welcome home. How was the trip?'

'Oh, fine, thanks.'

Stephanie took Bill's arm, and moved him across the room out of Jilly's earshot.

'Bill, did you bring the papers for me to sign?'

'Yes, I did.' Bill paused, hesitant. 'But I have to tell you that the Board weren't very happy about it.'

'I didn't expect them to be.' At such moments, Stephanie was very much a Harper, tough and unyielding. 'As long as you pushed it through.'

'Oh, I did. You can rely on me, Stephanie –' he hesitated again. She took him up calmly.

'So what d'you reckon, Bill? What's on your mind. D'you think I'm a complete fool?'

They had come to rest under a portrait of Max, a copy of the original which kept his presence so alive at Eden. Bill almost felt the old hawk-like stare on the back of his neck, and answered with a rueful grin.

'I haven't known a Harper yet who was. You could run Harper Mining and all the other companies single-handed if you wanted to. You've learned everything I've got to teach you, and you've got a great natural ability of your own too, if only you'd believe in it. You don't need my help.'

'Yes I do, of course I do.' Stephanie was excited, vehement. 'You know I couldn't have managed all these years without you.' She smiled self-consciously. 'I do seem to need a man to lean on.'

'Fair enough, I suppose. But I do think it would have been wiser, though – more discreet – if you'd . . . er . . . provided for your husband from personal funds rather than through the company. The Board's up in arms over making special provision for him as a regular part of the company like this.'

'Oh Bill.' Stephanie sighed heavily. 'Don't you understand? How do you think a man feels living out of his wife's handbag? My money is enough to put any man off marrying me.'

Not this man, thought Bill, if I know anything about anything. Stephanie, Stephanie, how gentle, trusting and naïve you are.

'It's been such a source of difficulty for me in the past,' Stephanie went on. 'I don't intend to make the same mistake again. I want my husband to be financially independent from the outset of our marriage, with his own funds, his own income. And I *don't* want it to look like a handout!' There was a dangerous flash in her eye and a commanding thrust to her chin. Bill read the signals.

'Don't worry, there's no problem,' he said soothingly. 'From this moment, Greg's on the payroll.' Stephanie relaxed.

'Thank you.'

'Your happiness is my only concern, Steph. Any help you may need, you have only to ask.'

'I know.'

Bill leaned in to kiss her. As he did so, her words froze him in his tracks.

'One more thing, Bill. I've been thinking about this, and I don't think I've gone far enough. I'd like Greg made a director of Harper Mining. Taken on the board. We need to give him a real function, not just a block of shares and a set of fancy titles. Will you see to it?'

Bill stared at her, trying to control his shock and rising anger. Stephanie looked back at him steadily. The realization hit Bill that this was Max's daughter, delivering an ultimatum. His opinion was not sought, nor was it considered necessary. He forced a light smile, nodded, and kissed her gently on the cheek.

'Leave it to me. Good luck, my dear, all the best.' He straightened and looked around him. Through the polished hall he could see the dining room, where long white-covered tables stood ready laden with food and drink for the celebrations after the ceremony. The hall itself was full of gift-wrapped presents large and small, and through the sitting-room lay the lovely garden where the groom and the guests awaited the bride. Jilly approached bearing a huge bouquet for Stephanie and a smaller one for herself. The air was heady with the scent of the flowers.

The stage was set. Bill had a helpless sense of events slipping beyond the control of mortal man, and taking their inevitable predestined course. He bowed to the force of circumstance.

'And now, my dear,' he said, taking Stephanie's hand in his arm, 'Let's get you married, shall we?'

Outside in the garden, the late summer air was warm and still. Earlier there had been rain, in a dismayingly sharp torrential tropical downpour, when it seemed that the scheduled garden ceremony might have to take place indoors with everyone cramped together. But the rain had gone away as swiftly as it had come, leaving the lawns and bright flowering trees fresh and newly washed. Mid-day, the hour of the wedding, had come and gone and the sun was high in the sky. From its zenith it streamed down on the guests who basked in the warmth, the fierce heat diffused by the sheltering trees.

At the heart of this green temple stood Greg with his best man in front of a simple makeshift altar table. To his

35

right, beyond the garden, lay the harbour, where the lawns ran down to the waterfront. In the harbour, yachts tacked merrily to and fro, or nearer in, rode quietly at anchor. Further off was the great gleaming arch of the Harbour Bridge with the city spilling around it on both sides. A million dollar view, thought Greg contentedly. He loved Sydney and though he had travelled all over the world on the tennis circuit, he had never come across a city to beat it. He looked out over the gleaming water and the cold still anger inside him, his constant companion since childhood, was calmed. At that moment the soul of Greg Marsden was as near as it could be to peace.

The little priest standing nearby with the best man regarded Greg with a curious eye. In all his years of celebrating marriage unions, the bride had often been late, but never the groom. He had borne the delay with Christian resignation, fortified by his faith that all would turn out for the best, and indeed it had. Here they were, and any moment the bridal party would emerge from the house and make its way down the velvet-smooth lawns to where the groom and congregation waited under the trees. He wished he could feel as confident that the handsome, arrogant-looking man lounging before him with easy grace was spiritually and emotionally prepared for marriage. Dear Father God, he prayed silently and sincerely, help him, be with him today, guide his steps. Opening his eyes again, the priest subjected Greg to a close scrutiny. He was clearly lost in thought. The priest's heart lifted. You never knew where the grace of Our Lord would descend. He had known a number of men brought to an understanding of their moral duties and the responsibilities of wedlock even at the altar. Was God even now welcoming one of His lost sheep to the fold?

Venice, Greg was thinking, Venice. That's the only place that can hold a candle to Sydney in the way that the water's part of the city and a facility for all the people to enjoy. But the canals in Venice stink, and they're full of crap. Even so, he thought, that's the place for a honeymoon.

That's where we should be going. And Paris, and then maybe down to Provence or the Dordogne . . . The shadow of a frown crossed his regular features. His assumption that he and Stephanie would honeymoon in Europe had been unconsciously destroyed by Stephanie in one of their first conversations about the wedding arrangements. 'I've got such a wonderful thing in store for you,' she had told him joyfully, 'Eden! As soon as we can get away after the wedding, we can honeymoon out there, just the two of us, as long as we like. Oh Greg, it'll be bliss!'

Eden? Greg had experienced a moment of real panic. That hole in the great blue yonder, cut off from everything that kept a city boy alive; the fun, the bustle, the bright lights, sweet music? But he fought the feeling off. Plenty of time, he told himself, plenty of time. I've been to Europe before, and I'll go again. He knew he could make out at Eden. He could ride a horse, in fact the ornerier the better, and handle a gun; skills from that part of his life that he had written off from the moment he picked up a tennis racquet and headed for Sydney. Officially now he was an orphan – Australia's an easy country to become an orphan in, he reflected with a grin. There would be no-one from his side at the wedding, he had seen to that. He was a man out of nowhere. That was his carefully created persona, and it suited him. He wasn't going back on that. But he decided it wouldn't kill him to spend a month at Eden, to go back to that life for a while. And it would make Stephanie happy.

Stephanie. Greg frowned again. He wasn't just humouring her. He really wanted to make her happy, and intended to start as he meant to go on. He was male enough to take it for granted that her happiness would spring out of and take second place to his. With both of them concentrating fulltime on the same bloke, he couldn't foresee any problem. Stephanie had as good as told him a thousand times that he was doing her a favour just by marrying her. And in his heart, for all her money, he believed he was. She was not a lot to shout about. She was gauche, unsophisticated and so desperately insecure that at times she got on his nerves by apologizing for her very existence. For Greg who liked his women cat-like, poised and daring, this was a big downer.

His mind flicked back to the French girl who, unknown to all his mates, he had arranged as a final bachelor treat for himself. When they had delivered him back to his flat at the end of his stag night, she had been waiting in the bedroom. He could see again the hard provocative stare, the sharp little white teeth, the shape of her body in the moonlight. His mind reached out to draw the skimpy dress down from her shoulders once again, to expose the tender breasts, the dark heavy nipples, to feel her skin, her lips, her tongue - sweet Jesus, her tongue! – his cock stirred lazily at the memory. Well, so Stephanie was not in that league. But she had passion, plenty of feeling, a bloody good body, and she could learn. Greg grinned. He was looking forward to teaching her. He resolved to be the best fucking husband that ever left his wife panting for more. He felt good. Everything was going to work out fine.

Within the house a string quartet struck up a delicate Bach air, grave and rather plaintive. The attention of all the congregation focused on the french windows giving out from the sitting room to the garden. The little wedding procession came into view, at its head Stephanie, leaning on Bill McMaster's arm. Behind her walked Jilly as matron-of-honour, and beside Jilly was Sarah, the fifteen-year-old daughter of Stephanie's first marriage. They were followed by Dennis, Stephanie's son, who had been persuaded to lay aside his treasured new movie camera just for the duration of the service. At Dennis's side was Matey, without whom no Harper ceremonial was complete, and bringing up the rear with superb dignity padded Kaiser the Alsatian.

Walking down the garden towards Greg, Stephanie was beautiful as she had never been before. In her eyes was a light it was a kindness to see. Her heart was singing, soaring away above the music, over the treetops like a bird.

Her mind was filled with just one thought, repeated over and over again – Greg, Greg, Greg. And there he was, waiting for her, smiling at her. A thought trailed across the back of her mind, but not unhappily – I should die now, now at this second, because I have reached the summit of earthly bliss . . .

The priest welcomed Stephanie with a smile of delight. He loved weddings, with their combination of human happiness and divine blessing. The bride was trembling with joy, and the groom had had the chance of a long and satisfying reflection on this solemn occasion. All was as it should be, in the priest's opinion. The ceremony could begin.

'Dearly beloved, we are gathered together in the presence of God and before the sight of this congregation, to join together this man and this woman in holy matrimony, and to seek on their behalf God's blessing and His grace . . .'

Standing behind Stephanie, Jilly dropped her head so that the brim of her picture hat could hide her flaming face. Only moments before she had been proceeding down the garden in Stephanie's wake, hardly paying any attention to what was going on around her. But she had been jolted out of her slumbrous inattention by the sight of the man standing at the altar. Tall, lean and powerful, with sun-lightened fair hair, smouldering grey eyes and classically superb features, he was quite simply the handsomest man Jilly had ever seen. But it was more than that. He was a magnificent animal, and the animal in him was only just below the surface. He was wild, feral, with a sense of danger about him – Jilly could sense it, almost smell it. His physical presence struck her like a blow. She felt as if she had been winded and could hardly breathe. The hot blood mounted to her face and ran like fever through her veins. Her body began to throb and to her horror she felt herself growing soft and moist between the legs. Her face began to burn. She dropped her head and tried to look as if she was praying. But even in those moments she felt she was lost. There was a madness in this man that called to a hidden madness deep inside her, and she knew that she would answer it. But why, oh why, did it have to be Stephanie's husband?

Next to Jilly, Sarah too was fighting a losing battle with warring emotions. Eyes cast down, Stephanie's daughter was as wretched as her mother was happy, weltering in misery. At fifteen she was woman enough to hate the couple at the altar with a pure and holy hatred, child enough to want to burst into tears and run away weeping. How *could* she, how *could* she, she kept demanding of herself with useless savagery, how could she, and with *him*? When he isn't smiling he's got eyes like a lizard, he's years too young for her, and he's loathsome, loathsome. Her brother Dennis behind her with a sensitivity surprising in a thirteen-year-old read the tension in her rigid shoulders and neck. Reaching forward, he felt for Sarah's hand and gave it a fraternal squeeze. With a furious gesture Sarah pulled away, and set her shoulders against him with even greater ferocity. And blissfully unaware of the witches' cauldron of feelings behind her, Stephanie Harper became Mrs Greg Marsden.

Afterwards there was music and feasting, the champagne flowed and the party began. Jilly lost no time in seeking the reassurance and solid presence of her husband Phillip and she found him in the dining room helping Dennis and Sarah to lunch from the groaning buffet.

'Now, Dennis,' he was saying amiably, as he loaded cold spiced chicken onto the boy's plate, 'what d'you think of your mother's new husband?'

'I hardly know him,' Dennis replied. 'I've only met him twice so far.'

'I think that goes for everybody, doesn't it?' Jilly joined in the conversation, determined to be light, but equally determined to turn the subject away from this danger zone. 'Hey, kids, did you have any trouble getting the day off school?' The children attended two of Sydney's best and most old-fashioned schools, and boarded there when Stephanie was away on business.

'It really wasn't any problem, Aunty Jilly,' said Sarah scornfully. 'Mother always lets us out for the things *she* wants to – so I suppose we should be pleased that included one of her weddings!'

'Sarah!' Phillip was shocked. Without another word Sarah stalked off.

'We get time off for good behaviour,' joked Dennis, trying to cover his sister's exit – then with an apologetic 'excuse me', he sprinted off after her, calling 'Sass! Hey Sass, wait for me.'

'Poor kids,' said Phillip feelingly. 'It may be the romance of the decade for Stephanie, but there's not much in it for those two, is there? Still, it'll all settle down when they're back from honeymoon, I daresay.'

Jilly made no answer. Phillip shot her a concerned look.

'You're very quiet. Hungry, are you? You must be. Let me give you something to eat. Have you got a drink? There's plenty of champagne at the bar over there, I'll get you one in a second.'

'Oh don't fuss, Phil.' Jilly's nerves felt like piano wires. 'I'll be OK. It's just jet lag.'

'Hmph.' Phillip took leave to doubt this explanation, but would not say so. Tall, slim and elegant in a well-cut dark suit, even in his late fifties Phillip was still an attractive man. But years of marriage to a much younger woman who had slowly fallen out of love with him, and whom he had never ceased to love deeply, had taught Phillip to tread carefully. He studied his wife quizzically, and tried another tack.

'Well, it's a marvellous party. The wedding seems to have gone off very well.'

'Ha! What do you expect? Let's face it, Stephanie's had plenty of practice.' Jilly reached in her bag and furiously fumbled for a cigarette. Taking her lighter, Phillip lit it for her.

'Do I detect a bitchy note, darling?'

'I'm sorry. I'm just tired.' Jilly brushed his cheek in thanks.

'We won't stay long.'

'No.' There was a pause. Jilly tried frantically not to think of—

'What do you make of Greg Marsden?' asked Phillip.

Jilly drew deeply on her cigarette and deliberated with herself before replying.

'Him? I wouldn't trust him with my loose change.'

Beyond the swirl of the party, on the edge of the Harper property right by the water's edge, Dennis finally tracked Sarah down under a great tree whose boughs came almost to the ground and formed a natural shelter. Clumsily he tried to comfort her.

'Hey . . . cheer up, Sass. It's not the end of the world. You've still got me!'

Sarah treated him to a withering glance, and was silent. Dennis tried again.

'The main thing is, Mum's happy. She's entitled to be.'

'Yeah.' Sarah continued to scan the far horizon. 'But why did it have to be *him*?'

'Why not him?' Dennis was baffled. 'He's all right really.'

'He bought you!' Sarah unleashed all her vitriol on her hapless junior. 'With that rotten camera. He's bought you, body and soul.'

'No he hasn't. Well, a bit, I suppose. But what have you got against him?'

'I don't know. I just know' – Sarah was struggling with ideas beyond her experience, beyond her vocabulary. 'I just know there's something about him . . .'

There's something about him after all, decided Bill. He had to admit that Greg had done very well today. He'd apologized gracefully to everyone for his lateness, been impeccably polite to the ladies and suitably robust with the men, he'd attended Stephanie devotedly and smiled on

42

one and all. 'I told you to give him a chance,' said Rina to Bill with wifely complacence, and Bill declared himself more than happy to suspend judgement, softened as he was by Stephanie's overflowing joy, the beautiful day, and the excellent chilled champagne. Now, in the garden, the guests were scattered about among the flowering trees, the women like so many flowers themselves in their bright dresses, and the late afternoon sun was releasing the heavy scents from the gardenias and frangipani. It was drawing near the time for the bridal pair to depart. Leaving Rina, Bill went down across the lawn towards the deep mooring at the waterfront where Stephanie's yacht was ready and waiting for the honeymoon voyage.

'Bill!' Greg was moving down to intercept him. 'Well, what d'you think? Went well, didn't it?'

'Very well. Stephanie tells me you've decided against honeymooning in Europe. You're going to fly out to Eden instead.'

'Ye-es, but not immediately. We thought a good rest on the yacht first. The last month's been pretty exhausting, what with getting ourselves organized, dodging the press—' Greg gave a rueful laugh – 'then we're off to Steph's beloved Eden for my introduction to the delights of the simple life.'

A good intention formed itself inside Bill's brain.

'Well, in that case – maybe you can drop by my office some time before you leave.'

Greg was instantly alert. 'Sure. I can come in when you like. Love to.'

'All right then. Let's say 11.30 one day. Give my secretary a ring. Afterwards we could have some lunch. Introduce you to Harper Mining, you're going to be seeing a good deal more of that than the outback. Get to know one another.'

'I'll look forward to that, Bill. Give us a chance to get better acquainted. Thank you.'

They shook hands.

'See you soon, then,' said Bill, nodding as he moved

away. Greg held his manly sincere smile, but inside he was exultant. Done it again, baby, he congratulated himself. It's so easy if you just take it one step at a time . . .

Smiling to himself, Greg turned to ascend the flight of stone steps leading up to the house. As he did so, a woman came out of the dining room onto the terrace at the top of the steps and leaning on the carved baluster she threw her head back and inhaled deeply as if to prevent herself from fainting. His attention caught, Greg ran the swift reflex appraisal over her – good body, nice breasts, thirty-fiveish but he wouldn't kick her out of bed for that . . . Suddenly, feeling his glance, the woman looked down. Her eyes! God, her eyes – cat-like, pale, almost yellow, and as they looked at him contracting almost to black slits, wild and defiant. Greg felt a stab of excitement run through him. The next second the woman turned and ran at speed back into the house. Who . . . ? What . . . ? Every nerve tingling, Greg slowly began to climb the steps.

Phillip had been more than a little alarmed to see Jilly, who had only wandered onto the terrace for a breath of air, come flying back in as if the hounds of heaven were on her heels. Swiftly he followed her, but was too late to reach her before she had locked herself in an upstairs bathroom, from which she refused to come out despite his pleas.

'I'm all right, Phillip,' was all she would say. 'It's just the heat. I want to bathe my wrists and forehead, and then I'll be down in a minute. Go on into the garden. I'll join you there.' With that he had to be content.

Inside the bathroom, Jilly listened to Phillip's feet receding. Then she dragged herself to the mirror and looked at her reflection. She hardly recognized the woman who looked back – wild-eyed, flushed and panting. Jilly had known she couldn't avoid him all afternoon. But she had not been prepared to meet him face to face at that moment. Again the sense of his physical presence came to her. Her nipples burned, and she soothed her breasts with both hands, watching herself in the mirror. But the hands that she wanted were not these little white things with

44

pink-painted nails, but the strong golden brown hands of – again she felt the throbbing in her crutch, the tell-tale moisture spreading below. In desperation, Jilly slid to the floor. Her caressing fingers found the centre of her urgent longing and within seconds she came. And came, and came and came, in a racking series of fierce sensations, murmuring one name over and over again under her breath.

Wandering disconsolately through the garden, Phillip came across Stephanie and Dennis. Dennis was proudly showing off his movie camera as Phillip approached, and precariously balancing a glass of champagne in the other hand.

'Phillip!' Stephanie called out, 'how about some footage of me with my big son?'

'Delighted,' Phillip obliged. 'But how about Sarah? Shall we make it a family trio?'

Stephanie grimaced. 'Seems I'm not too popular with my daughter. I'll just have to find the way to make all this up to her when I get back.'

'Don't worry, she'll get over it,' said Dennis loyally.

'Hope so. And how about you?'

'I'm fine. OK, Uncle Phil, shoot.'

Phillip began to film. 'OK, then, smile for the dicky-bird.'

Stephanie laughed, put her arm round Dennis, pulled him close and ruffled his hair. 'I love you,' she said. Dennis looked back at her with shining eyes. The camera whirred.

'Well, say something, Dennie, or we'll both stand here looking like a pair of shop window dummies!'

Dennis lifted his champagne glass with the critical air of a connoisseur. 'Good year, isn't it?'

'Are you drinking that champagne? I thought you were just posing! What will your headmaster say if I send you back to school sloshed?'

'He doesn't care,' replied Dennis airily. 'All the kids are lushes anyway.' Stephanie pealed with laughter and lavished a kiss on the tousled area she had created in Dennis's hair.

'Good stuff,' called Phillip.

'Thank you, Phil, that's fine.'

As Phillip was handing back the camera to Stephanie he was pleased to see Jilly coming up to the little group. She looked so much better, brighter, cooler, more relaxed, and she came straight up to Stephanie with an affectionate smile.

'Hey, kid! How are you, Mrs Marsden? How's it all going?'

'Wonderful, Jilly. I'm so happy. It's as if my other two marriages never happened!'

Dennis stiffened, torn between insult and hurt. Without a glance at Stephanie, he exited stiffly towards the house. Jilly squeezed Stephanie's arm.

'He knows you didn't mean it.'

'But that's the trouble.' Stephanie fixed Jilly with her great honest eyes. 'I did.' Suddenly her face cleared as she looked over Jilly's shoulder. 'But it'll all be all right. Look who's here.'

Greg made his way carefully across the lawn, scrutinizing all the females within range. After scouring through the house for the mystery lady with the wild pale eyes, he had become conscious of being away from Stephanie, and decided he had better return to her side to play the dutiful husband. Not to worry, he told himself. He'd find her. As he spotted Stephanie, he could see she was talking to some biddy in a huge hat. After today, he vowed, he'd never undertake to be polite to so many strangers again. Preparing a pleasant smile, he moved forwards.

'Darling!' Stephanie was bubbling with joy. 'You haven't officially met Phillip Stewart.'

'Phillip—' Greg shook hands.

'And this – this is my darling Jilly.'

Greg turned. The conventional smile froze on his face as he found himself looking into the cats'-eyes of the woman on the terrace. She stared at him unblinking.

'Hi, Greg. Congratulations.'

'Thank you.'

Totally unaware of the undercurrents passing to and fro, Stephanie bubbled on.

'You two – you're so special to me. Apart from my children you're the two people I love most in the whole world. I've so wanted to bring you together. I want you to be friends. You will be, won't you? For my sake?'

The irony lay heavy between them. Jilly felt as if she wanted to scream. She dared not look at Greg, even though she could feel that he had not taken his eyes off her.

'Come on, Jilly, Greg – stand together. I want a shot of you.' Stephanie had retreated a few paces and was focusing the movie camera.

'Steph – I've just got off a plane – I'm shot to pieces with jet lag.'

'You look beautiful, darling, like always,' Stephanie enthused.

'I don't feel it.'

'You look great, Jilly – just great.'

Jilly had felt Greg's approach, but was struggling to keep her attention fixed on Stephanie.

'Bit closer together now,' called Stephanie. With a practised grasp, Greg put his arm round Jilly's waist and pulled her close into his side. For the rest of her life she never forgot that first touch, the connection of their bodies standing hip to hip in the scented garden. Desire for him coursed through her so powerfully that she began to shake. The heady odour from the trees drowned out her senses. In the distance she could hear Stephanie's little cries of delight – 'oh, this is going to be real Academy-award-winning stuff' – but all her being was reduced to this arm round her waist, this thigh warm against hers, this man. She turned to look at him and saw in his eyes that he knew.

'Say something, Jilly,' said Greg.

'Cheeeeeeese?' said Jilly faintly.

*

At last night came. The happy couple had left for their honeymoon on the luxurious sixty-foot yacht moored at the private jetty at the foot of the Harper grounds. The guests had combined to give the newly-weds a triumphant send-off, and then dispersed to their homes. In her house on Hunter's Hill, Jilly rebuffed Phillip's diffident and gentlemanly advances on the grounds that she was too tired to make love, and then lay awake all night tormenting herself by picturing Stephanie transported to the heights of bliss, played upon, exhausted, satiated. Meanwhile, in the main cabin of the yacht, Stephanie too lay awake, rigid, tortured and alone. I'm sorry, I'm sorry, I'm sorry, hammered through her brain. She gazed at the sleeping Greg lying beside her in the darkness. How could anyone love a man so much, and yet be so little able to love him properly? Don't worry about it, he had said before falling asleep, and I love you, and there's plenty of time. But in the sick sinking sensation of failure and despair, Stephanie doubted that time would make any difference at all.

Chapter Three

Phillip came out of his office at the bottom of Macquarie Street late on Friday morning and turned right up the hill. Behind him lay Circular Quay with its old ferry wharves jutting out into Sydney Cove, and Bennelong Point with the Opera House thrusting flamboyantly from its tip. Normally keenly appreciative of his surroundings, Phillip paid no heed to them today. It had been a difficult week. Since the wedding the previous weekend Jilly had been so disturbed that he was seriously concerned about her. He had not in the least minded curtailing their American trip to return to Australia in time to share Stephanie's great day. His business was concluded, Jilly had been at a loose end having failed to find in Macy's and Bloomingdale's the distractions that New York had afforded her before, and she was ready to go. The dramatic news of Stephanie's impending marriage, plus the chance to play matron of honour yet again, had provided the excuse for a mammoth spending spree, and Jilly had boarded the plane with a whole new wardrobe, a hat so big that it called for separate stowage facilities, and a happy anticipation of an exciting event and a whole new change of direction in the life of her best friend.

Something had gone badly wrong for Jilly at the wedding, Phillip decided. On an impulse he swung left across Macquarie Street into the Royal Botanic Gardens, which stretched across the headland from Sydney Cove to Mrs Macquarie's Point. He was early for his lunchtime appointment in Elizabeth Street, and could afford to take time to sort out his feelings of concern. He ruled out any kind of upsetting incident, row or scene as the cause of Jilly's malaise – not that this was impossible, as she had a fiery temper when provoked, but because she had hardly been out of his sight for the whole time. He knew exactly whom she had spoken to and who had spoken to her, and she had collected nothing but welcomes back and compliments on her outfit. In fact Jilly had, as usual, made a hit, as an attractive woman in the prime of life who knew exactly how to dress to show herself off to the best advantage.

But something had happened, thought Phillip sadly as he crossed the gardens oblivious of the rioting hibiscus and oleanders in clusters around him. Since that day, Jilly had been very strange, alternating between depression and a grim 'what the hell' recklessness. He knew she lay awake at night, then stayed in bed in the morning, and had cancelled her exercise class and a coffee morning with friends this week. She was smoking much more heavily too, and eating hardly a thing. Undoubtedly something had happened to upset her equilibrium.

Phillip came to the edge of the gardens and paused, looking out on Farm Cove. Ahead lay the Tasman Sea, and beyond that the implacable wastes of the South Pacific Ocean. He turned, and wandered along the Queen Elizabeth Walk as it traced its way along the outline of the cove, working his thoughts out. Only one thing had changed, only one thing had been unexpected at Stephanie's wedding – Stephanie herself. Phillip could not resist the conclusion that what had happened to Stephanie was the event that Jilly was finding so hard to bear.

Phillip had long been aware that as in all women's 'best friendships' there was a proportion of jealousy in the feeling between Jilly and Stephanie, on Jilly's side, at least. This dated back to the dawn of their friendship, way before his time, and Jilly had not grown out of it as an adult. Stephanie could certainly be acquitted of doing anything to provoke it, so open and kind as she was, and so loving to Jilly. But Jilly could not forgive Stephanie for having the Harper fortune – though God knows, thought Phillip despairingly, we have more than enough and to spare. Phillip had been a well-to-do bachelor of forty when Jilly had married him, and since then he had prospered as a lawyer. Now he was doing even better, with business opening up for his firm in the US. Even with Jilly's extravagances there was, and always had been, plenty of money to support a very luxurious life for a childless couple.

Childless. The thought struck him like a blow and the shadow of an old pain crossed his face. He had long ago accepted that an irremediable hormone disorder made it impossible for Jilly to have a baby. But she had not. Privately Phillip doubted that Jilly would have made a good mother – she was hardly cut out for such a selfless role. He had lived happily for forty years without a thought of children and, apart from the odd pang of regret, did not miss having them in his life. But for Jilly the confirmation of her infertility had been a major blow and she had not got over it. Stephanie by contrast already had a daughter and a son, and with a new husband could be ready to embark on a new family. Still not yet forty, she was far from past childbearing, and with the proper tests and checks could reckon to have more than one child if she chose. Had that been a secret intention she had confided to Jilly upstairs? Had that been the source of Jilly's distress?

Or was it something more basic still, Phillip wondered, coming to the tip of the point and turning to retrace his steps. Jilly was a striking woman, with her heart-shaped cat's face, her widely-spaced eyes, her thick, honey-coloured hair and her smooth rounded body golden from the sun. Her power to attract men was very important to her – Phillip's heart shifted painfully within him as he recalled the occasions recently when he had had to look the other way, as the price of holding onto whatever remained of Jilly's dwindling love. Yet on the wedding day, her new outfit notwithstanding, Jilly had been quite outclassed by Stephanie. Not only the well-chosen laven-der-blue suit but her brimming sense of joy had made Stephanie not just pretty or attractive, but beautiful. Her

51

transfigured appearance made it seem not at all remarkable that she had managed to attract not only a tennis star but one who even Phillip could see was a terribly handsome man. Was Jilly just jealous of being left out in the cold by Stephanie, even on Stephanie's wedding day? Was she taking it as a personal blow that her ugly duckling of a friend was becoming a swan?

My poor darling, thought Phillip, in a sudden access of compassion, how can we get you through this one? It was entirely characteristic of Phillip that he always thought of Jilly before himself. Serving her needs was more important to him than anything else. He was not blind to her faults, but he could not bring himself to be angry with her for them, on the contrary they touched him and moved his heart. Her weakness called forth his protectiveness and her tantrums his tolerance. He saw through her completely but what he saw did not kill his love. Early in their relationship he had taken up the pitiable bundle that was Jilly, and he had not yet seen a good enough reason to lay it down.

With this reflection Phillip changed course and swung back decisively along the edge of the Botanic Gardens, across the park of the Domain, making for St James's Square and Elizabeth Street. If that's what it is, he thought, I can help her. His mind turned to treats or distractions he could arrange. Perhaps a trip to the East Coast of America, as New York was a washout this time? Or an exotic holiday in Papua? Bali? Preoccupied as he had been with Jilly he had scarcely noticed that the newly-married Marsdens had returned early from their boat trip. But now he recalled a tennis party arranged at short notice for this weekend – Jilly would enjoy that, she loved tennis and a languid summer day devoted to playing, eating, drinking, laughter and fun. The tennis party, he thought, yes, good. It'll make a start at taking Jilly out of herself, and if her problem is one of adjusting to Stephanie's changed status and prospects, the sooner she starts getting used to that the better. And with a consciousness that he had gone as far as he could go in the present state of his knowledge, Phillip hurried off to his business lunch.

While Phillip Stewart paced the Royal Botanic Gardens with a troubled soul, just across Macquarie Street at the headquarters of Harper Mining Greg Marsden was feeling unusually pleased with himself and life. He had known before the wedding that Stephanie was making a generous marriage settlement to ensure his financial independence and dignity. He had only subsequently learned that she had graced him with a proper function and a part to play in the company as a director. 'You'll be on the board, darling,' she had told him. 'About time we had some new blood about the place.' Greg had been exultant. No need to kow-tow to those old fogies of Stephanie's now – he recalled with anger awkward meetings with Harper Mining's financial director before the wedding and his obvious disapproval of the provisions for Greg he was having to carry out. From here on in they had better reckon with him as one of them, not an outsider any longer.

Greg had approached his meeting with Bill McMaster therefore in a buoyant mood, feeling confident and ready. He had arrived in good time, parked the Rolls without too much difficulty around the corner from Bent Street and ascended the massive Harper Building to the nerve centre of the Harper enterprise at its very top. Now he sat waiting for Bill in the reception area outside the Chief Executive Officer's suite, looking around him with approval. Tasteful and high-quality surroundings were important to Greg. So he registered and appreciated, though many did not, the subtle blue-grey of the deep-pile carpet offsetting the luxurious coral easy chairs to perfection, the paler coral colour of the silk fabric on the walls, and the solid mahogany desks and doors outlined in a fine gold trim. He was scrupulously careful not to look at the very fanciable secretary who guarded the access to Bill's office – this is no time to be picking up stray tarts, he told himself – even though he knew that she was looking at him and only needing the slightest encouragement to begin a conversation. Instead he concentrated on trying to read the *Financial Times*, to get in training for being a big businessman.

'Ah, Greg! There you are. Come on in.' Bill McMaster was not the kind of boss who buzzed his secretary to show visitors in, but preferred to give them a welcome himself.

'How are you, Greg?'

'Fine thanks. And yourself?'

'Never better.' Bill ushered Greg into the inner sanctum and relished, as he always did, the impact on first timers of what they saw as soon as they crossed the threshold.

From its eyrie on the fortieth floor of the skyscraper block, Harper Mining enjoyed one of the best views in Australia. It commanded the whole of the Sydney Harbour, with the Harbour Bridge and the Opera House as the centrepiece of the picture. To the right, the Union Jack and the flag of Australia fluttered limply in the damp air over the Livestock and Grain Producers' Association of New South Wales. Way below, the cars beetled to and fro on the Cahill Expressway like dinky toys, and a solitary tug puffed slowly down the bay.

The morning sunlight glittering over the dappled surface of the water reflected Bill's mood.

'Y'like the view?' he chuckled as Greg stared.

'Fantastic!'

'That's the best thing about being Managing Director. This corner office goes with the job. Dunno what I'll do for a view when I have to retire.'

'We'll just have to let you take the bridge with you, that's all.' Greg was keen to echo Bill's good humour and get their new business relationship off to a good start.

'What, the old coathanger? Na, she's better off where she is. I'll miss her though.'

'Who's talking about retiring? I reckon Harper Mining'll need you at the helm for a long time yet.'

'Sure. Well, have a seat, Greg.'

Bill crossed over to a mahogany sideboard and opening a door revealed a built-in fridge.

'Drink?'

'Beer if you've got it. Thanks.'

The two men took a moment to savour the cool beers, then Bill began.

'Let's talk about you a little, Greg – see how you could fit into the business now you're one of the family. Have you ever done –' Bill wanted to say 'a proper job', but substituted 'anything else but tennis?'

'Not since I was twelve,' said Greg with a boyish grin. 'But these days, of course, tennis is a business, and you have to run yourself like a business. Drawback is, you've got all your stock, your assets and fixed capital tied up in one body, and a tendon, a ligament, one weak spot can put you out of business.'

'But you've made some money,' probed Bill.

'Yeah, sure. But y'know the prize money for Wimbledon is peanuts – and you can't live off the glory. It's the same with the French championships. The Americans are best, but it's not what you'd call real money.'

Bill sat quietly for a good while as Greg developed this theme. It became clear that the sums he had come by either through his winnings or through various forms of sponsorship were not what Bill would have called 'peanuts'. Equally Greg's money had been 'real' enough to have afforded him a very luxurious lifestyle, and to have encouraged him to develop super-sophisticated tastes. Bill only had to hear Greg expanding on the subject of foreign wine, knowing from years of discerning drinking that Australia's own could see most of its competitors off, to realize just where and how Greg's considerable income had dwindled away. For gone it had, and apparently without leaving even the benefit of experience behind.

Still, he was young enough to learn, Bill mused, if the right niche could be found. At the moment he was an asset just by virtue of his name – the public relations department of the firm were dying to release the 'WIMBLEDON CHAMP JOINS HARPER MINING' press communiqué, and have Greg on parade for the various charities and public occasions, which were an important part of the

55

company's activity. He would be a great draw, and create a lot of good will. But that would only last for a short time. Something more solid than the role of Mr Wonderful had to be found. And it was years since the surprise Wimbledon victory, after all.

'So d'you have any ideas of where you might fit in with us, Greg?' asked Bill at length. 'There's any number of opportunities – not only the whole range of mining ventures, but the financial activities they've generated – plus of course all the subsidiary companies. Any suggestions?'

'You tell me, Bill, you tell me.' And over the leisurely lunch that followed the two men discussed at length the history, extent and prospects of every aspect of the company's operations throughout the globe. Greg finally departed from the penthouse office suite after 4.00 pm, weighted down with descriptions and reports of the areas which most interested him as possibles for the deployment of Greg Marsden's talents. He was in a high good humour as he walked to his car and edged out into the traffic of Pitt Street. Business? There was nothing about it he couldn't crack, he felt sure of that.

The same went for the home troubles, too – nothing serious to worry about there. Nothing to write home about, either. He grinned mirthlessly as he recalled the fiasco of his wedding night when Stephanie's tension, inexperience, and frantic desire to please had conspired to frustrate all hope of sexual pleasure between them. Then she had started her period, early she said, and practically gone into a decline from embarrassment and disappointment. Married a whole week and I haven't succeeded in screwing my own wife yet, he thought, unamused. Married life isn't what it's made out to be – I could die of frustration here. Still and all, things are bound to look up. Just take your time, boy, and don't rush the net. And the weekend would bring a welcome distraction – the tennis party Stephanie had fixed up, and with it the chance to get to know Jilly better. Greg felt a by-now-familiar stab of sexual interest at the thought of Jilly. He was curious, aroused. But he was also married, and trying to mean it. So he was careful to stop and buy a lavish bunch of pink and white carnations on the way home, and devoted the whole of his attention to a pathetically grateful Stephanie for the rest of the evening.

In the baking mid-afternoon heat, the tennis party was in full swing. Greg was partnering Jilly in a doubles match against the Rutherfords, neighbours of Stephanie's from further along Darling Point, while Stephanie and Phillip sat it out, Kaiser dozing at their feet. The tennis courts at the Harper mansion were superbly positioned within a sheltering square of cypress trees, so that no sidewinds could ever disturb the ball in flight. Nearby was the huge swimming pool, to cool off either the players or the spectators when the hot still air became too much for them. The four players, though, were abounding in energy. It was among the two watchers that the listlessness prevailed. Stephanie roused herself to conversation.

'Phil, what's it like being married to the same person for sixteen years?'

'It has its moments,' replied Phillip guardedly, 'both good and bad. With Jilly it's certainly never been dull. Of course . . . things might have been different if she'd been able to have children. How are your two, by the way?'

'They're fine – gone back to boarding school while Greg and I honeymoon. I wanted just these first few weeks alone with my new husband. Getting back to Jilly though – I remember how hard it was on her at the start. But Phil, she hasn't mentioned it for ages.'

'Maybe not. But she hasn't forgotten. It still haunts her, and she broods a lot. Actually, I'm worried about her. Her moods fluctuate so much lately.'

Stephanie carefully scrutinized her friend. Jilly was running around the court chasing every ball, laughing with animation, and clearly having a great time.

'Seems all right to me,' she said at last. 'In fact she looks

57

as if she's having the time of her life. I'm glad she and Greg get on so well. I must admit I was a bit worried she wouldn't like him.'

'You needn't have worried,' said Phillip drily. With the watchful eyes of a neglected husband, he had noted Jilly's long and elaborate preparation for the visit, her sparkle and vivacity when they arrived. He knew it was not for him, and he doubted it was for Stephanie. On the other hand, he had seen nothing other than conventional courtesies coming from Greg. And as the game came to an end, and the Rutherfords walked off court blocking the view of the other couple, neither Phillip nor Stephanie saw Greg pull his partner into him and bestow on her a winners' kiss that instantly became something harder and hungrier as soon as their lips touched. Jilly pulled away, frightened of being seen.

'Congratulations, partner,' said Greg calmly. 'You were fan-tastic.'

'Congratulations to you, too,' she whispered, shaken. 'It was . . . good to have a match with a . . . real pro. I didn't do you justice. I'm out of practice.'

'I can see I'm going to have to give you lessons, Jilly. Private coaching.' The innuendo was plain and provocative. Jilly felt herself tensing, rising to the bait. She would not look at him. But she could see his brown arm with its clustering fine golden hairs resting on the net, smell his body as he stood close to her, and she had to fight back the impulse to touch him, to make him touch her, there and then. She took her decision without thinking about it.

'Fine,' she said levelly. 'Are you expensive?'

'Very.' He grinned arrogantly. 'But I'm also very good. You'll see.' With a proprietary air he put his arm casually round her shoulders and led her off the court.

'Hello, darling,' he called to Stephanie, 'what d'you think of the dynamic duo of Marsden and Stewart, then?'

Stephanie watched Greg and Jilly coming towards her, and her heart rose. It was wonderful to see Greg having a good time. When she'd first thought of the tennis party,

58

she didn't know whether it was a good idea, or if Greg would find it too annoying to play with a bunch of amateurs. She'd finally risked it because she was so afraid of Greg being bored and at a loose end. She didn't know how to amuse him and had no confidence that she could hold his interest by herself. Especially after what had happened on their wedding night . . .

Stephanie felt a prickling on her neck and cheeks, and knew that she was blushing. She bent down to fondle Kaiser to hide her confusion. It's humiliating, she thought, that here I am at nearly forty, and I know less than some twenty-five-year-olds. And how could she have failed to respond to Greg, of all people, when she loved him so much? Maybe too much. She blushed angrily as she recalled her urgent kisses, her clumsy unpractised gestures, which it was so clear that Greg had not enjoyed. Stephanie was too honest to deceive herself, or to let herself off lightly. 'You-are-a-disaster' was the phrase that had been hammering through her head since that first night, her feelings of distress compounded by the misery of a heavy period in hot weather.

The only redeeming feature was how marvellous Greg had been. Tolerant and kind, he had been more like a husband of ten or twenty years' standing than a newly married man. He had soothed and comforted her, fallen in readily with her desire to cut short their planned cruise and return to the safety of the home base in the Harper mansion, gone off eagerly to his business meeting at Harper Mining just as her father used to do, and returned bearing flowers which Max had never thought of in his entire life. Stephanie looked at Greg as he stood relaxed and chatting with Jilly and the Rutherfords, and her heart swelled with love. I'll make it up to you, my darling, she decided fiercely. Love lessons, that's what I need. I'll learn, from you and for you. This is too important to me not to make it work. It's all going to be OK. Greg caught her glance and threw her a warm smile. She felt her spirits soar.

'OK, everybody,' she called gaily. 'Showers and cool

drinks up at the house, and then we'll get down to the serious eating and drinking.'

Later that afternoon the little group lay relaxed and contented on the terrace behind the house, watching the sun go down over the harbour in a fireburst of orange and red. 'Eine Kleine Nachtmusik' played quietly on the stereo inside the house, and Stephanie hummed snatches of it here and there. She was delighted with the progress of her party. Jilly had been on tremendous form and Estelle and Reg Rutherford had kept their end up with a flow of jokes and anecdotes. Only Phillip had been quiet, but then he always was. A general silence that had settled on them all was broken by Greg.

'Drink, anyone?' He rose and moved to the French windows leading into the sitting room, where the drinks were set up on a table just inside the door.

'Yes, please.' 'Count me in' – both Estelle and Reg were ready for a refill.

'For you, Phillip?' Greg really is a marvellous, considerate host, thought Stephanie joyfully. He seemed to read her thoughts as he turned to her with that same special smile.

'How about you, darling?'

'Just a Perrier water, thanks.'

Greg stepped into the sitting room to pour the drinks.

'What a glorious day,' said Estelle happily. 'You know, I've never played pro tennis before.'

'Got news for you, pet,' said Reg with heavy husbandly humour, 'you still haven't.'

'Come on, Reg,' Stephanie laughed, 'don't be mean. Estelle played a terrific game, put up a real fight.'

'Hear, hear' – this was Greg's contribution from inside.

'Well, I tried.' Estelle was not insulted. 'Anyway, you know what I mean. It's not everyday I get to play with an ex-champ.'

The sudden tense silence brought Estelle up sharply.

'What did I say?' she demanded, flustered. 'Oh, I didn't

mean "ex" – I meant – oh, what the hell did I mean?' Her voice rose to a wail. 'Will someone take my foot out of my mouth?'

No one seemed to feel up to the task. Greg stepped round the door with Estelle's drink in his hand. He was smiling pleasantly but the lines round his eyes were hard.

'There you go, Estelle. You mean it's been three years since Wimbledon for me, eh?'

'I'm sorry, Greg,' murmured Estelle.

'Don't be.' And he moved back indoors.

'I'll give you a hand, Greg,' called Jilly. She rose from her sun-lounger in one move. That stupid cow Estelle! She felt the need to ally herself with Greg after this inadvertent put-down and instinctively answered it. She crossed the terrace to the French windows.

'Greg's no ex,' said Stephanie rather too loudly. 'He has no intention of retiring yet, have you, darling?'

'No way,' called Greg from within. 'I can't afford to. I've got a wife and family to support.' And Estelle's gaffe was diffused by the general laughter which followed.

Jilly stepped into the shaded sitting-room. Greg raised his eyebrows and smiled a quiet smile to himself as she entered. Although a natural hunter and predator, he could honestly boast that he had never knocked off an unwilling woman in his life. They had to come to him. He knew Jilly would, from the first moment. He continued to pour the whisky for Reg, and revelled in the power of conquest, the sense of dominance that Jilly's appearance gave him.

Jilly stood before him, willing him with all her magnetism to involve himself with her. Greg could smell her scent, the freshness of her hair, see the outline of her body in the flimsy sundress she was wearing. Reflectively he reached out his hand and lightly drew his knuckles across the tips of her breasts. He could feel her nipples, already erect, respond like wildfire at his touch. He was instantly aroused. She drew in her breath with a sharp gasp and began to pant lightly.

'Steph' – this was Estelle's high, rather nasal voice. Jilly and Greg looked at one another, hardly daring to move, such was the tension between them. 'Don't you ever get jealous thinking of the hordes of women who turn up at Greg's matches not to follow the tennis but just to go after him?'

'Yes! of course I do!'

'Stephanie, you're an honest woman!' Reg said approvingly, 'no secrets, eh?'

'An honest woman – they're rather rare these days.'

Inside the sitting room Jilly clearly heard Phillip's gentle sarcasm and knew it was meant for her. But she could not draw back from the flame of Greg's attraction – she felt more alive than she had done for years, pulsing with excitement. Casually Greg picked up a bottle of Perrier water in one hand, opened it, and loudly clinked it against the glass as he poured it out. At the same time, with his other hand he slid the strap of her sundress off her shoulder and drew the top down, exposing the top of her breast. Her breathing grew shallower and her pale eyes dark. She lifted her hands to slip her top off altogether.

Danger time. Greg could feel the start of a massive erection. The hairs were standing up on his arms and body. Quickly he replaced Jilly's strap, turned away, and concentrated on the formula he had perfected in adolescence for dispatching lustful thoughts and their compromising consequences. Then without a backward glance at Jilly, he picked up the drinks for Reg and Stephanie, and moved out again onto the terrace. A moment later Jilly rejoined the group outside, and if Phillip noticed a dangerous glitter about his wife, he was certainly not about to mention it.

'So you're off to Eden tomorrow?'

It was the fag-end of the party. The Rutherfords had left an hour or so before, and Phillip had been making unavailing attempts to get Jilly to come away for some time. But Jilly was not taking any notice, and now pursued the subject she had started.

'How long are you guys going to be out there?'

'A month.' Stephanie beamed. 'Alone in the outback. Oh, Katie'll be there of course, Chris and Sam and the other people on the station, but really it'll just be us, the dingoes and the wide open spaces.'

'Greg, you're going to adore Eden,' said Jilly brightly.

'Mmm. I want him to love it the way I do,' Stephanie continued. 'It's the one place where I've always been happy.'

'Darling, I've got a great idea!' Feeling cornered, Greg entertained a wild, crazy impulse. Then with a clear awareness of the fatal danger involved, he gave way to it – 'why don't we get Phillip and Jilly to join us at Eden?'

Stephanie stared at him, unable to hide her shock and hurt. Swiftly Greg covered for himself.

'Well, for the last couple of weeks anyway?'

'Phillip won't be here.' Jilly's tone was neutral. 'He's got to go back to New York again soon.'

'Well, how about just Jilly then? She could come by herself. You'd love it. It'd take the curse off being stuck with me all the time.'

Greg was turning all the power of his persuasive charm on Stephanie. Jilly felt the ground going from under her feet. Did she really want this?

'Oh don't be silly!' she burst out. 'It's your honeymoon. God!'

Stephanie smiled weakly. Greg took her hand and raised it to his lips.

'Our lives together,' he said in a low, sincere voice, 'are going to be one long honeymoon. Aren't they, darling?'

'I'll hold you to that,' Stephanie said nervously.

'It's just that I want you to have the two people you love on this trip – and everything to make you happy.'

Stephanie scolded herself for being selfish and silly. Greg was only thinking of her. She tried to cast her mind back.

'Gosh, Jilly and I haven't been at Eden together for – oh . . .'

'Donkey's years.' Jilly was curt, unsure.

'What do you say, Phillip?'

'It's up to Jilly.' Phillip knew with great sadness that events were moving out of his control. 'I'm afraid I'll really have to be off now – past my bedtime. You can get a cab back, Jilly, if you're staying on for a bit.'

'Oh, Jilly'll stay for a nightcap,' Greg assured him expansively. 'The girls can have a final natter while I take Kaiser on his night-time trot around, then I'll run Jilly home. Don't you worry about her.' He moved to show Phillip to the door.

'Oh do come, Jilly.' Stephanie had taken her decision. If Greg wanted Jilly there, that was good enough for her. He obviously liked her, and it would be someone else to divert him in case he got bored. And Jilly could play tennis with him, which she couldn't.

'Oh, I don't know.' The conflict within Jilly was enormous. Then Greg re-entered the room, and standing behind Stephanie, looked straight at her with a mocking, provocative grin.

'Well – maybe. Yeah.'

Jilly too had taken her decision.

Chapter Four

A cloud of red dust moved over the hot, dry landscape of the Northern Territory. At the wheel of the landrover sat Greg, beside him Stephanie. Behind, seated bolt upright and staring straight ahead was Katie Basklain, Eden's housekeeper for over forty years. An indomitable country-woman of almost seventy, she gripped her ·22 rifle as if she knew how to use it. At her feet a clutch of dead rabbits tied together proved that she did.

The flat, sundrenched wilderness stretched from horizon to horizon, with one lonely gum tree breaking the expanse. Greg scanned the arid scrub idly, in a good mood. He was enjoying Eden more than he had anticipated. Careful not to annoy him, Stephanie studied his expression covertly. Already she had learned to keep a weather eye on Greg's uncertain temper and to avoid provoking what she had come to think of as his dark side. Something must have happened in his past, she decided. Well, in time he would tell her. And she would make it all up to him with the power of her love.

Suddenly the landrover cut out and stopped without warning on the dry and deserted road.

'When did you last fill her up, Katie?' Stephanie asked 'Have we run out of petrol?'

'No, gauge says not,' said Greg. 'Maybe the air filter's come loose. Or out here – probably dust in the carburettor. I'll have to pull the whole bloody thing out and clean it.' He swung down out of the driver's seat, swearing under his breath.

From under her battered old hat, Katie surveyed him with scorn. Then she made her pronouncement.

'Vapourlock.'

'What's that, Katie?'

'Vapourlock.'

'Don't worry.' Greg appeared from under the bonnet. 'I think it's the carburettor.'

Katie rolled her eyes majestically to Stephanie, then with surprising agility hopped out of the vehicle, strode to the front, and elbowed the astonished Greg out of the way.

'It's vapourlocked,' she said emphatically. 'You've been dawdling, that's what caused it. Will you leave it to me?'

'Katie's awfully good with engines, dear,' Stephanie put in nervously. She stood in such awe of Greg that she could not bear anyone to treat him with disrespect. But Katie had been no respecter of man or beast for the last fifty years, and she was not going to begin with Mr Marsden.

Katie peered into the engine and fiddled about.

'I was right,' she announced. 'We might as well take it easy. Nothing to do but wait for it to cool.'

'It's a wonder you haven't opened a garage,' said Greg sarcastically. He had felt the old woman's antipathy from the moment of his arrival, and despite all his efforts to be charming she hadn't budged an inch. But his barb passed her by.

'Don't you worry, son, I could've,' she said simply. 'If I'd wanted. But there's no money in it these days. Buggers won't work the way we used to. Everyone's looking for the free handout, the meal ticket.' Stephanie's apprehension grew. Greg was so sensitive to any aspersions about money.

'Come on, darling,' she cried gaily, 'let's go for a walk.'

'If you insist. But does she really know what she's doing?' asked Greg as they moved off, loud enough for Katie to hear.

'You can always trust Katie, darling.'

'Oh, I do. I do.' Greg was grinning now, nudging her and pulling faces. Stephanie struggled to suppress her laughter and broke into a run.

'Effie!' Katie's piercing outback halloo came after them. 'You git y'self under that tree while you're waiting – sun'll ruin your skin, d'you hear?'

The two of them headed for the solitary tree, giggling

66

like children. They arrived at the base of the huge gum in high spirits. Out of breath, Stephanie leaned her back against the warm bark, and Greg faced her, a hand on either side of her head. How handsome he is, thought Stephanie, as she gazed with adoration at his face. Reading her expression, Greg moved gently into her to kiss her upturned mouth. As he did so, there came the crack of a rifle, and the bullet whistled past Greg's head.

'Jesus Christ!' Greg was almost comical in his shock and horror. 'The old – she's *lethal*.'

'Best behave ourselves, darling,' said Stephanie demurely. 'I don't think Katie likes the idea of any hanky-panky.'

Stephanie was so glad that she had answered her instincts to cut short the boat trip and hurry Greg off to Eden. Here she had always found peace, and the welcoming old stone house, with its rose-hung porch and arbours, its magnificent shaded gardens and vast rolling acres beyond, had not failed her this time. Here there had been plenty for Greg to do. He had enjoyed hours of solitary knocking up on the tennis court, his tennis balls retrieved by an endless train of willing children from the Aboriginal tribe living on the station. He had been particularly delighted to discover that Eden boasted a superb swimming pool, although even more surprised to discover that Stephanie couldn't swim, the legacy of a bad experience in childhood. There's so much we have to learn about one another, she thought contentedly. Well, here we have the time, and the peace.

She had had to accept, of course, that there were some things about Eden which could not mean as much to Greg as they did to her. He had no time for the local people, and had hurt her by his ability never to speak to the Aboriginals unless to issue an order. Stephanie by contrast had known them as part of her emotional world since childhood. She had been reared on their haunting stories of the dawning of the world in the great Dreamtime, when the ancestrals' spirits wandered at will over the land, and as they passed they made the people, the plants, the animals, hills and rivers. Since her father's death, when they had drifted in with other members of their tribe, Stephanie had grown particularly close to the two Aboriginal brothers, Chris and Sam. Chris, the elder, had in abundance the mystical gift of his people, and with him she enjoyed an almost wordless communion. Apart from herself, Chris was the only person who could handle her stallion King. Now over twenty, the mighty horse was in the prime of life. He was one of the elements that pulled Stephanie back to Eden again and again. Riding him had been one of the major loves of Stephanie's unloved girlhood – and the devoted Chris almost always knew when to get him ready for her without having to be asked.

All these thoughts were running through Stephanie's head as she contentedly toured the house at the end of the day. Overcome with the day's events Katie had succumbed to her weakness for cooking sherry and had dropped off leaving Stephanie to do the rounds and check that all was at peace. Satisfied, she turned down the long corridor, and entered the bedroom. Greg lay reclining on Max Harper's bed, his hands behind his head, naked, waiting. Stephanie looked at him with love.

'I'm afraid it's the lantern tonight, darling,' she said, indicating the hurricane lamp she was carrying. 'Katie's a trifle indisposed, and she's the only one who ever understood the generator.'

'I'll bet it's vapourlocked,' said Greg lazily. 'If that generator ran on sherry like she does, we wouldn't be in the dark.'

'Oh Greg, have a heart – Katie's nearly seventy,' said Stephanie, laughing. She gathered up the nightdress and negligée from her trousseau set and made to go out to the bathroom.

'Hey – Steph.' She turned to look at him. 'Come here.' Apprehensively she crossed to his side of the bed and sat down. She settled the hurricane lantern on the bedside

68

table and leaned forward to blow it out. Greg's grip on her shoulder prevented her.

'I want to look at you,' he whispered.

Sitting up, he unzipped the back of her dress, and eased it forward away from her body. Gently he kissed her neck and shoulders, stroking her heavy hair away from her head and softly tonguing her ear, licking the lobe and probing deep within. With both hands he slowly slid down her bra straps from her shoulders and with infinite tenderness exposed her breasts.

'Look at them,' he murmured. 'Aren't they wonderful?' His hands sought their silky fullness, stroking, caressing. He found the nipples and squeezing gently drew them out to their full extent from the rosy areola. Lowering his head, he drew one into his mouth and ran his tongue around its dimpled circumference. And as he did so he felt Stephanie growing ever more rigid with tension and dread.

Rage shot through him like a fire. What the *fuck* was wrong with her? Greg had never in his life made love to a woman who was not groaning for him, on the point of orgasm just by thinking about him, ready to come with his first kiss. He had learned how to stave off the first swift climax in a woman, and then to bring her again and again, because he so enjoyed the power he could have over the soft, yielding bodies. He loved to make a woman moan and writhe, cry 'oh please! more! don't stop'. He loathed to feel a woman's muscles set under his hand, see her eyes wide with dread as he did now.

But hatred can fuel the so-called act of love, and Greg was a determined man. Patiently he helped Stephanie out of her clothes, laid her on the bed, and to make her feel happier blew out the lantern. With all the resources of his skill and experience he explored her body, playing expertly on her clitoris, insistently opening her tight little cunt, until at last, when he was on the edge of his restraint, he had eventually readied her to the extent where she would accept his straining cock, and in a disappointing, juddering

69

finale, he came. That was always good for him, even now. But his heart was cold.

Stephanie lay beside him on the bed overwhelmed with grief and frustration. Her aroused sexuality, unreleased, tormented her. But worse was the renewal of her old fear – I am not a woman! She stared at the ceiling, struggling to control her feelings. Eventually she spoke.

'I'm sorry. I'm so sorry.'

'I keep telling you—'

'I know.'

'Go to sleep.'

'I love you, Greg.'

'And I love you. OK?'

And clinging onto that age-old exchange, Stephanie watched out another sleepless night.

From the air, Eden was easy to miss. The one inhabited spot for hundreds of miles around, it was a tiny speck in the flat red wasteland extending out of sight in all directions. But the pilot of the twin-engine Beachcraft Queenair had made the journey a number of times. The little plane made good time through the still, shimmering air.

'Here she comes!' Alerted by Chris, Stephanie had been ready for Jilly's arrival when the plane touched down, and eagerly ran to greet her friend.

'How are you, Jilly? Oh, I'm so glad you're here. It's going to be wonderful!'

Jilly hopped down from the plane into Stephanie's waiting arms. Over Stephanie's shoulder she could see Greg striding loosely away from the house towards the airstrip to greet her. She smiled.

'Yes, darling, I do believe it is.'

A few hours later, as the harsh day softened into a technicolour sunset, Stephanie and Jilly sat side by side in the rose garden. Stephanie idly played with a deep red tea rose she had picked, and the scent of summer hung heavy between them.

'You know, Jilly,' she began dreamily. 'If I ever had any doubts about why Greg married me, I haven't any more.'

Jilly stiffened.

'How d'you mean?'

'He's wonderful to me. He makes life so much fun, and he's so considerate. He really tries to make me happy. You'll never guess what he's lined up for us while you're here.'

'Tell me.'

'He's arranging a crocodile hunt.'

'What? Fantastic! But I thought you—'

'Couldn't bear killing things?' Stephanie finished for her with a wry smile. 'It's true. But Greg didn't know that when he planned it. And he was so full of the idea I hadn't the heart to pull the rug from under his feet.'

Crocodiles. Jilly repressed a shudder of excitement and dread.

'Where is he now?' she asked, trying to steady her voice.

'Trying to call Darwin on the radio to hire a guide for us. Apparently the good ones are few and far between.'

'The radio? Still no phone, then?'

'Too far out. So it's still the old pedal radio – nothing's changed!'

'So when's the hunt?'

'As soon as Greg can finalize the arrangements. He couldn't believe I'd lived so near to croc territory and had never been before. He's so excited he can hardly wait.'

'And how about you, Steph?'

'Oh, me.' Stephanie sighed. 'The brutes terrify me. But . . . I suppose a woman in love will do anything for her man.'

'I suppose so. Yes. Anything.'

The sun went down over Eden in a blaze of blood red and gold. As night deepened, one by one the inhabitants settled to their rest in the rooms leading off the wide shaded verandah that ran three sides of the house. By the French windows leading to Jilly's room, a shadow flickered and was gone. Nothing moved in the warm, still air. The house slept.

In the stables across the paddock the stallion King stirred restlessly. From his box he caught a scent in the night air, something that disturbed him. The man with him spoke a few words softly in the liquid Aboriginal.

'Gwandalan, yarraman, bana nato, barra. Be quiet, horse, I hear it too.'

Outside, an almost soundless footfall, and the figure of a man darkened the doorway, and slipped inside. He moved lightly to the back of the building, where the hay was stacked against the wall, and blended into the darkness, became invisible. Soon another footstep, and a woman's shape flitted in. She hovered in the entrance, then plunged into the thick blackness within, turning to face the door as if expecting someone. The man approached her soundlessly from behind and in one swift movement grabbed her roughly, and crushed her body into his.

'Aaah! Greg . . .' Jilly's breath escaped in a soft wail.

There was no light inside the stable. But Chris, looking over the side of King's box, could see Greg perfectly where he stood holding Jilly close to him. Unhurriedly he stepped from the box. He knew that any small sound he made would be covered by those of King, or the other horses. He knew too that the pale untrained eyes of whites could never pierce the darkness as his did. One shadow blended into another, and Chris was gone. Only the animals remained as witnesses of the primal drama about to be re-enacted in their midst.

Greg cupped his hands around Jilly's breasts from behind and found her nipples already hard with longing. Teasingly he ran his hands down her body and with the fingers of both hands traced the outline of the V at the top of her legs. She trembled under his hands. Tearing herself away, she turned round and grasped at him hungrily for the first desperate kiss. Greg felt her prehensile little tongue flickering round his mouth and a shaft of excitement stabbed through him. Her fingers sought the front of his

72

jeans and he felt the blood spurt into his cock as she delicately traced a tattoo on the shape stirring there. She groped for the button on the waistband of the jeans.

'Oh no, you don't,' he hissed with delight. He picked her up, and moved confidently through the pitch darkness to the back of the stables, where he laid her down on the sweet-smelling tightly-packed hay. She pulled him down beside her, and taking his face between her hands, she kissed him again and again, exploring the inside of his mouth with her tongue. He fought back, thrusting his tongue so deep that she grew dizzy with excitement. She pushed him back, and began to undo his shirt, slipping her hand inside to find the contact with his body which she was so longing for. Greg lay back and laughed aloud with delight as Jilly skilfully caressed his nipples, fuelling his strong excitement, covering his chest with little kisses like butterflies' wings, then taking her white teeth to nip him sharply here and there. Compare this with screwing a lump of dead wood like Stephanie!

His hunger growing, Greg felt for the silky wrap she was wearing, and pushed it off her shoulders. The feel of the strong masculine fingers on her breasts sent Jilly into a spasm of excitement, and wriggling her arms free of the negligée, she jumped on top of him and squatted down on his hips. She trembled at the sensation of his cock between her legs as he took her breasts in both hands. Confidently he traced the smooth as satin contours, teasingly brushing her nipples then moving away again, until almost maddened she took his hands and crushed them against her hard, at the same time thrusting down with her hips to rub against the thick shaft of his penis straining against the fabric of his jeans. She worked her way skilfully to and fro, her tempo increasing with the mounting rhythm of her own excitation, until she could tell from his breathing that he was almost ready to come.

'You fucking little witch!' Greg could hardly believe the speed of his response. Reaching up, he took her by the hips and threw her down on her back on the bed of hay. Tearing at the sash which still held the wrap around her waist, he freed her from the flimsy folds and began to discover the whole length of her body. He crushed her breasts together, nuzzling each of the nipples in turn, allowing one to pop slowly out of his mouth as he moved on to the other. Then he turned his attention to the swelling mound between her legs, already moist and creamy to his satisfied touch, the silky curling hairs damp with sex dew. Tantalizingly he stroked her clitoris with deliberate slowness, and when he could feel the onrush of her first orgasm, abruptly he stopped, laughing softly.

'You – you bastard!' Arrested on the brink, Jilly juddered to a grinding halt. Rousing up, she pushed his shirt from his shoulders, and unzipped his jeans. Forcing them free of his hips, she released his pulsing cock and took it in both her hands. God, it was marvellous, unbelievable. Jilly had been fantasizing about this for so long, the reality almost overwhelmed her. He was beautiful, all the way down. Her senses whirling, she leaned over and very gently kissed the head of the penis, kissed it all down its length, absorbing the strong and unmistakable scent of his manhood as she did so. His balls were wonderful, tight and full. One by one she held them in her hands, then began to caress them with her lips, alternating with playful love bites. Then she moved back to the top of his cock and took it in her mouth, excited almost beyond bearing by the restless rhythm of Greg's hands and the nearness of fulfilment. At last he reared up, threw her backwards, took her by the hips, and jammed his cock into her, thrusting away at the centre of her being. Together they came to their first long-drawn-out shuddering climax, higher and higher till, spent at last, they lay together like one.

Later, much later, finally sated, they conversed in broken whispers as the horses shifted restlessly in their stalls, made uneasy by the nearness of creatures on heat.

'You're pretty bloody sexy, y'know that?'

'Oh Greg, I couldn't have stood to be away for another minute.'

'I missed you too.'

'I thought I was going to die. Greg – I can't bear the thought of you touching her.'

Me neither, thought Greg mirthlessly.

'It won't be much longer,' he said.

'I love you so much. What are we going to do?'

'Trust me, baby. Just trust me. OK?'

And watching by his campfire on the other side of the station Chris felt the age-old mystery of mankind evil germinate and flower in the hot, moist air.

'Well, Jilly, how are we going to entertain you at Eden?' Stephanie anxiously raised the question in an attempt to brighten up what seemed to her to be an unusually gloomy breakfast time. Opposite her across the table Greg sat glowering, lost in his private thoughts, while Jilly was nervous and abstracted, pouring down black coffee but obviously unable to face any of the magnificent breakfast Katie had provided for them all. Stephanie's concern had been awakened the previous evening, when over dinner Greg and Jilly had hardly had a word to say to one another. With the close scrutiny born of her love and insecurity, Stephanie had noticed that they would hardly even look at one another, but if their eyes met both of them would hastily look away and abruptly begin a new topic of conversation. Never a practised hostess, Stephanie had had to work very hard to try to counteract the atmosphere of strain, and all her old worries had swum back to the surface. I was afraid they wouldn't get on, she mourned to herself. I can see they're trying, because they know it's so important to me, but it isn't working. Her fears were confirmed when Jilly had pleaded a headache as a transparent excuse for going to bed early, while Greg had taken so long making the nightly round of the homestead and outbuildings that it was quite obvious he couldn't sleep, poor darling. Surely Jilly can't be getting on his nerves already, Stephanie worried – she's only just arrived.

'Entertain me?' Jilly returned, rather too sharply. 'Don't

you go bothering your head about me, Steph. There's plenty to do at Eden. I'll . . . entertain myself!' She stared straight ahead and laughed unnecessarily.

'Well, there's the pool . . . plenty of walking . . . and all the good books you could ever read in the library,' Stephanie said brightly. But inwardly her heart misgave her, for although she loved Eden for the chance it gave her to rest and relax, she couldn't kid herself that any of these pursuits held any charm for the sophisticated Jilly. Then a more promising idea struck her. 'And don't forget the tennis court! I'm such a rabbit, someone has to get out there and give the champ some practice!'

'Will you stop fussing, Stephanie?' Seeing the look of admiring love on Stephanie's face instantly turn to one of hurt and shock only encouraged Greg to go on. 'Y' behaving like a broody hen this morning, what's wrong with you? Jilly's a big girl now –' Stephanie noticed his mouth tighten on this '– she can look after herself, OK?'

'Oh yes, Greg, I know. I was only . . .' Her voice trailed off.

Greg looked at her with disfavour. Christ, when she sat there gazing down at her hands and twisting them in her lap she looked like a schoolgirl, not a grown woman. Getting to know Stephanie better at Eden, where she could be completely off-guard and natural, had shown Greg for the first time just how unsophisticated and unschooled Stephanie really was, and he did not like it. He had had to fight so hard for his own entrée into the world of wealth, glamour and privilege that he was subtly outraged by someone who had been given it all on a plate, and had thrown it away. She could have been a world leader of the beautiful people, he thought with contempt. But now he recognized that she simply did not have it in her. He would have to abandon the idea he had cherished before they married that he could turn her into the sort of woman who would be a worthy consort for Greg Marsden, elegant, soigné, gracious and cosmopolitan. He felt the explosion of that little dream like a personal injury, and he was finding it hard to forgive her.

Brooding resentfully, he looked across the table at Jilly. There sat everything a woman ought to be. Poised, confident, bright, sexy – oh yeah, *sexy* – with great self-discipline Greg kept a smile from curving his lips and maintained his expression of injured irritability. Even sitting carelessly in her housecoat this early in the morning, with no make-up on and the hard sunlight pouring in on her, she looked terrific. He watched her closely as she tore a roll to shreds, inserting only tiny portions of it in her mouth. The restless movements of her fingers, the flashing glimpse of her small white teeth, excited him. Jilly looked up and caught his eye. A gleam passed between them, instantly suppressed by Greg as his sense of caution made him glance at Stephanie. She was still staring down at her hands, and Greg felt a spurt of anger; at himself for behaving like a schoolboy in fear of being caught out, and at her, as one who now had the power to crack the whip over him. Fuck you, Stephanie, he thought – then, immediately afterwards, if only I didn't have to. Stephanie meanwhile had decided to put her own hurt feelings aside and concentrate on her loved ones.

'Sorry if I've been fussing you two,' she said with a generous smile. 'But I still reckon you could enjoy a game of tennis together – better than either of you could, playing with me. Why don't you have a game this morning before it gets too hot to play?'

As the days went by Greg and Jilly seemed to be finding a way of getting on with each other, much to Stephanie's relief. Things were still far from easy. She could not blind herself to the awkwardness that ensued whenever the three of them were together, the sudden silences, veiled glances and air of tension. She blamed herself for not being able to bring the two of them closer, and her solution to this was to make sure that Greg and Jilly spent as much time as possible together getting to know each other properly. And she was pleased and heartened to observe that when they returned from playing tennis, walking or driving round the station or the famous local beauty spots, they were always more cheerful and relaxed with one another. It was only in her presence that they became strained and stiff. With her built-in habit of self-deprecation, Stephanie did not find that at all strange. With two people as bright, attractive and interesting as Jilly and Greg it was only natural that dull, clumsy Stephanie should be the odd one out, as she had been all her life.

There were things that puzzled her though, things she worried away at in the darkness of the night and could not find the answer to. She knew, for instance, that Greg did not appreciate Eden's Aboriginal people the way that she did. She had had to accept, although with some sadness, that he had no time for them and would never bother to learn their ways and try to share their wisdom. But now he seemed to be developing an active and irrational hatred of them. One day when Greg and Stephanie were going out to ride, after Jilly had announced that the two newly-weds must spend some time together or she would feel like a cuckoo in the nest, Stephanie had asked Chris if he would have the horses ready for them. At the prearranged time they had left the house and gone across to the stable yard to find Chris standing waiting with King, the great black stallion deceptively demure in Chris's gentle hands, while nearby Sam was holding the leggy chestnut Greg had chosen to ride. It was a glorious morning, the outback was beckoning, and Stephanie was in the seventh heaven at the thought of having Greg to herself for the next few hours. But as she took her horse from Chris and began to mount, her happiness was unexpectedly dispelled by the sound of Greg's raised voice.

'What the hell are you staring at?'

Stephanie glanced over her shoulder in alarm. Chris was standing quietly behind her looking at Greg with an expressionless gaze.

'And you, y'bastard! What are *you* staring at?' Inexplic-

78

ably Sam had now incurred Greg's anger, although he too was simply standing unmoving by the horse.

'The pair of you! Get back to y'work! Y'lazy buggers, loafing round here all day, with nothing better to do than hang around gawping—'

'Greg!' For herself, Stephanie would never dare to challenge Greg, whose very frown held her in anxious dread. But it was quite beyond her to stand by and let the two brothers be abused. Leaning down along her horse's neck she spoke softly to Chris in Aboriginal, to apologize for the incident and reassure him that it would not happen again. Although his eyes as always greeted hers in friendship and understanding, there was something in them that Stephanie could not fathom – a kind of pity? Sam, too, normally much more communicative than his brother, kept silent and aloof.

'Y'ready, Steph?'

Greg's call, in effect a command, reached her from further down the yard where he had drawn back in disdain while she spoke to Chris and Sam. With a hasty farewell, she moved to join him and they rode out together. Greg was brooding furiously, his mind in a turmoil. Just as he was getting onto the horse, he had happened to catch sight of Chris's face across its withers. As their eyes met, Greg received some kind of message. He knows! was the thought that flashed through Greg, *the bastard knows about me and Jilly*! He did not waste time trying to work out how. Although not an outbacker himself, Greg was aware like all Australians of the strange and metaphysical power of Aboriginals, their super-normal skills of knowledge and intuition. What was suddenly giving Greg very unpleasant food for thought was the question, would he tell Stephanie?

He had not told her so far, of that Greg was positive. Work it through a step at a time, he told himself, fighting down the panic surging up inside him – she doesn't know yet. The Stephanie he had got to know at Eden could never play the double game that some women manage to, concealing their knowledge of their husband's infidelity,

79

behaving as normal no matter what it cost them, in the hope that his love would return to them at last. No, Stephanie was as madly in love with him as ever, and nothing had happened to disturb that. But for the first time Greg entertained the idea that something might. Like the opportunist that he was, Greg had taken Jilly because she had chanced along. He had never thought that what for him was just a casual fuck, although a bloody good one, could seriously threaten his situation. Now he saw very clearly that what was almost meaningless to him would be the very opposite to Stephanie. It would be the one thing she could not forgive. Oh, her besotted love would make allowances for almost anything else, he felt sure, from crashing the white Rolls to bankrupting Harper Mining. He could get away with any other infidelity too; he felt pretty confident of that. But this, which linked breaking his marriage vows to her as soon as they were made with the classic ultimate betrayal of screwing her best friend – how could any woman be expected to forgive that?

Greg broke out into a prickly sweat on the back of his neck. Although only a short while earlier he had been basking in his false security, now he suddenly saw himself as a man staring ruin in the face. If Steph found out . . . The risk he had been running, which previously had put an exciting edge of danger on his stolen escapades with Jilly, now seemed to him frankly terrifying. To lose all this now . . . Greg had only known Stephanie for a few weeks, not even a matter of months, but already he had slipped into the luxury of her wealth and lifestyle, like a hand into a glove. If it were all to be snatched away again now . . . Sweating more, he pushed the fear away, and concentrated on trying to think his way out of the trap he had run himself into. As they rode along Stephanie stole many an anxious loving glance at Greg, in the hope of breaking in on his mood of black introspection. But Greg's newly-awakened concern was not to be lightly laid aside and he hardly spoke a word to her all the time they were out.

What's getting to him, Stephanie asked herself in deep distress – oh if only I knew!

Possibly because she knew that Greg had somehow lost his peace of mind, that one gift which above all Eden should have given him, Stephanie became more and more inclined to indulge him in every way. She had always been afraid to cross him for fear of provoking his anger. Now she became unable to withstand him even when she knew he was in the wrong. Not long after the day of their disastrous ride together the outside world broke in on them unexpectedly when the ancient radio in the kitchen emitted a cough and splutter, then sprang to unaccustomed life. It was Bill McMaster calling from Sydney to speak to Stephanie, hastily summoned from the poolside where she was watching Greg and Jilly disport themselves.

'Steph? It's Bill. Look, I really hate to break in on your honeymoon like this . . .'

'That's OK, Bill. Go ahead.'

'It's just that there could be something rather big about to blow up, and I want you in the picture. I want your say-so on which way we jump. I've had an interesting hint from a mole of mine in one of the big brokers that a hefty chunk of Harper shares are coming up for sale.'

'Our shares on the market? Why?' Out of the corner of her eye Stephanie saw that Greg had followed her in from the pool and now approached the radio receiver, dripping water all the way, to pick up the other headset and listen in on the conversation.

'Oh, combination of circumstances, all routine, no reflection on the stock,' Bill reassured her. 'But I don't think we want a packet of our shares floating around the international markets just now.'

'No, certainly not.' Stephanie's face was thoughtful as she worked out the angles. 'It's vital to keep up confidence in the company with the new projects still at such a tentative stage.'

'Yeah, nothing at all's come in on that exploratory

drilling yet, by the way.' Bill's voice crackled on with the latest news while Stephanie made her decision.

'I take it you want to buy?'

'Yeah, I do. It'll cost us, sure, because the shares are good and high right now – I've just got the latest figure if you want it – but we can stand the pace if we have to.'

'Then later, if we want, we can release the shares in dribs and drabs to re-secure capital without any risk of a run, or a loss of confidence. Yes, you're right Bill. Let's buy.'

'Steph!' To Stephanie's astonishment Greg leaned forward and switched the radio from 'transmit' to 'receive'. His eyes were glittering and he looked alive for the first time in days. 'Hey, Steph, let me handle this, OK?'

'How d'you mean, Greg?'

'Well, you told me I had to play a real part in Harper Mining,' Greg said gaily, 'Not just be your sleeping partner, so to speak. And this is my first chance! Let me take this decision for you – for us, darling.'

Stephanie was bewildered. Her heart almost melted with gratitude for his expression of love and faith in their future. But this was a major issue, and he was so inexperienced in business. While she sat there, bemused, Bill's voice broke the silence with an angry crackle.

'Hello, Steph? Steph? Are y'still there?'

Calmly Greg spoke on 'transmit'. 'Hello Bill, Greg here. I'm handling this now. We don't buy – it'll tie up too much of the ready we need for development – I've got a few ideas of my own on that score. We can afford to let the market find its own level. There won't be a run on Harper's. We're too strong. A good burst of buying could push the shares right up, anyway.'

There was a thunderous silence from the receiver. Then Bill spoke.

'Put me back on to Steph for a moment, will you?'

'He wants to talk to you again,' Greg informed the trembling Stephanie, momentarily cutting off the Sydney end. 'You'll back me up on this, won't you, darling?' He smiled at her lovingly.

'Greg – I . . .' He was wrong, Stephanie knew, foolish and wrong, taking this decision simply to go against her and Bill and somehow make his own mark on the company. 'It's not as easy as that,' she managed finally. 'If our shares—'

'I want you to back me, Steph,' he interrupted. His voice was still pleasant but his face was bleak and his eyes threatening. 'Because if you don't . . .'

'Oh Greg . . .' It was almost a whimper and Greg knew he'd won. Immediately he reconnected Bill, who heard in stunned disbelief Stephanie's broken instructions that matters should be conducted according to Greg's way of thinking. His vociferous attempts to change her mind were quietly cut off, and to his fury he had to bear a lecture from Greg about the inner workings of the stock market and the importance of not losing your nerve in business. But Bill had no option in the end but to knuckle under. Despite his importance to Stephanie, he was still only managing director, while she was owner and chairman of the company. So if that was her wish – *if* it was – all he could do was to carry it through.

Bill did so, but it was one of the most difficult things he had ever had to do in his business life. For although in theory Greg could have been right, in his bones, like Stephanie, Bill instinctively felt that the more conservative course would have been the wiser one. Within twenty-four hours he was vindicated. When the shares came on the market, the unexpected size of the block released, together with the natural jitteriness of any stock exchange, produced a rapid crisis of confidence. Other investors were panicked into jumping on the bandwagon and enough movement was created to give Harper Mining shares a very bad time for a short while. Eventually the basic strength and soundness of the company came through and the shares, assisted by some judicious third-party buying by Bill on his own initiative, rallied and held up. But it had been an extremely unpleasant patch, as bad as any Bill could remember in a lifetime in business. It had also been very damaging – money, time, and perhaps most important of all business confidence had been lost and would take a lot of repairing. Bill would gladly not have been right at such a price as this.

When the news was communicated to Eden, Bill did not need to spell it all out to Stephanie. With her years of experience, she understood every detail. She was agonized at Harpers' loss of capital, and of face – the company had become very dear to her in the years she had worked in it, and she felt the damage like a personal sorrow. But even more acutely she felt for Greg's loss of face, his rash judgement, his need to make an impact more than to make a sound decision. She could not bring herself to be angry with him, feeling his failure as a scalding shame and an ominous portent for the future. But Greg had no qualms about getting angry with her, with Bill, with almost anybody in fact except himself.

'Y'didn't put me in the picture at all!' he attacked her hotly when the bad news found its way to Eden. 'Y'just crumpled up like a frightened mouse and didn't tell me a damn thing! And McMaster – he must have played it wrong in Sydney for everything to go haywire like this. He's dropped a bundle on this one all right. God! – I can't go on like this, Stephanie. I've got to have a free run. I'm boxing with one hand tied behind my back here. When we get back they'll have to see I mean business – and *you'll have to show 'em I do*!'

Abandoning the stricken Stephanie without a backward glance Greg stormed off to find Jilly, where he knew he would get an enthusiastic reception as a welcome change from Stephanie and her reproachful cow's eyes. Together they went for a drive through the outback in the landrover, ostensibly sight-seeing, in reality to hammer away at what had become an over-riding preoccupation for both of them, what are we to do? Jilly was now hooked on Greg with a deeper and more compulsive feeling than she had felt before for any other man. If she had not been so blinded she might have had a better chance of seeing that Greg was paying only the scantest lip-service to the idea that any plans for the future included the two of them. Much, much more than Jilly could ever dream of in suffering and loss might have been averted had she realized that the panic thrumming through Greg's head sounded only as 'what am *I* to do?', or that he was rapidly approaching the edge where much more stable men than he ever had been do dangerous and dreadful things.

'There he goes!' The probing spotlight stabbed through the darkness of the tropical night. A huge crocodile caught in its beam froze for a second, then with a convulsive twitch of its entire frame jerked away from the bank and slid into the water. The heavy spear grazed its hide, but it was gone.

'Lost'm, the bastard!'

The crocodile hunt was in full swing. In the large canoe, laden with hunting gear, were the guide, Reeder, his son Malc, and his Aboriginal Denny. Stephanie had cried off at the last moment, but behind the three hunters sat Greg and Jilly.

'Again! There! Get it, Malc.'

The floodlight had picked up another crocodile gliding through the slimy water. Spear at the ready, Malc threw, and hit the beast on the side. Mortally wounded, the creature began to thrash around, opening its jaws wide to tear at the spear with its terrible teeth.

As Greg caught a glimpse of the sharp white teeth, he felt again a reminiscent stab of excitement, thinking of Jilly and their lovemaking. Already aroused by the thrill of the hunt, he was electrified by the enormous power of the quarry, and secretly stimulated by their vicious killing urges. Now he leaned forward intently, totally absorbed as under Reeder's curt direction his assistants succeeded in dropping a rope around the crocodile's jaws. Even then, the struggle was far from over. Rearing up on its tail, the creature made a determined attack on Malc. Only the swift intervention of Denny, warding it off with a heavy pole, saved him.

'Jeez-us!' Greg was aghast. Reeder chortled with amusement.

'Oh yeah. An old saltie'll eat anything – even him,' he said with an affectionate glance at his son, now engaged in hauling up the crocodile and securing it to a long board. 'Fish, mostly. But crabs, wallabies, cattle, buffalo even. And people. They'll have a go at anything when they're hungry enough. And they're hungry this season. Attacks on humans by the crocs have been so frequent in the last year, we're getting to be the endangered species, not them.' Greg nodded thoughtfully.

'This one's tight, Dad. Any more?'

Reeder turned to Greg speculatively. 'Had enough, or d'you want to go for another?' Greg looked at Jilly. Her eyes were glittering, and he felt her body tense and aroused.

'Why not?' she said gaily, 'why not?

Back at the camp, Stephanie tossed uneasily on her light bed. How much longer would they be? She could not regret the sudden decision to leave Eden and embark on a safari up through the Alligator River territory. Greg and Jilly had both been so keen on the idea, and their enthusiasm had carried her forward. She had hoped too that the adventure would help Greg to put the fiasco of his first sally into Harper Mining business behind him, so that he would smile at her again, and be nice – she wanted so desperately to please him. In spite of all her worries she had enjoyed the journey, and the fun of making camp on a cleared section of bank beside a salt-water estuary with the dense bush protecting them all around. She loved the basic camping life, sleeping rough, washing in the river, hanging clothes on a makeshift washing line and keeping house in the wilderness. After the arid starkness of the scrubland around Eden, the Kakadu parkland formed a stunning contrast of salt water swamps, eucalyptus forest, weird sandstone escarpments and primeval lagoons undisturbed by any except the resident crocodiles since time began.

But the killing – she hated that. Her whole nature as a woman who would always instinctively pick up the lost creature abandoned by its mother and give it life, fought against it. And in Greg's fascination with the hunting and death of the great reptiles she had a glimpse into a darkness in his soul that she shuddered to contemplate. Oh God, what was she to do?

At last she heard them returning. As she hurried out to greet them Chris emerged silently from the shadows and moved forward to the bank to help to moor the canoe and unload the catch. Reeder hailed her jovially.

'Mrs Marsden! Come and see where one of 'em has taken a bite out of the boat. And nearly out of m'son and heir, too!'

Crocodile after crocodile was being unloaded from the canoe. Stephanie shuddered at the size of them.

'Y'think these are big? There's an old salty named Gindy Baru, wait'll you meet him on a dark night! Seventy year old, twenty foot long – I've been after him for years. They reckon he's killed seven people already.'

'Joe –' Stephanie protested weakly, 'you're giving me goose-bumps.'

'You'll be all right, darling.' Greg had joined them, elated by his night's sport. 'I'll look after you.'

'Yeah, but watch your step,' cautioned Reeder. 'Get too confident, y'wind up as croc tucker.'

'Greg – darling –' Stephanie took a deep breath. 'Let's not kill any more – please?'

Greg smiled. 'Don't worry, Steph. I'll think up another form of entertainment.'

At eveningtide of the same day, Stephanie sat clutching her camera in the prow of the canoe as it nosed its way out through the swamps. She was blissfully happy. Greg really did love her, after all. He had arranged this trip to shoot not alligators but the fabulous sunset. He'd been determined to take her, in spite of opposition. She had heard him arguing with Reeder, who had vigorously criticized his desire to take the boat out by himself, with darkness due within the hour. And he had had to get angry with Chris, to make him get the boat ready. Mysteriously the Aboriginal had neglected Greg's instructions until it was almost too late to go out. But Greg had got round them both.

The sun was sinking in bands of searing yellow, orange and brown across the sky. On every side the trees, silhouetted against the lurid light, composed strange, distorted shapes, sinister, threatening. Behind Stephanie in the boat, Jilly shivered. Her feeling for Greg had now become so intense that she lived in daily wonder that Stephanie had not noticed it. We can't go on like this, she thought desperately. She shot a glance at Greg, steering the craft from the back. He stared back impassively, lost in his own thoughts.

The narrow waterway widened as they joined a large lagoon. The dark slimy water, like oil, scarcely rippled at their passing. All around motionless gnarled shapes indicated the presence of the malignant denizens of the estuaries. Occasionally a hooded eye would slip open to show the cold life within. But Stephanie did not notice, her eyes fixed on the skyline. Through a break in the trees, the spectacular sunset was caught in a natural frame, changing from moment to moment in a dazzling kaleidoscope of colour.

'Oh look! Look there. Can we stop here, please Greg?' Excitedly Stephanie reached for her camera, and as the canoe came to rest she quickly focused on the brilliant scene. Babbling happily, she stood up to compose the shot.

'Oh darling, that's just wonderful, it's quite breathtaking –' She did not hear Greg as he moved down the boat, past Jilly, to stand behind her. Her eye was caught by an insignificant movement in the water.

'Greg! Oh my God, it's a crocodile! It's huge! It must be that Gindy Baru that Reeder was talking about!'

The hideous reptile was making straight for the canoe, its shiny black eyes fixed on her.

'Greg' – Stephanie half turned. The next instant she felt a heavy blow between her shoulderblades. She flew through the air and hit the water with a splash, going straight down.

Panicking, flailing her arms and legs, she drew in water instead of air and felt her lungs constrict in terror. She fought her way to the surface and came up screaming.

'Greg!' She could hear another woman's voice screaming as if in a cruel echo of her own.

'Steph! Steph! Steph!' Frantic, screaming, Stephanie reached out hopelessly for the boat. She could see Greg standing there, motionless, yet exalted, a pale fire in his eyes she had never seen before. In that second she read both his heart and her doom in his face.

'Jilly – Jilly, help me!' She turned her eyes to Jilly sitting paralysed with horror in the middle of the boat.

The crocodile took her from behind, grasping her arm and shoulder in its huge jaws. Its teeth ripped down the side of her face and neck, and the blood poured from the gaping wounds.

'Aaargh!' Eyes wide and bursting from her face, Stephanie slowly went under as the crocodile dragged her down.

Suddenly Jilly was released from the paralysing grip of her terror. She jumped up and grasped Greg's arm.

'Greg – for God's sake! She can't even swim!' He did not move. Desperately Jilly grabbed for the canoe pole and leaned over the side, attacking the killer reptile where she could reach it. Sobbing, swearing, she fought for Stephanie's life, till she felt Greg's hand on her shoulder, she was thrown back into the bottom of the boat, and the pole, wrenched from her grasp, was tossed over the side. Greg stood over her with a rifle. Calmly he turned to the water.

With its jaws clamped firmly on its victim, the crocodile

was tossing her body to and fro. Her naked legs waved about like waterweed, her bloody face surfaced from time to time, eyes anguished, like a revenant. Her screams, choked by the water grew fainter, her frantic movements weaker and weaker. At last, with the instinct of its kind, the crocodile took her into the final death roll. As the daylight disappeared in a last sunburst of crimson red, Stephanie sank out of sight in a boiling cauldron of mud and blood. It was finished. Darkness covered water and land. With great deliberation, Greg turned, and emptied his rifle into the air.

'Oh, you bloody bastard!' Back at the camp, Reeder wept with rage. 'Fucking amateurs, I warned you—'

'Reeder, I've lost my wife!' Greg had been quick to raise the alarm. 'We're wasting time. She may be still alive out there. What do we do now?'

'Call Darwin on the radio. But they've no hope of getting in here before morning. And alive? If you really love your wife fella –' Reeder paused, heavily '– pray she's not.'

And in the stillness of the long night nothing stirred except, deep in the bush, the flames of the sacred fire that Chris had raised to charm Stephanie's spirit wherever it roamed and keep it warm.

Chapter Five

The next day's sun rose sluggishly, bathed in blood and lowering through heavy bands of thick swamp mist. Before dawn Reeder and his hunters had been astir, readying all their boats and equipment for the search, a different kind of hunt now and one devoid of any fun or excitement. A grim sense of purpose gripped all the inhabitants of the camp save two. Within her tent Jilly still lay prostrated, sobbing and screaming and muttering to herself as she had done almost non-stop since Greg had brought her back last night – she would be quite unfit to join the search. Likewise Chris, despite the open abuse, threats and intimidation of Reeder and Greg, could not be persuaded to leave his fire which he had raised the night before, but squatted before it impervious to everything except the need to keep that warm glow alive by constant care.

Greg had set off with a small advance party as soon as the earliest streaks of the dawn light were making themselves felt in the charcoal sky. He was impatient to be gone and would brook no restraint.

'You should be here when they come,' Reeder told him. 'You'll need to tell them the exact spot where the accident occurred so they can pinpoint the search area.'

'Reeder, I want to be the first to find my wife,' Greg said, with such emphasis that Reeder couldn't doubt him. 'You can tell them where to look. I'll fire off my rifle at regular intervals to let you know where to make for. I can't just sit around here doing nothing, now can I?'

With that Reeder had to be content. He had a certain rough sympathy with Greg, even in spite of his angry conviction that he had brought all this on his own head. And he had to admit that waiting at the camp, as the Kakadu rangers, searchers and helpers made their way in in odd numbers and small groups, was frustrating work. Besides, the wailing of that woman and the silent vigil of the blackfella would give any man the creeps. Shivering, distressed, Reeder had to admit that Greg had had the best of the morning's bargain, but he could hardly begrudge it to him.

The day was well advanced before the authorities in Darwin could succeed in getting help into the remote swamp in any significant way. Around noon Greg returned after hours of combing the lagoon where Stephanie had last been seen and all the area around it. He was dirty and tired, and to Reeder's anxious query he simply returned a dispirited shrug. The leader of the searchers was hardly inclined to be sympathetic to anyone whose rank amateurism, as scrupulously retailed to him by Reeder, had resulted in a woman's horrible death. But he saw no point in hitting a man when he was down, and confined his dealings with Greg to brusque questions about the precise location of the boat at the time when Stephanie had fallen in. Meanwhile, angry and frustrated, Greg went to make a call he had been putting off on the radio.

'Bill? Bill? Whatever is it?'

Sundays were very highly prized days in the McMaster household. It was quite understood that Harper Mining ate up all Bill's working days, spilled over into most evenings, and often gobbled up Saturdays too. But Sundays had always been sacrosanct, kept as family days despite all pressure, and defended all the more vigorously because there was only a small family to defend. Apart from Bill and his wife Rina, the only other member was a dearly loved son, young Tom.

Rina had realized that something was up as soon as Tom had come running into the kitchen on his own. Admittedly lunch was almost ready, and her son had a young boy's healthy appetite, but normally nothing would prise him away from his father. Tom idolized Bill, and never got enough of his father's company. So he had to take every advantage of Sundays to stock up for the coming week. Leaving her cooking, Rina went to investigate.

She found Bill sitting motionless on a sofa in the living room, the telephone purring idly in his hand. Rina rushed forward to take it from him before it fell, and replace it on the receiver stand. His face was grey and tears of horror stood in his eyes. Rina had never seen him so devastated and though all her dear ones were safe with her, an answering sense of dread woke at once in her heart.

'What – is – it?' she breathed, grasping his hand for comfort. Slowly Bill seemed to come round, focused his eyes and looked at her as if seeing her for the first time.

'Y'not going to believe this,' he said, dazed. Painfully he rubbed his face, dashing the water from his eyes. 'Y'not gonna . . .'

'Oh Bill, *tell* me – what? what?'

But Bill just sat there, like a man suddenly gone deaf, shaking his head, and repeating with imbecilic slowness the same phrase.

'Y'not gonna believe this, you aren't . . . y'not gonna . . .'

It was the second day before the hydrofoils could be brought up. Apart from the slow flat-bottomed boats these were the only way of moving across the sluggish waters and Reeder's heart lifted a little as he saw the stately little twentieth-century galleons skimming across the swamps. The very sight of the skilful operators, their hearing guarded by ear-protectors from the powerful whine of their machines, raised his spirits – they'll find her if anyone can, he thought. Besides, some top brass from Harper Mining was arriving today to take charge of the whole thing, and many more men were due in from all over the territory. There's plenty of hope left, he thought. I ain't giving up yet.

He felt better too when Greg had taken charge of 'that woman' as he privately thought of Jilly. He didn't know what had happened, but last evening after sunset had made any further searches impossible Greg had gone into her tent with a bottle, and when he came out again some time later the banshee routine had been suspended for the first time in over twenty-four hours. 'Good on yer, mate,' he told him, but Greg had brushed him aside and strode off. Only natural, I suppose, Reeder thought philosophically. Greg later unbent enough to inform Reeder that he was making arrangements to get Jilly flown out as soon as he could arrange for her husband to be at home in Sydney, or to come to Darwin to collect her. 'Well, she ain't fit to shift one leg in front of the other by herself, and that's a fact,' Reeder privately related to his son Malc. 'So the sooner he can get her lifted out the better.'

So the long day wore on, the hydrofoils sweeping tirelessly to and fro, increasing their range on every sweep and still finding nothing. Wearying at last of being tied to the camp, Reeder deputed his son to take his place as the search co-ordinator and went out with one of the parties returning to the hunt after a rest break. For hours they plodded forward, step by step, investigating every hollow at the root of every tree, probing deep pools with long poles, wading through the shallows, turning over every log, every leaf. Nothing. Reeder's confidence waned as the sun did, diminishing a little more with every minute that passed. As a second spectacular sunset since the one that the ill-fated Stephanie had set out to photograph gave its technicolour finale, Reeder came at last to the end of his optimism. Returning to camp he encountered Greg coming in with another party. None of the men even greeted one another with the ghost of an enquiry. Privately they had all given up hope.

'Is this it, then, Dad?' asked Malc, to whom Reeder had unburdened his feelings.

'That's it for the poor cow, anyways,' said Reeder gloomily. 'That ain't it for the search. It's just that what they're looking for now won't be a woman – it'll just be chunks of remains – or bones.'

*

The dawn mist hung low over the river and crept in among the trees. A solitary bird cried, with a strange, croaking call. Half concealed by the wreathing mist, a figure made its way through the swampy shallows, poling along in a flat-bottomed boat. Dave Welles, prospector and recluse, had lived alone here for many years. Visitors never disturbed him. He simply lay low till they had taken themselves off again. Now he was out and about, foraging as usual, his fishing gear and hunting tackle thrown together in the bottom of the boat.

On a far bank, his attention was caught by a flash of red among the brown of the mud. Changing course to investigate, he heard a heavy splash up ahead, and noticed that a large crocodile had taken to the water, its interest apparently aroused by the same object. Getting nearer, Dave saw a mound, streaked in crimson and the dark slime of the river, and nearby, to his horror, what looked like a human hand. Skimming towards it at about the same speed came the crocodile. Doubling his effort the old man came up to the inert form. The body of a woman, scarcely recognizable as a human being, lay face downwards in the slime, her arm outstretched and hand digging into the mud where she had clawed her way out of the river before collapsing.

Desperately Dave struggled to free her from the clinging mud, his stringy muscles grappling with the dead weight as he dragged her clear.

'No breakfast for you today!' he yelled at the crocodile, now beaching on the small inlet and beginning its sinister waddle towards them. Panting, heaving, he tumbled the woman into his boat and jumping in, pushed off from the bank.

'Don't you worry, girlie,' he addressed the inert figure. 'Old Dave knows. Y'll be all right.'

'Come on, then' – 'Here we go' – Dave kept up his cheery banter all the way back to his hut miles deep in the secret heart of the bush, though he had no way of telling if his find was dead or alive. Only after he had with difficulty brought her indoors, carefully cut her free of the torn rags of cloth that still clung around her body, washed her clean and wrapped her in warm rugs, did he begin to hope she might live. As the day wore on, and the rising sun warmed the interior of his shack, the woman lost her deathly cold and he could feel a faint pulse flickering inside her wrist. Dave pushed his battered old hat to the back of his head. She was alive. Right then.

Crossing the hut he took the hurricane lamp, lit it, and suspended it from the roof right above the bed where the woman lay. By its golden glow he found an old tin, opened it, and withdrew a length of cat gut and a large needle. He stood for a moment, regarding her with a world of pity in his piercing blue eyes. Then he settled to his work. Best to do it now while she was still unconscious. He leaned forward, and with infinite care began to sew together the flaps of torn and savaged skin.

'Aaaargh!' She started, moaned, and her hand flew up to grasp his shoulder. Dave held steadily to his task.

'Hold on, girlie, hold on,' he murmured. 'Old Dave'll see you right. Easy now.'

At length he was done. Sitting up, he rubbed his tired eyes. Then delving into a jar beside the bed, he gently applied a thick yellow paste liberally over the wounds. She had relapsed into unconsciousness long before he had finished. Allowing the paste to dry, he tucked her up again as tenderly as a mother, and sat by her for a long while before he too slept.

Stephanie never knew afterwards how long she remained hovering between life and death, drifting in and out of consciousness in a haze of pain. Only by degrees did she become aware of the wiry old hand supporting her head to offer her a drink, the kind face that swam into her vision from time to time, the comforting presence who guarded her night and day. As her eyes adjusted to her surroundings, she saw a cluttered primitive interior, its roof low over her head, and a man sitting beside her, watching her with the light of compassion in his eyes.

'How y'doin', girlie?' he asked quietly. 'Good t'see you coming round. Didn't know if you'd make it. M'name's Dave Welles. Reckon that's all y'need to know f'now. Try a sip of this, and rest again.'

As the days went by, he filled her in on events in casual snatches, much of which she could make no sense of, for there were gaping holes in her memory and she did not know who or what she was.

'Pulled you out of the river a week 'n more back, I did. Bloody living miracle you are. Them old crocs, the big'uns, they've got a habit of storing their prey before they get around to eating it, and if I hadn't snatched you from his larder, you wouldn't be here to tell the tale . . . Y'jaw's broke, so don't try t'talk. Keep 'im still and he'll heal, I learned that back in the opal mines at Coober Pedy, years ago . . . take another little drink now, for old Dave, come on . . .'

By degrees her body regained strength, though her mind remained far from whole. One day she felt strong enough to explore her body, and discovered she was wearing a man's shirt and trousers.

'Them's m'clothes,' explained Dave. 'Nothin' of yourn left but rags. I kept'm to remind you who y'are.' But the sight of the mud-stained blood-dried fragments of cloth meant nothing to her. 'Y'feel like a walk now?'

Pain was her constant companion. Slowly, with Dave's strong old brown arm as her support, she learned to walk again. By night, in bed, she traced with her fingers the raw sites of her various hurts – the tearing on her face, neck and throat, all down one side, the ugly scarring on her shoulder and breast, the huge weals on her thigh. Dave was ever supportive.

'Y'healing well, girlie,' he would proclaim. 'Good flesh y'got there. And I got this concoction for wounds from my Abo mate. S'special. They make it out of flowers and clay.

Pongs a bit, but I've never known it fail. Y'get no infection, see?'

One day Dave appeared at her bedside, looking impish and full of himself.

'Going t'town today,' he volunteered, 'leastways, that bunch of shacks down the road. Get y'some clothes. Get you up and about again. Sooner we can get you right, sooner y'can contact y'family and friends. Now don't worry. I'll be gone a few hours. Back before dark.'

After Dave had gone, she lay there wondering, pushing the ideas round in her mind. Family? Friends? What was it made her shudder at the phrase, made her feel that here was the only place she was safe? Where had she come from? Who was she anyway? I don't even know what I look like, she thought with numb despair. Dave's hut did not boast anything like a mirror. Who am I? hammered through her head.

At last, weary of her morbid thoughts, she decided to get up. Dave would be back soon. She would take the kettle to the water tank outside, as she had so often seen him do, and have it ready for their afternoon cup of tea when he came back. Moving with difficulty she got the kettle, and slowly crossed the floor to the doorway. She stood on the threshold and her bruised soul revived a little under the influence of a perfect day. Outside the sun rode high in a cloudless heaven, the birds called from tree to tree, and Dave's little hideaway seemed a perfect paradise. Allowing the first faint tendrils of hope to unwind in her heart, Stephanie came out of the hut and walked to the water barrel at its corner beneath a rough drainpipe. Leaning forward, she plunged the kettle in to fill it, disturbing the placid surface of the water.

As she did so, through the distortion of the shimmering circles, she caught sight of a reflection within. A horribly twisted face looked back at her, and a sick terror began to dawn in her mind. Surely she did not, could not look like that? She forced herself to be calm, gripping the water barrel till her knuckles turned white as the ripples subsided.

98

There could be no mistake. Mirrored in the still surface of the water was her own face, hideously disfigured. The razor teeth of the crocodile had ripped down one side of her head, tearing the flesh into shreds, now healing in gross red welts. By a cruel irony, the other side of her face was quite unmarked, so that one profile mocked the other like a caricature. On the damaged side her eyelid and the corner of her mouth were dragged down as if by a stroke. That was the face of an old woman, a witch, a stranger . . .

'No!' Stephanie's scream rang out through the bush. The birds struck out squawking with alarm from their perches and little animals ran for shelter to their burrows at the wild intensity of this cry of despair.

'No, no, no!'

And the madness of darkness and despair rose up and overwhelmed her.

Hours later, Dave found her on his return, cowering beside the water barrel and mourning to herself in broken muttered snatches. Gently but firmly he picked her up and led her back into the hut, where he tucked her up in bed. Then he sat himself down beside her.

' 'Sbad, girlie, I know. But it's got to be faced,' he began ' 'Cos when a thing is faced, 'tain't never so bad as when we're still in fear. That old croc messed you up good. But y'cheated him of his dinner. You're alive, when you could've been lining a croc's belly by now. That means something. Y've been saved for *something*. Or somebody. Now y've got to find out what that is.'

Dave's voice reached her dimly at the bottom of a pit of despair. Something? Somebody? She croaked out a response.

'I don't even know my name.'

'But y'wearing a wedding ring. Y'could be married. I seen the police all over in town. Rangers're looking for somebody and I guess it's you.'

'Oh Dave, I'm so frightened to leave here. I don't know where to go, where to begin.'

Dave paused before replying, and his voice took on a sad, husky note.

'Give it time, girlie, give it time. I'll give you a name, if y'like. Long time back, before I lost m'taste for human company, I fell in love with a little girl from Mount Isa. She was a publican's daughter, and her name was Tara. Y'see, her mother only ever saw one moving picture in her whole life, and that was *Gone With The Wind*. Well, I liked it fine. It suited her. Well . . . we were sweethearts until . . . till one terrible day when she shot through to Townsville and married a butcher!' Dave broke out into a guffaw to cover his expression of emotion. 'So if it's all right with you – I'll call you Tara!'

She smiled with gratitude and squeezed Dave's hand.

'And we've got to get you moving, Tara – back to real life. Y'could be safe here with me f'the rest of y'natural. But y'came from out there –' he gave an expressive nod with his head towards the door '– and that's where y'll find the answers to y'questions. I done a good raid today – gotcha some women's things to wear, stead of my old duds.' He moved across to a bundle on the table, and unwrapped a pink dress, bra, pants a straw hat and scarf, even shoes.

'Oh Dave! Where did you get these from?'

'Found 'em,' he said, twinkling. 'On lines, outside back doors, setting on chairs on porches. 'Course, there's no telling 'bout size. But it's something to wear when you go to town y'self.'

A week later, she stood with Dave by the side of a dirt road, waiting for the road train, the only mode of transport through the vast desert wastes, to come by. After hours of discussion with Dave a plan had emerged. A strange and inexplicable dread made it impossible for her to go to the nearest town and ask for help from the police or rangers. All she knew was that she had to get away. A long way. And then? She didn't know. But she knew her first move, and resolved to take it a step at a time. The sun beat down fiercely from directly overhead, so that she was glad of the straw hat Dave had provided, which with her heavy hair brushed well forward helped to hide her ruined face. Awkwardly she smoothed at the ill-fitting pink dress, and shivered slightly inside the strange underwear.

'Road train's coming,' said Dave. His bushman's eye had picked up the tiny puff of red dust on the horizon signalling its approach. 'He'll get y'to Darwin, and then it's up to you.' He turned to face her, his weatherbeaten face crinkling with affection, reached inside his shirt and produced a nondescript old tin like a tea caddy.

'Here y'are,' he said off-handedly, passing it to her. 'Going away present. It's a tin of old dreams I've got no use for any more. Have a look.'

She opened the tin. Inside, in a nest of grubby cotton wool, lay a heap of magnificent opals. The smallest was the size of a man's thumbnail, the largest like a baby's fist. All were of the finest quality.

'Look at the colour,' said Dave proudly. 'Like fire at night. Opals like that'll give you a start.'

'Oh Dave – I couldn't.'

'Course y'could. They're no use to me. Oh, I meant 'em as insurance f'my old age, when I mined 'em first, so I sold the others and always kept back the best. But now –' he smiled contentedly. 'I don't need 'em, girlie. I've got all I want. I ain't goin' nowhere. You can take 'em back into life for me.'

Tears stung her eyes. She didn't dare to speak, but nodded.

'And Tara – mind y'get a good price for these when y'take 'em into Darwin. Don't let 'm rob you!'

The road train was coming steadily nearer, its huge bulk churning up the dirt surface. Dave removed his battered hat with an old-world air of courtesy.

'It's goodbye, then, Tara. Do me a favour, will you? If'n you run up against anybody looking for me, don't you tell'm where I am. And don't be bringing the world and his wife back here to me, either. When y'go, y'go. No look-backs, no heel-taps, right?'

'Right.' She gave him a watery smile.

The road train pulled to a halt, covering them both with a fine dust.

'Goodbye, Dave.' She was fighting to hold back the tears. 'And thank you.'

'Remember, Tara,' he called after her, 'something. Or somebody. You'll find it.'

The driver of the road train was delighted at the prospect of a female passenger to relieve the endless boredom of the long haul. Hurling the monster vehicle round the tight corners took up most of his concentration, but he had thrown two or three glances her way and liked what he saw. She had carefully concealed the bad side of her face by dipping her head as she entered the cab to hide behind the brim of her straw hat. Now she presented to him her good profile set in deep lines of reflective sadness he was at a loss to understand.

'What ya doing out here all on your own?' he inquired, 'your car break down?'

She nodded.

'Well, y'don't want to worry about that,' he continued, expansively. 'I'll get you all the way to Darwin. I'm glad of the company. Especially female company.' There was no response. The driver, who had had a lot of success with what he thought of as the direct approach, was encouraged to pursue his advantage.

'We could have a nice conversation, you and me. 'S a long way to Darwin. You gotta break up the monotony.' He paused. Then he reached out a hand and grasped her thigh, squeezing it heavily. 'You and me could have a nice time together. A very nice time.'

To his surprise, he felt her muscles contract under his hand and set like iron. Slowly, and with great deliberation, she turned to face him. His ingratiating grin died on his

102

lips as he took in the extent of the ravages of her injuries. Shame, irritation and disappointment fought within him.

'Darwin it is then – all the way,' he said at last.

Diagonally across the great island of Australia in Sydney, Bill McMaster was at that moment bidding goodbye to Stephanie Harper with a grieving heart. The second he had heard the news of Stephanie's accident he had stopped only to order all Harper personnel within a thousand miles into the area to help with the search before flying north to take charge of things himself. Every waterway, every lagoon for miles had been scoured by men in boats, canoes, hydrofoils, and the search had been extended back as far into the bush as a severely wounded woman could possibly hope to crawl. Nothing.

Obediently, patiently, the men had kept on till there was nowhere else to look. Even then, hoping against hope, Bill had ordered those places in the estuary where the tide came and went to be searched again. He was not a man who accepted defeat easily. Finally he had been forced to return to Sydney, where the company could not manage for long without his direct attention. From there he had continued to receive reports of the searchers' lack of success. The latest lay before him on his desk at that moment. It left him with no sane option but to call off the hunt.

He thought of Greg Marsden with great bitterness, recalling his arrival at the camp in the Alligator River territory. There wasn't much to be expected of a woman – he didn't blame Jilly for being a jittering wreck, nor even for her sudden night wails that disturbed the whole camp, and her equally sudden silences that followed them. But Marsden – by turns arrogant and aggressive, at others maudlin and sentimental – for him Bill had conceived such a profound loathing that he was simply glad he had got through that agonizing period without violently assaulting him. What a prick, he muttered to himself, feeling his fingers bunch together by reflex. Oh Steph, why him?

Then there had been the task of breaking the news to Sarah and Dennis, something that naturally Greg had felt would come better from Bill than from him. Bill's heart turned over as he recalled the painful little scene – both children aware that something frightening was afoot, or they would not have been recalled from school, but neither dreaming that the news he had to give would be that bad. Well, it was over now, Bill thought heavily, and please God I'll never have to do anything quite so dreadful again. He renewed his private vow to be the father to the two children that he knew Greg would never be, and made a mental note to keep their birthdays, Christmases and celebrations in exactly the same way that their doting mother Stephanie always had.

Stephanie . . . Bill sighed heavily. In the weeks since her loss he had mourned her as he had never mourned Max, who had had his respect and admiration, but never his love. To his surprise, Bill found that he was missing the tall, coltish woman with her large sad eyes, and her honest smile. He missed, too, the professional Stephanie – the businesswoman with her shrewd, intuitive grasp on the market and on Harper Mining. But most of all he missed her as a person, warm, vital, loyal and trusting. Well, she was gone now, and he had to let her go, just bearing her loss like a toothache. Goodbye then, my dear, he thought with great love – but I won't forget. I won't forget.

At Darwin Airport the ticket clerk was intrigued by the smartly dressed woman who entered the booking hall at a slow pace, looking around her as if to check where she was going. Unlike most Australian women, she wore an elegant hat, with heavy veiling that completely covered her face. Stiffly she approached his desk, walking cautiously as if she had been in an accident. Maybe that's why the veil, he thought idly. But there was something attractive about her all the same.

*

She paused in the middle of the hall to study the flight departures notice board, then approached his desk.

'Ticket to Townsville, please.' Her voice was low and husky.

'Single, or return?'

The woman hesitated.

'One way.'

The clerk punched up the flight times and availability on his desk computer and gave the price of the ticket.

'Could I have your name please?' There was a pause. The woman opened her bag to pay, and to his amazement the clerk saw that it was literally bulging with dollars carelessly thrust in anyhow. Oblivious of his scrutiny, she lifted her head.

'Tara Welles,' she said proudly.

Chapter Six

On the plane, Tara Welles sighed with relief, slipped off her shoes under the seat in front, and sat back, closing her eyes. She did not enjoy being the veiled mystery lady. But anything was better than the stares, some horrified, some pitying, some frankly insulting, that greeted her when she tried to walk the streets unprotected. And soon . . . and soon . . . her chin set into the firm resolve reminiscent of the woman who had been Stephanie Harper as she thought of her life to come.

Since leaving Dave, Tara had been through a maelstrom of emotions that had left her buffeted, but oddly strengthened too. Her trip to Darwin in the road train had turned into a strange nightmare as without any warning, the suppressed episodes of her recent history began to return to her in lightning flashes of pain and terror. The first had struck as the massive vehicle plunged into a ford that crossed the road not far from where they set out. As the water splashed up by the wheels struck the windscreen, Tara found herself throwing up her arm and screaming, she had been so sure the water was going to hit her, come over her head, blind her eyes and fill her choking mouth. She fought for control, drawing in huge juddering breaths, aware of the curious scrutiny of the driver but powerless to explain.

In the wake of that first memory, the others had stolen up on her implacably like thieves in the night. She saw again the sunset over the swamp, felt the boat under her feet and the camera in her hands. Surfacing in a sobbing panic she saw the cold eyes of her killer – Greg! my husband, oh my God! – and behind him the other woman – the woman who sat hypnotized as I screamed to her for help – Jilly. Then the pain, the unspeakable agony of the razors in her arm, the hot blood spurting down her face, and going under, going under, till finally oblivion. As the road train thundered onwards through the northern wastelands, piece by painful piece she reassembled the jigsaw of her life. By the time they arrived in Darwin, she knew she had been Stephanie Harper.

But Stephanie Harper was no more. Her husband had wanted her dead, and he had killed her. Shaking, weeping, she recognized herself as a woman with no face, no name, no life. All these he had taken away. She was nothing.

With the onrush of memory, Dave's last words came back to her as a bitter irony. 'You've been saved for something. Or somebody.' Saved? For a husband who had been the author of her disaster? She smiled savagely, her twisted face crumpling with distress. Well, he wouldn't get another chance to have a crack at her. Saved? For what? Why, oh why, had fate reached down and plucked her back from the death which at this moment would have been preferable to such unspeakable suffering? In a spasm of loathing, she tore off her wedding ring and flung it through the window.

Why . . . why . . . why . . . was the insistent refrain that kept returning to her as she sat in the cab of the road train weltering in misery and hot anger for hour after hour. *Why*, Greg? I loved you so, no woman more. Why did I lose that love? Why did you want me dead? Why did you hate me so? Round and round she went, down and down, till at the very bottom of her grief and rage she found the thread by which she began to inch her way up again. I have to have been spared for something, she thought wildly, Dave said so. This must be it – *to find out why*. And then, what comes after? The answer was with her as swift as the wings of thought – *revenge*! I shall have my revenge. Furious ideas of the form it might take coursed through her brain. But she was totally clear and cold about the decision. She entertained the notion of committing him to the police only to dismiss it at once. That wouldn't be enough, she thought. I should never know why. I must know. And I will.

The woman who dismounted at Darwin was shaken, weak as from a long illness, and raw and jangling in every nerve. But inside her there was a core of steel, a newly-forged strength of purpose which she knew would carry her through all the trials that lay ahead. She desperately needed that strength, for it was all she had. But it would be enough, she knew. Her first test had been the conversion of Dave's opals into hard cash. She had forced herself to enter one by one all the old army huts that housed the gem merchants and jewellery manufacturers in Darwin, pricing here and here, withstanding the prying eyes, the probing questions, the attempts to beat her down. By the end of the day she was sick to her stomach, and the effort was almost too much for her. In the workshop of the dealer she had finally selected for the purchase, she had given in to an attack of panic and had to rush out to the fresh air. The dealer came after her, concerned.

'Hey, lady!' he cried, 'don't run off without your money. Very good stones you got there. You all right?'

She had shrugged off his offer of assistance, taken the money and scurried away, almost at the end of her tether. But the results had exceeded her wildest expectations. She had entered the gemstone traders' quarter as a penniless derelict. She left with a sum of money that would make possible anything she chose to do. I'm back in business, she thought. A business of one. Me. Tara Welles.

She went immediately to the best hotel in town, where the bad impression produced by the strange-looking woman in the faded unfashionable ill-fitting dress was immediately counteracted by the payment in advance for the best suite in the place, and the dispensation of generous tips all round. From the privacy of her rooms Tara sent out to all the fashion stores for clothes on approval, and as the word went round that a rich eccentric had hit town, they were eager to comply. Yet the choice and fitting of the new clothes was no pleasure to her. Here, with a full-length mirror and the chance to examine herself, she had been forced to come to terms with the horror of her injuries.

And she had cried, for the first time since the day she had had a glimpse of herself in Dave's water barrel, lying on the bed for hours and giving herself up to the agony of grief, mourning not just for her ravaged face and body, but for the loss of her self.

Then in the midst of her sea of sorrow she had found the bright hard pearl of anger. This she used to drive forward with a singleness of purpose quite new to her. From the comfort of her bed she had telephoned to hospitals, doctors, consultants all over Australia, enquiring for a plastic surgeon who could help her to take the first step in rebuilding her life. One name had come up again and again. Which was why she was now en route for Townsville, as a stepping-off point for the Great Barrier Reef. There, on Orpheus Island, was the man who would make her whole.

Single life had a lot to recommend it, reflected Greg Marsden, as he lounged at his ease in Max Harper's king-sized bed in the Harper Mansion in Sydney. No need to get up just yet – nobody to please but himself. When he was ready, a leisurely shower, and Matey would bring him his breakfast. Not so bad, he thought.

But in another way it was not so good, either. For he was not truly single, but newly bereaved, and he wondered how much longer he was going to have to play the part of the grieving widower. As he had anticipated, the story of Stephanie's terrible accident had had worldwide press and TV coverage, and from the moment they had left the shelter of the bush camp to return to civilization they had been hounded by reporters, cameramen and film crews. He had pleaded his deep grief as a means of getting out of giving any interviews. Even more important, he had convinced a hostile Phillip that Jilly must be shielded from any pressure and knew that she was safe from prying newshounds up in the big house at Hunter's Hill. Finally, since he knew from experience that you had to give the press something to keep them happy, he had handed over

Stephanie's photo album and all the pictures of the wedding to an agency who had succeeded in raising some very satisfactory sums for each and every snap. So far so good.

But Greg still had to be very careful, and his was a nature that chafed under any restraint. Nobody knew about him and Jilly, of that he was sure, and there was no reason why it should come to light. Jilly had been in a bad way immediately after the accident but he had managed to bring her round. In fact the shock had put a new edge on her desire for him, and he had deliberately taken the risk of visiting her tent night after night, even when Bill McMaster was in the camp, to taste again the intensity of her passion. His audacity both outraged and enthralled her. She was his, body and soul.

With this thought came the familiar stir of sexual interest. He could do with her here right now. He let his mind roam over her body, her hands, her tongue . . . With a start he caught himself up. Come on, boy, he chided, are you going to throw all this away for a fuck? Even for Jilly, undoubtedly the best fuck he had ever had? He thought back to his arrival at the Harper Mansion, the slow struggle he had had to establish himself with Matey and the rest of the house staff, so devoted to Stephanie that their unspoken reproaches hung in the very air he breathed. Well, he had done it. They were eating out of his hand now. Even her kids were tolerating him.

And then there was what the lawyers tastefully called 'the Harper Estate'. Nothing could be finalized till Stephanie's body was found – Greg frowned in irritation. He had no doubt she was dead. He could see again that long, slow death roll as the croc took her under for the last time. He could see the whites of her eyes rolled up, and the last breath bubbling from her bleeding mouth. He had stood guard over the spot for a long, long time and neither Stephanie nor the croc had resurfaced. He knew her body must be tangled up somewhere in the roots of one of the twisted trees that cluttered the lagoons. It would have been so convenient if it could have popped up and been brought home for a spectacular funeral. Still, no matter. The money due to Stephanie now rolled in to him. He had full access to it, since Stephanie had been so scrupulous to arrange that they should hold everything jointly. He had, too, his own funds as a director of Harper Mining. He had the house, the yacht, the service of the staff. And he had his freedom. First a slap-up breakfast, he decided. Then for the sex thing, he could wait. He'd find the way to work it off. Anyone for tennis, he thought with a happy grin. My serve.

The small boat made its way carefully out of the busy Townsville harbour. On its deck Tara, alone with her thoughts, scarcely noticed the beauty of the natural scene around her. On the flight south-east from Darwin to Queensland she had been so lost in her plans and reflections that she had not even looked out of the window at the country unfolding below. Of all Australia's states, each beautiful in its own way, only Queensland boasts the biggest natural wonder of the world. Other people come from far and wide to admire the stunning magnificence of the Great Barrier Reef. But Tara Welles was otherwise engaged.

Still, as they neared Orpheus Island her interest stirred in spite of herself. She could see it ahead floating on the aquamarine sea, its low hills clustered with palm trees, its gleaming white beaches and friendly huddle of cabins, all basking in the brilliance of the tropical sunshine. From a substantial building in the centre of the complex of dwellings a large woman was making her way to the jetty clad in a bright-coloured mu-mu and bearing aloft a gaudy parasol to protect the new arrival from the sun. As the launch pulled in, she was there to help Tara alight.

'Welcome to the Marshall Clinic!'

Tara saw a capable woman in her fifties, cosy and maternal with a grin like a split watermelon. Undeterred by Tara's silence, she bubbled on.

'Oh, isn't it a great day! I wouldn't be dead for two bob, and I could do with the money. I'm Elizabeth Mason, but everyone calls me Lizzie. It's Tara, isn't it?'

'Yes.'

'Is that all your luggage? Let's be having it, then.' Lizzie hoisted Tara's small suitcase without effort, and together they turned up the jetty in the direction of the main building.

'Doc Marshall's in surgery, otherwise he'd have met you himself. But I'm part of the staff, sort of a general dogsbody. How do you come to be with us? How did you hear of the clinic?'

'Oh,' said Tara vaguely, 'through a magazine article.' She took a deep breath. 'I'm here because I believe that you specialize in . . . reconstructive surgery.'

'Sure do,' said Lizzie cheerfully. 'Doc Marshall's just about the best plastic surgeon in the whole country, y'know. Put himself through Med School – worked nights and all. Then some old duck – an aunt, or something – died and left him a whole packet of money. Course, he could have retired. But he opened this place instead. Looks after the Aboriginals who need him for free. You'll never hear him go on about it, but that's the kind of bloke he is.'

Lizzie's vitality, and her obvious joy in her work, struck some kind of chord deep in Tara, quickening her deadness and bringing her back to reality.

'This here's your cabin,' said Lizzie, stopping outside a small bungalow and opening the door. Inside was a beautiful little sitting room, simply but elegantly decorated in duck-egg blue, with stylish bamboo furniture in keeping with the palm tree island outside. Beyond lay the bathroom and bedroom. It was the perfect house for one. Tara felt a relief she could not explain.

'You'll be all right here,' said Lizzie confidently, 'the beds are really comfy, there's peace and quiet, and you'll be able to do as you please.'

She led Tara outside again, and pointed across the lawn to where a swimming pool, carefully shaded by tall waving palms, glittered in the sunlight. Patients lay around on sunbeds, or walked gingerly to and fro as if exercising themselves. Others stood around chatting, or swam and played in the pool with varying degrees of assurance. Some were bandaged, while those who had had recent surgery wore sun hats and kept in the shade to protect tender skin. All were scarred while some poor souls had lost fingers or limbs or suffered other deformities too. It's like a freaks' convention, Tara thought bitterly – a holiday resort for cripples. God, if I ever get out of this . . .

'Don't you worry, love,' Lizzie broke in, eyeing her shrewdly. 'Don't feel sorry for them – they don't feel sorry for themselves. And they all leave here smiling. Doc Marshall sees to that.'

The doctor lost no time in seeing to his new patient. Tara felt an unaccustomed nervousness when Lizzie came to fetch her for her first examination. But her fears were partially allayed by the sight of the tall gentle man awaiting her in the consulting room of the main clinic. Sensing her dread he made no attempt to engage her in idle chat, but concentrated on a minute inspection of her face and body scars under a microscope, recording them all one by one.

At last he sat back, and regarded her with kind brown eyes.

'What kind of an accident was it that caused injuries like these?'

Tara hesitated.

'I know it must hurt you to talk, Miss Welles, with the damage you've suffered to the vocal chords . . . But I do have to ask these questions.'

'A car crash – collision.'

'How long ago?'

'Six weeks.'

Neither of these statements could be true, the doctor knew. He leaned forward to the inert figure on the examination couch.

'Can you tell me anything more about your . . . accident?'

'An old man . . . a friend . . . he knew something about
Aboriginal herbal remedies . . . a paste, made of flowers
and clay . . .'

'Oh yes. We use some of them here. Well, your friend
seems to have known what he was doing. Your jaw's been
badly broken, but it's knitted again perfectly.'

Tara grew impatient.

'Doctor Marshall, I want to look like a human being
again. Can you help me?'

Marshall took his time before replying.

'Your injuries are extensive, severe and . . . unusual,
Miss Welles. You'd require more than just one operation.
There'd be several – reconstructive, cosmetic. There would
be pain – a great deal, I'm sorry to say – and afterwards,
extreme discomfort for some time.'

'I'm not afraid of pain!' Tara flashed out angrily.

The doctor was unperturbed.

'Another thing. We couldn't begin to operate until the
scar tissue softens. That could be several weeks.'

'That's all right,' said Tara, carelessly. 'I have the
money, and nowhere else to go.'

'Money is not actually the primary consideration with
us here.' Tara ignored the gentle reproof, and the quiet
voice went on. 'But certainly, rest and recuperation after
an accident, when the organism has suffered such a severe
trauma as you have, can only be for the good. Now, more
to the point – do you have a recent photograph of yourself?
One taken as shortly as possible before your accident?'

The sudden hot tears pricked her eyes as she remembered her wedding day. Gritting her teeth she regained
control.

'No, I don't. And anyway—' shaking again, she plunged
on with the decision she had taken lying on her hotel bed
in Townsville '—I want more than having these scars
covered up. I want to look different. I want a new face, a

new me. *When I leave here I want to be a completely different woman!'*

As the days on Orpheus passed Tara's strength of purpose did not relax. But her injured body and overwrought mind began to, slowly. In the unique peace of the unspoiled tropical island, the days unfolded in pure splendour as they had done since the dawn of time, and the nights came down as a protective purple dome spangled with myriads of twinkling stars. All was fragrant, clean and undefiled. She felt like Eve in paradise, beginning again, this time in full knowledge of the serpent.

Part of the peacefulness of Orpheus emanated from the personality of the genius of the place, Doctor Marshall. As she grew to know him Tara realized that his consideration for others was no mere bedside manner, but sprang from his deep feeling for all the sufferers who came to him for help. He had dedicated himself to supplying not just medical advice, but the total healing environment. And he was always on hand to offer his patients a human – not a cold professional – contact. Tara came upon him one day pulling his small dinghy up the gently shelving beach as he returned from a fishing expedition.

'Would you mind grabbing that rope?' he hailed her. 'Could you just tie it round that log for me? Thanks, that's great.'

Silently Tara made to walk on.

'Hey, don't go,' he called, still engaged in securing the dinghy, 'come over here.' Reluctantly she joined him. He reached into the bottom of the boat and proudly displayed two large fish.

'What d'you reckon? Not bad for a couple of hours' work, eh? D'you fish at all?'

'No.'

'Here it has its practical purposes,' he continued merrily. 'Helps with the food bill!' He gestured about him. 'Well, what do you think of Orpheus?'

Tara looked around. Her mind felt blank. It was so long since she had held anything like a normal conversation.

'It's . . . nice.'

'It has a natural healing power, you know. I'm very proud of my tiny paradise. It's the perfect place to practise medicine – especially my kind.' Tara made no reply.

'Are you a seaside person?' he asked. 'Where were you born?'

'Inland – in the country.'

'Ah – I envy you that. I'm a town boy. What about your family?'

'No one.'

He laughed. 'You don't like talking about yourself much, do you?'

Indignation made her vocal, though with the injuries to her throat she still found it painful to speak.

'Doctor Marshall, I understood that you guarantee your patients' privacy!'

He smiled. 'OK, if I promise not to ask any more leading questions, then you're going to have to stop calling me Doctor Marshall. My name's Dan. All right?'

Dan. She tried the name around her mind. It seemed to suit the easy, smiling man standing before her in shorts, t-shirt and friendly old sunhat, with the smell of the sea coming from his lean, brown body. She wriggled her bare toes in the hot white sand and relaxed a little.

'OK, Dan,' she said.

Later that night Dan found himself remembering the way she had said that, the struggle he had sensed taking place within her whether or not to let those well-kept defences down. What had happened to make her so mistrustful, he wondered. Closely attuned to all creatures in pain, he nevertheless felt in Tara a hurt deeper than any he had experienced before. What was her story? Well, the first step had to be to rehabilitate her body with diet, exercise and swimming, a planned programme due to begin very soon, and to rebuild a face. The time for the first round of surgery was drawing near. It had better be good. So much –

even her sanity – was hanging on it. With a sigh Dan reapplied himself to the study he had been taking of x-ray pictures of Tara's skull. Around him lay sketches, three or four different versions of possible faces for his mystery patient, beside a plaster model of her face as it was. It can't matter, really, which of these faces she finally has, he decided – anything is better than the one she's got.

Not far away in her little house across the warm, night-scented compound Tara too was working late. Carefully she was taking cuttings from a pile of magazines and newspapers and pasting them into a scrapbook, her expression hard as granite.

Before her on the table of her bungalow lay pictures and articles, all on one theme. 'HEIRESS IN HONEYMOON TRAGEDY' screamed the headlines, 'SYDNEY WOMAN LOST IN CROC ATTACK'. 'Shortly after the wedding of the year,' ran the copy, 'Stephanie Harper, Australia's richest woman . . .' All the reports were illustrated by photographs, of the wedding, of Greg, of the hunt in the alligator swamp land. But there were others, of her as a child, her on King at Eden, her as a fat, plain teenager. Greg must have sold her family photos. Well, she was keeping the score.

She had begun keeping her record when, in a magazine picked up idly in Townsville, she had first come across the news coverage. It was her way of trying to make sense of what had happened, and of keeping in touch with later developments. Her scrapbook provided her with another life-line, too. Her expression changing, she turned to the snaps she had of Sarah and Dennis, and pored over them for a long time. Would her children ever understand, she wondered, that their mother was ill, and had to be away from them till she was better? More than that – that their mother could not re-enter their lives till she had made herself over from the weak, foolish woman who had allowed such a terrible thing to happen in the first place? Silently, desperately, she sent messages to them through the air, talked to them often in the solitude of her own brain: I have to learn to be a real person, my darlings, my own person – not Max's daughter, or anybody's wife, not even your mother – but me. For the first time in my life, I'm not leaning on a man. I'm learning to walk alone. You deserve better than an emotional cripple for a mother. Till I can walk properly, I can't come home. You understand?

Tears stood in her eyes, and she allowed them to fall; allowed her overburdened heart the relief of weeping. She missed them so much. She laid her head on her arms and wept a good while. Then, purged and tempered, she cleared her things away and went to bed. There she slept a peaceful sleep in which, for the first time since the accident, she did not dream of Greg. Instead a lean and handsome face, with kind brown eyes and a quizzical smile hovered over her, asking her if she would like to come out fishing with him.

Hunter's Hill is generally agreed to be a highly desirable area of the highly desirable city of Sydney. Its lovely old sandstone houses ornamented with lacy ironwork, its tree-lined avenues, private tennis courts and swimming pools were the admiration and envy of less well-to-do Sydney-siders. But to Jilly Stewart, trapped in the big house where she lived alone with Phillip, it was a prison. Oh, no one held her there against her will. On the contrary, she was an entirely free agent. Since her return from Eden, Phillip, always a busy man, had been busier and busier, as if contriving to leave her to her own devices. Nothing had been said between them about Stephanie's death. But she felt that he knew. And she could not blame him for holding aloof from her. She would have given anything to be able to hold aloof from herself.

Since that night in the alligator river Jilly had been living in a crazy world where hideous storms of terror alternated with wild sensations of joy and exultation. She had not wanted Stephanie to be killed. She knew she would remember to her own dying day the last beseeching glance from Stephanie's eyes before the crocodile took her under, hear the despairing screams, 'Jilly! Help me!' She knew, because she heard them every night, in her raging, technicolor nightmares, if she permitted herself to sleep.

But she had wanted Stephanie to die. That had held her paralysed in the boat, unable to intervene until it was too late, a desire that she recognized from a long way back to have Stephanie Harper dead, out of the way. Most immediately this was because of Greg – her passion for him, her dependence on his particular brand of love-making had become an addiction with her. Oh, it's terrible when you get a man into your blood, she moaned. Until Greg, she could comfortably feel sorry for Stephanie in the marriage stakes – Stephanie, for all her money, saddled with two horrible fuckless wonders, while she had had in Phillip not only an attractive and distinguished man, but a good provider, a sensitive partner, and one who was doomed to be a one-woman man forever. 'Poor Steph,' she used to remark patronizingly to mutual friends, 'she just doesn't know how to pick a man.' But suddenly it all changed. She had found the one man who Jilly's soul cried out to her was *her* soul's partner, not Stephanie's. It's not fair, the child in her wailed, *it's not fair!*

But then, it never had been, had it? The Harpers had always had it all their own way. Reaching deep into the roots of her bitterness, Jilly thought of her father, who had committed suicide after a deal with Max Harper went wrong. Wrong only for him – Max had profited greatly out of it. This, never acknowledged, had been the start of her friendship with Stephanie. The older girl, honourable and warm where her father was tough and cold, had taken the orphaned Jilly under her wing and loved her sincerely ever after. For Jilly, the friendship was more complex – love was there, but always a tiny sliver of ice lived in the core of her heart towards Stephanie, and nearer the surface, jealousy; jealousy of her money, her freedom, and now, her husband.

Greg. Jilly shivered. Like a child she went mechanically

through the catechism that Greg had forced her through in her tent during the long night after the accident.

'It was an accident. Wasn't it? *Wasn't it?*'

'Yes.'

'Good girl. Remember that.'

'It was an accident.'

'Remember that for the inquest, baby. And another thing.'

'Yes?'

'It's just you and me, now. The way we wanted it. OK?'

'Oh Greg—'

'Ssssh, baby. Just remember. All over now. Have a drink.'

And weeping, cursing, raging with sexual longing and all alone, Jilly had a drink.

Chapter Seven

'Almost time for your op, now. Y'ready?'

Tara was enjoying her weekly massage with Lizzie, when under the older woman's kind hands, she could feel her knots and tensions being smoothed away. The tall, quiet woman had become a favourite with Lizzie, as despite the extent of her mutilation and her obvious suffering, she was never once heard to complain.

'Almost – no. Not really,' Tara answered truthfully.

Lizzie cackled. 'Wassa matter, got no faith in Dan?'

'He's a very good doctor.'

'He's more than that. He's a bloody miracle worker. Look at me. I was a heavy boozer when I met him. Busted marriage, in and out of institutions. He offered me a job. Yeah, Dan Marshall's a good bloke all right.'

Preoccupied with her train of thought, Lizzie worked away at Tara's damaged shoulder.

'I asked him once why he never got married, y'know. He said there'd been a couple of special ladies – and that's not hard to believe, him so kind, and handsome and all. But they just couldn't cope with the kind of life he leads. This place may look a bit like a posh resort. But there's no one here without bad problems and it takes up all your time. And Dan's the dedicated type. Whoever married him'd have to be willing to adjust their life to his.'

Just like any good wife, thought Tara. Just like I did. She shifted restlessly under Lizzie's hands.

'Am I hurting you?' Lizzie asked, instantly aware.

'Not so's you'd notice,' cracked Tara. 'It's OK.'

In truth Tara was not really ready for her operation, if being ready meant being totally prepared and accepting of whatever would befall. But she was as ready as she would ever be. Under Dan's carefully worked out programme she had taken exercise, of the kind that her injured arm and leg could stand, she had stuck conscientiously to the island's diet of fresh fruit, vegetables and fish, and she had even begun to work on overcoming her fear of the pool. This last phobia had given Dan another clue to the mystery of the patient who was coming to engross more and more of his interest every day. It had come to light when Lizzie had persuaded Tara to leave the seclusion of her bungalow, where she spent almost all her time, and come to the pool to watch another patient completing a length. This boy, Ben, had lost his father in a terrible car crash that had cost him also his arm and the lower part of his leg. So his valiant attempts to swim a length had been hailed as a victory by all the little community. But Dan could not help noticing that as Ben triumphantly came to the side, he threw up a spray of water that happened to fall beside Tara, and she instinctively sprang back, her face a mask of horror.

'Are you all right?' he asked.

Instantly she was in control again.

'Perfectly. It's just that water makes me . . . nervous.'

'We'll have to do something about that,' he said pleasantly. 'Swimming is an important part of the rehabilitation programme here. We'll help you.' And they had. By degrees she had progressed from dangling her feet in the pure liquid blue at the shallow end, and now at least could immerse her whole body without succumbing to panic. After her operations, Dan promised her, she would learn to swim.

Other preparations had been equally important, too. With the aid of specialist catalogues at the clinic Tara had sent off for wigs, cosmetics and beauty preparations, and with the assistance of a beautician who came in once a week from Townsville to advise the patients, Tara had experimented with different looks until she had been able to tell Dan what she wanted to be like. Her guiding light throughout was that she wanted to look as little like

Stephanie as possible. Yet it was terrible how Stephanie came back to haunt her. One of the wigs in particular was Stephanie to the life. Tara pulled it off in horror as soon as she looked in the mirror. Yet afterwards she put it away carefully, and kept it. Lest I forget, she thought, lest I forget.

On the night before her first series of operations, Tara slipped away from her little house and went for a solitary walk to the other side of the island to think and be alone. Reaching the sea, she sat down on a rock to gaze out over the reef to the Coral Sea beyond. Ahead of her the sun glinted on the blue jewel-like water. Behind her wild goats grazed on the rocky hillside, and a languid breeze puffed among the grasses. A tiny bird of purple and yellow flitted fearlessly about her feet, and all was stillness and tranquillity.

'Mind if I join you?' It was Dan's voice. 'Lizzie said I'd find you here.' He sat down beside her and regarded her with his kind, serious scrutiny. The warm brown eyes in the sun-gold face were full of concern. The light wind ruffled his hair.

'Tomorrow's the big day,' he began. 'I just wanted to say this one last time. I've always been straight with my patients, and . . . it seems to be even more important with you. You know, once we start – there's no turning back. And there can't be any guarantees, either. I'm not a bloody miracle worker, even though Lizzie tells everyone I am.' He fell silent.

'That's all right, Dan. I understand.'

Gently he took her hand in his, and held it for a moment. Tara felt the reassuring pressure of his muscular, capable hands and was strengthened.

'It's OK, Dan, really. I'm ready.'

The next day in the operating theatre, Dan's staff, accustomed to working with him always on difficult cases, and always under pressure, noticed that he was unusually strung up. His tension expressed itself in a tendency to keep going over instructions which had already been obeyed and a habit of grilling his hapless junior.

'Has her head been shaved? Good, good. Now you know that if the mouth injury has been caused by a ruptured muscle, we can repair it. But if the nerve is severed, doctor, what then?'

'That's it, sir,' replied the young assistant promptly, glad that the question had been no harder. Dan continued, impervious.

'Similarly, there may be just scar lesions dragging across the throat to prevent free movement of the vocal apparatus. But if the voice box itself is damaged –'

'That's it again, sir!'

'Don't keep saying "that's it",' said Dan, irritably.

'No, sir.'

'Oh, let's get going. We might as well know the worst.'

But Dan's pessimism was unfounded. To his great relief, the major part of Tara's deformity was created by the heavy scarring produced by such deep wounds. With ever-increasing optimism he made the precise, fine incisions and repairs, aided by the silent squad of green-gowned minions working all around him. The ruin of the eyelid and the downturned mouth called for every ounce of his skill and concentration. By the end of the afternoon, when finally he peeled the rubber gloves from his hands, they had begun to tremble with exhaustion.

This had never happened to him before in all his years as a surgeon. Hours later, showered, rested and refreshed, Dan was still trying to work out the implications of it. He did not have very far to seek. This patient was more than ordinarily important to him. And yet he knew nothing about her! On an inpulse, he picked up the phone.

'Hello, this is Doctor Marshall here, from the clinic on Orpheus Island. Could I speak to Sergeant Johnson, please?'

In the pause, Dan could hear his own heart beating through the silence of the night.

'Hello, Sam? Marshall here, Dan Marshall. I was

wondering if you could track down a missing person for me? No, not a friend, exactly. It's a patient of mine. She is suffering a temporary amnesia – loss of memory . . . Yes, sure – about five foot eight, hundred and thirty-odd pounds, brown hair, blue eyes . . .' Later, he had a chance to check her particulars again, when he checked her along with all the other patients on his last round before turning in. Who are you, he silently asked the unconscious, heavily bandaged form. Do you even know yourself, Tara?

Greg Marsden was suffering no such doubts as he hit the freeway out of town towards Hunter's Hill. He knew that he had been both clever and careful. After this length of time a duty call to enquire after the health of his wife's best friend should not give rise to comment. Such a pity that Phillip was in New York again, so he'd miss him. Greg grinned. He drove the Rolls hard to hurry through the depressing outer suburbs of Sydney till he came to the great span of the Gladesville Bridge arching elegantly over the Parramatta River. From there on it was a green and pleasant drive. He took the left off the freeway, turned right over the bridge, and was there.

'Greg! Oh my God!'

Jilly came flying out of the house as soon as the car was heard on the drive.

'Hey, baby! At least let me switch the engine off.'

'Oh Greg, I've missed you so much, I've been going crazy out here on my own . . .'

Greg looked at her. There certainly was a heightened manic glitter about her. Her heart-shaped feline face was flushed and the yellow cats' eyes were wide, dilated. Greg found the hint of madness indescribably attractive. Excitement stirred within him. He looked around. The big old house was totally shaded by mature trees and they were not overlooked. He reached out and brushed the outline of her breasts with the back of a careless hand, then took her by the waist, pulling her to him and grinding his thumbs into the soft flesh above the hips. She could feel the hardness of his cock and almost sobbed with longing.

'Welcome home, baby,' he said. 'Let's go inside.'

The first series of operations on Tara Welles had undoubtedly been a success. Dan permitted himself to feel a professional pride and gratification. But they had inevitably been largely of an exploratory nature, and what Dan thought of as 'clearing the ground'. The real work, of building the new face, had yet to be done. This was the worst phase for the patient, he knew – all the pain of repeated surgery, with nothing as yet to show for it. Wounds healed well in Orpheus' magical climate, but the heat undoubtedly added to the discomfort of a heavily bandaged head and body. Accustomed as he was to dealing with individuals who had borne some of the worst of life's blows without flinching, Dan had nevertheless been deeply impressed with Tara's stoicism.

'How's the pain,' he asked her after one examination. Unable to speak, she gestured with her hand. 'So-so.'

'No, you don't. It must hurt like hell under there.' She did not move. 'Well, we'll give you something to help with that. It's important that you sleep well. I'll have Lizzie bring you some sedatives.'

Inside the blind white world of her bandages, Tara heard the concern in his voice. He really cares, she thought, and a tiny seed of joy took root in her heart. This thought was worth a million times more to her than any painkillers. The sedatives duly arrived. But she did not take them.

Tara went into the second wave of her surgery. Days and nights passed now in a warm haze of alternating pain and oblivion. Sometimes she dreamed herself back in Dave's hut in the bush, and babbled and wept in her sleep. At such times she would often wake to find Dan at her bedside, reading her chart, his hand on her pulse, his whole presence a rock of reassurance after the nightmares. He had the habit of going round all his post-operative patients himself in the blackness of the tropical night, armed only with a small flashlight to avoid awaking the sleepers. Somehow on these rounds he always found that he was leaving Tara till the last, so that he could linger by her side for as long as he wanted. On these occasions she knew that her present pain was the price of her new growth and change. Without it she could not emerge from the dull cramping chrysalis of being Stephanie Harper. *I am making myself what I want to be*, she repeated fiercely again and again. Every time she did so an uprush of pride spurted in her heart. What I want to be. A new face for a new woman for a new life. Hold on. Just hold on.

As the moment came when the bandages were due to be removed, Dan found himself as nervous as Tara herself was. He was not worried about the surgery. That had worked fine, and she was healing well, he had monitored that meticulously. What he was concerned about was Tara's reaction. He realized that he desperately wanted her to be pleased with her new appearance. She had as yet seen nothing of herself, since she had been continually bandaged since the first operation. The night before the unveiling he took her for a stroll along the beach. The still-glowing indigo sea stretched before them, and the incoming tide plucked softly at their bare feet. Dan was silent for a long while.

'We're taking the bandages off tomorrow, Tara,' he said at last. 'I want you to be prepared for . . . a shock. I mean a hell of a shock.' She held her breath.

'When you look in the mirror for the first time tomorrow morning, there will be your eyes looking back at you. But that's all you'll recognize. They'll be looking out at you from the face of a stranger.'

The face of a stranger . . . the phrase stayed with her all night long. At dawn the next day she was pacing the beach again, and not long after Dan arrived at her cabin.

'How did you sleep?' he asked.

'Not very well.'

'Neither did I.' His tone was brusque. 'Let's not prolong the suspense then, shall we?'

Together they entered the cabin, and Tara seated herself tensely, gripping the arms of the bamboo chair. Dan drew up the coffee table before her, laid out his scissors, and squatting down on the table set to work. He cut through the external dressings, lifting free the layers of cotton wool and lint. Tara kept her eyes tightly closed, but she could tell from the soft sensation of his breath fanning her face when at last her skin was free to the air. Dan's voice reached her from far away.

'Remember, I never knew how you looked before your accident. Nor even how you sounded. I've just done the best I can to arrive at your idea of your new self.'

Tara heard him sit back, releasing his breath in a sigh.

'You can look now.'

She opened her eyes. Dan was holding a mirror up before her. With a deep sense of shock, mounting incredulity and at last overwhelming delight, she registered the face in the glass. It was lovely. Gone forever were the dragged-down mouth and eyelid, the raised weals of scar tissue. But gone too were all the traces of Stephanie, who she now realized in a flash of insight had always had a sad, careworn expression. All the signs of anxiety and strain had disappeared. A much younger, more buoyant woman altogether looked back at her.

Oh so gently she raised her hands and explored the tender skin round her eyes where before the tiny crows' feet had borne unmistakable witness to her age. They had disappeared, and she looked at least ten years younger than her real age.

'How about . . .' Dan's voice was tentative, unsure. 'How about if you like what you see . . . you just nod?'

Tara raised her shining eyes to him. She nodded vigorously. Dan laughed aloud with delight, punching the air in triumph like a boy. Her heart soaring, Tara Welles smiled her first smile. Then she burst into tears of joy, and hurled herself into Dan's arms. Happy beyond words, they clung to one another for a long time.

Now began Tara's real programme of rehabilitation.

With ever-increasing confidence in the weeks that followed she exercised, danced, and even swam. With the inviting pool almost at her cabin door, and the languid sea just beyond, she learned first to relax in the water, then to enjoy it, and finally to trust her body to it completely. The physical freedom and sheer pleasure she now found in swimming she had only ever before known on horseback. Now she came to love the sensuous feel of the warm waves caressing her body, lapping her with delicious sensations from head to foot. With her programme of swimming and dance exercise, her body became more graceful as well as more confident, and with the weight loss produced by the island's healthy diet, she gradually shed forever the last vestiges of awkward, ungainly Stephanie.

Tara also worked on herself in the privacy of her little bungalow. She still kept her scrapbook record of her 'accident' – it was a story the papers were unwilling to let go, but kept alive with 'CINDERELLA HEIRESS – HER DEATH STILL A MYSTERY' headlines. She had not weakened in her determination to seek revenge. On the contrary, as she recovered her purpose took on the hardness and clarity of a diamond. But now she used the newspapers and magazines which she had brought in daily by the morning launch to study fashions, clothes and latest trends. A new woman wants a whole new look, she told Lizzie happily. So she pored over the fashion shots, made rough sketches of herself in the newest lines and garments, rehearsing colours and ideas for when the time came to buy. For the first time in her life, she realized, she was free to concentrate on herself, and becoming confident enough to do so. She meant to make up for all those wasted years.

The board meeting at Harper Mining was not going well. There had been no significant fall in the annual profits. Stephanie's sound instincts and sense of the market had been very much missed, but when the losses produced by her absence were spread across the worldwide operations of the mighty conglomerate that Max Harper had created, the company was sound enough to absorb them without difficulty. The trouble answered to another name.

Bill McMaster, from his seat at the head of the smooth slab of boardroom mahogany, looked at the source of the difficulty, reined in his temper, and tried again.

'OK, Greg. Maybe we didn't give your idea a proper hearing. Let's have it once more.'

Greg glowered at him, and threw a contemptuous look around the table. Bunch of has-beens! Bloody old bastards! He was flushed with rage. When Stephanie had made him a director of Harper Mining, he had been determined to make it a real job and no mere sinecure. Life was offering him a chance to be more in the years ahead than just an ageing tennis bum. He meant to take the chance with both hands. He had made what was for him a real effort to get to grips with the vast range of Harper Mining's activities and, though he had come rather unstuck on the finance side, he was not deterred. That's what accountants are for, he decided. *He* would be an ideas man. He had in fact had plenty of ideas. Each one had been courteously received and discussed by the sober-suited men who kept Harper Mining on its tracks – and then, just as courteously, thrown out. The same fate had just befallen Greg's latest brainchild.

'You've all heard all you need to know!' he flashed out. 'There's deposits there just waiting to be lifted out of the ground. No one else is after them. They could be ours for the taking. And you lot are sitting on your arses doing nothing!'

'And doesn't it occur to you to wonder why our competitors have so obligingly left the field free for us to clean up?' The sarcastic question from lower down the table expressed the general mood of the meeting against Greg.

'Yeah, the feasibility study—'

' 'Snothing to do with feasibility, y'drongo!' Another of the board members had had enough. 'Tell'm, Bill!'

'You can't imagine that we haven't looked at this one

before, Greg,' Bill began with a mildness he was far from feeling. 'The problems are not engineering problems, not transport nor cost, nor manpower. It's a political minefield out there, and the multinationals have learned to be very careful with operational intervention. The whole thing could blow at any time, it's so unstable. And if the pieces came down in favour of a Marxist government when the explosion comes, we've paid for the privilege of establishing their mining industry for them. You're asking us to risk capital, equipment, and worst of all our men's lives, on a venture so half-baked, half-cocked—'

'Ah, get stuffed!' Greg was on his feet, glaring round him with white hatred. 'That's the trouble with y'all – dead from the neck up! Y'aren't worth a can of camel's piss!' And without a backward glance he strode from the room.

'Delete that last observation from the minutes would you, Mary,' instructed Bill imperturbably. 'OK, gentlemen, shall we carry on?'

Some people take a lifetime to discover the magic of the islands of the Great Barrier Reef and the Coral Sea. Tara afterwards thought that she had packed a whole lifetime of happiness into the few weeks she spent there after her surgery was over, building up her strength, confidence and determination for the world outside. For the first time since her arrival she was able to enjoy to the full the stunning beauty of the natural playground, the towering palm trees, white-golden beaches and endless, endless good Queensland sun. Every day came to her like a gift, shining and new-minted, and she spent each one freely, as only the truly rich in happiness can afford to do.

She was very soon aware that a major part of her new-found delight in life centred on a certain Dan Marshall. Almost without noticing it she had come to look for his daily appearance round the bungalows, listen for his step, wait for his special smile. The realization came to her without strain or anxiety for her friendship with Dan was

like the man himself – easy, warm, relaxed and unde-
manding. He was the perfect companion and, when his
day's work was over or he was taking a break from surgery,
the perfect guide to the tropical paradise of Orpheus too.

Together, deep in conversation, they would explore
every corner of the isle from one set of gently-shelving
beaches to their opposite numbers across on the other side.
From the seaside fringe of fronded palms they struck
inland to the backbone of Orpheus, a rocky outcrop gaunt
with a riot of different trees, bloodwood, ash, wattle and
gin-gee. Tree-ferns, thousand-year-old mosses and vibrant
flowers sprang from the chocolate-coloured soil, small
creatures watched them on their way with bright unblinking eyes, bees filled the air with a lazy drowseful hum and
the whole world of nature seemed theirs to enjoy.

Together they were like Adam and Eve before the Fall.
In the peace and purity of this island clean and green,
Tara rediscovered her lost innocence, her trust and faith in
her fellow men. It was a world without corruption. Dan
was an eager companion, responsive and committed,
indeed with her he seemed to be able to lay aside
temporarily the heavy burden of responsibility for other
peoples' lives and well-being that he carried as a doctor,
and enjoy himself as a man. But with his almost boyish
enthusiasm for her and her company came no pressure, no
demands. She sensed that Dan was one of those rare souls
who had scotched the serpent in him long ago; it was not
lurking there somewhere to sting her. So she was able to
abandon herself without fear to the sights and sensations
of this garden paradise, and did so without restraint.

Chief among their delights was the underwater exploration, the snorkelling and scuba diving which Dan
encouraged her to undertake as she grew bolder and bolder
in this new element so warm and inviting. Can anyone
who lives in a cold climate appreciate how blessed by the
sun's beams the water can become? For Tara, swimming
expeditions with Dan were more than a physical pleasure
– they were a series of heightened sensations and a passport

into a new world. Beneath the surface of the water lay revealed to her delighted eyes all the denizens of that strange universe; infinitely fragile manifestations of marine life, sparkling, twisting, darting about. Some were splashes of startling colour, others scarcely less limpid than the sea itself, translucent creatures who revealed their presence only by the shadows moving below them on the sandy bed. Yet all were alive, vital, daring and quick with the very essence of life – Dan would scarcely have time to draw her attention to a brilliant flash of silver but it was gone, only to be succeeded by another and another. In their strange and silent world the inhabitants busily came and went, impervious to the large human creatures moving slowly amongst them.

A restful day in the sea would usually be followed by an evening's barbecue when they cooked and ate the fish that Dan managed to catch. 'Have dinner with me tonight?' he would ask merrily, popping up beside her with a succulent fish on his spear. 'I wouldn't miss it for quids' was Tara's prompt response. Then when they came ashore he would build the barbecue and cook the fish while she collected fruit for afterwards, eating utensils and chilled beer in a cool box and brought them all down to the beach again. Dan loved to barbecue, and did so with great flair and dash. After one particularly successful meal, Tara remarked on this.

'Are all surgeons good cooks?'

Dan laughed. 'As a matter of fact, no. We great chefs are born, not made.'

'I really must learn to cook.'

'I thought all women could. How have you avoided it?'

Tara stiffened. How could she explain to Dan her 'poor little rich girl' situation, where she had never learned to do any of the ordinary things, because of always having someone to do them for her? Dan sensed her unease, and moved on to another topic.

'Well,' he said deliberately, 'if you ever decide to try, and you need a guinea pig, give me a call. I rather fancy being around . . . when you serve up your first bacon and eggs.'

This was the first time he had ever made any reference to feelings of more than friendship for her. She was furious, delighted, confused. She had never in her life flirted, or been flirted with. She sat tongue-tied and raging at herself.

'Dear me,' said Dan, obviously enjoying her discomfort. 'I didn't know forty-year-old ladies *blushed*. Or is it just the glow of the fire?' Tara could not help laughing.

From among his fishing things, Dan produced a sea-shell, a perfect crescent of gleaming mother-of-pearl.

'A present,' he said shyly.

'A going-away present.' There was a painful silence between them at her reminder of the inevitable parting to come. 'It will always remind me of Orpheus. And you, Dan.'

'You really are so beautiful,' he said under his breath.

'You should be proud then,' she came back lightly. 'You did it.'

'Hey!' Dan was taken aback. 'Your face is only a reflection of who you are. You're still the same lady I met months ago, and don't you ever forget it.'

'Thanks, Dan. I won't. Well, it's time for the lady to go.'

'I just wish you'd trust me enough to tell me what it is you're running away from.'

'Oh Dan.'

'Well, at least tell me you've got somewhere to stay and enough money when you land up in – where will it be? Sydney?'

He was growing angry, and she was too.

'I'll be fine. I'm a big girl now, you know. I'm allowed out on my own!'

Dan took the warning in her voice and changed tack.

'I'm going to miss you,' he said heavily. 'You must know by now I think of you as . . . someone special.'

Tara took a deep breath, conscious of a pain stirring somewhere deep around her heart.

'Dan, there are some things – I have to do – alone. I'm

134

sorry, but I just can't talk about it. Not even to you. So please. No more questions. OK?'

And that was how they left it, right up to the end. Dan honoured his promise, though his soul was tormented with unanswered questions about the woman he was falling in love with more deeply every day. With the humility of the genuine lover to whom the beloved's happiness is infinitely more precious than his own, he set himself to make perfect the remainder of Tara's stay on the island, and to return her to the world outside fully restored both in mind and body.

Tara meanwhile was engaged in systematically hardening her heart against him. Since that first shy indication of his love, she had been alarmed to feel her purpose wavering, her plan of discovery and revenge fading under the impact of the warm joyful life offered her on the island. She reapplied herself to her scrapbook to stiffen her resolve. It did not fail. The cruel images of Greg burned from her mind the stirrings of love for Dan. The time came when she was not only ready to depart from Orpheus, but beginning to burn along the whole long length of the touchpowder which would lead her at last to her revenge.

Dan noticed the change in her, and his heart saddened more from day to day. At last they stood together on the jetty, beside the launch that would return Tara to Townsville and the world outside. Tara had taken a painful leave of Lizzie, smiling bravely through her tears. 'Didn't I tell you they all leave here smiling?' Lizzie had cracked, on the verge of breaking down herself. But now both Tara and Dan were dry-eyed.

'This is it for you then, Tara,' he said. 'Scared?'

'A little.'

'You don't have to go—' It was his only appeal and it hung in the air between them.

'Promise me one thing—'

Tara raised her eyebrows in question.

'If you ever need anything – *anything* – you'll call?'

'I'll be all right.' And I will *not* call, she thought. I will prove I can manage on my own. On my own, Dan, don't you understand? I've leaned on men all my life. I'm growing up now.

Out loud she said merely, 'Goodbye, then.'

'Good luck, Tara.' Gently he tipped up her chin for their first and last kiss. Her lips were cold. Without another word she turned and climbed down into the launch. She did not wave in answer to his last farewell. But impassive, unmoving, she kept her eyes fixed on the tall lone figure on the jetty until long after he had faded out of sight.

Chapter Eight

In Sydney, nature created one of the world's most beautiful harbours. And for the last two hundred years, man has been dumping his refuse in it, reflected Bill McMaster, in sombre mood. He stood at the window of his corner office at the top of Harper Mining, looking out over the Harbour Bridge and of waterside Sydney spread out below him. He had been at work early, early enough to have seen the water garbos going about their daily task of collecting the tons of garbage that Sydneysiders fling into their harbour every day. Could do with one of those boys up here, thought Bill angrily. Got a major garbage problem of my own.

The intercom buzzed on his desk. Bill stabbed at it in exasperation.

'Yes?'

'Excuse me, sir – just to let you know that Greg Marsden is still here. It's been over half an hour . . .'

'I know, I know. All right, show him in.'

Immaculate in a cool suit, white shirt and pale lemon tie, Greg wasted no time on the courtesies.

'This is a surprise visit, Greg,' began Bill equably. 'What can we do for you?' But Greg brushed him aside.

'I've tried to get you on the phone all week.'

'Yes, I know. I've been out of the office quite a bit. This is a busy time of the year here. Won't you sit down?'

Greg took a seat, but did not relax his attitude of controlled aggression. He fixed Bill with a level stare.

'It's been months now since Stephanie died, Bill. The press had a field day there for a while. You'd have thought the world was coming to an end. But it's over now. And somehow it seems as if Stephanie Harper never existed.'

What's he driving at? thought Bill irritably. Aloud he said, 'She hasn't been forgotten.'

'Certainly not by me.' Bill found the pious response very hard to swallow, but he held himself in, and waited.

'Thing is, Bill, I'm finding it very difficult to believe that after three separate searches, two masterminded and controlled by this company from start to finish – still her body hasn't been found.'

So that's it! thought Bill with rising anger.

'Something – a skeleton. Remains.'

'I assure you,' said Bill evenly, 'that everything that could possibly be done has been done.'

'Well, I'm not satisfied.'

'Oh really.'

'Do you honestly mean to tell me' – Greg was warming to his theme – 'that this huge organization with all its resources, that can manage to find uranium, gold, iron ore, oil, can't even manage to find a handful of bloody *bones*?'

Bill's anger burst the bounds of restraint at last.

'You stinking hypocrite!' he shouted. 'Your only reason for wanting Stephanie's death legally established is so that you can get your paws on her money. Well, I loved Stephanie Harper! She was like a daughter to me.' He paused, and carried on more quietly. 'It's a pity that you never took the trouble to get to know her properly before she died. You might have learned something from her. She wasn't perfect, but she was warm, and she cared about people. She'd give, and give, and all she ever asked was to be accepted for what she was, rather than who she was. She tried damned hard, and that's epitaph enough for anybody.'

'I never said—'

'Shut up and listen! Yes, I'd love the chance to give Stephanie Harper a proper funeral. But I'm glad they didn't find her body!' He rounded on Greg, now looking much less self-assured. 'D'you know why? Because I want you to sweat out every moment of the next seven years.

After that, you'll be legally entitled to a slice of one of the biggest fortunes in Australian history, it's true. But – there's a but you never knew about, sonny boy, because no one anticipated this would ever come to pass.'

Greg was suddenly alert. What was this? He fought back the sudden fear that stabbed at his stomach. He'd got it all worked out . . . hadn't he?

'I should point out to you' – Bill was beginning to enjoy this – 'that before she married you, I persuaded Stephanie to add a clause to her will. In the event of her pre-deceasing you, and you re-marrying – you *forfeit the lot*!'

The silence was electric. Greg sat mute and unbelieving in his chair. He could not seem to take in what was happening to him. Bill leaned back, his anger spent.

'So that's it. In the meantime, you could try getting a job. I don't think that your . . . usefulness to Harper Mining would prevent us from releasing you from your directorship if the right opening came along. Working for your living might prove to be a very pleasant change.'

Lifting his head Greg turned eyes full of hatred on Bill, who knew that his opponent would have killed him without hesitation at that second if he could. Suddenly Greg sprang like a panther from his chair, and for the first time in his life Bill knew the sick lurch of physical fear. Then without a word Greg raced from the room.

Bill was inexplicably shaken. But he was also experiencing a sense of the lightening of a burden. I know I'm not through with you yet, Mr Marsden, he said to himself. But there's not much longer to go.

By day or night, Sydney's Mascot airport never sleeps. But on a busy weekday morning, it is at the height of its bustling activity. To the woman who had been out of civilization for many weeks and months, the raw energy and movement of the crowds was a severe jolt after the tranquillity of Orpheus Island. Half shy, half fearful, she pushed her way through the people and came out of the main exit, looking lost.

'Taxi, lady?'

Without thinking, Tara fell gratefully into the back of the sloppy old sedan.

'Where to?' They were already headed for the city nearby, and she had not yet given him any directions.

'Oh—' She had made no plans, preferring to let events unfold in their own course. 'I need a place to stay. Somewhere cheap. I don't know . . . those parts of Sydney. Can you make any suggestions?'

When the taxi dropped her in the part of town known as the Rocks, Tara experienced for the first time life as it is lived by people without money. Grimy, urban, under the shadow of the Harbour Bridge, the area boasted cheap accommodation, with all that that implies. Yet Tara knew that somehow she had come to the right place. She was running out of funds, after the expensive and prolonged stay on Orpheus Island. But even if she still had a bag full of money, she knew she would not have put up at the Sydney Regent. That was Stephanie Harper. Tara Welles would do it her way.

Struggling with her suitcase, and wearying fast in the sticky heat of the afternoon, Stephanie came to a private hotel, built on a corner site and jutting out imposingly into the roadway. Through the grimy windows of the bar, she could see the publican serving drinks to his rowdy, all-male clientèle. Tara saw the mass of singletted male bodies, the unappetizing beer bellies, the eyes turned her way, and her heart began to drop. But the publican noticed her there, and signalled to her to come to a side door.

'Y'wanting a room, girlie?' he began without preamble.

'That's right.'

'It'll be fifty dollars a week.'

'That's fine.'

'—payable one month in advance, and there's a hundred dollar bond—'

'Bond?' Tara was aghast. She had never heard of such a thing.

'Well, landlords have got to protect themselves, you

know! A small, middle-aged man with thinning sandy hair, he looked as if he was in need of all the protection he could get. 'I've trusted people in the past – let them run up arrears – and then they've done a moonlight flit on me.'

'It's just that I wasn't prepared to have to pay a bond – or so much in advance . . .'

'Well, them's m'terms. Take it or leave it.'

'I'll have to leave it. I've arrived in Sydney with four hundred dollars, I've still got things to buy, I haven't eaten all day, and I haven't got a job yet. I'm sorry for wasting your time.' She turned to go.

'Hold on, there. I could forget about the bond.'

'Could you make it two weeks in advance?'

The landlord hesitated.

'All right. Two weeks in advance. Payable directly.'

Tara smiled. My God, she's a looker when she wants to be and no mistake, he thought admiringly. Well, she won't be bad for business.

'Would you like to see the room? This way.' He picked up her bag and escorted her in, opening up chattily.

'It's a nice old pub. A real chunk of Aussie history, this. Built in 1915. There's lots of old photos down in the bar y'can see later on if you're interested.'

They climbed a dark staircase to a narrow landing. He pushed open a door. Ahead lay a window, and athwart it the huge shadow of the Harbour Bridge. Inside, the room was dirty, depressing and poorly furnished. Its tiny grimy kitchenette was partly concealed by a torn curtain. Tara stifled her feelings of dismay.

The landlord read her reaction.

'I'll be honest with you,' he said defensively, 'it's been empty for months, and I've let it run down. I was hoping to let it to a bloke, y'see – the right type of bloke, I hoped one'd come along. But some of the types about these days, y'could end up with a druggie or a basher. And I can't afford to get into trouble with the police.'

He paused, and studied her carefully.

'Well, y'look like a nice girl. I can help you get it . . .

fixed up. M'name's Sandy, by the way. I'm right above you on the top floor and I haven't got a lot t'do in my spare time. I'm on my own now. My friend died end of last year – cancer – we'd been mates for twenty-seven years . . .'

He came to a rambling halt. Impulsively Tara squeezed his hand, then moved to the window.

'Well, after all, it does have a harbour view!' she said.

Standing in the hall of the house on Hunter's Hill, Phillip Stewart carefully checked passport, airline ticket, currency. His smart set of matched luggage was waiting by the door, his overcoat on the chair nearby. He looked at his watch, and entered the sitting room.

Looking strangely forlorn in the large, open plan area, Jilly sat watching the television, the now-familiar glass of whisky by her side. But the phone was on the floor by her chair, and Phillip guessed that she was waiting for a phone call – which, he also guessed, would not come until he was on his way to the airport. Jilly showed no interest in his imminent departure. But she was obviously not really watching the television either. Oh Jilly, he thought, what's become of us?

Still he went through the motions of being half of a couple.

'You won't forget then, Jilly? Tuesday?'

'Tuesday? What?'

'The pool engineer's coming to see about the pump. And there's that insurance thing to see to – you won't forget?'

'I won't forget.'

They had come to the end of their matrimonial smalltalk. Phillip used to say when he had to go away on business, 'And what are you going to do with yourself while I'm away?' Now, he never dared to ask, because he knew the answer. From a thousand-and-one of the tiny giveaway signs, he knew that Jilly was having an affair. From her desperate absorption in it, her tension and bouts of misery, because he also knew *who*, he could guess *why* she was so wretched. And he felt quite unable to help her.

In the past, because he loved his wife, Phillip had not only tolerated her infidelities. He had loved her enough to support her through them, and rescue her from despair after them. They had never been so numerous, gross or humiliating that he had felt his own position compromised, and he drew a sad kind of satisfaction from being the man who, at the end and after all, Jilly came back to. All that had changed when she had returned from Eden with the news of Stephanie's death. He did not know what had really happened, and he did not want to. But intuitively he had felt that somehow now she had put herself beyond the pale. It was the end.

He was therefore in the strange situation, as he was well aware, of a man who mourned the loss of his wife while still living with her in the same house. His pain had been real, and her presence was a daily reminder of all he had lost. But his period of mourning was drawing to an end, and he was preparing to move out of it. Partly this took the form of increasing the physical distance between them. He was more and more in New York, and when in Sydney he tended to dine and even sleep at his club, keeping out of the empty house as much as possible. Mainly, though, he had by degrees put such an emotional gap between himself and Jilly that there was no bridging it. When the time came for a parting, their marriage would be found to have died of a sheer lack of nourishment.

Phillip was still the old Phillip enough to feel that he should not make the first move to collapse the relationship. Their marriage was finished as an emotional reality. But it still had an important social function as a shelter for Jilly to live within. After all, as a divorced woman, where would she go? How would she live? She had never done a day's work in her life. To turn her out would be like asking a wheelchair case suddenly to get up and walk. Jilly was effectively disabled for real life. Perhaps that's why she's so dependent on Marsden, he thought. Well, there's nothing I can do about that.

Outside came the hoot of the taxi to take him to the airport.

'Goodbye, then, Jilly,' he called as he crossed the hall, picked up his bags and opened the front door. Without waiting for a reply, he left the house. Jilly hardly heard him go, though her ears would have picked up another footstep, another man's call, with the sensitivity of a bat's. But she had nothing to listen to, since she sat all night listening for a telephone that would not ring.

That same night, in the battered hotel in the Rocks, Tara sat on the hard narrow bed of her room and struggled to hold back the tears. She was coming to the end of a far from perfect day. Returning to Sydney had been a very emotional experience for her, coming back to what had been 'her' city, but with a new identity and an uncertain future. Everything was rich in memories, both sweet and bitter. She had felt herself drawn to the old familiar places, but had resisted that temptation – that was why she had come to the Rocks, after all, not one of her old stamping grounds. But it had been a struggle.

This was on top of the struggle she was having to do even the simplest everyday things of life for herself. As the life-long mistress of two great houses whose provisioning had always been the care and concern of others, she had never even been in a supermarket. To purchase a few basic necessities of life for the next few days had been an ordeal not made any easier by the rude, impatient attitude of the woman on the check-out.

But worse was to come. As she came into the kitchen with her shopping, she noticed something moving on the table. To her horror she discovered that she was about to deposit her box on what looked like a whole family of cockroaches. She recoiled in horror. But then her anger came to her rescue and she brushed them vigorously away, making a mental note that the next shopping list would include cockroach powder at the very top. The final straw came when she knocked over a carton of just-opened milk and saw it splash everywhere. Feeling thoroughly defeated, she sat down on the bed and fought against the temptation to have a really good cry.

Then to her joy her eye fell on a clutter of cleaning things that she had not noticed when she came in. Sandy had made good his offer to help, and had provided detergent, disinfectant, a brush and pan, and a mop. She fell on them eagerly. Scrubbing floors was another thing that Stephanie Harper had never tried her hand at. But Tara Welles turned to with vigour, and when she fell asleep that night she slept the just sleep of those who have laboured well and are satisfied.

As the days went by, Tara's situation at the hotel improved steadily. Once thoroughly cleaned, the room was much more inhabitable. Sandy came through with new curtains for the windows and the kitchen alcove, and provided odd bits and pieces to make it more homely and comfortable. Best of all, though, she found someone to make it home, someone to come home to.

He had attracted her attention when she went out the first morning to take her rubbish to the garbage cans behind the hotel. She had heard a faint miaow, and looking down saw a tiny cat cowering behind one of the bins. She picked him up and he sat trembling on her hand.

'You poor little thing,' she said wondering. 'You lost? You don't look as if you belong to anybody, or as if you've had anything to eat for days.' The cat regarded her trustingly and sat quite still.

'Do you want some dinner, then?' she continued. 'Come on, puss.' She took the cat in, and its starving hunger when she fed it, as well as its bedraggled look, confirmed her conviction that he was a stray. 'Well, you're not any more,' she told him. 'You're mine, and your name is – Max!' She giggled at the absurdity of naming this shivering scrap after the mighty industrialist, her father, and in doing so realized that she had never ever before dared to laugh at this man. 'I must be getting better,' she decided. She made Max a bed of newspapers, and fed him as much as he could eat till at last, sated, he slept on her knee, purring quietly even in his slumbers. He was more than a cat, that was clear to her. He was, although not black all over, a good luck omen to her. He was a helpless scrap, he was something to care for, he was a positive reaffirmation of new life.

'Oh Maxie,' she sighed. 'I'm glad we found one another. No one knows how I've longed for someone to talk to.'

Greg was not normally interested in billiards. To a man accustomed to the smash, lob and volley of top-class tennis, it was a game singularly lacking in action. But the Harper Mansion boasted a fine mahogany slate-bedded professionally-sized billiard table, in a fully-equipped billiard room. And when he had the right kind of partner, for the right kind of game, Greg was willing to play a few frames.

He needed to relax, anyway. Nothing was quite as easy as he had hoped it would be. Greg was still trying, months after the event, to establish some kind of regular life for himself. But at every side he came up against the situation of being neither a married man nor single, neither Stephanie's partner nor her inheritor. So although he received a good income by virtue of her arrangements, he could not raise a penny under his own steam, or touch a farthing of the estate. It was a curiously powerless position to be in.

Similarly, although Greg chafed against the frustrations of the single life, he was determined not to get too deep in with the all-too-available Jilly Stewart. He had not wriggled his neck out of one matrimonial noose to thrust it straight into another. He liked Jilly well enough as a woman – he found her love-making fantastic and only had to think of her to feel an erection stirring. He would have been happy to pursue a discreet but steady affair. But Jilly had pushed too hard ever since the return from Eden – 'When shall I see you again?' – 'Why didn't you call me?' – 'Oh Greg, there's got to be more than this!' She didn't seem to realize, *he* called the tune, not her. So he deliberately distanced himself from her, was cold towards her, played hard to get. Yet at the same time he knew better than to alienate her. He had to keep his hold over her, to make sure that their unspoken secret remained locked within her brain. He therefore saw her enough to continue her dependency on him, without ever leaving her happy and satisfied.

Greg fobbed Jilly off with claims that he was very busy at Harper Mining, sorting out Stephanie's estate, running the Harper mansion, a thousand and one things. In reality he had almost nothing to do with himself all day long. He could not revert to his bachelor life – its raffish conviviality would have been quite inappropriate for the grieving widower role he had chosen to play. He had no contacts now with the Harper business – he had got the message loud and clear that he was *persona non grata* to the men at the helm there. And Matey, major-domo of the mansion since time immemorial, would have been massively insulted at the suggestion that the master of the house had to do anything towards running it. His whole life had been dedicated to doing this with such streamlined efficiency that it really looked as if the house ran itself.

This afternoon, almost out of pure boredom, Greg had taken himself back to his tennis club and played a few games. He was out of practice and out of condition, but there were always people who were delighted to knock a ball about with a big-name champ. He had watched Lew Jackson, his best man, whom he had not seen since the wedding, win a scorching victory in a practice match and felt once again the chilly wind of competition he couldn't handle. Well, at least he was out of that rat-race. Afterwards he bought Lew a beer.

'How y'been, Greg?' Lew was, in his way, expressing sympathy.

'So-so.'

'Good t'see y'back in circulation.'

'Yeah, well. You can go out of your mind, on your own too much.' Greg sipped his beer.

'So will y'be coming back on the circuit then?'

'Nah, mate, no chance. I can't keep up with you young blokes!'

Lew thought of a number of jokes about creating a geriatrics' challenge cup for Greg's especial benefit, and decided not to risk it. Diplomatically he took a neutral tack.

'So what are you going to do with y'self?'

Greg tried to sound light and noncommittal. 'I shall just have to take up other amusements.'

'Talking of which . . .' With Lew, diplomacy could only go so far. He raised his eyebrows suggestively and nodded across the room to the door.

Greg followed his gaze. There in the doorway stood the French girl who had gladdened Greg's last bachelor night before his wedding. As a tennis groupie, her thing was to hunt down the leading players; success turned her on. She had had the hots for Greg, but she had them for any winner. Looking at Lew and the grin on his face, it flashed through Greg's mind that he had had her too. He found that thought oddly exciting and his interest stirred sharply. It was also several days since his last visit to Hunter's Hill.

Nevertheless he had feigned a lack of interest, and turned back to the bar. He would not let Lew share his thoughts. He knew that the tart would come to him before too long, and was already planning how he could fix her up for tonight, ostentatiously take his leave on his own, then have her come out to the house after him in a taxi, when the staff would all be in bed. No problem. Greg Marsden could do it if anyone could.

Which is how, later that night, Greg came to be playing billiards with his French guest. She had arrived to find a bottle of chilled French wine already opened, and the lights of the sitting room turned down low to keep company with the soft music emanating from the stereo. Greg could be romantic when he chose. But his visitor had other ideas in mind. Her proposal for a good evening of family entertainment took Greg by surprise.

'Strip snooker? That's a new one on me.'

148

She bared her small even teeth. 'I show you.'

'I don't know the rules.'

'I teach you.'

Amused by her managing little ways, Greg led the way into the billiard room and under her direction set up the balls.

'Is simple. Every time you knock the ball off the table, I take something off. And you too.'

Greg did not need her explanation. He had figured it out for himself. He had a feeling he was going to enjoy this. He looked at her carefully for the first time since she had come in. She was wearing a white shirt, with a red scarf, tight red trousers, earrings and high sling-back white shoes. It was clear to his scrutiny that she was wearing no bra. He grinned. Carefully he placed the white on its spot, selected two cues from the rack, chalked them, and handed one to her.

'OK, then,' he said. 'Shall we start?'

Her skill, or luck, had taken him by surprise at first. She had had his shoes, watch and shirt off before he had managed to strip her of the red scarf and earrings. Determined to have her trousers off her before he had to part with his, Greg fought back and slammed a red into a pocket.

'OK,' he ordered, 'shirt!'

Slowly she unbuttoned her shirt as he watched her. He had been right about the bra. She dropped her shirt to the floor and stood before him. She had small, firm, well-shaped breasts whose silky feel he remembered very well. Her nipples were large and dark, slightly tip-tilted, jutting towards him. He reached out to touch them. Swiftly she backed out of his reach, and impudently declared. 'No touch! Is not in the rules.'

She leaned down to play her shot, and her breasts swung forward like ripe fruit. The single central pool of light over the table played on her gleaming skin. All the rest of the room was in darkness. The tension mounted within him. Impatiently he watched her shot go awry, and then in a

149

single flurry of shots dispatched all the balls left on the table into the pockets. Breathing heavily, he turned to her. She stood smiling at him mockingly.

'You are cheat!'

Without a word, he lifted her bodily onto the table, and peeled off the bright red pants. Urgently he sprang up beside her and almost in one movement jammed into her and came. Afterwards he made up for this adolescent conduct. But he also made her atone in full for what he considered to be her less than respectful attitude towards him. These activities went on for a long time, and none of them were according to the rules of snooker.

Just as soon as Tara had sorted out her room at the hotel, she was ready to begin on the purpose for which she had come not only to Sydney but back to life. She did not have the details worked out totally in her mind. But her twin objectives were as clear and as firm as they had been from the moment she first conceived them – to find out the truth, and then – to revenge! Now, for the first time, she felt strong, well, and settled enough to begin. But there was another vitally important piece of business first.

Schoolboy soccer matches are usually not well supported by parents. Especially when a high proportion of the boys are boarders, fathers and mothers are not to be expected. At Sydney's most ancient and distinguished boys' school the following Saturday, Dennis Harper was not the only boy who noticed the tall slim lady hovering outside the school gates as his football match was in progress, taking photographs of the game. But he was the one who got the best look at her, when the runaway ball, well over the line, bowled almost up to her feet. She seemed mesmerized by his approach, staring at him as he ran up, till at last she turned away, seeming covered in – what? Confusion? Dennis noticed that she had a kind face, very little else. It was, after all, in the middle of a close-run game. So he retrieved the ball, ran back again, and promptly forgot her for the rest of the week.

At the weekend, though, he tried to raise the subject with Sarah. She was both uninterested and scornful, so Dennis dismissed it from his mind. Unlike Dennis, Sarah had not seen the woman in the third row at her school concert taking photograph after photograph of her piano solo from the darkness of the hall. She had been absorbed in the fingering of a very difficult piece and had no thought for anyone out there in the audience. She did not hear the strenuous burst of proud clapping that came from the third row, nor notice the woman who fixed her attention on her at the curtain call with shining eyes.

That night, tremulously happy amid her sadness, Tara leaned against her window nursing Maxie and recalling the events of the day.

'Oh Maxie,' she cried softly, 'it's only been a few months, but they've grown so. You should have seen how tall Dennis is getting. And you should have seen my little princess. She was so beautiful. And in the whole damn difficult thing, she only missed three notes!'

Chapter Nine

'Harper Mining, good morning, can I help you?'

'I'd like to speak to Mr McMaster, please.'

'Hold the line.'

Matey gripped the receiver in his wrinkled old fist, and looked out of the hall window. The white Rolls-Royce Corniche could just be seen disappearing down the drive of the Harper mansion. Matey had wasted no time getting on the phone. A second female voice sounded in his ear.

'Mr McMaster's office.'

'Could I speak to Mr McMaster?'

There was a pause.

'Mr McMaster's rather tied up at the moment. I'm his secretary. May I help you at all?'

'It's him I've got to speak to. Look, it's kind of urgent. Can you tell him it's Matey? From the mansion?'

Another pause. Matey tried to subdue the turmoil of emotions within him. At last, to his great relief, Bill came on the line.

'Hello, Matey, what can I do for you?'

'It's a difficult matter, Mr McMaster. I hardly know where to begin.' The old man's voice was trembling.

'Just take your time, take your time.'

'Well, sir, you know that myself and all the staff here have made every effort to adjust to our . . . changed circumstances. The loss of Miss Stephanie—'

'I know, Matey.'

'—but everything we could possibly have done for Miss Stephanie's husband, has been done for Mr Marsden. Everything!'

'I'm sure it has been.' Bill was baffled.

'But there are bounds, sir – bounds of decency that no

gentleman should overstep. As in this case—' Matey knew that he was not making good sense, and tried again.

'Last night, after all the household was in bed, Mr Marsden received a visitor. A lady visitor.'

Did he, the bugger, thought Bill heavily. Well, it had to happen.

'Well, there's not a lot we can do about that. Technically he's—' Bill searched for the right word '—a free agent.'

'It's not that, sir!' Matey was offended that Bill should think him the kind of snoop who rang up with tittle-tattle. 'It's what happened. We don't know the full story, as the – lady – was gone by the time we all got up this morning. But the maid reported an occurrence in the billiard room. The housekeeper went to investigate and she drew the matter to my attention. The remains of a bottle of wine have been knocked over on the billiard table. There were glasses, too.'

Bill waited with his habitual restraint. He knew there had to be more.

'That wasn't all. There were other marks on the table, sir, indications—'

'What marks?'

'Scoring, sir, and stains . . . the baize, the entire surface, is ruined.'

'I'm not with you, Matey.'

'Mr McMaster, I have every reason to believe that certain activities took place last night on that billiard table – on the table itself – that would be beyond decent people anywhere!'

The picture of the billiard room at the mansion came vividly before Bill's mind's eye. He saw the handsome table, the fine fittings that Max had insisted upon, the assortment of cues to suit players of any preference as to length and weight. When he, Max, and Harper Mining were all young, the only kind of board meetings ever held took place between him and Max around that table over a game of snooker. Major decisions would be taken, policies would emerge, easily and painlessly between frames. And this punk . . .

Bill found himself shaking. Matey's voice rang hollowly in his ear.

'Mr Marsden's out at the moment, so I've taken the opportunity to check with you, sir. What would be your instructions?'

'Jesus, Matey—' Bill's instructions at that moment could not have been carried into effect, since judicial castration was withdrawn from the statute books as a penalty some time ago.

'Let me think,' he resumed at last. 'First step has got to be to see if the damage can be made good. Get onto some specialists, have them look at it and get some opinions, estimates. Then send them to me.' He paused. 'And about Mr Marsden—'

'Yes, sir?'

'You can leave him to me. Sounds as if he's due to have his wings clipped. You'll be interested to know that something along those lines is already in the pipeline. We'll sort it out, don't you worry.'

It is frightening how completely our attitude to a place is governed by the presence or absence of one of its occupants. Dan Marshall had been entirely and totally happy on Orpheus Island, fulfilled in equal proportions by the man-made creation of his clinic and the wild, unspoiled natural beauty of its setting. But now his technicolour paradise seemed reduced to a flat monochrome. The sun shone as brightly as ever, but the gloss had gone off everything for him. He lacked any real incentive to get up in the morning. At the end of the day he never felt any enthusiasm for his lonely bed but would find excuses to stay up and burn the midnight oil till he had gone past tiredness.

In a determined effort to forget Tara, or at least to put that chapter of his life behind him as a pleasant memory, Dan worked harder than ever, taking on extra patients till he had hardly any time to be alone and brood. During this period he achieved some of his greatest triumphs of reconstructive surgery. He had the satisfaction of seeing a young girl who had come to him with her leg crushed out of all recognition by an accident with farm machinery, walk out of the clinic looking forward to her first disco. Yet somehow it was all dust and ashes to him now, without someone to share it with. The faithful Lizzie, who watched him closely, deeply troubled about him but powerless to help, would try to cheer him up.

'She's doing well in cabin ten – found her doing her exercises when I took her breakfast in this morning! Says she's gonna cheat you of your profit and get right in half the time. She will, too.'

Dan would smile obligingly at her banter, but it never removed the sadness in his eyes. For however hard he worked, however deeply he immersed himself in the problem in hand, he could not expunge Tara quite from his thoughts. Her image would creep up on him unbidden, and he would see her again, walking, swimming, barbecuing, smiling – he pushed the memories away. He had not been out snorkelling since she left, had no delight in the world about him, but withdrew like a hermit crab into his shell.

How long would this dull misery go on, he wondered. How long do you take to 'get over' someone? It had been so easy to fall in love with her – her stillness, her fortitude had won his respect, later her gaiety and zest for life had won his heart. Lovingly he recalled her tall, slender figure, grown relaxed and graceful on the golden island, her honest glance and vulnerable mouth he had kissed so fleetingly and dreamed of so often. He would never fall out of love, he knew. He would just have to climb out, the hard slow way. He sighed and returned to his paperwork. It would be a long haul.

High in the sky, the sun beat steadily down. Beside the translucent blue of the swimming pool, the bronzed figure stretched lazily, like a cat, and slowly turned over on the sun-lounger. Greg Marsden was maintaining his tan. In the days when he was on court every day from dawn to dusk, it had taken care of itself. But now he had to work at it. He sat up languidly, reached for a chilled beer from the cool bag beside him and sipped it appreciatively. Then languorously he settled back to work some more, eyes closed, prostrate at the altar of sun-worship.

Lower down in the gardens he could hear the low whirr of the mowing machines as the gardeners tended the smooth lawns. It pleased him to think that while he took his ease, others laboured for his benefit. He loved being the master of the mansion, and from the first had had more pleasure from the position in a matter of months than Stephanie had had in all her years as its chatelaine. He felt that he was rising, growing into the situation. The staff were responding well to his demands.

Of course, he had to be careful. Should've been more careful the other night he told himself chidingly. Silly to screw up the billiard table for the sake of a screw. Still, it had been stupendous at the time. His face creased into a smile as he remembered. And they were getting it fixed. He had seen the minions coming to and fro and knew that without any pain or fuss everything would be made as it had been, and a discreet item would appear on the household accounts for the month. That's the beauty of good staff, they take the worries right off your shoulders. And there wouldn't be a repeat performance of last night. Though he had a feeling he had not seen the last of the French girl. Suddenly he laughed out loud. He realized he did not even know her name. But just thinking of her he could feel the familiar tingling in his cock. He reached for it affectionately, then changed his mind. Maybe later, he thought. Not now. Time for a little snooze.

The telephone sounded disagreeably loud even on 'purr'. Reluctantly he picked up the receiver.

'Hello.'

'Greg! I've been trying to get through to you—'

'Jilly – how are you?'

156

'Missing you like hell.'

'Me too, darling – it's been a busy week . . .'

'Greg, I must see you.' Instantly his mental defences, already on the alert, sprang to battle stations.

'Sure, baby.'

'And don't tell me we have to be careful! I'm sick of being careful. I might as well be dead!'

There was a hysterical note in her voice that Greg was coming to know.

'I want us to be able to go out together – do ordinary things, like a normal couple,' Jilly was rushing on. 'I hardly ever see you, and it's always up here, when you can make it, never when I want. Well, I want to see you *now*.'

'And I want you, you know I do.' She's been drinking, he thought. Watch out – it makes her reckless.

'Well, I'm coming down to see you.'

'Now?'

'Why not?'

'I'm just getting ready to go out for a meeting,' he improvised smoothly. 'Big Brazilian mine owner in town, gotta lunch him at the Hilton.'

'Greg' – Jilly's voice took on an ugly note – 'I want to see you, and I want to see you today.'

A sense of threat hung heavily in the air.

'Sure thing.' Greg was thinking quickly. Matey's night off, housekeeper goes to bed early . . . 'Come round tonight, can you? About . . .'

'I'll be there,' she cut him off. 'Oh Greg, I love you so much. I'll show you how much tonight.'

'Yeah, baby. See you tonight.'

He replaced the receiver. Jilly was an unstable component in the situation, and needed to be handled with care. But he knew he could handle her. He could do literally anything with her. Anything. He grinned lazily to himself. He found himself looking forward to tonight.

From her offices in the attractive twisting Liverpool Lane, not far from its intersection with Crown Street in Darlinghurst, Joanna Randall had run Sydney's top model agency for the last twenty years. An ex-model herself, she had lost none of the looks and flair that had put her on the covers of all the top international magazines in her heyday. The bright red hair was even redder these days, and her dark brown, almost black, eyes had lost none of their snap. When she came whisking into a photographic studio, a tall rangy well-shaped figure, everyone sat up, and the private joke among the photographers was that old Jo could put any of her own model girls into the shade.

But it was not easy to stay ahead. As the boss, she bore the responsibility not only for keeping up a constant flow of good creative commercial ideas – as a top model-maker, she virtually dictated the look of the season, the trend for the forthcoming year. But she also had to run the business, and found that wrestling with income tax returns, staff salaries, future projections, profit and loss, did not come any easier as she got older. And by its very nature, the world of fashion is a constantly changing market. There's always somebody treading on your heels, and they don't get any younger, she thought uneasily.

Joanna Randall, the woman and the agency, were in fact in their prime. But with the high level of self-criticism that keeps top people on their toes, she never accepted this fact, but worried in private if she had reached the top only to find herself over the hill. You've gotta remember it's a young person's business, was her constant credo. So she scrutinized her work and ideas for any signs of staleness or 'that tired feeling', with the same eagle eye that she turned on her own signs of ageing, the tiny wrinkles round the eyes, the remorseless little frown indentations, the deepening of the nose to mouth lines. She revamped her fashion concepts as briskly as she slapped the special creams into her face and neck. But she did not know how long she could keep it all at bay. And secretly she dated the onset of middle age from the time when she had started to feel hassled by what she called BYAs, Bright Young Assholes.

A prize BYA now sat in her office arguing about the

model girls Joanna had set up for a major shoot the following week.

'The client is spending rather a lot of money on this campaign, Miss Randall. And we've put a lot of man-hours into it down at the agency.'

'Get to the point, will you?' Joanna did not like being patronized. Especially by a young man in a pin-stripe suit and horn-rimmed glasses, with a supercilious look on his face.

'These girls—' He leafed disdainfully through a sheaf of head-shots which lay on the desk between them, all showing different shots of three girls, a blonde, a brunette and a redhead.

'Yeah, they're my best girls all right. Cream of the crop.'

'Except—'

'Except what?'

'Except they're totally wrong for the campaign as we've devised it.'

'Totally wrong? You must be joking!' Joanna let out a cross between a laugh and a guffaw. She just didn't believe this. Smoothly the BYA tried again.

'Miss Randall, there's a whole new market opening up, especially in the USA and in England too. We're looking at the new woman of the late '80s, and the new woman is a career woman. A number of our clients have suddenly woken up to the fact that there are a lot of ladies with careers now, a lot of ladies in top jobs, and they've got money. They've got lots of money, and they spend it on themselves. A whole new market, as I say.'

Privately Joanna didn't think the 'new career woman' was all that new – in fact *this* career woman is feeling very old, she thought – but whatever the man says . . .

'OK, so what's the problem?'

Sighing elaborately, the BYA picked up one of the photographs and handed it to Joanna without a word. She could feel her temper coming up to match her extravagant red hair.

'What am I supposed to be looking at?'

'That.' He pointed. 'It's the face of a girl. A very lovely girl, and I'm sure she's a wonderful model, quite wonderful.' No need to overdo it, buster, thought Joanna irately. 'But she's too young. What is she, nineteen, twenty-one? Our target in this campaign is the woman in social class AB1, age 25–44. The model's got to have a more mature look. And don't forget these are executive women, woman in management. We're not looking for just another clothes horse. The model must have an air of intelligence, capability . . .'

'Gotta look as if she could run General Motors, right?'

'Something like that.' Joanna's sarcasm was lost on him. 'So you see, it's not just a question of an older-looking model girl. It's a new type, a different *type* of model we want from you.'

Joanna's heart sank. A new type? Sure, I'll have two for you before breakfast, tomorrow. To cover her feelings of dismay, she picked up the photos of her girls and stared at them blankly. Too young? Dear God! It wasn't so long ago, when the 'pretty baby' Brooke Shields look had taken off, that everyone was on at her because the models then were too *old*. And in one big account she had lost out to a rival because that agency did not scruple, as Joanna did, to sink to peddling thirteen-year-olds. And now it's the rediscovery of the older woman, is it? Fine, I'll go back to work myself, she thought mirthlessly, and felt like screaming.

'OK, so come back to me on this, will you?' The BYA felt he had made his point, and sensed that this was the moment to ease out gently. 'Of course, we'll have to pass the request round the other model agencies, broaden the field, as it looks as if you might be going to have difficulty in sorting this one. But let's talk? Let's talk soon?'

'I'll give you a ring,' said Joanna dully. The intercom buzzed on her desk.

'Jason's here – wants to see you,' came her secretary's voice.

'I'm on my way,' said the BYA, making his exit.

'Hold Jason a minute or two, then show him in.'

She simply had to have a tiny oasis of quiet between appointments, even though what she had just heard would take more thinking about than this. But one thought was uppermost in her mind. She could not afford to lose this account. It wasn't only the money, though God knows the fancy studios in the super-chic artistic quarter of Liverpool Lane took a lot of shekels to keep up. No, it was more a question of her credibility, her right to claim the title of Sydney's top model agency. Just gotta be up there with it and ahead, she told herself. If there's a new-look woman, Joanna Randall's got to find her. Or create her. But come up with her. And soon. That's all there is to it. Sighing, Joanna reached for the intercom to buzz Jason in. She could do with someone to cheer her up.

In the privacy of his room, Matey was getting ready for his evening off. Since he had first undertaken a job which required him to live in, he had made it a private rule that he always spent his evenings off away from the premises. It was the only way to have a proper break, in his view, the only way to keep yourself fresh for the job, and to show that you had a life outside your work, however much you enjoyed it. So come rain, come shine, winter or summer, Matey went out. Sometimes he would go to the theatre, or a concert – he loved the Opera House, which he considered with justification to be the eighth wonder of the world. Sometimes he would take in a film, or eat out, when he would scrutinize the activities of the waiters and the maitre d' with a professional's attention. Fairly often he would go in search of those adventures which have made Sydney famous among the community of international gays – another reason, so he firmly thought, for keeping his off-duty life both personal and private.

With a final check in the mirror, he left his room, and hurried down. Time was getting on and the taxi he had called twenty minutes ago had not arrived. It was not outside the front door when he opened it. Perhaps it was waiting at the gates, though he had thought they were open. He moved on down the drive to check. Almost at once, he could see that they were closed. Annoyed, he sped down the drive, and opened the electrically-locking gates exiting to the avenue beyond.

To his surprise, a woman was standing outside in the avenue on the pavement before the Harper mansion. Nobody walked in well-heeled Darling Point, where the Porsche Turbo was as likely to be a second car as a first, not unless they were exercising the Borzoi or the Bichon Frise. This woman had neither dog nor car. But it was clear she was not coming to the house as a visitor – she was not attempting to ring the bell or approach the gates. She was just standing there, looking.

Matey looked at her carefully. She was a fine-looking woman. Did he know her? There was something familiar about her. But it was hard to tell, as she turned away as soon as she saw him and slipping on a pair of dark sunglasses, started to hurry off. Maybe she was just sightseeing. Anyway, Matey had worries of his own. Hailing her, he stopped her dead in her tracks.

'Excuse me!'

'Yes?' Her voice was low and husky.

'I wonder if you can help me. I'm expecting a taxi. I don't know how long you've been here . . . but it hasn't been and gone, has it?'

The woman seemed relieved by his question. She shook her head.

'No, I don't think so. I've been here a little while.'

'Well, they said it'd be twenty minutes, but you never know. I used to get the bus into town, save all this bother, but I reckon a taxi's a better idea nowadays.'

He paused and again looked at the strange woman carefully. She seemed to be looking down, unwilling to meet his eye. Perhaps she did not feel too well. Suddenly the taxi, an old blue saloon, entered the avenue at the bottom and came roaring up. Matey approached it to get in, then a thought struck him.

'Miss?'

She was still standing where she had been when he came out.

'I can't give you a lift anywhere, can I?'

She shook her head and smiled. 'No, thank you.'

He hesitated, then spoke out. 'You all right?'

At last the woman lifted her head, gazed at him steadily, and smiled again.

'Oh yes, thank you. I'm perfectly all right, I promise you.'

Tara stood in the road and watched the taxi bearing Matey away to the town until it was out of sight. He hadn't recognized her! She had been so startled to see him, since of all the inhabitants of the mansion he was the one who went out least. But she need not have worried. As far as he knew, she was a stranger to him. Tara now felt completely confident that if Matey did not know her, no one would.

She leaned against the wall, musing. She was not sure what had drawn her here, to haunt the exterior of the house – she simply knew that she had got up that morning and her urge to go and see her former home had been irresistible. Well, she had seen it. She had had too the unexpected bonus of testing out her new face and appearance on one of the few people in the world who really knew her well and finding that it worked perfectly. She had no trace of Stephanie Harper about her now. She was Tara. And the woman who was Tara had drawn admiring glances even from an elderly gay, like Matey. She smiled affectionately. Good old Matey. And good old Tara!

She shivered. Evening was closing in with the characteristic antipodean swiftness. The day had been hot, but the nights could strike very chill. Time to be going. But not just yet. She stood with her back against the rough-cast wall, enjoying the emergence of the brilliant night-time crop of stars in the southern skies. Home time. She turned to go. As she did so, the headlights of a car swept into the avenue from the top, and the car came tearing down the hill. Instinctively Tara shrank into the ample foliage which overhung the wall, and shielded herself from view. Then, making sure she could not be seen, she looked out. The car had come to rest not far away, in front of the wrought iron gates to the drive, which Matey had carefully closed after him. She could see the driver quite clearly. It was – Jilly! As Tara watched, Jilly got out of the car, and pressed the button of the speaker that connected the gates with the house.

'Yes?' With a shock Tara recognized the voice crackling out of the small black grille as Greg's.

'Darling, it's Jilly. I've arrived, I'm here, let me in.' Jilly's manner was urgent, seductive. Tara heard the buzz which activated the remote control on the gate lock, Jilly pushed them open, returned to her car, and accelerated up the drive as the gates swung behind her.

Jilly? Why was she –? How –? Tara could make no sense of this. She sank back into the comforting shadows, her senses reeling. *Jilly?* In slow motion, like a drowning woman, Tara saw in flashes images of past events – Jilly at the wedding, standing with Greg's arm around her, weakly saying 'Cheese!', Jilly playing tennis with Greg, and the winners' kiss they shared, Jilly hanging on Greg's looks and words as they all talked that night. With a pain that was almost physical, new ideas forced themselves into her mind, rupturing, tearing – Jilly had not wanted to leave the party that night, Phillip had gone home without her, nothing strange in that, but when Greg had run her home he had been gone a long, long time . . .

And then, Jilly at Eden – Jilly had been the one to swim and play tennis with Greg, go out shooting with him, while she, *his wife*, had moped on her own, Jilly had been the one who wanted the crocodile hunt while she – *the crocodile hunt*! She remembered the final damning piece of evidence in a searing flash, as her memory delivered up what she now realized she knew all along but had suppressed so totally – Jilly sitting paralysed and unmoving in the boat, her face a mask of shock but her eyes alight with wild death-lust—

Tara threw back her head and screamed. Her soul's

164

agony released itself in a visceral, animal howl, the age-old lament of a creature in torment. Stumbling, shaking, she started to run, anywhere, away from the place. After a few yards she pulled up sharply to answer the racking, juddering spasms of her body – she leaned against the wall, bent double, and clutching her stomach vomited violently, again and again. Afterwards, spent and exhausted, she ran on and on till her legs would go no more, and suddenly she stumbled and fell down.

She fell awkwardly and painfully, cutting her leg. But the pain brought her to her senses as she crouched on the pavement, huddled against a wall. She groped in her bag for a tissue, and tried feebly to clean the vomit from her mouth and clothes, to wipe the blood and dirt from her knee. How long she sat there she did not know. But at last, sick, shaking and chilled to the bone she picked herself up and quite unable to catch a bus or train where she would have to bear the scrutiny of others, walked all the way back to the Rocks and the sanctuary of her little room.

All night she lay huddled in her narrow bed while her wounded mind absorbed this new blow. She had not thought she could suffer any more than she had already, with the knowledge that her beloved, adored husband had hated her so much he had wanted to kill her. But this – another betrayal, another kind of murder – was in its way no less agonizing. 'I loved you, Jilly,' she mourned to herself over and over during the night. 'Why did you hate me so?' Jilly had been her only friend, a central feature of her life, of her heart, and the tearing pain as that part of her which had been Jilly's was ripped away was almost more than she could bear. She had thought she'd hit her lowest point and, with the efforts to get better, the long healing on Orpheus Island, she was on her way up. Now she knew that there were new depths, and the climb out had to begin all over again. Lying there, hurt, humiliated and degraded beyond all her worst fears, she not only doubted if she could, but if she wanted to.

*

Where was the new woman? Seated at her desk in the stylish clutter of the Liverpool Lane agency, Joanna Randall was still fighting mad, but growing close to despair. I've turned over every bloody woman in Sydney between the ages of twenty and sixty, she thought grimly. Through her huge web of contacts built up over the years as a model, stylist, fashion coordinator and top agent, she sent out the word that she was seeking new talent. Almost immediately waves of it had broken over her head – girls had been ringing, writing in, descending on the agency and even on her private address at all hours – so much so that she had now issued firm orders that no-one, repeat *no-one* would now be seen without an appointment. And nothing had come up.

Nothing, she repeated wretchedly. Some were very promising newcomers in their way. But it was all more of the same. Once the brief had been given to her properly by the BYA from the advertising agency, she knew exactly what they were looking for. But that extra look – she just couldn't find it. Still, she was going to have to come up with something if she was going to make some kind of attempt to win that important account. With a sigh, she turned again to the photos and headshots scattered on her desk. Maybe if this one with the long hair wore it pinned up . . .

In the midst of her meditations, the door opened, and Jason Peebles breezed in. Only the presence of an advertising man ever caused Jason to wait in the outer office, for he respected the money men and knew that he who paid the piper called the tune. But as Sydney's top photographer, he reserved the right to penetrate Joanna's inner sanctum at will. 'She has no secrets from me,' he would assure the terrified receptionist. 'She and I – we're like *that*!' And crossing his fingers in a dramatic gesture, in he'd go.

As always, Joanna was delighted to see him. They had worked together for a long time, and she had a close professional dependence on his subtle skills, his unerring eye for the photogenic quality even in an apparently dull face, and his exacting standards which invariably delivered the goods. But she also loved him as a person, for his high spirits, impish humour and outrageous sense of fun. All this was expressed in his physical appearance, for he was small and puckish with thin fair hair standing up on his head and bright little eyes forever darting here and there, missing nothing.

'Morning, mother!' came the customary greeting, along with the customary smacking kiss on the cheek. Joanna groaned as she made the customary reply. 'Really, Jason, one of these days someone will think I *am* your mother!'

'They all do already,' he assured her, settling himself down on her plump brown and pink sofa.
'Now what's new?'

'Big calendar job,' said Jason carelessly. 'On-going, like life itself, mother – keep you and me going for a good while, the way it looks.'

Joanna brightened. 'Now *that's* what I like to hear!'

'Yeah, it's a biggie. Lots of work for lots of girls. And you and me, of course. It's the Grenadier chain of hotels. They're doing a promo to try to persuade people to stay more in hotels all the year round. So they want lots of cheery pics of lovely ladies disporting themselves in the different Grenadier hotels throughout the country.'

'Sounds good,' said Joanna, already running through her mental file of the models on her books.

'Yeah, 'tis. Only two catches.'

'Catches?'

'Number one, it's very upmarket stuff – they're doing a face-lift on their image – so the girls have got to be not just stylish, but classy. *Classy*, mother – out of the top drawer.'

'I know, I know, Jason,' said Joanna irritably. 'Don't teach your grandmother to suck eggs!'

'Number two,' continued Jason unruffled, 'is that we're working to the theme of the seasons. You know? Seasons? Spring, summer, autumn and winter? So I want some older, more mature faces for the autumnal and wintry shots – not just your usual run of bright young things.'

'Not you too, Jason!' Joanna felt like howling.

He looked at her in surprise. 'What's up, mother?'

Before Joanna could reply, the voice of the receptionist crackled on the intercom.

'There's a model here to see you, Miss Randall.'

Joanna's screeching reply could be clearly heard throughout the outer office. 'I don't care if it's Bo bloody Derek, *tell her to stuff off!*'

An hour later, Jason was feeling that he had done as much as anyone could be expected to do, in cheering up Joanna Randall. He had chaffed her, made jokes, helped her to put this current problem in perspective, and reminded her of how many worse crises she had risen above triumphantly in the past. But he had not been able to solve her problem for her. It was a tough nut to crack and no mistake. He was thinking hard as he took his leave, coming through into the outer office in a brown study. Suddenly he heard a crisp, authoritative voice.

'I'd still like to see Joanna Randall, please.'

The receptionist was at the end of her tether. Wearily she pushed her glasses more firmly onto her nose, and ran a hand through her hair, mechanically repeating lines she had obviously said many times before.

'Look, I've told you, she's very busy at the moment. You don't have an appointment.'

'I'm afraid I don't.'

'Miss Randall isn't able to see anyone without an appointment.'

Jason looked up. Carefully, taking his time, he made a thorough professional appraisal of the woman standing at the desk. Then he went into action.

'Appointments, sweetness,' he said to the receptionist, 'are for small fry. I think the Queen Bee will see this one.' He turned to the woman. 'I'm Jason Peebles, and this is my winning smile.' He flashed her a brilliant grin. 'Like it?

I'm the power behind the throne round here. Have dinner with me tonight?'

Without waiting for an answer, he took the startled woman by the wrist, towed her towards the inner sanctum, pushed the door open unceremoniously, and shouted, 'Joanna! Cop a load of this one!' Then he shoved her in and closed the door.

'Terrific!' he pronounced to the bemused receptionist. 'Jaw a little square but I can light that, mouth far too big but it's wonderful, eyes like Bambi's – God! I love her!' As he swept out a thought struck him. 'Did she leave her name?'

Chapter Ten

'I need an agent. Someone who can get me on the cover of *Vogue* in six months.'

Joanna Randall never forgot that moment when the answer to her prayers materialized and stood before her. Tall, elegant and well-groomed, yes, those were the very basics – not young, but strangely not old either, and a lovely face, superbly proportioned yet with something more. That something was expressed in the eyes – huge glowing orbs, mysterious and sad – and the mouth, which was at once generous and guarded, as if conveying emotions that its owner did not wish to reveal. Above all there was about her a quality of determination, of the will triumphing over all, that made her, in Joanna's instant surge of hope, the 'new woman' she had been searching for in vain.

Joanna was not a woman who played games. She was sufficiently confident in herself and her own judgment not to worry about having to look cool, and she never hesitated to show when she was pleased or impressed. So she raised her eyebrows in undisguised approval of the new apparition, and simply said, 'Have a seat.' She was human enough to take pleasure in the flash of discomfiture as the lovely lady looked round for a chair – she's not superwoman then, she thought. But once they were both settled, Joanna like the real pro she was, simply got down to business.

'Where're you from?'

'Queensland. A little island, Orpheus, on the Great Barrier Reef.'

'Where've you been working?'

'I was in England for a few years – then in the Northern Territories.'

'So you thought you'd better get a crack at Australia's big apple, then?'

'Yeah, sort of . . .'

The interview proceeded without too many hiccups. Tara was amazed and delighted as she listened to her own voice, answering Joanna's professional probing with smoothness and skill, fielding certain questions, evading others, as to the manner born. She had been careful to work out her cover story in every detail – she was a woman who had done a little modelling here and there, and had now come to Sydney in an all-out attempt to launch her career. She was banking heavily on making a terrific impact with her first appearance – you never get a second chance to make a first impression, she had reminded herself grimly, as racked with nerves she had made her way to Joanna's office for her make-or-break interview. She was also gambling on something even Australians often forget or take for granted, the huge size of their island. She knew that if she claimed to have done some in-house or photographic modelling in western Australia, Queensland or the Northern Territories the chances that Joanna would catch her out were remote.

The main thing had been to get the look right so that Joanna's first eyeful was so stunning that her instant response would be 'yes' rather than 'no'. This had been the work of hours and weeks, during which Tara scoured the glossy magazines and toured the top fashion boutiques, painfully putting together a look that was contemporary without being too topical, youthful without being too young, and arresting without being over-dramatic, at a fraction of the cost of the advertised garments.

Then there had been the question of makeup and hair. Again came the hunt through the magazines to identify the current styles, then the personal modification in such a way as to put her own accent upon it, not just echoing but improving upon the prototype. The last of her funds had been swallowed up on the basic make-up requirements, and a very expensive but very good cut and re-style with

Sydney's top crimper. At first she had been horrified as swathe upon swathe of her heavy hair fell to the ground to be trampled under careless feet. But as her rich dark mop was released, so she could almost see it spring to life, as skilful club-cutting gave it a vitality she had never known it possessed. The same was true of her eyes and skin. Under the guidance of a free consultation with almost every beauty specialist in the big Sydney stores, Tara learned how to highlight her cheekbones to shape her face like a heart, to bring out the piquancy of her features and, above all, to shadow her lids in every shade of blue from indigo to periwinkle, to flatter the colour of her eyes.

She carried out her programme of exploration and self-discovery with great determination, treating it as her work, and doing something towards it every day, and in the evening too. Yet always there was a sense of excitement, of wonderment, that she was doing it at all. She thought back to the woman who had been Stephanie with a painful pity. How had that woman, who had been so agonizingly shy about her appearance, who had had so little self-confidence that even when she saw something stylish she didn't dare to buy it, turned into the Tara who was now so deeply resolved not only to make herself into the best-looking woman she could, but to prove it at the highest professional level?

Finally the time had come when she knew she was ready to launch herself on Joanna Randall. After a lot of thought she decided to make a full-frontal assault, not even phoning for an interview in case her nerve failed her. It was to be one do-or-die attempt to take the top agent by storm. And like all military campaigns, it had been planned to the last detail. Tara prepared herself literally from the skin out-wards. The first item of importance, and one of her most expensive purchases, had been a good bra, which gave her breasts shape and definition even under the heaviest clothes. Next came a good pair of tights – she could not risk snagging a cheap pair on this day of all days. Proudly she smoothed down her flat stomach and slender thighs.

Can anyone who has not been overweight ever really enjoy the delight of being slim? she thought happily.

Reaching for the wardrobe she took out a white shirt in heavy, gleaming silk. In fact she had bought it very cheaply from a stall in Sydney's Chinatown, but it looked much more costly than it was by virtue of the fine detail on the front and cuffs, the tiny pearl buttons of the fastenings, and a stylish little stand-away collar that emphasized the grace of her neck. Her skirt was another find, one of the newly fashionable full-skirted flower-prints, with soft pleats to the waist and big patch pockets, an attractive and wearable style. But the main feature was the design, in which chrysanthemums, peonies and honeysuckle rioted in and out of one another in subtle gradations of rose-red, pink and peach on a white background that succeeded in being arresting but was never brash. The whole outfit was set off by a neat boxy little waist-length Chanel-style jacket which perfectly picked up the hottest, most glamorous pink in the skirt, so that the three separate pieces cleverly gave the effect of being all co-ordinates in the same range, rather than random items laboriously teamed together after weeks of patient hunting.

With pink as her theme, Tara began on her makeup. First she applied a strong foundation in a rosy tan, then set about defining her distinctive features. Her cheekbones she contoured with a carnation blusher and brought out the contrasting blue of her eyes with a midnight-blue eyeliner. For eyeshadow she chose a rich and dramatic shade of plum, fading it skilfully through to the palest glowing pink below the browbones. Blue-black mascara and a rich crimson lipstick a couple of tones darker than the predominant pink of the outfit completed her turn-out. No jewellery – the impact had to be strong and simple. Quickly running a brush through her springing, glossy hair, Tara was ready.

Before leaving she paused to scrutinize her appearance in the glass of the wardrobe door. Every detail passed before her intensely critical survey and at last she was satisfied. Satisfied, but far from confident. As she set out, Tara realized that this would be almost the hardest thing that she had had to do since she came to Sydney. To have to go for the first time at her age for an interview, to subject herself to the appraisal of an uninterested outsider, suddenly seemed to be a far greater ordeal than she had imagined. As she walked through town, bumped and buffeted by careless passers-by, afraid at any moment that she might spoil her outfit or ruin her tights, Tara had never before been so tempted to abandon all her plans, give up, and quit. But as she reached the Liverpool Lane and entered the attractive reception room of the agency, she forced herself to ignore the twisting gripe of her anxious stomach. Stonily she outstared all the photographs of Joanna's top models hung intimidatingly round the walls. As she stood before the receptionist she made a secret mad vow that she wouldn't leave – they'd have to drag her out! – before she had got something from the great Joanna. And it had worked! *It had worked!*

Looking back, Tara always saw her new self as born like a phoenix from the last flames of what had been Stephanie. As she lay on her bed, scarcely moving, not eating nor drinking for days after the revelation of Jilly's betrayal, she felt like one meeting a slow death at the stake. She burned with anguish, grief, rage and humiliation for a long time, the hot tongues of agony wrapping themselves around her and consuming all within. At last she was all worn away, there was nothing left, and she slept. When she awoke, she awoke as a different woman. The last tie that had held her to Stephanie, that part of Stephanie's life which had been so important, was burned out of her. And though her whole body still throbbed like a cauterized wound, she felt the onset of strength that comes with the knowledge that the infection is driven out and gone for ever.

And out of all evil cometh forth good, she reflected. For the blistering impact of this final piece of information had made all the other bits of the jigsaw fall into place. Unravelling the factors behind her cruel 'accident' helped her at last understand the form her revenge had to take. And it all tied in with her fanatic determination now to live in and for herself, making the most of the new life that fate had given her, and the new appearance she had won with so much pain and courage on Orpheus Island.

Quite simply, it came to her in the watches of the night that the most perfect revenge on Greg would be to inflict upon him the misery that he had inflicted upon her, to make him fall in love with someone who did not love him, and then find himself spurned, scorned and cast off, his love rated as less than the dust beneath his feet. And that someone, who would never be in danger of falling in love with him, would be her. She would ensnare him as he had ensnared her, with no more pity than hunters feel for the small rabbits they catch in their cruel traps. Then she would wound and reject him spitefully, killing his heart as he had tried to kill her body. That would be the most perfect poetic justice, the most perfect triumph, and she would enjoy her revenge to the full.

To do this, she had to make herself into the kind of woman that Greg went for. That meant glamour, glamour in a big way. I should have smelt a rat, she thought bitterly when he of all men was ready to pair off with plain, frumpy, overweight Miss Stephanie Harper. I need to be a fashion plate. It was then that an idea came into her mind which she realized she had been storing up since Orpheus Island, when she was both creating a new face and immersing herself in glossy magazines – she would become a fashion model. She had the looks, the figure, the height – and now, above all, she had the reason and the will to do it.

And that would be the most perfect irony of all, she concluded. For in annihilating Greg, she would be liberating herself. She had it within her, she knew, to become the beautiful woman she always had been inside, to break away from being the woman who had lived like a tenant in the lodging of her body, instead of owning it with pride. Perhaps only those who have felt ugly and despised can understand the craving of a starved nature to be beautiful. Tara had felt that craving like hunger pangs all her life. Now at last that hunger would be fed.

'. . . get some test shots done as a first step –' Joanna's hard, rather nasal voice brought her back to reality. Privately Joanna was nurturing not a few reservations about the mystery arrival. *She admits to being over twenty-one, but she won't tell me her age,* she pondered. *She claims to have done some modelling but obviously knows no more than the average beginner. And there's something else strange about her I can't put my finger on. I oughta throw her out. I'm crazy to bother with her at all.* But then Joanna thought of the BYA, and her resolution stiffened. *Who the hell else have I got,* she thought grimly. *And what can I lose?* She leaned forward to her new find. 'I know just the guy. No offence, but he can make Dracula look meltingly lovely. D'you have a phone number? I'll be in touch.' Joanna leaned forward to buzz her secretary.

'Get me Jason on the phone.'

'No need,' came the disembodied voice of the man himself through the intercom. 'I'm still here!'

There is no paradise yet discovered that is free of evil. The Garden of Eden itself came equipped with its own snake. Sergeant Johnson of the Townsville Police was not a philosophical man. But he did often wonder what excuse any individual could make for giving way to human wickedness and weakness here, in one of the most beautiful spots in the entire world. He also had the normal policeman's normal desire that as little crime as possible should take place on his patch. He was proud of Townsville, the city in the sun, as it styled itself. He loved its blend of old and new, the historic pubs rubbing shoulders with the spanking modern pedestrian mall, the stylish beachfront boulevard and the waterfront area going back to the early days. *Best bloody city in Queensland,* he thought, *if not in the whole bloody island. What more do people want?*

But they did want more, or at least a proportion of them

did, and set themselves to various illegal ways of obtaining it. So even in his tropical paradise Sergeant Johnson was a busy man, which was why he had not had much time to pursue the inquiry Dan Marshall had made some months back – a fact which was borne in on him when he received a gentle reminder over the phone.

'Hello Sam? Dan Marshall here, from Orpheus. I was wondering if you'd had any success in tracing that missing person for me?'

Dan had decided that his only hope of peace of mind now or at any time in the future lay in forgetting Tara Welles. With that end in view, he had made a point of resuming all his previous activities, such as snorkelling. He had barbecued on the beach with congenial patients; men, women and children. He had cleared out his office and reorganized his filing system – 'a proper old spring clean!' said Lizzie, who regarded it as a very hopeful sign. He had even taken a vacation, the first for a number of years. He had flown west across the whole unimaginably massive bulk of the great island of Australia, straight across the dead heart of the country that has claimed so many lives. For the first time he saw the great sacred symbols of the Aboriginal dreamtime, the huge red rocks shaped into rounded minarets, giant domes and cupolas, which have stood like miracles in their flat and wasted desert world since countless aeons before time was even measured. He flew on to Perth, the capital of the west, and hiring a car drove down to Cape Leeuwin, through the beautiful national park that graces the whole length of that coastline. There he stood upon Australia's extreme south-western tip, as far removed as he could possibly be from his home in the north-east. There he walked upon a different beach, beside a different sea, picking up the different shells that the Indian Ocean brought to those shores. And there he thought the same thoughts he had thought all along – of Tara.

It was hopeless. He could not get over, away, or past her. He still loved her so much that her loss was a daily bereavement; that fact came into his head before all others at each morning's waking. He knew that he could not make her love him. But at least he knew now that his feeling for her was real and enduring, not just a summer season's infatuation. Is that a gain? he asked himself wryly. He had made his bid and lost. He knew nothing about her – he did not even know where she was in Sydney. But he could not wipe her from his mind, or write her out of his heart. All he could do was to continue to travel his road, to pick up what he could en route, and to hope against hope that somehow, by some miracle, he might find Tara again at the end of it all. So he picked up the phone to Sergant Sam Johnson, less in any expectation of news than in the desire to do something, anything.

'Not a lot to report, I'm afraid.' Sam did not want to hold out too much hope on this one. ' 'S a bloody big place, godzone country – an army c'd go missing here and nobody any the wiser. And y'didn't give me a lot to go on.'

'That's true. But I've got something more now, something that might help.' Dan had been thinking. With the aid of his sketches, his photographic record and his memory of Tara's injuries, he was prepared to put an estimate on the exact date of her accident. It was only a guess, he knew. But it was a very highly educated guess, and he knew he would not be more than a few days out. 'So you're looking,' he told Sam finally, 'for a woman who had a grievous accident – not a car, you can rule out all the car smashes – between those two dates. Can't be *that* many, can there?'

And impressed with the doctor's obvious determination, Sam Johnson decided it was about time he made the time to start to find out. Back on Orpheus, Dan was idly flicking through the latest edition of his medical magazine when he saw the notice of a forthcoming conference. 'Medicine Today' was not the most compelling title to flush a busy doctor out of his demanding practice for a week-long symposium. But the venue was Sydney. Brush up on the modern trends, keep in touch, thought Dan. 'Medicine Today' – sounds like a good idea.

Whatever Jason's talents as a photographer, they did not extend to teaching. He had no patience at all, but would bully and screech until he drove anyone under his tuition to rage or despair. But somehow, his method worked for Tara. This was the third photographic session they were having in his large airy studio, and Tara was enjoying it hugely.

'Flow! Let it flow!' Jason howled from behind his camera. 'Nice and easy, like good sex. That's it! That's put a look in your eye, I like it, good, keep it coming, make love to the camera, make love to *me*!'

Tara lost her concentration and began to giggle. Jason leaped into the air with rage, his puckish good humour converted into a goblin malevolence.

'You're hunching your shoulders! DON'T HUNCH! You look like a bloody great camel. Concentrate now, *work*, *think*, that's more like it. Think happy now, something that gives you a great buzz. You just won the lottery – what are you going to do with all that money . . .?'

Money. Tara nearly laughed out loud. That was the last thing she needed.

'You ought to know,' she said ironically, 'that money is the root of all evil.'

'Good, good, keep it,' he pattered on imperviously, 'Keep that cockeyed look, it suits you. Moving now, slow turns. God help us, she's only got one leg! Try to move like a normal human being for Jason now, will you?'

Across the city from Jason's studio, in the business quarter, Bill McMaster was negotiating what he dearly hoped would be one of the last encounters he would ever have to have with Greg Marsden. Up in the nerve centre of Harper Mining Bill studied Greg's back closely as the younger man gazed out of the window, blind to the superb view, struggling to absorb the information Bill had just given him. Suddenly he turned round, his eyes black with rage though his voice was under control.

'Just like that, eh? I'm off the board, and no more income. I'm not even sure you can do this, you know. Stephanie did leave very strict instructions . . . and I am still her husband.'

He finished defiantly, but he knew that Bill and his fellow directors must have found legal and binding ways to trump that ace.

'It was decided at last week's director's meeting. The vote was unanimous.' Bill's manner was quiet and calm. But he was enjoying this more than he had enjoyed anything for a long time.

'I assure you that it is all entirely within the law, Stephanie's arrangements, and the terms of her will. But get advice by all means.' He paused, then administered another thrust. 'Why don't you consult Phillip Stewart? He's a very good lawyer.'

Greg chose to ignore this barb, and returned to the fray.

'How come I wasn't informed the meeting was on?'

'This was not a special arrangement but the normal board meeting, whose date was arranged at the last meeting of the board. You haven't attended one for months, or else you'd know. Anyway, your presence there would hardly have changed things.'

Greg fell silent, musing angrily, then muttered, almost to himself. 'Dammit, there are bills to be paid!' His adversary was urbane, in control.

'Staff salaries and household expenses will continue to be met by the company. Except, of course, your personal expenses. From here on in those will be your responsibility.'

Greg's eyes widened with shock.

'Oh, you can go on living at the house.' Another pause to increase the impact of what was coming. 'For the time being, anyway.'

With a nervous start Greg began tensely pacing to and fro.

'You never approved of me marrying her, did you?'

Bill made no response, but kept a steady impassive gaze fixed on Greg.

'Well, did you, you bastard?' Greg was shaking.

With outward dignity and inner glee Bill rose from behind his desk, moved to the door and held it open for his visitor to leave.

'I think this meeting is concluded,' he said.

'More! More! That's it. Come again, forward. Only glide, glide – don't hobble, think smooth and easy and *glide* towards the camera.'

Tara's instruction was proceeding apace at the hands of the ebullient Jason. As Joanna had hoped, her face did have that special thing that the camera loves, and as soon as the shots from her sessions with Jason were made available, everybody else loved her too. Like the good agent she was, Joanna did not rush to snatch at every offer that Tara received at this stage, taking care to pace her new discovery so that she was not doing too much, too soon. Joanna had realized from the first, from the way she walked into the room, that Tara was very inexperienced. That did not worry her, it could be made up. But it had to be watched, and this obviously promising career developed at the right tempo. Tara also had to have time to polish up some of the basic modelling skills, particularly of movement. So Joanna had insisted on dance exercise classes, disco dance classes, jazz dance classes, until Tara really was beginning to look like 'a smart little mover', in Jason's phrase.

Now Tara was fulfilling her first major assignment, an all-day shoot during which she had to model an entire range of day and evening wear. This was gruelling enough in itself, and to add to the difficulties Jason had decided on an outdoor city-centre location, 'to give it that urban patina', as he said. So they were working their way down the fashionable centre of Elizabeth Street, the wide thoroughfare that runs due north-south through the heart of Sydney. Jason was the ultimate professional, decisive, focused, and utterly demanding. Tara had learned a lot, fast, but there were moments when she faltered, not quite sure of herself. Jason was quick to sense those moments and would be there with his instant support, offering cheery banter or wheedling and cajoling instead of his usual tyrannizing.

'Lean against the wall there, Welles, take a break, never mind the garment,' he ordered now, seeing a weariness and lack of confidence come over her. They were opposite the city's lush green Hyde Park, and Jason paused to do an instant travelogue.

'Notice the wonders of the Mirvac Trust Building to your right, a little brownstone marvel distinguished by its Corinthian pillars. And next door we have Sydney's answer to Notre Dame de Paris, at present being propped up by Miss Tara Welles, seen here as a flying buttress . . .'

Incredulous, Tara straightened up, moved away and looked back at the building behind her. Jason was right – the tiny church with its rose window did have a crazy look of Notre Dame Cathedral about it. The thought was so ridiculous that she began to giggle.

'That's better,' said Jason approvingly. 'How are you feeling?'

'Dizzy.'

'Right! Back to work before you fall over. If camels can fall over, that is? Or do they just lock their long ungainly legs into the "hold" position and pass out standing up?'

'You are a slave-driver, Jason.'

'Me?' He pretended to be shocked. 'I'm kindness itself, I am. See how thoughtful I was, asking you how you felt. I really care. So back to work, Welles, and no messing about.'

'You're so considerate, Jason . . .'

They carried on down the street, past the department store of David Jones, a huge brownstone building with purple plate glass windows and bronze canopy, to the St James' Centre, twenty-one floors of green glass with a row of slender plane trees outside. Jason was in his element, spotting a promising background here or an interesting shot there, thinking aloud or talking to himself, his brain working all the time. Opposite the St James' Centre he discovered a little ochre-washed courtyard with a flight of wrought iron steps that he decreed to be 'utterly blissful', and undeterred by the fact that this was the back entrance to the District Court of New South Wales, he had Tara walk up and down them a thousand times, swing right, swing left, and do everything except stand on her head. At last even her professional obedience to the demanding little gnome scampering around her clicking incessantly began to fray.

'Jason, I've had enough!'

'Wait a minute, come on. You can't stop now. You can't wilt this early . . .' He was continuing to snap away, privately thinking that the sullen, mutinous look on her face made her appearance wonderfully brutal. 'I mean you're young, fit – for your age, that is –' Jason had long ago learned the stimulating power of the well-timed insult – 'and in any case, I've paid you in advance, till midnight. So come on – tilt that head.'

'You are merciless.' Tara groaned, but complied.

'Certainly. And worse. Right. Now let's go again.'

This exchange, and variations upon it, were repeated at intervals throughout a long day. Tara went through her paces till she felt she had no more to give.

'Jason, I'm cold, I'm tired, and I want to go home!'

She leaned her back against a lamp post and closed her eyes.

'Princess!' Feigning mock dismay, Jason moved up to her. 'OK, we'll do lamp post shots. No problem. It's all right. Just calm down. This is a perfect spot, classic in fact. Leaning on a lamp post . . . OK, keep those eyes closed. Relax. Eyes closed, body relaxing. I want you to think . . . think you're with your lover, think of him, now there's the man that really gets your blood boiling, gets your juices flowing. He really makes you hot, feel that heat, good, keep that feeling, think of him, God, how I hate him . . .'

In spite of herself, in spite of trying to tune out Jason's chatter, Tara felt a hot ugly wave of memory wash over her when she thought of her unsatisfactory love-making with Greg.

'Wella wella wella – I do believe you's blushing! Yeah? Now that's lovely, that's great. Are we feeling passion, though, or embarrassment?'

Tara was even more disconcerted by Jason's shrewdness. 'I'm sorry,' she mumbled.

'Stop apologizing!' commanded Jason. 'It was fantastic. You're a very strange lady, do you know that? Every time I mention sex you have hot and cold flushes. You obviously need to be taken in hand, and Peebles is the man to do it, n'est-ce pas? Now I want you to think of something sad now. I mean, real sad. Feel your poor little heart breaking into a thousand tiny pieces, give me the pain now . . .'

Through his viewfinder Jason could see Tara responding as if hypnotized. Slowly the tears welled up, stood in her eyes, and spilled over down her cheeks. Jason was beside himself.

'Great! Marvellous! God, you're wonderful. I could really go for you, Tara Welles. Is the world's most eligible man about to lose his heart? I wonder if old Professor Higgins had it off with Eliza Doolittle? Did Svengali ever get into Trilby's knickers? Food for thought, eh?'

The roll of film complete, Jason allowed himself to notice for the first time how exhausted Tara really was.

'Enough of this idle chit-chat!' he said to her scoldingly. 'You talk too much – keeping me here intellectualizing about life and love when you ought to be carrying me off home to bed Come on. Let's go. Tomorrow is another day.'

The Stewart mansion on Hunter's Hill was not overlooked, but its neighbours were not deaf. Recently they had become more and more accustomed to hearing rows and brawling of a kind that their genteel neighbourhood as a rule never knew. Tonight's occurrence was taking its predictable course.

'Greg! Greg! Where are you going? Don't go!'

'Get off! Leave me alone! Do you think I'd stay here?'

'Greg! Oh darling – Greg!'

Jilly Stewart was clinging onto Greg's arm, physically preventing him from opening the door of his car. Behind them the open doorway of the house bore witness to the running exit Jilly had made to try to arrest his departure.

'Come back into the house. Please!'

'Will you let go of my arm!'

Cowed by his rage, Jilly released her hold. Although these days she seemed always to be driven to provoke Greg, she feared his cold rages terribly, as one who knew what he was capable of in such moods.

'Please, Greg.' Humbly she tried again. 'I didn't mean to annoy you. It's just that—'

'You're drunk!' He turned away from her in disgust. Immediately she fired up again, her control so fragile that anything could break it.

'Yes, I am! I am! Can you blame me? Whose fault is it? You got me onto the sauce in the first place.' In an angry voice she mimicked the offer that Greg had made to her in her tent the night that Stephanie had been killed. ' "Have a drink, baby" .'

As always when Jilly reached a certain point of drunken hysteria, Greg heard the warning bells going off. Taking her arm, he brutally pushed her back into the house, and slammed the door behind them. He rammed her against the wall and held her prisoner with his arms, then made the effort to speak to her as pleasantly as he could.

'Better forget that, baby. Forget it, OK?'

Sensing an advantage, Jilly went with it. 'I am not putting up with this any longer!' She raised her fists and pummelled him violently on the chest. 'I am not your whore!'

A look of contempt passed over his face. By way of answer, he reached down between her legs, took the soft fold of flesh he found there between his finger and thumb through the thin fabric of her clothes, and slowly twisted it in a vicious tweak. Then he turned back to the door.

Sobbing with pain, Jilly threw herself against the door to block his way out.

'Don't leave me, Greg, don't leave me!'

He paused, perfectly still. Hysterical, deranged, she poured her heart out.

'Just stay with me, you can have the money, I'll give you all I've got, I can get some more tomorrow when the banks open – but please don't leave me here on my own tonight. You can have anything you want, anything. Stay, darling please . . .'

Greg was won. But he did not let Jilly see how much he was softening, nor the smile of satisfaction that he felt inside him. He just nodded curtly. Jilly was pitiful in her relief.

'Oh darling, come back in, yeah, that's right – I'll fix us a drink . . .'

Jason Peebles was very careful about what he drank. Never spirits, always wine, champagne when he could get it and lots of that golden sparkling liquor if possible. Today was a day calling for both quantity and quality of the blessed brew, for Tara Welles had made the front cover of *Vogue*. A shot from the punishing but highly successful city centre shoot had been selected to lead the fashion story for autumn, and Joanna had fulfilled the brief that Tara had given her in the first sentence she ever spoke to her agent.

Now the congratulatory party was in full swing in Jason's studio, as he, Joanna and Tara pored over advance copies of the magazine, revelling in their triumph. Elated, Joanna raised her glass in a toast.

'Ladies and gentlemen, hot off the press – I give you Tara, the exciting new face in the fashion world!'

'Well, she excites *me*,' said Jason, coming up behind Tara and slipping an arm round her waist. 'You know that, don't you? I find you very exciting. Grrrh!'

'We don't wish to know about that, do we Tara?'

'Oh well.' Jason did his little boy lost look. 'My own toast then – here's to the flavour of the month!'

'And here's to us!' Joanna was really enjoying herself.

'To us!' Tara clinked her glass enthusiastically with Joanna.

'To *us*?' Jason was incredulous. 'Don't you mean to Jason Peebles, starmaker extraordinaire.'

'Thanks a lot, you horrible little man!'

Tara was quick to pour oil on troubled waters.

'Here's to both of you,' she said with quiet sincerity. 'Thank you both so much. For everything.'

'Six months to the day, almost.' Joanna was studying the cover again. 'And here you are. Not bad.'

'Not bad?' Jason was sending her up as usual.

'All right then, fan-bloody-tastic!'

Jason turned to Tara. 'Now my darling, how does it feel to be one of the beautiful people? On behalf of the local trendies, I'd like to say welcome to the elite.'

Tara burst out laughing. 'Oh, good grief!'

'Tut tut tut.' Jason pulled a disapproving face. 'Local trendies don't say "good grief". Much too provincial. Your vocabulary must become urban, sophisticated. So you cultivate a few juicy oaths and—'

'Jason!' Joanna cut him off in mid-flight. 'I don't want you corrupting my top model.'

'Sorry, mother.' Jason was unrepentant. 'Should have remembered that in your day they kept the legs of pianos covered up to protect the innocence of the young.'

Joanna held up her glass of champagne at a dangerous angle.

'D'you want this over your head? In your lap? Up your nose? Just choose.'

Jason shook his head sorrowfully. 'She would, you know, she would.'

Tara beamed at them, loving the jokey byplay and the strong sense of comradeship she drew from both of them.

'I owe it all to you two,' she said honestly. 'You taught

187

me everything. I practically had to learn to walk all over again.'

Joanna looked at her with affection. 'I knew the day you came into my office you had a different kind of quality – a sort of mysterious something, indefinable. But whatever it is, it's bloody original, darling.'

'That's it!' Jason had had an inspiration. 'The Sphinx! Ageless . . . the picture of maturity and wisdom, contradicted by a youthful façade. That's a very potent mixture. Don't look now, but all the blokes are after you.'

'I read your comments on the TV contract,' Joanna continued. 'You know, you really are incredible. I mean, you'd picked up on all the things that I wanted to question. Where did you learn about contracts?'

Tara smiled evasively. 'Just gut instinct, I guess.'

'Well, if you ever decide to pack up modelling, there's always a job for you backstage.'

'Backstage?' Jason was horrified. 'Leave off, mother, she's hardly had a chance on the front stage yet! Dear me! And you're supposed to be Sydney's top agent?' He snuggled up to Tara and squeezed her tight. 'Give old mother over and come to my casbah, little one – I can be your Pygmalion, your agent, your demon lover, or anything – any offers?'

Chapter Eleven

It was the end of a long, wearing day. Tara looked at her face in the dressing-room mirror and with a critical eye observed the tell-tale signs of tiredness. Early night for you, my dear, she said to herself contentedly. Straight to bed as soon as you get home with a light supper and a good book. She picked up her bag, made one last check around to see that she had not left anything, switched off the lights, and came out into the stillness of Jason's deserted studio.

Tara was exhausted but satisfied. After the happy start to the day with the celebration of her success, she had put her glass aside and got down to the day's shoot. Jason, however, had stayed on the champagne, and was now not drunk, but definitely in a state of exaltation. She stood in the doorway and watched him affectionately as he moved around the studio unconscious of her scutiny, switching the powerful lights off and putting the studio to bed. He came to a motor bike that had been used as a prop in part of the session, and mounted it dreamily, his champagne glass still in his hand.

Tara came forward and stood before him.

'G'day, sphinx,' he cried merrily. 'D'you know, I know your face now nearly as well as I know my own – yet I don't know the most basic thing about you. I could light you with soft light, and diffuse it . . . and you'd look twenty-one. But in hard sunlight – what? Thirty-five? Twenty-nine?'

Tara kept very still.

'Not saying, eh? Well, that's the sphinx, isn't it? An eternal female beauty who took her secret with her into immortality. Now that old girl kept her cards up all right, for centuries . . . the way you do.'

He was looking directly at her now. Tara met his eyes and was disturbed by the depth of his gaze.

'What do I know about you? Nothing. I feel as if I've known you for ever, yet all I know are your eyes, and your wonderful smile. I find you a puzzle, Miss Tara Welles, and I find myself puzzling over you more and more.'

There was no mistaking what Jason was trying to say. Tara hid a sigh. She had had faint inklings that something like this might be coming, but was not sure. She had never met a man like Jason before, and with his passion for raillery and fooling she never knew whether he was serious or not. She steeled herself to try to handle this well.

'And why do I think about you all the time?' Jason's expression was quizzical. 'For the same reason that every boy has thought about every girl, since Adam and Eve – Romeo and Juliet –'

Time to intervene. 'Abbott and Costello,' said Tara lightly. All her instincts told her to head him off now, before any kind of declaration was made, to avoid the pain and difficulty of trying to extricate them both from it.

'You know what you are, Jason,' she continued in the same light vein. 'You are a romantic. You see something in a poor ordinary working girl that just isn't there.'

'Well, that's my secret.' Jason gave her a rueful smile, the most serious that Tara had ever seen from him. It was clear that he had received her unspoken message. He would not press his suit. He raised his glass in a flamboyant gesture.

'Here's to us, then – and well-kept secrets.'

Tara smiled at him affectionately and moved towards the door.

'Goodnight, Jason.'

'Hey –' His voice arrested her. She turned and looked back.

'Sure you don't want a ride on my bike?'

She shook her head. 'I'm going home.'

In the lonely studio, Jason lifted the glass high above his shoulder level. Then, in the age-old gesture of farewell, he slowly turned it upside down and let it fall to the floor where it smashed in a thousand pieces.

Tara made her way through the city, bright with the bustle of countless Sydneysiders out on the town, towards her home. In the wake of her success as a model, with the sudden influx of high earnings, she had moved from the rundown hotel in the Rocks and had found herself a smart new apartment in fashionable Elizabeth Bay, where the residents all enjoyed one of the glories of life in Sydney, a harbour view. Weary in body and sad at heart thinking about Jason and the vagaries of love's dispensations, she took the lift to her floor and let herself into her new home.

Immediately she heard a welcoming miaow, and the erstwhile scrap of fur, now a big fat cat, came strolling up to greet her.

'Oh hello Maxie, my boy.' Tenderly she scooped him up and cuddled him close to her. 'How are you this evening? Had a good day?'

Stepping into the flat, she kicked her shoes off and with a sigh of relief padded down the carpeted hallway into the sitting room.

'I'll tell you a secret, Max. My face may be twenty-eight, but at the end of a day like this, my feet are definitely forty!' She put the cat down on the thick carpet and moved to the stereo. Since coming here she had been able to enjoy again one of the delights of her life, her music. Now, following her crash course in disco and jazz dance, her musical taste had broadened and it was no longer her beloved classical pieces that she reached for. She pressed a button, and the poignant lament of Barbra Streisand and Neil Diamond, 'You don't bring me flowers any more', filled the air. With a sigh, she sank into the capacious receptive sofa and looked around her.

She had to admit that she was pleased with what she saw. In the elegant restful room, the only strong colour was provided by a warm coral carpet, set off by plain white walls. The furniture was of glass and chrome in a brilliant Italian design, and the starkly modernist effect was softened by the rich full drapes which hung floor to ceiling at what Tara had already christened 'the wonderful window'. This was not so much a window as a fourth wall, since the whole space was taken up by a sheet of plate glass giving an unimpeded view of the harbour beyond. It was this which had sold the apartment to her, and she never tired of gazing out on the ever-changing panorama. The waters of the bay reflected the sky's moods as closely as a faithful lover, and she delighted in them all. She took as much pleasure in the onset of a dancing rain as she did in the relentless sun. To sit at her wonderful window and rest her eyes on the world beyond was her favourite form of relaxation.

'I worked hard today, Maxie,' she told the inattentive cat. 'Worked like a dog. That's a joke, little one. You're supposed to laugh.' Maxie was not amused, his entire attention being focused on his mistress's languid movement towards the kitchen, which as he knew promised that his supper was imminent.

'So what do you think of our new home?' she continued, reaching for tin and tin-opener to feed the cat. 'It's a bit expensive, but I reckon we've earned it. Earned it, Maxie. It's the first time in my life that I've ever been able to have that feeling and d'you know what? It feels damn good! You ought to try it sometime.'

Lovingly she placed the dish down on the floor for the cat who was winding himself round her legs in pleasurable anticipation.

'So, shall we get you a job? Maybe you could do some modelling? Or shall we get you a lady friend to keep you company while I'm out at work? Only one thing, though. You mustn't run off and leave me, Maxie. I'll get horribly lonely if you leave me on my own.'

As she talked, she moved round the luxurious flat tidying rather vaguely. Housekeeping was another skill that Stephanie Harper had never learned, but this one Tara seemed to be able to manage fine without. She crossed into her bedroom to change out of her working clothes, and stretching, sighing, slipped into a comfortable old house-coat that if it ever had been fashionable, certainly wasn't now. 'I'm too old for all this kiddie caper,' she told Maxie, 'that's my trouble. Still, if it serves its purpose . . .' She let this dark thought hang in the air. She would think about all that later.

Comfortable at last, she returned to the hall, where she had dropped her bags in a heap behind the door when she came in. She found a parcel that she had picked up from a shop on her way home from work, and taking it into the bedroom, opened it. The stout wrappings came off to reveal two blown-up, carefully framed photographs. Tara gazed at them intently. In the first, a girl sat at a piano, her head thrown back as if in inspiration as she tackled the piece before her. In the other, a schoolboy footballer made a determined effort to get his foot to the ball nearby. Sarah and Dennis. Tara fed her eyes upon the photos of her children for a long, long time. Maxie came to ensconce himself on her lap, but soon departed in a huff, put out by the wet salt drops that would keep descending on his nose. 'Soon, soon, my darlings,' she whispered, kissing the cold glass of the photoframes tenderly. And to herself she repeated her well-worn formula for endurance – *hang on. Just hang on.*

Much later, Tara made herself a tray of tea and carried it to the small table that served as her desk. She switched on the desk lamp, which shone down on her now much thicker scrap-book. Tara Welles had continued to keep her record. Today she had achieved her first objective, to become the glamour woman she needed to be. Now she was ready to embark on her revenge. The active phase, she thought to herself, the time is ripe. Next to her scrapbook lay a copy of a sporting newspaper, *The Sports Review*. The headline read 'CHAMP FOR CHARITY'. 'Greg Marsden', read the copy 'ex-Wimbledon champion, is to play in a charity match to raise money for disabled sportsmen and women. It is hoped that the cream of Sydney will be there to grace what promises to be a glittering event, with the tennis star greeting the distinguished guests at a champagne reception following the game. Marsden, still mourning the tragic and mysterious loss of his wife, heiress Stephanie Harper . . .'

Tara reached for the scissors. Methodically she cut out the news item and photograph, and detached the accompanying form on which those hoping to go could apply for tickets. Then she carefully fixed the cutting in her scrapbook. The face of Greg looked out at her, handsome, vital and evil. Nothing had changed. Vengeance, vengeance, vengeance throbbed through her mind.

On the centre court at the Hordern Pavilion, Greg Marsden was giving a demonstration of the world-class skills that had taken him all the way to Wimbledon. The powerful serve came across the net with a kick like a mule, so that if the hapless opponent actually succeeded in getting his racquet to it, he was lucky not to have it spun out of his hand. The forehand drive raked the court, hurtling to within a hair's breadth of the base line, but somehow miraculously always coming down inside rather than out. The same was true of the tormenting lob, which would soar over the head of the man foolish enough to try to rush the net, and drop as if dead in the farthest corner, while the backhand smash had more bite in it than others' forehands. Every stroke was true and sweet, every point was securely tucked away for Marsden, and the whole pavilion rang with the enthusiastic buzz of his ardent fans.

Unfortunately this magnificent performance was taking place in Greg's imagination rather than in the game he was actually playing. In his mind he would shape up for the mighty Marsden serve, and instead would release an unimpressive ball that his opponent had no trouble in converting into a blistering return. Mentally he would plan the scorching smash that would pulverize the opposition, and then be unable to give it any of the old drive or spin. He had known he was out of condition, out of practice, but not that it would be like this. He had been playing pretty regularly at the club – had even beaten Lew Jackson, the rising wonder boy on one occasion, much to his delight. He had accepted the invitation to star in the charity match because he had thought he would do just that – star. He anticipated wiping away the youngster they had put against him, the organizers having deliberately chosen a player who would offer him a game that was just good enough for a contest, but not good enough to overcome the champ. And he thought the charity touch would be good for his image, while the reception afterwards would be a chance to meet the rich and ritzy of Sydney society. Who knows? He might even pick up another Stephanie Harper – a sexy one this time.

From the first encounter with his opponent in the dressing rooms he had had the feeling that it might go wrong. The kid had been really tense and psyched up, gripping his racquet and muttering to himself. Once on the court, he had been like a tiger unleashed. He had been all over Greg in the first five minutes. From the outset, Greg knew he was sunk, and simply concentrated grimly on not going down to a humiliating defeat.

'Forty-fifteen'. The voice of the umpire rang sonorously over the hushed crowd. All eyes were riveted on the fast-paced singles, but most of all on the tall, arrogant, tousled figure of Greg. Unlike the young man opposite him, Greg was hyper-aware of the gallery of his fans all around, women of all ages, watching with eager concentration, reacting audibly to every shot; all for Greg, all willing him to win. He flashed a dazzling smile here and there as often as he could. Above all, he knew not to look like a sore loser, although if the truth were known, there was none sorer.

In the midst of Greg's adoring fans beat the one heart which hated him with a passion even greater than that of those who loved him. Tara was watching the match seated next to the comforting presence of Joanna Randall, in a maelstrom of conflicting emotions. The first sight of Greg as he entered the court, a moment she had been dreading, passed off fairly painlessly since the entrance was far away and the distant figure burdened with racquets and towels seemed remote from the man who had tried to take her life, and had almost succeeded in condemning her to the life in death of hideous deformity. But as he drew nearer, she began to feel again a rush of painful emotions and during the course of the match she grew increasingly agitated by his proximity to her. She made herself sit very still and look calm.

'He had quite a good career then.' Joanna's voice broke into her ear. 'Showed a helluva lot of promise when he was younger. Something went wrong.' She paused and laughed drily to herself. 'Don't think he could drag himself out of bed if you get my meaning.'

Tara felt a pain in her heart like a stab of ice.

'Anyway, he blew it.' Joanna yawned and looked at her watch. 'God, he's blowing this, too. Look at him. I must be nuts, letting you drag me off to watch a tennis match in the middle of a good working day. I'm a busy woman. Now if it'd been football – then you'd be talking!'

'Game to Mr Whiteman. Whiteman leads two sets to love.'

Tara took a deep breath. 'Jo, did you say you'd met Greg Marsden?'

'Me and half the female population of the island, darling. Met him at another do like this, a fashion show for charity a year or two back. Why?'

'What's he like?'

'Greg's an alley cat with a touch of class. He had one lucky break – he married Miss Moneybags, Stephanie Harper. You must have read about it. She died in an accident when they were up north on their honeymoon – a croc, a real killer . . . hideous.' Joanna shuddered.

Oh yes, it was hideous all right, thought Tara tonelessly.

'At the time everyone was saying he married her for her money,' Joanna went on. 'I never met the lady. She didn't mix in society, though with her money and position she could have been one of the leaders of the beautiful people.

But God! I felt sorry for her when I heard about it. Actually, it wouldn't surprise me if he bumped the poor bitch off.' She looked round idly. 'Mind you, there isn't a female here except us two who wouldn't jump under a train if Greg Marsden told her to. Will you look at them! All having their private little fantasies about the great tennis star and what he's got inside his pants!'

'Ssshh!' came the angry hiss of a spectator. Tara coloured faintly. Joanna looked at her out of the corner of her eye.

'I don't believe it. Not you too! Are we here because of Greg Marsden?'

Tara reacted angrily. 'No, of course not. I love the game, that's all.'

'Oh.' An idea struck Joanna. 'We should get Jason to do some shots of you on a tennis court – remind me.'

'Ever the pro.' Tara smiled faintly, and gave her attention to the drama on the court, now reaching its climax. Spinning and dashing around, chasing the last few balls of the game, Greg was losing. The applause that greeted the victor was less than lukewarm. But he didn't care, transported with delight, the triumphant underdog made good. With his unerring instinct for his own PR, Greg made a show of offering magnanimous congratulations, flashing the famous smile around for one and all. Then the two players left the court.

At the reception afterwards, Tara found that she was feeling totally calm. Her earlier agitation had subsided, and she now felt in control of the events which she strongly sensed were about to unfold. Oblivious of her part in this drama, Joanna came bearing down on her with two glasses of champagne she had collected from the bar.

'Tickets cost an arm and a leg, we might as well get our money's worth of the free booze,' she announced cheerfully. She sipped it, and her expression changed. 'Uugh! Not exactly a fine vintage, wouldn't you say?' She gazed around her in some disdain. 'Talk about a bunfight!' The room was heaving.

Suddenly there was a change in the noise of the crowd,

signalling an important arrival. Greg Marsden made his entrance through the door to the players' quarters. He had not bothered to change or shower, well aware of the effect that his tennis star's presence and odour of fresh sweat would have on his female fans. After a lull, the noise sounded louder than ever, and the groupies gravitated towards him adoringly. Joanna snorted in disgust.

'Huh! He might as well have walked in stark naked! Will you look at that pack of daft sheilas?'

Tara looked carefully across the room. Greg was signing autographs, flirting casually as he did so. He seemed to feel her gaze even among so many others, and looked up. He caught her eye, and she looked away with assumed nonchalance. But she knew he had seen her, and every fibre of her being was concentrating on willing him over to her, drawing him to her side.

'Greg Marsden has a reputation,' came Joanna's voice again, 'for being attracted to new faces, particularly those in the public eye. And I hear he thrives on challenge. Don't say I didn't warn you. Don't look now' – she threw a glance across Tara's shoulder. 'Here he comes. Like a bee to a honeypot.'

'Hi there.' The smooth caressing tones were unmistakable. As cold and hard as stone inside, Tara turned to face him. She found herself looking into those same eyes as in her last frantic moments in the water before the crocodile took her down for the last time.

'I'm Greg Marsden.' His face split into a boyish grin. 'I don't believe we've met.'

This is the man who tried to kill me. This is the man who took my innocent existence and blasted it apart. This is my own beloved husband, dearer to me than my heart's blood. This is the man who –

'No,' said Tara offering her hand with a charming smile, 'we haven't met. I haven't had that pleasure.'

A receptionist's lot is not a happy one, thought Suzie, Joanna's best girl. Here she was, the only one at the agency with the phone going like the clappers, the cleaning not done from yesterday and to cap it all flowers arriving every five minutes so that she had to run down to the street door all the time from the first floor where the work proper was carried out. She was relieved to see Joanna arriving as she received yet another basket of flowers and signed for its delivery.

'Good grief!' Joanna was staggered to see all the flowers in her upstairs office. She was accustomed to receiving floral tributes after a successful fashion show like last night's. But nothing like this had ever happened before. As she stood there examining them, Tara walked in. Joanna enjoyed her amazement, then dropped the bombshell.

'They're for you.'

'What all of them?'

'Almost all. It seems we were a big hit at the show last night, and a few are from our advertisers or whoever by way of congratulations. But practically all of these' – Joanna waved an arm over banks of carnations, chrysanthemums, roses and gladioli – 'are for you. Guess who?'

Tara approached the nearest basket and looked at the card on it. 'Have dinner with me,' it read, 'tonight, any night, every night.' It was signed with a simple 'G'. Her heart burned in triumph. Outwardly cool she turned to Joanna, whose curiosity knew no bounds.

'What happened to you two last night? I saw you leave the party with him.'

'He walked me to my car –'

'Car! Since when have you had a car?'

'Since yesterday. I figured a top model who was about to star in the town's greatest fashion show ever ought to have a car. If we were a big hit I'd have deserved it, and if we flopped, I'd bloody well need it!'

'How terrific! First a new apartment, now a new car. You must have a good agent.'

'The best,' said Tara with an affectionate hug.

'So what do you want me to do with these? Your loverboy has made working today impossible in this office.'

'Give them away,' Tara ordered carelessly. 'Just get rid of them. Give them to any of the girls who'd like them. And he's not my loverboy. I went home alone. Having refused his invitation to dinner.'

'Oh my God, hay fever!' Jason made a characteristically flamboyant entrance, miming the dying antics of a man suddenly affected by nerve gas. 'This stuff's got to go. Who's your admirer, mother?' He picked up the cards and began to read them, his face darkening as he did so. Then he turned on his heel to go. He paused at the doorway.

'If I'd known you were so interested in tennis, I'd have bought a racquet.' And he was gone.

'He's mad!' said Joanna quite bewildered. 'But forget about Jason. What about you and Greg Marsden?'

'What about me and Greg Marsden?' replied Tara, very calm.

Joanna had not built a business on being mealy-mouthed.

'D'you fancy him?' she demanded bluntly.

Tara turned away, unsure of how to respond. Joanna thrashed on.

'You must have a sex life. You do have a sex life, don't you?'

Tara looked at her and shyly her lips formed the shape of the word 'No'. Joanna looked bewildered.

'I don't have time,' declared Tara. 'You know what it's like. Or, to be honest, the inclination.'

Joanna let out her breath in a long 'pheeeeew!'

'You never stop amazing me, d'you know that? Most girls today are dizzy from playing musical beds and my top model has this quaint old-fashioned attitude that's . . . well it's positively antique! I don't believe it!'

She paused, and thought for a second.

'And neither will he. Greg Marsden's not the type for maiden modesty and bashfulness. You want to be careful, kid.' Her strong open face was troubled. 'Gotta watch out for yourself in this wicked world. And keep your old mother in the picture, eh? Tell me if you're going to see Greg Marsden again?'

Tara smiled enigmatically. 'I will, I promise you – as soon as ever I know myself!'

*

Chapter Twelve

Tara left the agency and drove off recklessly down the narrow Liverpool Lane, her heart singing wildly in exultation. I've done it. I've got him, she thought. A great sense of triumph filled her. Her mind returned to last night, the gala fashion show which Joanna had devised and staged as a showcase for the latest trends among the top designers. Attendance was by invitation only, and as space was limited, and the show promised to be sensational, tickets were like gold. As one who had begun to fear that his star was on the wane, Greg Marsden had been delighted to receive an invitation, with its implicit suggestion that he was still one of the beautiful people. What he did not know was that the most beautiful of them all, the one who was to be the star of the show, had arranged for him to be put on the list.

Tara had very good reasons for wanting Greg present at the fashion show. As the newest, hottest property among all the city's model girls, she would get to wear all the most stunning outfits and original creations. She also knew that as Joanne was running the show down to the last safety pin, she would ensure that Tara was presented to her very best advantage throughout. Tara could hardly think of a better way of attracting Greg's attention, or impressing him with her glamour and style. She had to get him to the show.

This idea had come to her as she was standing talking to him at the champagne reception after the charity tennis match. She could see that he was attracted to her, and curious about her, so she had played the Mona Lisa to the hilt, putting herself over as enigmatic and inscrutable. And as soon as she was sure that she had caught his interest, she had hurried Joanna away.

'Now that I've met him properly, I can understand why he has women eating out of his hand,' Joanna said thoughtfully as they walked to the car park. 'He could charm the birds off the trees.' She gave Tara a look full of meaning and added with a knowing grin. 'You watch out, little bird. After the way you virtually walked out on him there, I'm ready to take a bet that it won't be long before you hear from him again.'

Tara continued to stride along as if she had not heard.

'OK, OK, I get the message,' said Joanna finally. 'But just one thing – I'm not sure you can afford the disruption right now that a man like him would mean. Maybe in another six months? And for God's sake stay loose for the fashion show, or I'll scrag you!'

Tara devoutly hoped that Joanna was right about her hearing from Greg again, even though she disclaimed any such ideas to Joanna's face. She was counting on it that the large white square of card, gold-encrusted with 'A GALA FASHION EVENT' and 'MISS TARA WELLES' would draw the fox from his lair. As the night drew near, she felt less certain, and losing confidence under the strain of the performance itself, she was not surprised to see that he had not made it. As she was due to make her first parade down the catwalk she was nerving herself up for his scrutiny, for she had checked the seating plan and knew exactly where his table was. But as soon as she emerged from backstage into the glare of the lights, she could see beyond the edge of the long walkway that the table was empty.

Perhaps it's as well she thought miserably, once she was back in the shelter of the models' changing space, getting ready for her next appearance. I really need to concentrate on what I'm doing tonight. All around, other models were rushing to and fro, with dressers, make-up artists and hair stylists frenziedly assembling each girl and her total look for the next part of the show. In the midst of the creative chaos was Joanna, in her element: half harpy, half mother hen, alternately terrorizing and soothing, a human dynamo of tireless energy.

'Keep it moving, now – Cleo, that's *not* your rack, get over there, that's where you'll find it. No laughing now, *concentrate*, this is work, not playtime. Kim, you were out of step with the music when you went out front, for God's sake get it right, you *can* count, get it wrong again and you've got big trouble, honey chile . . . Jennie, do remember to keep your eyes up – *wrong hat* with that green number! – come on, darling, hurry that change . . . Now out you go, don't forget everybody, enjoy it, *enjoy!*'

Tara's part in the evening's entertainment was to appear as the highlight and grand finale of the three distinct sections when in the *pièce de resistance* she would have a complicated routine, half walk, half dance, to display the garment off to its best perfection. Twice she ventured onto the catwalk, and twice returned smiling brilliantly but inwardly crestfallen at Greg's continuing absence. By the third time, she was not looking for him. And there he was, watching appreciatively as attended by two male models dressed as life-savers, she came out like a pillar of silver under the lights in a stunning slender sheaf of an evening dress, which glittered like the pure metal itself under the lights and drew every eye.

Behind the scenes, Joanna was winding up in a terminal frenzy.

'Come on, come on. Jesus Christ, who's smoking? PUT THAT OUT AT ONCE! If you've burned a hole in that gown I'll take a box of matches to you myself and make you think you're Joan of Arc, you silly bitch! Right, I'm watching you all now, this is the grand finale coming up girls, give it your best shot all of you, OK? Right, heads up, out you go, listen to the music . . .'

Yet frantic as she was Joanna noticed a new vitality when Tara came back inside, and a suppressed air of triumph, which she attributed to Tara's excitement at the success of the show. The party afterwards provided another opportunity to bewitch, bother and bewilder Mr Marsden.

He appeared out of nowhere as she was having the first dance with Jason, and ruthlessly cut in to take her from him, something which the little man resented bitterly but was powerless to prevent. However, Tara had already had one tiny revenge on Jason's behalf – murmuring to Greg, 'would you excuse me just one second?' she had moved swiftly from the dance floor, from the room and from the building, leaving him standing there before he even realized she had gone.

That had been a calculated risk – he might have been so mad at being ditched that he would never speak to her again. But she was gambling that he would be more intrigued than annoyed, and that her evasion would arouse his thrill of the chase. And now the flowers, which by their extravagance proved her hunch had been right. Deeply satisfied, she composed in her mind the reply she would send to his invitation. 'Friday, 9.30, Chez Solange in Rowena Place'. With flowers, of course.

The telephone shrilled urgently, but the dignified figure was not going to be seen hurrying to pick it up.

'This is the Harper Mansion. Good afternoon.'

Matey prided himself on his telephone manner, confident that he could deal successfully with anyone on the phone. Even he, however, could not hope to satisfy the woman who had been trying to reach Greg Marsden for over two weeks without success. Jilly was convinced that Greg simply *had* to be there even on occasions when he wasn't, and her demands to speak to him would grow so urgent that even Matey found his diplomacy stretched to the limit.

'No, I'm sorry he's not here at the moment. May I take a message? I assure you, madam, that Mr Marsden receives all his messages the moment he comes in. I'm afraid I cannot say why he has not been in touch with you. Perhaps you'd care to leave another message . . . No, I'm sorry, I simply cannot say when he is likely to be in. He comes and goes at all hours. Shall I ask him to call you?'

And so it would go on for a considerable time, as Jilly took out on the imperturbable Matey her frustration at being unable to get to grips with Greg. Eventually she accepted defeat, with urgent instructions to Matey that Greg was to be told of her call and her request for him to call her the second he set foot in the house, she rang off. Oh dear, oh dear, thought Matey heavily, what a come-down for the house to have a master who's involved in all this after Miss Stephanie . . . He stood for a moment lost in thought, and when he went his way, it was with a heavier tread than he had come.

'You're a very beautiful woman, do you know that?'

Greg and Tara were having a dinner date in one of Sydney's most exclusive and expensive restaurants. For Tara, the sense of her triumph was almost palpable. How can he not feel it, she thought, as her heart surged at his words. That's the first time he has ever said that to me, she thought recklessly, and for a second her eyes glowed with something of his pale fire. But quickly she veiled her lids, and looking down murmured modestly, 'Thank you.'

'All the men must tell you that,' he pursued.

'A few.'

'Oh yeah . . . How many?'

She pretended to make elaborate calculations.

'Well, let me see now. There was . . . and . . . oh and . . .'

'Mmmm.' Greg expressed a sarcastic disbelief.

'And don't let's forget . . .' Tara continued

'What, him too?'

'And . . . and . . . and . . .'

'Here hold on. Slow down there, will you? I'm jealous of every damn one of them.'

'Jealous?' Tara's lips surved in a demure smile. 'We hardly know one another, Mr Marsden.'

Greg looked at her carefully across the table. Her deep blue evening gown set off her eyes and skin to perfection. Her slender graceful figure expressed all the vitality of her personality, and her conversation had held his interest for hours. Tara returned his gaze frankly. Since the meeting with Matey, she had no fear that anyone would recognize her, and knew she was safe from discovery with one so self-absorbed as Greg anyway. Another husband would have sensed out his wife by a thousand tiny things that nothing could ever change – Greg Marsden, never.

Besides, she had prepared with great care for this evening's encounter. She was not surprised that she was making a big impact on Greg – she had, quite literally, dressed to kill. And she knew her man. She made full use of this advantage, going for an outfit that was extremely seductive, but very classy and understated at the same time – nothing obvious or cheap would ever attract this one, she knew. The dress she had chosen came from the latest range of one of the top design houses which pressed their garments on Joanna so that her models would wear them elegantly around the town in all the smart places. The surface of its shimmering fabric changed every time it caught the lights so that it seemed to be not just blue but every shade from cornflower to sapphire by turns. Now, in the warm light of the candle burning on the table between them, she seemed to give off a soft radiance of her own, like a glow-worm.

Tara caught Greg's glance, and flirtatiously looked away, feigning indifference. Greg felt that he too should now be playing it cool, filling up her glass, introducing some casual topic of conversation. But he could not take his eyes off her, and Tara knew that the heavy-lidded regard meant that he was well on the way to being hooked. Fascinated, he studied her as she sat opposite. The liquid blue evening gown plunged in a bold V to the waist, clinging softly to her fine breasts. Around her neck she wore a heavy silver choker, the cold metal a tantalizing contrast with the warm flesh of her throat he was longing to kiss. As she moved her head long silver earrings danced beside her face – he wanted to rip them off and make love to her on the floor. Slowly she crossed her legs, and his aroused senses heard the whisper of sheer stockings brushing past one another, and picked up the almost silent rustle as her silky underslip rearranged itself around her legs. To a man of Greg's highly-developed sensuality such sounds were the call of Tara's womanhood to him, an even sweeter torture because he could not answer. He wanted to have the undressing of her for a week, take her to bed for a month. He felt as if all the fucking he had ever done had been only in preparation for her. He could imagine those carmine lips playing over his body, see those deep blue eyes drowning in sexual love. Oh, he must have her! He couldn't let her get away.

Now he picked up her last remark with an unmistakably seductive intonation.

'You say we hardly know one another. But I feel I've known you a long, long time. It must be . . . what d'you call it? . . . déja vu.'

'Or perhaps,' Tara said softly, keeping the irony out of her voice, 'perhaps we were meant to meet.'

'Tell me something.' He picked up her hand as it lay on the table, and gently caressed the back of it. 'Is there a boyfriend or husband in the picture?'

Tara took her time before replying, and chose her words with great care.

'There was someone once. Someone I loved very much. He really was the fairy-tale prince that I'd dreamed about ever since I was a little girl.' She fell silent.

'You obviously loved him very much,' prompted Greg gently. 'So what happened?'

Tara's voice was cold and flat. 'The dream turned into a nightmare. I woke up.' She directed a searching gaze at him. 'How about you?'

'Me?' He was startled. 'Oh, no you don't! It's not fair.'

'Oh come on. Of course it's fair. I told you.'

'Oh, well . . . of course you know I was married and lost my wife . . . but nothing really, nothing serious.'

Nothing serious. Tara had to fight for control. No, not serious at all to a man like you, I suppose. She hung onto her sympathetic expression with the greatest effort. He was lost in his own act, and did not notice. With a sincere

208

smile, he resumed. 'I'm just a guy who's searching for that special one . . . and when I find her, I could be tempted. I could be tempted now, in fact – by you . . .'

Tara sat very still.

'What is it, after all? Love is life's greatest mystery. I'm not talking about sex – that's nothing. But regard for one another, mutual respect, real closeness, friendship . . . Tara, I want us to be friends, more than anything else in the world at this moment.'

For the first time in her life Tara experienced the pure joy of playing with a man, hooking him like a fish, drawing him in . . .

'Just – friends?' She murmured in a low voice.

'Whatever.' Greg raised her hand to his lips and bestowed the faintest butterfly kiss on the back of it. He was well satisfied. Once you get them starting to play the game, you've got them, he thought. And I'll get this one. It's not going to be easy – there's something there – for a moment his mind worried away at a feeling he could not put a name to. But with his usual arrogant disregard, he brushed it aside. You've never failed yet, boy, he told himself, and you won't now.

Their quiet moment was interrupted by an unexpected greeting.

'Greg!'

'Phil!' Greg was completely taken aback.

'I wasn't sure if it was you or not, the light is so dim in here.' Phillip had been strongly tempted to slip past without acknowledging Greg, but had sternly repressed that impulse as cowardly and unworthy. Greg favoured Phillip with his silkiest smile. Here was a fine chance to dispel any suspicions that Phillip may have about him and Jilly. He turned to Tara with a possessive and caressing air which he could see was not lost on Phillip.

'Tara, this is Phillip Stewart, an old friend of my wife's, Phillip, Miss Tara Welles.' So, Phillip thought, this is the latest conquest. No wonder Jilly has been fretting so badly, losing weight. She's been remaindered. Last year's model.

His heart moved with pity, in an echo of what he now knew to be Jilly's pain. His greeting of Tara was polite, but perfunctory.

Tara was practising one of her most useful new techniques, that of keeping very still. Phillip's appearance had been a real shock for her, concentrating as she was upon Greg. She still had not quite got used to people from her old life popping up again in her new. In addition, she was shocked still further by the change in Phillip. His tall body had taken on a discouraged stoop, his face, which used to be attractively lined was now just worn, and he looked like a man who had forgotten how to smile. Poor Phillip! Another casualty of Greg's greed and lust. Her heart went out to him. But she sat poised and motionless, holding an empty smile of greeting like a mask on her face.

'So Phil, how's Jilly,' Greg asked breezily.

'She's . . . quite well . . . the last time I saw her, anyway.' He looked Greg straight in the eye. 'I'm away a lot these days. We've rather lost touch, I'm afraid.'

'Oh, that's too bad.' Greg's air of surprise and boyish concern was totally convincing.

'I think so,' said Phillip evenly. 'Well, I must be off. Enjoy your evening. Nice to have met you, Miss Welles.'

Phillip always had dignity, thought Tara. And now he really has need of it. She watched him fondly as he made his way out.

'Nice bloke, Phil,' Greg observed. 'The Stewarts were my wife's best friends.'

Tara felt a stirring of excitement within her, and moved forward to pounce.

'Tell me about your wife, Greg. What was she like?' She was tingling with anticipation.

Greg took time arranging his thoughts and answered with great deliberation. His reply was couched in warm and touching terms.

'She was a nice person – wonderfully loving and honest. The most generous human being I've ever met. I still miss her, so much . . .'

He allowed the tears to well up to his eyes. Tears! *Crocodile tears*, thought Tara, in a spasm of fury. She could have sunk a stiletto in his black heart. But she waited.

'But she was her own worst enemy,' Greg went on. It wouldn't do to convey the impression that his dead wife was too wonderful. It frightened women off, to think of competing with a departed saint. 'Anyone who worried as much as Stephanie did about what people thought, was crazy.' He paused, obviously following a train of thought for the first time. 'You know, it's bizarre. The first thing that struck me about you, is that you reminded me physically of Stephanie. But she . . . the comparison's ridiculous. She was an ugly duckling. You are the swan she always wanted to be.' He fell silent while the waiter refilled their glasses, then raised his in a graceful gesture.

'To us, Tara. To your beauty. To the future, and whatever it may bring.'

'To us.' Tara echoed the toast with meaning. To us, she thought, with a vengeance. The waiter reappeared with their first course and set it before them. Smiling sweetly, Tara picked up her knife and fork, and decapitated her trout with a hidden sense of purpose renewed.

The white Rolls-Royce Corniche sang sweetly as it ran them towards Tara's apartment at the end of the evening. Simply to ride in that car, her lovingly chosen wedding present to Greg, had been another little ordeal for Tara, in an evening of alternating knife wounds and pinpricks. They drew to a halt outside one of the large apartment buildings in Elizabeth Bay. Greg got out, came round to the passenger side, and opened the door for Tara to alight.

They stood facing one another on the footpath, the warm breeze off the harbour fanning their hair; the air between them electric with unspoken questions, tensions, desires.

'Thank you . . . for a lovely evening.' She looked down.

'Hey . . .' He took her under the chin and tipped her face up to his. 'It's a long drive home . . . don't I get a cup of coffee?' His eyes were full of invitation and promise.

She stepped back. 'I don't think so . . . not tonight. I

have an early call.' There was a silence, then Greg surrendered gracefully. He gave a regretful grin, and nodded.

'OK. Maybe next time?'

'Maybe. Goodnight, Greg.'

She stood on the footpath watching the rear lights of the Rolls till he was out of sight. Then she walked briskly to the safety of her own apartment, several streets away. She had not been ready to let him know where she lived. Not yet. Coming home felt like coming into sanctuary. Within these walls she could let the mask fall from her face. To the severe discomfort of Maxie, his mistress was to be seen shaking, crying, laughing, talking wildly in a stream of curses, threats and promises. But with the age-old patience of his race, he simply waited for it all to pass over, and at last it did.

Jason's studio staff were all inclined to get nervous when the maestro was giving birth to a new creative concept. Extravagant demands would be succeeded by frenzied rejections and the whole place would be in a ferment till the new theme had finally emerged in the way the little tyrant wanted it. Today's shoot was to launch a new range of ultra-sophisticated late-late wear, and Jason was working to the idea of the denizens of the night, those who emerge to enjoy the world of darkness after ordinary folk have taken to their innocent beds. In the middle of the newly-created night scenario, Tara and a male model were doing their best to comply with Jason's orders and realize his vision.

'You're a vampire,' screeched Jason, his thin hair standing up on top of his head, 'you're a lovely lady vampire, he can't resist you. Now go for his neck – go go go!'

Lying on top of the unresisting hunk, Tara obligingly nibbled away at the bronzed adam's apple just below her.

'No no no!' howled Jason. '*Bite*, damn you! Sink your fangs in his neck, don't worry about him, he's getting paid for this, and I want to see the pain . . . that's better! Again. And keep your eyes up, tilt your chin, I can't see your eyes. What's the matter now? Look at me, watch the birdie, come on, concentrate, concentrate, you've lost it . . .'

Tara had indeed lost all interest in the nice masculine neck she had previously been chewing with some enjoyment. Behind Jason's back, and unseen by him, Jilly Stewart had just walked into the studio. Tara broke away from the male model, and stepped off the small stage.

'I need a powder down,' she improvised, putting her hand to her forehead as if to detect the perspiration there.

'OK, take five, powder down,' Jason conceded. 'Makeup, come on, get in here, double quick. Now while we've stopped, I want some blood on this boy, real gore oozing all down his neck from the lovely Tara's love bites, the whole vampire number, can you do it? And take his nose down, he's glowing like Rudolf the Red-Nosed Reindeer.' He moved about the studio firing orders like a machine gun. 'OK, let's change those gels. Get the pink out, I need more blue for sure, and perhaps a bit of green to heighten the sinister effect . . .'

In the midst of the hurly-burly Jilly stood looking shaky and extremely forlorn. Tara studied her as she looked wildly around her, obviously not knowing who to speak to. Like Phillip, Jilly had suffered with the passage of time. Her cat-like poise, which used to be her most pronounced feature, had given way to a bedraggled all-alone look which reminded Tara of the pitiful little stray that had been Maxie when she first picked him up. Her once-immaculate grooming had quite deserted her: her hair was a hastily-combed mess and her makeup applied as if in the dark. But there was more than a flash of the old Jilly in the way she tossed her hair out of her eyes and threw her head back like a horse before the off. And after all, thought Tara grimly, you have still come out of your entanglement with Greg Marsden in one piece – more than I did. She moved forward very deliberately.

'Did you want to see me?'

'You're Tara Welles? I'm Jilly Stewart. Can we talk?'

Tara could tell from the excited manner, the glassy glitter in the eyes, that Jilly had taken something by way of fortification for this encounter. But she was not going to make it easy for her.

'Are you a reporter, then?'

'No, no.' The denial tumbled out eagerly. 'I'm . . . a friend of Greg Marsden.'

'I see.'

'A close friend.'

Tara made no reply. Close friend, she was thinking. Yeah.

'Er . . .' Jilly was twisting a tissue in her hands. 'You met my husband the other night. Phillip Stewart.'

Tara pretended to remember.

'Oh yes, that's right. Greg introduced us at the restaurant.' A silence fell. Jilly had obviously got stuck. At last she blurted out, 'Are you having an affair with Greg?'

'I'm sorry?' Tara was shocked and contemptuous of Jilly's lack of shame.

'I know he's been seeing you!' urged Jilly, very agitated.

'Oh . . .' Tara made herself as cold and distant as she could. 'We met at a tennis match. We've been out to dinner once. That's all.'

Jilly cracked, lost control. 'You're lying,' she charged, white with passion. 'I know Greg Marsden, don't forget. He's quite incapable of being around a beautiful woman without getting his own way with her. If a lady really said no, he wouldn't waste his time. And they don't anyway. You're his mistress!'

Even in the workaday frenzy of the studio, heads were turning and people were beginning to take notice. Tara moved to dispel the aroused curiosity of the bystanders.

'Look, would you like to talk some more? Talk properly?' she asked softly. 'There's a bar round the corner, I think we'd find that more private.' Jilly's face bore a woeful hopefulness like a beaten child's. 'I've got a couple more shots to do and I could meet you there if you like.'

Jilly grasped at this like a drowning woman. 'I'll be there.'

Jason's voice cut through all the studio babble like a chainsaw.

'Is anyone going to do any *work* round here? Or am I paying you for the pleasure of your company? Let's get some asses into gear – *now!* No I can't speak to Joanna, pet, and I don't care if she's in mood indigo. Hey, that light's wrong – not a-fucking-*gain!* Tara! Tara! Where are you?'

Tara smiled, and turned to go. 'See you soon, then,' she said. Had Jilly looked back as she left the studio, she would have seen a look very like a vampire's come over Tara's face as she went back to the set.

The fine fury of Jason's creative rapture took a long time to express itself that afternoon, and it was much later than Tara had thought when she was able to get away. Cursing, she hurried round the corner to the bar, preparing herself to find Jilly gone. She need not have worried. Jilly had found the natural home-from-home of any drinker at any watering-hole, and was well ensconced. Tara could tell at sight that she had been drinking heavily.

'Sorry I'm so late,' she said as she approached Jilly's table. 'It all took longer than I expected. I'm relieved to find you're still here. I wasn't sure if you'd wait.'

'Don't worry about it.' Jilly made an expansive gesture, and her words were slurred. 'What'll you have?' she caught the waiter's eye with practised ease.

'Oh, I think a beer would be nice – a cold beer.'

'Beer, and another scotch,' Jilly ordered, then caught sight of the empty glasses on the table before her. A defensive look passed over her face.

'I only drink when I'm down, you know. When Phillip's away it gets lonely in an empty house.'

'It must do,' agreed Tara, then prepared herself to move in. 'Still, you do have Greg.'

'Do I?' Jilly squinted at her drunkenly, then her mood swung suddenly into boastfulness. 'Yeah. Yeah, I do. He needs me. But –' another swing '– I need him too. Yeah, Greg Marsden's addictive. Like this stuff.' She took a large swig of the whisky, and grimaced as it went down. Tara returned to the attack.

'He . . . told me a bit about his wife. I gather you and she were best friends.'

'Since we were kids. Our fathers knew one another. They did business.' The shadow of a bad memory crossed Jilly's face. Of course! A flash of insight illuminated that past episode for Tara. *Jilly's father killed himself when the deal with my father failed! Is that what she has been thinking of for all these years? Is that what she was punishing Stephanie for? Oh Jilly!*

'So I suppose it was his wife's death that brought you and Greg together?' Carefully she probed her way forward.

Jilly considered this, and found the suggestion a very convenient lie. 'Yeah, yeah it was,' she said carelessly. 'But look, I don't want to keep going on about her, OK? I'm sick of talking about it.'

'Oh sure.' Tara's voice was ice-cold. Jilly looked at her speculatively. 'You know, Stephanie was a beer drinker. She used to prefer a beer to wine or champagne.'

Something was ticking away in the back of Jilly's fuddled brain. Tara swiftly brought her back to the subject.

'So – you were saying?'

'What? Oh yeah. What I meant was, Greg never really loved Stephanie, you know.'

Tara's face expressed her feelings. 'Never? At all?'

'Yeah,' Jilly went on in her self-absorbed way, 'He told me. So it wasn't like I was doing anything disloyal when I fell in love with him. He was fancy-free, as they say.'

'But what about Stephanie?'

'What about her?'

'Did she love Greg?'

The question obviously struck Jilly as completely irrelevant.

'Did she – well, yeah, I suppose so. But that didn't—'

'Matter?'

216

'Well . . .' Jilly was not so drunk that she couldn't see how awful this sounded. 'Not after she was dead, anyway. Can't make any difference now she's dead, can it?'

Oh, you'd be surprised, thought Tara.

Suddenly Jilly looked at her watch.

'What time is it?'

'Going on for seven.'

Jilly let out a wail of anguish. 'Oh God, I'm late, I've got to go.'

'Go?'

'Yeah.' Jilly's face was alight with triumph, and her yellow cat's eyes were gleaming. 'Greg's waiting for me – at the house. Gotta dash.' Tara thought quickly.

'Did you drive here?'

'No, I took a taxi. Always seem to take taxis these days.'

'I'll drive you home,' said Tara, remembering to add, 'where do you live?'

'Would you? It's Hunter's Hill, and Greg gets so angry if I'm late.' She giggled fatuously, like a teenager in love.

'My pleasure,' said Tara, and meant it.

Outside the Stewart house on Hunter's Hill, Greg waited with his temper mounting like a boiler under pressure. Stupid fucking bitch, he was thinking with great bitterness, persecutes the life out of me to see her and can't even be here when I've fixed up to come. He loathed the feeling of knocking on the door of an empty house, the realization that no one was coming to let him in. He was used to the very opposite; his whole nature craved ecstatic welcomes and loud ovations. Raging with the habitual cold fire, he stored up his anger and waited.

The drive out to Hunter's Hill had given Tara the opportunity to work her way into Jilly's confidence, and to extract without difficulty more and more of the details of her relationship with Greg. By the time they swept up Hunter's Hill to Jilly's house, they were fast friends, in Jilly's confused brain at least. As she got out of the car, struggling for sobriety, she was lavish in her thanks for the lift, and professions of friendship.

'Let's keep in touch, hey? Ring me, I'm in the book.' Oh I will, thought Tara, I will. For through the trees at the top of the drive she had caught a glimpse of the white Rolls, and Greg's tall, lean figure lounging in the doorway.

'Better get off to your date, Jilly,' she said brightly. 'I'll see you. That's for sure.' Then she let in the clutch, roared away, and did not look behind as Jilly ran wildly up the drive to another appointment with misery.

Chapter Thirteen

To say it had not been a good night was an understatement. Tara had lain awake for hours mentally replaying her meeting with Jilly, painfully fitting the new pieces of information she had gleaned into the jigsaw she had been building up for so long. When she did manage to doze off, she slept fitfully and woke again wretched and unrefreshed. At times like this she felt the lack of the twenty-year old's ability to do without sleep and still bounce up bright-eyed and pink-cheeked in the morning. The apparition that greeted Tara in her bathroom mirror almost made her cancel that morning's shoot – but she dared not bring down Jason's wrath upon her undefended head by such unprofessional conduct.

She compromised by arriving early, so that the makeup girls would have plenty of time to iron out the evidence of the night's ravages. Even so, she was not ready to begin when Jason was, a fact which frayed his temper considerably. Jason had never again reverted to the topic of his feeling for her since she had managed to deflect his declaration of love some time ago. But he had made it plain that he still cared for her, he had never failed to express a jealous dislike of Greg, and it was clear that he was doing what a lot of men have done before, playing a waiting game. All this made for a tension between them that had not been there in the early days of their comradeship – and Tara mourned the passing of a friendship that had gone without bringing anything else in its wake.

Now Jason burst without knocking into the model's changing room at his studio, a tiny cubicle which meant that he over crowded the cramped conditions even more.

'How much longer are you going to be, Nicole?'

'Five minutes, that's all,' replied the makeup girl mechanically.

'What have you been doing in here?' Jason's irritability had to find an outlet. 'Discovered some new sexual variation, have you? Something to keep girls amused on a wet afternoon?'

'Five minutes, Jason, all right?' There was a warning note in Nicole's voice. 'Unless you want to see the dark circles, bags, *portmanteaux* under her eyes—'

'Five minutes then,' said Jason, retreating, 'No, that's *not* all right, but I suppose it's the best you can do. We're all ready to go out there, so give it a bit of chop chop, will you? Thank you, your ladyship.' And he swept out with an injured air.

'I hope your camera . . . self-destructs,' she yelled after him, and returned to her work. 'Hmmm. Not a lot we can do about late nights, madam — and yours looks to have been a Roman orgy!'

'I'm sorry,' murmured Tara. She was kicking herself for not taking a good dose of the sedative that Dan Marshall had given her to help her sleep when she was recovering from her surgery on Orpheus Island. She still had it, tucked away at the back of her medicine cupboard. But she had been afraid to take it in case it had left her dopey and sluggish the following day. All Joanna's phrases and attitudes were burned into her mind: Gotta be on the ball! Gotta stay ahead! She felt like having a damn good cry. But it would ruin her makeup. She closed her eyes.

A loud knock sounded on the door.

'Bugger you, Jason!' bawled Nicole cheerfully. 'It ain't five minutes yet. Sod off!'

The door opened.

'Did I hear "Come in"?' The voice was gentle, familiar, dark brown. 'Hello, Tara.'

She opened her eyes, and looked straight into those of the man she had taught herself to forget.

'Hello, Dan,' she said weakly.

He looked wonderful, in a new, well-cut suit and an

excellent shirt and tie. He wore a red carnation in his button-hole, and this fragile symbol of love and hope touched Tara almost more than she could bear. He stood filling the tiny cubicle with his presence, his kind brown eyes fixed upon her as if he were feeding a great hunger.

Suddenly Jason's head popped round the side of Dan's arm. He ignored Dan and Tara completely and addressed himself to Nicole.

'When the model has finished receiving her boyfriends and turning my studio into a *knocking shop*,' he said viciously, 'would you please remind her that there's work to be done today?' There was no mistaking the jealous fury in his voice. He stalked out. Tara reached hurriedly into her bag for one of her little private address cards.

'Sorry, Dan,' she whispered, handing it to him. 'Tonight. Eight o'clock? OK?'

By eight o'clock that night Tara had got through a working day made unusually difficult and long by Jason's foul temper, shopped hastily for the ingredients for a good dinner for two, and still got home in time to do a lightning tidy-up and get herself ready before Dan arrived. At eight o'clock on the dot he rang the door to her flat, having tired of pacing the wide avenues of Elizabeth Bay as he had been doing for the last three-quarters of an hour. His need to see her was now a physical ache. And somehow this last day had been harder to get through than any of the months since Tara left him.

Those months of waiting, hoping, longing and despairing had eventually taken their toll not only of his nerves, but finally of his resolution to forget Tara and put that whole episode behind him. Eventually it just wore away and he knew that he had to come to Sydney and make one more attempt to see Tara, to offer her his love, and to persuade her to accept it. He had arrived last evening, and spent the night in alternating states of hope and fear like a schoolboy before a big exam. The sight of Tara as she opened the door made his heart melt. She looked so lovely that he faltered momentarily, and could not think of anything to say.

'Come in, Dan, come in.' She sensed his confusion, and covered it with more sophistication than she had had before, he noticed. Her greeting was warm, but there was a tension there. Take it easy, he told himself crossly, you're trembling like a fool.

She took his coat, then led the way into the sitting room where, as she had hoped, he was immediately entranced by the wonderful window. 'What a view!' he cried, and she flushed with delight. She busied herself with drinks while he prowled around, releasing his shyness by degrees in this pleasantly relaxing atmosphere. He came to rest by her desk, where he was secretly overwhelmed to notice the shell he had given her on Orpheus, in the centre, in pride of place among a few others.

'I see you've kept your shell collection,' he said noncommittally, trying not to build too much on this.

'Yes. I simply never tire of them.'

Dan reached into his pocket. 'I'm glad to hear that, because I brought you a little something.' He handed her a tiny shell, exquisitely formed in mother-of-pearl, its whorls and swirls catching the light in its soft diffused bloom.

'Oh Dan, that's beautiful.' He could tell she was genuinely pleased. 'Thank you so much.'

'Echoes of Orpheus,' he said lightly. But the meaning it all held for him was plain in his face. Tara quickly excused herself.

'Shan't be a sec – just going to check what's in the oven.'

In the kitchen she leaned her back against the wall and let out a long sigh. Dan's unexpected appearance had knocked her sideways. In a life full of uncertainties, this was one she had not been anticipating. To see him again was marvellous, no doubt about it – his handsome, expressive face, those eyes that seemed to focus on her to the exclusion of all else, his wide-shouldered figure now more lean and angular, she thought. Had he lost weight?

She must remember to ask him. Had he been unwell? The thought stabbed at her. Did she care about him then? No, she couldn't let that happen. Everything I've planned is just starting to work, I can't go back on it now, if I get involved it will just foul the whole thing up—

With a start she saw that he had entered the kitchen and was standing regarding her with that quizzical expression she remembered so well. He moved forward and took a glance around, approving the compact little kitchen, like a ship's galley, with its interesting range of herbs and spices standing around.

'Need a hand?' he asked.

'Yes!' Tara grabbed the nearest jar. 'I can't seem to open this.' She moved to the oven and checked the meat dish inside.

'You seem to have taken an interest in cooking since Orpheus.'

'Some, yes.' She laughed. 'But to tell you the truth, most of these herbs and things are here for decoration, not use. Still, you will get a good plain dinner.'

'I thought,' he said quietly, 'that the first meal we were going to share was bacon and eggs.'

'Bacon and eggs at dinner time?' Tara put him off firmly. 'You do have an uncultivated palate, doctor.'

'Well, whatever it is, it smells good.'

'Let's hope it tastes good, too.'

She busied herself assembling the vegetables, getting the rolls and butter on the table, trotting to and fro between the kitchen and the dining area of the sitting room in front of the wonderful window. Dan revelled in the opportunity to study her at length, and took his fill of getting to know her again.

'D'you know, you're getting to be quite famous,' he said at last. 'Lizzie noticed your debut in your new career – now I think I must be the only doctor in North Queensland who buys copies of *Vogue*.'

'You reading *Vogue*?' Tara laughed. 'I can't imagine!'

'You know, Tara. I've never seen you look lovelier.'

'I warned you you should have charged me more.'

'Oh no – I don't just mean in a physical sense. There's a . . . new kind of ease about you. You're more confident, so poised. More at home with yourself somehow. And that has been all your own doing.'

'Don't be so sure, doctor. You and your handiwork had more than a bit to do with it.'

Tara felt good. Dan was not going to pressurize her – on the contrary, his presence made her feel very calm and at peace. She remembered now how soothing she had always found him on Orpheus, soothing yet never boring, simply fully involved with her in a very caring way. She began to relax, as she sensed that he was doing, slowly and pleasantly.

'Are you happy?' he asked after a while. She considered her answer, with that painful honesty he had always so admired in her.

'Yes. Yes. I think so. I love my work.'

'You can tell that from your photographs. But I don't just mean your modelling – your success—'

'No, I know. It's a lot, and it's wonderful, but it's not everything.'

Dan could not think of a way to wrap up the question he wanted to ask in polite nothings.

'How many men do you have in your life?' he asked bluntly. He had to know, though he felt he had no right to ask. Tara stood stock-still before the fridge, caught in the act of reaching for the bottle of wine they were drinking. She considered lying to him – another skill that Stephanie Harper had been severely deficient in, but which Tara Welles had made up on rather successfully – then she looked at his face, and ruled it out. What was the need to lie to this gentle troubled man who so obviously was not fighting his corner, but instead wanted only what would make her happy?

'None.'

Dan laughed. Relief or disbelief? she asked herself.

'Well, I'll be – I believe you Tara, but it's very hard to

do so. I've . . . thought about you . . . a great deal.' Tara found it convenient at this point to don oven gloves and delve into the depths of the cooker to investigate the mystery within, emerging at last pink-cheeked to say with infuriating casualness, 'You haven't told me what you're doing in Sydney yet.'

'Well – it's a medical conference.' In spite of herself Tara could not help throwing him an enquiring look. He needed no more encouragement.

'I'm really here to see you, Tara.' His voice was very low. 'I couldn't just let you . . . disappear. I tried. God knows I tried. But it didn't work. I just had to find you again. Oh, you weren't hard to track down, now that you've got one of the most famous faces in town . . .' He came to a halt, then made a tentative but heartfelt appeal: 'Something happened between us up there in Queensland – didn't it?'

His question hung in the air. Tara was floating in a state of suspended animation, unwilling to do or say anything that might dispel the mood of the moment, so infinitely delicate and poignant. She pondered the true answer to Dan's question – how could she express all her feelings, old and new, let alone her hidden purpose? As she mused, the silence was pierced by the timer on the oven, its insistent buzzing overriding all other considerations.

'Looks as if we're ready!' Tara said brightly. Dan gave a rueful shrug. The moment was shattered.

'Where's the bathroom?' he asked.

'Through the bedroom, turn right.'

Dan put his wineglass down on the work surface and left the kitchen. Tara flew to the cooker, and relieved her feelings in a flurry of activity, getting the meat out of the oven, loading a tray with the hot dishes to be carried through to the table. Suddenly, as she was working, something struck her like a blow – the photographs of Sarah and Dennis! If Dan passed through the bedroom, as he had, he could hardly miss the two pictures so prominently displayed at her bedside. For a second Tara was

225

frozen with horror. Then thinking furiously she sped into the bedroom on silent feet. The door to the bathroom was closed and Dan was not to be seen. Working soundlessly but very fast, she picked up the photographs one by one, carefully folded down their stands, and slipped them into the shallow top drawer of the bedside table. Immediately she whisked back into the kitchen and immersed herself in the last-minute tasks. Dan found her there, humming inconsequentially, acting like a woman who didn't have a care in the world. But he now knew about two more of Tara's cares than he had done before he had entered her bedroom. His heart was as heavy as lead that on a subject as important as this, a part of her life that must mean more to her than any other, her children, for God's sake, he couldn't even ask their names.

After this the conversation, by mutual consent, restricted itself to safe neutral topics.

'Will you serve?' asked Tara as they settled at the table.

'Yeah, sure.'

'Well, how do you like my flat?'

'You've got everything – and a great view.'

'Yes, it is, isn't it?'

'You were lucky to find a place like this.'

'I've always loved Sydney Harbour, and I knew I had to live somewhere where I could see it, beside it, if not on it.' So you *are* a Sydneysider, thought Dan – maybe that's where Sam Johnson should be looking for his missing person . . . But he allowed none of this to show on his face. 'Me too,' he replied. 'Though my enjoyment has been more through postcards and picture books than the real thing in recent years. It's a treat to see the old girl in the flesh, so to speak.'

'Were you born in Sydney, then?'

'Sure was. Lived here all my life till I opened the clinic on Orpheus. But I'll tell you a funny thing.' He laughed.

'What's that?' Tara could not help dimpling in response.

'Do you know – a real confession this – I've never been inside the Opera House.'

226

'Never been inside the . . .' Tara mimed mock horror. 'That's *terrible*. Seriously though, you should try to go while you're here. There's a marvellous season on at the moment – some of my very favourite operas –' Her face wore a dreamy look.

'You do love your music, don't you?' asked Dan affectionately.

'I think there have been times . . . when it's saved my sanity.'

'I've had a great idea. If I can get some tickets while I'm here – would you come with me?' He hesitated, unsure.

Tara gave him a warm, glowing smile. 'I'd love to.'

'Good. That's settled then.' Dan reached for his wineglass. 'Here's to the Opera House, music and – having a good time,' he concluded lightly.

'To all those things,' Tara echoed. She wanted to add 'and to us'. So did Dan, desperately. But neither of them dared. So the toast was never given life but stayed as an unspoken desire trembling on the brink of a fulfilment it could not quite achieve.

Joanna always dreaded it when Jason decided to do an outdoor shoot. The conditions, especially the weather, were always so difficult to control. 'Why the hell do they call this a land of sunshine?' she would wail to her offsider when instead of the expected eight hours of brilliant ultraviolet the elements delivered the equally familiar heavy overcast grey skies and thick banks of cloud. Even worse was one of the typical rainfalls, which would come out of an empty sky in seconds, not creeping up on you with a warning mist and mizzle, but simply coming straight down in streaks of continuous water guaranteed to turn the most expensive designer dress into a dishrag before the model could even sprint for cover.

Yet she had to admit that Jason's outdoor shoots almost always delivered that little extra something that made the finished result great – the sensation of silk and chiffon against brick or concrete, rather than the bland white-out of the studio. Sometimes it was the expression of a passer-by caught in the shot, innocent, curious or outraged. At times Jason even used his mercurial charm to persuade or bully the bystanders to be part of the shoot – Joanna still recalled the memorable occasions when he had involved a whole gang of street labourers in a shoot for ladies' lingerie, with models in negligées, bras and pants languidly draped across half a dozen Aussie superhunks, all bleached hair and naked brown torsos – and it was just one of those things, thought Joanna, stifling a reminiscent sigh, that they all had to be gay.

So she was preparing herself and her girls for an action-packed but rewarding day as she drove into the stylish suburb of Paddington towards the street of elegant terrace houses that Jason had chosen for the location. Sydney's a proper old jigsaw, she thought fondly. She surveyed the lovely old houses, each with its unique frosting of delicate filigree ironwork, with an approving eye. Good old Paddo – dead handy for the city centre, and yet Bondi beach only ten minutes down the road. She found herself looking out for 'For Sale' signs as she drove along.

The location of the shoot advertised itself from a great distance. Joanna had no trouble spotting the sprawl of Jason-type props about the place, especially the centre-piece, an antique Bugatti convertible that his assistants were obligingly hopping in and out of as he sized up shots with polaroid pictures in preparation for the real thing. Most highly visible was the man himself, for he was dangling dangerously from the top of a pair of step-ladders, the extra-tall kind used by paperhangers, snapping away and issuing orders as chirpily as if he were still on the ground. He spotted Joanna from his perch before the others did, and offered a shrill greeting.

'Morning mother! Wonderfully well preserved quarter, this, don't you think? You should feel at home here among the antique restorations, no?'

'Stuff off, Jason,' she responded amiably, and after the ritual exchange of insults they got down to work.

By the time Tara came on the scene at eleven o'clock, Joanna had departed and the 'juices', in Jason's choice phrase, were really flowing. He had completed the shots involving several of Joanna's girls in groups together, 'the crowd scenes', as he called them, and was ready for Tara, jumping up and down with impatience. So she had been hurried into the first gown, and then into the Bugatti, already occupied by two male models, in double-quick time, to avoid frustrating the master in the act of creation. Jason was certainly bubbling along as he began to arrange the trio in what he had decided would be appropriately glamorous and seductive poses.

'OK you, the blond one, lean back against the seat, and Tara, lean onto him . . . onto not into, darling, this is family viewing . . . Johnny in the front, one hand on the wheel, the other arm behind you, looking back at these two, good, good. Now start working on the mood, you'll get a glass of champagne but that's for show not to drink, so I want you to work up the champagne feeling by yourself, so let's think of something golden and good that gives you a buzz – money! how about that? You've just all committed the bank robbery of the century, you've really pulled it off and now you can settle back and enjoy the fruits of your plunder—'

As always, Jason's absurd patter had the effect of relaxing the models and they all began to giggle. Jason carried on quite unperturbed.

'Good, you're getting it, that's the feeling we want in it. Tara, forward a bit, and straighten up, he's not a double bed, and you, Blondie, straighter too, try to look more Germanic about it, pretend you're Von Rippemoff or whoever. Tara, look to camera, boys, look at Tara, fine, we're almost there, be ready to go in just one second . . .'

Holding her pose with the professionalism that had become second nature to her in these few short months, Tara looked idly out at the street as it wound away behind Jason towards a leafy turn at the bottom. Suddenly to her horror she saw a white Rolls Royce convertible come slowly into view, and accelerate when its driver spotted the shoot. In seconds Greg drew up on the other side of the road, his face inscrutable behind heavy sun-glasses. Outwardly cool, inside Tara was in a panic. She had not seen Greg since the night they had had dinner, partly because she wanted to play hard to get, but mainly because she had found the evening with him so disturbing that she wanted to put a little space between them before she tried it again. She knew he could not trace her at home – he did not know where she lived, and she had not been in Sydney long enough to be in the phone book. She trusted the girls at the agency implicitly not to reveal her private address, and they had not done so. But she had not thought that he might track her down at work through one of the thousands of people who know where and when a major shoot is going to take place.

Much to the surprise of the two male models, the centre of the composition suddenly detached herself from the picture. Tara stood up, swung herself out of the car and walked to the foot of Jason's ladder.

'Jason, you need a re-load,' she called.

'Eh? What? I haven't shot anything yet!'

'Give me five minutes,' she called as she hastened off.

'What is this? We only just got going?' Baffled, he looked about him, and anger darkened his face as he saw the white Rolls, the unmoving occupant, and Tara streaking across there as if her life depended upon it.

'Anyone for tennis?' he said bitterly. 'Rippemoff, you don't happen to know any old Nazi tortures do you? Be a good boy, work on it, eh?'

In the Rolls, Greg made no attempt to greet Tara as she approached, but gazed ahead coldly. This was his last throw. He enjoyed the chase – no man more – but when the quarry goes to ground and adamantly refuses to be flushed out of cover, even the keenest sportsman can lose interest in the hunt. He could not be mistaken – he knew Tara was giving him some kind of a come-on on the night they dined. He had at first been intrigued, by her disappearing act, then annoyed, and now angry. One last attempt, he promised himself, then finito. Trouble was, he couldn't stand a woman not giving into him, even though he so utterly despised those who did.

Tara approached at a run, rather in the spirit of the ancient fighters who preferred to hurl themselves upon the swords of the enemy rather than wait to be cut to pieces. She came to rest by the side of the car, out of breath.

'Why haven't you answered my calls?'

She did not reply but looked down at her hands.

'I've left messages all over town for you. And what's with the lady vanishes routine? When I went to your apartment house, you don't live there!'

'I never said I did. I just asked you to drop me there at random because I felt like a walk that night.'

He spoke deliberately and coldly. 'If you're trying to get rid of me, say so. I'm not a complete moron. I can take a hint.'

'It's not that, really.' Time for some sweetness and light, she told herself warningly, I'm in danger of losing him. 'It's just that it's all been frantic. New cover shots, a TV commercial – other things. It's a dog's life. I've been flat out . . . but I've thought about you . . .'

From behind her came the screeching voice of Jason, who had obviously decided that two minutes was as long as Tara was entitled to by way of a break.

'I am a highly strung creative artiste, I work my knackers off to magic into being the world's most wonderful shoot, and the most highly paid person on the set starts holding a fucking *open day*!' His voice rose to a wail. 'Tara – my heart's darling – come back to me!'

Greg eyed him with bilious disfavour.

'Who's he?'

'A friend.' Some instinct told her not to give too much, too soon, to this man.

'How close a friend?'

'Not that close. We have a professional relationship.'

'We have two minutes before the sun goes behind that cloud.' Jason howled.

Tara giggled. 'I also really like the man. He's mad.'

Greg softened. No rival there. And she was pleased to see him.

'Have a coffee with me?'

'Tara! Tara!' Jason had reached the soul in torment stage of his performance.

'I have to get back to work – but sorry.'

'How about the weekend?'

'Haven't planned anything.' She kept her expression neutral, but a tingling began inside her – something's coming, this is it . . .

'Come and spend it with me. At my house.'

Tara felt as if the breath had left her body. With difficulty she got out, 'At . . . your wife's house?'

'Yes.' He was not pleased with that description, she could see.

'I don't know . . . I hadn't thought . . .'

'If you're worried about your reputation, forget it. You'd have your own suite, and there's masses of staff around, a butler type and all. He's an old fart but you'll probably like him.'

Her resolution hardened. 'OK, fine.'

'Terrific.' He was clearly delighted. 'I'll pick you up on Saturday at ten o'clock – if you'll trust me with the secret of where you live.'

'I'll give you a ring to fix in all the details.'

'Don't change your mind now.' He gave her a marvellous smile. God, Greg, you are still the best-looking man in the world, she thought. What am I doing? Can I handle this?

'I won't change my mind,' she said.

'Till Saturday then.' He blew her a kiss, engaged the clutch and drove off. Tara looked around. Behind her the Bugatti was as she had left it, the male models still draped around in their positions inside. But no Jason, not up his ladder, not anywhere. Wildly she looked around. In the distance, a small wiry figure was to be seen stomping off. Jason was quitting the shoot in disgust.

'Jason! Oh Jason! Come back!' And in her high-heeled shoes and designer gown, Tara set off down the road as fast as she could after him.

Chapter Fourteen

Waiting for someone you love, when they are late, has a certain exquisite melancholy to it. So Dan thought as he roamed about the forecourt of the Opera House, looking and longing for Tara to appear. With his usual vice of over-punctuality he had in fact been there unnecessarily early to collect the tickets, order interval drinks, and be ready to welcome her. The first quarter of an hour had passed easily enough in pleasurable anticipation, simply thinking about Tara and the changes in her since Orpheus – the new grace and swing to her walk, the well-styled clustering hair, the delicious enamelled fingernails – like all lovers Dan found that he could think about each of those ten little pearlized shells individually, and indulged himself with the thought of kissing every one.

Then came the disagreeable realization that if she didn't come soon, she would be late – then that she *was* late – then the creeping fear that maybe she wasn't coming at all. All the glitterati of the city swept into the auditorium in a buzz of excited anticipation, and Dan was left behind like a piece of flotsam abandoned by the tide. There is nothing so lonely as being the only person in an empty foyer. Dan stuck it for about thirty seconds and then went out.

Prowling around the reaches of Bennelong Point, where the Opera House rests like a great bird that has just come to land, Dan thought about Tara. What else did he do these days? And yet how little he really knew about her. Leaning on the railings of the forecourt he looked across the water towards Campbell's Cove. At the terminal on Circular Quay an ocean-going liner rode serenely at her berth, brilliantly illuminated from stem to stern. Farther down across the harbour to his right were the lights of

Luna Park, the great funfair coming into its own after dark. All was peace and loveliness, and it left Dan cold. Normally a man who was highly attuned to beauty in any form, Dan found tonight that nothing could shift the burden of love from his heart. Of all the stupid, ridiculous, idiotic things, he told himself angrily, to be falling deeper and deeper in love every minute with a mystery woman who hasn't even told me her real name!

At that moment he heard running feet behind him, and turning saw Tara, flushed and anxious, arriving with much less than her usual poise.

'Oh, I was so worried you would have gone!' she burst out, and Dan was immediately won over by this evidence that she did care after all. 'I could murder Jason. It's all his fault I'm late. He had one of his bees in the bonnet and just kept making me go again and again.' She paused, almost out of breath, and took his hand. 'I'm so sorry.'

Dan's hand in hers felt warm and strong, and she felt an almost irresistible urge to bring it to her breast and hold it there. Instead, suddenly conscious, she dropped it rather abruptly and forced a smile.

'It's OK, it's fine, really. Don't worry about it.'

'Am I too late? What's the exact time? I've lost count!'

Dan looked at his watch. 'Well, the opera has begun, I'm afraid – I couldn't persaude them to hold the curtain for you—' he flashed her an affectionate grin '—so we can't go in till the interval. But I could buy you a drink in the bar.'

'Oh heck—' Tara was crushed. 'I really love this opera. I didn't want to miss the first act.' Her lower lip jutted like a motherless foal's.

Dan came to a decision. 'Look, let's go and see it properly another time. We'll do something else. How would that suit you?'

'That's a great idea!'

'What do you want to do instead?'

'What do *you* want to do instead?' she returned teasingly.

'I'd like to take you somewhere. That's if you don't mind . . .'

Tara groaned. 'I don't mind what we do as long as I can sit down and take the weight off my feet!'

'Done!' Dan was delighted with the turn of events – 'and I'll get tickets for another day – when you aren't working for that little twerp!' Laughing, they turned back towards the city.

Dan's proposed destination was not far away geographically, but in every other way it was a journey into another world. Wherever the tracks are in Sydney, Pyrmont is definitely on the wrong side of them. Situated at the tip of the inlet of Darling Harbour it received all the huge cargo ships at its busy wharves, and dispensed goods to all over the island via its network of roads and railway lines. The whole area looked like an abandoned building site, with huge cranes sleeping drunkenly in the moonlight, and the rough little houses and stone cottages crouched under the concrete flyovers as if they had no right to be there. Its desirability had not been improved by the siting there of a massive power station, now closed down, and the fish markets, where even the freshest of the luscious fat fish which fed the tables of the city flavoured the air with their unmistakable smell. Stephanie Harper had never been to Pyrmont.

Dan directed their taxi unerringly through a warren of back streets till they reached a run-down-looking pub. Tara's curiosity grew. Dan caught her look of interrogation as he paid the driver, and said, 'Thought it was time to fill you in on a bit of my background.' Without elaborating further he took her by the arm and led her into the place. Inside a row of gnarled old-timers propping up the bar surveyed the intruders with the resentment of regulars. The walls were tiled in a noxious green and hung with lifebelts, there was a thick stink of beer fumes and cigarette smoke, and there was no carpet on the floor.

'A real waterfront dive,' Dan said with a grin as he conducted her in, 'and a piece of my past.'

'Tell me.'

'I was a Pyrmont boy,' he said simply. 'This was my Dad's local. The hours I've spent sitting on that step as a child, waiting for him to come out . . . talk about a misspent youth—'

They moved up to the bar where a wizened old codger grudgingly made room. Tara was fascinated, absorbing the whole thing without comment. So this was Dan's boyhood! She contrasted it with her life at Eden and felt a spring of pity for the child he had been.

' 'S funny,' Dan commented, puzzled. 'The place always used to be so crowded.'

'Times change,' she said gently. She did not want to spoil the mood of this unusual moment.

'That was my old man's spot over there,' said Dan, nodding. 'You know, he'd be here every day after work, every single day except for Sundays. He kept this business going. I was supposed to bring him home, but I never could get him away. Then Mum'd come in herself in the end, and drag him off home for his dinner.'

'Hey, you!' A raucous cry interrupted Dan's recollections. 'I know you!' It was the barmaid, bearing down on Dan with a beam that split her face from ear to ear.

'Hello, Dot.' Dan's greeting was easily outdone by hers.

'Danny Marshall! As I live and breathe! Well now, don't tell me – it must be thirty years! Frank Marshall's boy. Well I never!'

'That's right.'

'Didn't you want to be – hang on – a doctor?'

'Yes, I did.'

'God, I remember – you were always bandaging my bloody cat!' Tara had to join in with Dot's infectious guffaw. Dan sat quietly smiling, obviously enjoying himself. He's wonderful, she thought, at home on any level.

'I've been promoted since those days, Dot,' Dan spoke up merrily. 'They allow me to practise on people now.'

'D'you meantersay—' Dot's eyes widened '– that you actually ended up being a real bloody doctor?'

'That's right.'

'Well, fancy that! You hear more pipe dreams and wishful thinking on my side of the bar than actual achievements. I'll have to get you to look at my bunions!'

They all laughed together in companionship.

'Dot, let me introduce you. This is Tara.'

'Pleased to meet you, Tara. Now how about a drink?'

'Beer for me,' said Tara.

'Make it two, would you Dot?'

Their conversation was interrupted by a discontented punter clearly unhappy with the attention that the newcomers were receiving.

'Ey Dot! How about a beer down here?'

'Just a minute!' Dot roared back majestically. 'I'm talking! Stick yer tongue down yer throat for a minute, can't you, and just wait?' She turned back to Dan and Tara, rolling her eyes melodramatically. 'No bloody manners, this bunch.'

'You must have known Dan longer than anyone else?' Tara felt at home with this large motherly woman in her dress striped like a deckchair, and wanted to pump her for whatever she could glean about this man who interested her so much.

'Danny Marshall?' Again Dot's laugh treated them to a complete survey of her array of gold teeth. Outsize chunks of amber clunked together on her outsize bosom. 'Used to know him when he was knee-high to a sparrow. Cheeky little devil, though. Used to steal all the milk money people left on their step in the street!'

Tara looked at Dan, stunned.

'It's true,' he confessed, a little shame-faced. 'Until I got caught in the act. Scared the living daylights out of me, that did. I never did it again!'

'Even so,' said Tara, amused, 'it's hard to think of you as a juvenile delinquent.'

Dot had gone off on another track. 'Didn't you used to live round in Wetherill Street?'

'Yep . . a little weatherboard house down there . . .'

'Dot!' It was the discontented customer again. 'Look, I'm dying of flaming thirst down here. M'skin's cracking! I'm spitting chips!'

'I'll be with you in a minute!' To Dan and Tara she said, 'No more for *him*, or he'll finish up in the deadhouse. You two sit yourself down comfy at a table. I'll get your beers to you in a shake of a lamb's tail. On the house!'

Together they crossed to a small table and sat down. There was a new mood between them, warm and trusting. Tara felt completely relaxed, and without caring what it looked like, slipped off her shoes under the table and enjoyed the relief. What the hell! Dan of all people knew how old she and her feet were. She had no physical pretence to keep up in front of him. As Dot came up with the beers she noticed the fine leather high-heeled shoes cast aside, their tailored elegance in strong contrast with the bare, cigarette strewn floor.

'Ooooh, I know just how you feel love,' she cried.

'Cheers Dot.' Dan raised his glass to her in greeting as she moved off, like a galleon among the tugs and barges of the withered old men around her. Then he mused quietly.

'You know, we used to have a backyard so small that I could spit across it in a strong wind. Every weekend throughout the summer a mob of us kids'd go down to the harbour, and we'd dive for the pennies that were chucked to us by the tourists. I guess the sharks felt too sorry for us to bother.'

Tara sat very still, entranced.

'Either that, or they weren't hungry. My old man used to say there was so much other garbage in there that the garbos didn't fetch out, that the sharks wouldn't have us when they could get something better! But later I found out that he never stopped bragging about me to his mates. "My Danny," he'd say, "Bravest bloody kid in the neighbourhood." Fact is . . . I kept him in cigarettes.'

'I wish I'd known you then,' she said softly. 'I'd like to have been able to dive for pennies with you.'

'Well . . .' he took her hand, understanding the feeling in her heart. 'It still has fond memories.'

They sat in silence, very close, their spirits at peace with one another. Tara had never before experienced this sensation of being perfectly at home with a man, open, trusting, unworried and so drawn to him for his love and courage. She could find only one honest expression for it if she listened to the voice of her heart.

'Dan,' she whispered, 'when we leave here . . . let's go to your hotel.'

He looked at her in total astonishment, which gave way to a deep joy when he read her face and knew that she meant it. He leaned across and kissed her. They sat together, holding hands for a long time before they left.

The gentle mood of glimmering understanding between them persisted all the way back to the hotel. Together they ascended to Dan's room and he opened the door. Across the room the window stood open to his balcony, and the night was bright with stars.

'Don't put the light on,' Tara said. She walked out to the balcony to enjoy the beauty of the night. Dan joined her there and for a moment they stood side by side. Then he placed his hand on her shoulder and turned her to face him. She was very conscious of his nearness now. With a sigh he put his arms around her and drew her into him. She could feel the hardness of his body and the warmth of his arms round her waist. He held her gently, then lowered his head and kissed her.

His mouth was marvellous – she felt she had wanted it for a long time. But without warning she found herself trembling, and suddenly all the old fears rose up to haunt her. She pulled away from him.

'Dan . . . I don't think I . . .'

She turned to look out over the sleeping city, unwilling to see the hurt in his eyes. A moment passed, then Dan stepped up behind her and lovingly folded her in his arms. A very sad feeling trembled in the air between them. After a while he spoke quietly in her ear.

'Tara – my darling – you don't have to prove anything. Just be yourself. It's not the glamorous successful model who attracts me. It's the warm, intelligent lady I met up in Queensland – who had time then for a rather withdrawn banana-land doctor – who loves good music . . . barbecuing . . . and sea shells.'

Lightly he kissed the springing hair on the top of her head, marvelling at its fragrance. She listened spellbound as he continued.

'And I'll bet that when she was a little girl she was the bravest kid in the neighbourhood too. I've come to care for her – care about her – more than all the world.'

Tara was very close to tears. Yet in her sadness was a sweet joy of great intensity. Her soul filled with the wonderment of it, her body responded to his closeness in ways she had never felt before. Turning within his arms she reached up and kissed him, kissed him fully, possessed herself of that mouth that she now realized she had longed to know since first she met him. Then she took his face between her hands and ran her fingers lightly over his wide forehead, his silky eyelids, the hair curling above his ears and the roughness of his jaw. In a passion she traced the outline of his mouth with one index finger, then kissed him, again and again and again.

Tenderly Dan stroked her neck and shoulders, murmuring words of love. The satin of her skin seemed to scorch his fingers, such was the strength of his desire for her, but he schooled himself to patience and consideration. Unhurriedly his hands found her breasts beneath the thin fabric of her evening gown, and he was touched to the depths of his unassuming soul to feel from her engorged nipples that she was aroused already for him. Tara let out a deep shuddering sigh, and feeling for the long, strong hands on her breasts held them there rejoicing. Then she placed her hands round his waist so that he could continue with the delicious caressing, soothing, exciting sensations rising up in her.

She allowed herself to be led across the room to the bed, where Dan sat her down, removing his shirt before he joined her. With infinite gentleness and patience he made love to her, kissing her all over her face, her eyes, her neck and shoulders, never forcing, never hurrying. She felt a tingling anticipation, longing for each touch before it came, then longing even more for the next. Yet at the same time she was at peace, as trusting of Dan as Maxie had been of her when she first took him up in his sorrowful state of neglect. Slowly, and fumbling rather, he began to undo the fastening at the front of her dress, his normal deftness quite overwhelmed by the strength of his love. Eagerly she shrugged out of the light garment and waited for him to slip off her bra.

Dan never afterwards forgot his first sight of the perfect beauty of Tara's naked breasts, gleaming white in the moonlight, perfect globes, the nipples tilting towards him in irresistible invitation. He bent his head and tenderly brushed the soft skin with his lips, marvelling at its smooth sheen, then kissed the delicate nipples. She put her hands on his shoulders and lightly traced the arch of his back. I love every bone in his body, she thought dreamily. He lifted his head to search out her urgent mouth once more, then pushed her back on the bed. One thought formed up in her mind irresistibly, come on top of me, Dan, come inside me, I want you so—

She caught herself up, in one second flying from love to fear. What? Love him, want him so badly my whole body aches for him? Dear God, no! In a piercing flash of insight Tara recognized for the first time the passion she was capable of with the right man, the power of her love and her desires. But not now, her mental voice was shrilling, not him, I can't let this happen, I'll ruin everything . . . She was rigid with terror and panic. To his growing dismay Dan felt her suddenly become as stiff as a board under his hands and along the length of his body as it lay beside her.

'Dan!' she cried out, and again 'Dan!'

'My darling?' He was horror-struck. 'What is it?'

Feverishly she leapt from the bed and began to struggle back into her clothes, once again in her own mind the ugly, ungainly woman she thought she had buried in the swamps of the Alligator River.

'I'm . . . I'm sorry,' she muttered, almost laughing with bitterness at the inadequacy of this, Stephanie's habitual phrase. 'I'm sorry—'

Dan had not moved. 'What is it?' he asked, very low. 'Please – if this means anything to you at all – please *trust me*?'

'I do trust you,' Tara said monotonously. 'It's just all a mistake, that's all.' She was dressed now and bolting for the door. Galvanized into action Dan leapt off the bed and intercepted her before she could get across the room. She could feel the pain and anger emanating from him in waves.

'Mistake?' he cried. 'I don't understand this. I don't understand anything. Trust me enough to tell me what the *hell* is going on!'

It was the first time she had ever heard him swear, unlike Greg who scattered oaths as freely as smiles. Shocked and frightened as always by men's anger, she tried to collect herself.

'We can't see one another again. I'm sorry. It was all my fault. It was unfair of me.' Painfully she began to cry, already suffering the anguish of losing him, the torture of tearing him living from her heart. Her vision misted with tears, she fought her way to the door, striking away his restraining arm, found the catch and was through the door.

'Tara!' Dan's despairing appeal followed her down the corridor.

'Forgive me, Dan, forgive . . . goodbye,' escaped from her as she fled stumbling away, but never knew if he had heard. And nothing, nothing, could bring peace or under-standing to the man who lay all night in a lonely bed hugging his emptiness in place of the woman whom he now knew he could not live without, even at the moment when it seemed that he would have to.

*

'Too slow! It's too slow. And the snow isn't falling right. Doesn't look like snow at all. Looks like bird shit!'

Jason was not in a good mood – but then he rarely was these days. Secrets have a life of their own, and a way of getting out, even when two people who share one keep it silent and unspoken. So Jason's staff had noticed that he was always more than usually short-tempered on a Tara day, when other times he could perform the most boring or demanding work with his normal high spirits. Today was due to be trying anyway – the craziness of the fashion world demanded that they had to do a winter wear promo while wilting under the heat and humidity of Australia's best summer weather. And Jason was not happy with the snow. But he was even less happy with his top model.

Days now had gone by since Tara had seen Dan, but the passage of time had not made his loss any easier to bear. Tara was like one bereaved. She had lost all her joy and though she clung even tighter to her secret purpose it was cold comfort for the destruction of Dan's warm love, the living dismemberment of that miracle of new birth. But she could not allow herself to be deflected, turned from her chosen path, not while Greg like a killer tiger roamed free, free to stalk and bring down new prey. And what she had not realized till the night in Dan's bedroom, she could not be free until she had freed herself of him – could not give herself to another man while the dark shadow of the one who in spite of everything *was still her husband* haunted her waking hours and talked like a demon lover through her dreams. Vengeance had to be all her passion. She had to repay. But it was hard, and it hurt so much, her soul was bruised and bleeding to its core. And Jason kept after her like a pickpocket.

'You! Madame in the fur. Tara Welles, is it?' Jason's sarcasms were hurtful, but mere pinpricks in the face of everything else. 'You are too *slow*! I want you to spin, dance, revolve in this snow like the snow fucking fairy! Got it? Get with it!'

'I'm sorry, Jason,' she mumured mechanically, plucking a handful of the snow flakes from her mouth.

'Oh, you're *sorry!* She's sorry,' he informed the studio at large. 'OK, go again.'

There was an intermission of hostilities while Tara diligently spun, danced, and revolved, and Jason clucked frenetically. Then his fragile patience snapped again, and Tara felt she did not have the strength to deal with him.

'Tilt! Up! Look *up*, damn you, are there any eyes in that face? OK, stop, cut, finish, kill the so-called snow.'

Tara came to a halt. Jason spoke very coldly and deliberately.

'You couldn't manage a little more? I mean, is there any more to give? Look, I don't know what's the matter with you today, I don't know where your mind is – but it certainly isn't here on your work, is it? You know, you've got about as much spontaneity as a two-year-old *corpse!*' He was winding himself up to a frenzy of irritability, and Tara was not the only hapless victim. 'I said kill the snow,' Jason screamed to his assistant 'kill that bloody snow out there, or I'll kill *you*. You have to switch off the wind machine, you cretin – God, how do I come to be employing such *morons*, just get it shut down!' He turned back to Tara. She could see that he was seething with rage. 'Just one thing for you, and I hope you're listening to it – this is my profession and I am a professional and *I have got no time to waste on amateurs!*' With a gesture of abandon he addressed the whole studio. 'Well, don't all stand there like virgins at a wake! Go home. You're finished. *GO HOME!*' He turned blindly and charged into the little room off the studio that served as his private office, and slammed the door with a vicious thud.

Minutes passed. Nobody moved. Tara felt too exhausted to stir. I'm all used up, she thought. I've got nothing left. Then quietly Jason's door opened and he re-entered. His rage had left him and he looked like a chastened little boy. He walked up to Tara and took her hand.

'We'll all have a good long weekend, OK? Take Monday

to rest, and be here nice and early on Tuesday. We can crack it, kiddo. Don't forget – I love you. Let's be friends, eh?'

It's not hard to feel sorry for most of the people who find their way into a police station. Even in a city centre there are still more weak than wicked, more people with bad luck than bad dispositions, and a lot of what society calls crime is what most of us get away with most of the time. So thought Ted Druitt, station sergeant of Circular Quay Police Station. It was this philosophy that helped him to get through an often difficult job, and still have enough basic humanity left to offer a solitary soul banged up overnight the comfort of a cigarette, or to make contact for them with someone at home who would be worried about their absence.

But some people you just can't help, and you don't want to. The well-dressed woman brought in screaming drunk that night was one of them. She'd smelled like trouble from the word go. Usually the experience of being brought into the station sobered them down straight off. Not this one. It had taken two good blokes to bring her in, and even then they couldn't leave her on her own with the police-woman – she'd had a crack at her would've broken her jaw if it had connected. In the end they'd just locked her up and left her to get over it.

'Looks as if you were lucky to get out of there alive,' Ted observed as the officers returned.

'Who, her?' Barry, the senior of the two policemen, threw a contemptuous look over his shoulder in the direction of the cell. 'Honestly, she's that pissed she doesn't know Arthur from Martha. Y'oughta hear the things she's shouting – "You can't arrest me, my husband's a lawyer".' He mimicked an affected female voice, his hand on his hip.

'Where'd you find her?'

'Trying to attack another woman she said had pinched the taxi she hailed – lucky for her that one wants no trouble, won't prosecute.'

'Well, if she swipes an officer again,' said Ted, '*we* will, and that's for sure. What a mess!'

'She's not a bad-looker though, sarge,' said Barry reminiscently, 'not bad at all, as tarts go. When she quietens down y'could get your end in there, no problem, she'd cock it up to anyone tonight.'

Ted sighed. 'Y'know, sometimes I think you came down in the last shower, son. Let me just forcibly remind you that there's nothing like that in the Police Manual. Go by the book, son, that's the name of the game. And don't forget – it's just possible her husband *is* a lawyer.'

Tara drove home from the abortive snow-scene shoot in a state of emotional exhaustion, almost completely drained. Tomorrow was her weekend with Greg, which she had firmly determined would bring her much more closely to her goal. But it would be a major ordeal to be with him for so long, and also to undergo a reunion with the staff at the mansion, especially Matey, even though they would not be party to it. Thank heavens Sarah and Dennis would not be there! That she simply could not face. But she knew they would definitely be away at their boarding schools at this time of the year. Her reunion with them . . . that was something else. For now, she had to get herself in the right frame of mind for what was coming. It was time to cosset herself, somehow shake off all these dreadful nagging anxieties and become the Tara whom Greg Marsden would expect at ten o'clock the next morning.

So she treated herself to an evening of the purest idle luxury: first of all a deep, hot, scented bath in which she simply lay like a statue and allowed all the tension to drain out of her tired limbs, then a deliciously sinful supper, crusty brown bread and gooey cream cheese, crisp cucumber, peppers and tomatoes, with a glass of dry white wine, followed by a rare treat, a rich, succulent slab of dark chocolate cake. All this she ate in bed while catching up on her fashion magazine reading with the comforting weight of Maxie on her feet as he snoozed and purred all in the same action. Then feeling dreamy and relaxed she prepared for bed and slipped easily into a restful slumber.

Restful, but not long enough. Tara was definitely not ready to come back to the world when her telephone woke her, shrilling aggressively into her ear at six o'clock in the morning. Fighting her way back up to consciousness she experienced that blend of anxiety and resentment that any call at an unseasonal hour produces. Wearily she picked up the phone.

'Hello?'

'Tara, hello, it's me.'

'Who . . . who . . .?'

'It's Jilly.'

'Jilly . . .?'

'Oh Tara, I know this is awful, I'm so sorry to wake you this early – but I terribly need a favour.'

Tara gathered a few of her wandering wits. 'Where are you?'

'At Circular Quay Police Station. Could you pick me up?'

'Yeah . . . yeah. Look. I'll be there in . . . say half an hour.'

'Oh thanks. Thanks so much. Oh Tara, you're a real friend—'

' 'Bye, Jilly.' She put the phone down with a crash. Oh Jilly. Whatever next?

But the Jilly whom Tara picked up at the police station half an hour later was far from contrite about her escapade. Tired, cold, and far from well, yes, but still the desperate defiance that had landed her in trouble hung about her like a bad odour.

'It wasn't anything really serious,' she said defensively. as Tara helped her down the steps of the station to the pavement. 'It was only drunk and disorderly – it's not a crime!'

Tara made no comment. Jilly was still unsteady on her feet and it took all Tara's efforts to keep her upright. Jilly

248

stumbled and swung heavily on Tara's tall but slender frame, and they had to fight to stay upright.

'Oh Tara, I'm sorry – I shouldn't be doing this to you.'

'It's all right.'

'I'm grateful to you, really I am – thanks. It's just that there doesn't seem to be anyone else left to call any more. Phillip's away – and I haven't seen anyone else for ages. I used to have lots of friends,' she added mournfully. 'But . . . they just went.'

Tara asked the one question she wanted to know the answer to.

'Why didn't you call Greg?'

Jilly's voice rose hysterically. 'Oh, I couldn't. I simply couldn't. This . . . isn't the first time, actually. It makes him so angry and . . . he gets violent when he's angry.' Her hand rose to her cheek as if in memory of a blow.

They had reached Tara's car and she helped Jilly into the passenger seat before letting herself into the driver's side. In the privacy of the car, Jilly waxed maudlin, confidential and threatening by turns, spilling her soul in her habitually self-centred way.

'I should be able to count on Greg Marsden! But it's been awful lately, it seems to be getting worse and worse. He hasn't made love to me for – oh God, I forget the last time. I don't know what to do.' She turned to Tara with a frantic air. 'D'you know, I've been giving him money since Stephanie died? The past few weeks I've had to pay all his bills. Oh, he can't treat me like this!' Her tears began and she wept loudly in self-pity, then her mood changed again. 'I could tell a lot of tales about Mr Marsden if I wanted to,' she said vindictively. 'But I wouldn't. Oh, Tara, there isn't really anything between you and him, is there? I'm so frightened of losing him. That's the worst thing of all, to lose someone you love . . .' She tailed off into a feeble snivelling.

Tara sat stock-still, consumed with contempt. Jilly's pathetic weakness was fast bringing her own punishment on her head, she thought. She looked at the dishevelled figure beside her, her hair a mess, her dress soiled and torn, and one knee out of her tights where she had fallen over. In the cold light of the early morning, she looked like something that had been washed up – she wore a greenish pallor and her eyes had a dull and fishy stare. She thought back to the wedding, Jilly in her Fifth Avenue outfit, bandbox neat and smart, and felt a passing sensation of something that could have been pity. But with professional swiftness she knocked it straight on the head.

'Come on then, Jilly,' she said evenly. 'Let's get you home.' She switched on the engine.

Chapter Fifteen

'Ten o'clock! How very punctual you are, Greg!'

'On the button for Miss Welles – the chauffeur-driven Rolls. Here, let me give you a hand with your bag.'

Tara allowed herself to be ushered into the front seat of the splendid motor and they were on their way. Greg was in high spirits, humming a little tune as they drove along. She knew he was thinking of her as virtually won, the conquest secure except for the simple act of mastery. I may surprise you yet Mr Marsden, she thought coldly, even while her face wore a look of eager attentiveness.

Tara had not found it easy to pull herself round for the effort of this weekend after the lowering encounter with Jilly some hours earlier. But fortunately she had got back in time to do her full morning's routine of half an hour's brisk work-out – she still did the exercises she had learned at the clinic on Orpheus Island and they now had become second nature to her. This was followed by a toning bath, then full body rub, and finally a facial. By ten o'clock she had been groomed and ready, even anticipating the forthcoming duel of wits with a sense of real excitement.

Greg drove out to the Harper mansion on Darling Point at an easy speed – there was no need to hurry. This gave Tara a chance to adjust more slowly to the thousand and one remembered features of the route, without the danger of suddenly betraying herself. At last the familiar gates came into view. Greg operated the remote control from inside the car, and the great white house lay before her once again.

'There it is,' said Greg expansively. 'What do you think of it?'

'From what I can see,' she chose her words with care '– it looks very nice.'

'The house is all right,' said Greg as he engaged the clutch and the car moved off, 'but I'm planning major changes inside. The interior décor was my wife's testimonial to being her own person after her father died. She got a bit pale, I think, living in the old man's shadow.'

Greg was pleased with this statement. He felt it expressed just the right amount of solicitude for his late lamented, along with just the right degree of distance from her memory.

'I like the house fine,' he continued. 'But I just can't wait to get rid of all her stuff inside. You'll see.'

Oh I will, thought Tara, I will.

'Before we arrive – I just want to tell you I've arranged a surprise. I didn't tell you you'll be meeting Stephanie's children.' Tara froze. 'I asked their schools to let them come home for the weekend – they're home a lot anyway, Bill McMaster takes them out and has them round to his place.' She could not speak. Greg threw her a look and caught her concern.

'I hope you don't mind,' he said hastily. 'I thought it might help to convince you I'm a family man at heart.'

They had arrived at the house. Greg pulled up, and turned to look her full in the eyes.

'You see, Tara,' he said with a sigh, 'you're the first woman I've ever brought here since Stephanie died. So . . . be prepared for a cool reception from the kids. Don't let it get you down. By lunchtime you'll have them eating out of your hand.'

With a reassuring smile and a squeeze of her hand, Greg jumped from the car and moved round to the passenger seat to open Tara's door. As she got out of the car, she caught a movement on the balcony above the main doorway, looked up, and saw a girlish form whisk back into the master bedroom within. Sarah, it had to be. Tara stood still, to subdue if possible the wild beating of her heart.

Meanwhile, Matey had come out to give a hand with the bags. He glanced at Tara as Greg introduced them, then looked at her more closely. Surely she was the woman he had seen outside the mansion all those months ago? Ah, now he had his explanation. She must have been sweet on Mr Marsden then and came to suss out his house and territory. Well, she's landed him at last. He turned away and entered the house. Tara heaved a huge inward sigh of relief. She had quite forgotten the encounter she had had with Matey so long ago, before she began modelling. At least that had passed off without awkwardness. Was there anything else she should have remembered?

As if in answer to her unspoken thought, a deep bark sounded from within the house, and in a second a huge Alsatian came bounding through the door. In a frenzy of welcome, he hurled himself upon Tara, almost knocking her over, and made much of her in every way that he could find to express his feelings. Greg regarded this pantomime of affection with astonishment.

'My, you are special,' he said slowly. 'That's Kaiser. He was Stephanie's dog. He doesn't normally like strangers.'

'Oh, I've got a way with animals,' Tara dismissed it lightly. But bending down to pet Kaiser, she tried hard to soothe the almost demented dog before he gave her away – and if a few tears fell onto his smooth sleek coat, who noticed them but Kaiser?

'In we go, then.' Greg took her arm and steered her towards the door. They crossed over the threshold with Kaiser still at Tara's heels, or gambolling joyfully about her feet. As soon as they were inside, Greg turned on the dog, and disregarding the creature's pitiful whines, booted him out of the door and slammed it in his face.

'There you are, Tara,' he said. 'You won't be bothered with him any more. I'll show you to your room.'

Tara looked around her. Everything was just the same as she had left it. She felt a stab of physical pain at the thought of all the happy hours spent here before – before Greg. All this was the same, but she? She was almost a stranger, in what was still her own home.

'I'll show you where you're sleeping,' Greg pursued,

quite unaware of her inner turmoil, 'then I'll disappear to chase up lunch. I've had to let most of the staff go – still got Matey of course, and for today I've brought in a temporary – she's stumbling round the kitchen somewhere – it's so hard to get good help these days.' He thought he was doing rather well at the domestic stuff. 'Still, just as long as everything's all right for you . . . I want this to be perfect . . . in every way . . .'

He led her upstairs and along the corridor, past the master bedroom that had been Stephanie's until they reached the guest suite. Tara stifled a sigh of relief. Greg put down her bag and moved to the door.

'I shan't be far away' – he paused, to allow this to sink in – 'so if you want anything, day or night, don't hesitate . . .'

'I'm fine, really.' It struck her forcibly that she was alone in a bedroom with him for the first time since their parting.

'I'm glad you're here.' He only needed a tiny bit of encouragement to move towards her, she knew. She was as taut as a violin string.

'I am too, Greg,' she said with a smile. 'Now if you'll just give me a moment to sort myself out –'

'Of course. See you later.' And he was gone.

Tara crossed to the open window and gulped in great draughts of the fresh air, heaving out huge sighs of relief. Then she grimly pulled herself together. It's going to be a long weekend, she told herself. Hold on. Just hold on. As she stood there, she heard a quiet knock at the door.

'Come in!' she called.

The door opened and there stood Dennis. In an instant Tara ran through a whole gamut of emotions, as joy, rapture, delight, were chased away by the fear of discovery. She longed to rush forward and take him in her arms, but knew she could not. What she could do, though, was to feast her eyes on him, take in every detail of his appearance, and feed her starving heart with the food she had been lacking for so long.

'You're Tara Welles, aren't you?' he asked brightly.

'And you must be Dennis.' Her voice sounded strange even to her own ears.

'I know who you are,' he went on, with the confiding manner of the young. 'I know everything about you. My sister used to cut pictures of you out of magazines. She loves clothes and things – you know, like girls do. Would you like me to show you round?'

Tara looked at him. He was taller than she remembered, but in every other way still the same – the bright friendly eyes, so interested in everything and everyone, the cropped hair, the same freckles, even the same brace on his teeth. There was a new sense of sadness about him, but he did not look like a boy who had deeply suffered. Soon, soon, my darling, she promised him in her heart as she had done so many times in the privacy of her bedroom, talking aloud to his photograph and kissing his image behind the chill glass. Soon, soon, we'll be together again. In the meantime, I'm doing the best I can.

'A guided tour?' she said. 'I'd be delighted.'

They left the guest suite and walked down the corridor. As they passed the master bedroom, the sound of music was apparent.

'What's that music?' Tara asked.

'Oh that's Sass – my sister Sarah. She digs good music, just like my mum did.'

'How about you?'

'I'm kind of a protestant with catholic tastes, really.'

Tara smiled. He was so easy to talk to, she might never have been away. 'Do I get the feel of a rock 'n' roller?'

He grinned. 'Sort of.'

Together they descended the wide stairs and came to a halt under the great portrait of Max Harper hanging at the bottom.

'That's my grandfather,' Dennis indicated. 'Some people reckon I'm like him, but I don't think I am. I'm not ambitious like he was. I'm not really into money and power . . . just into whatever makes me feel good.'

'Well, I don't suppose he was at your age,' Tara said amused. 'Just give it time!'

Through the sitting room lay the terrace, inviting in the morning sunshine.

'Would you like to see the garden?' Dennis quizzed her.

'Why not?' As they moved down over the smooth lawns, she asked quietly, 'Dennis – do you mind my being here?' He thought about it.

'No, I don't mind. It's Sass, my sister, I told you – well, she's my half-sister really – she really is taking it hard.'

'I gather that you and Sass don't like Greg too much?'

'Not very much.' He hesitated, then as if deciding that he could trust her, rushed on. 'To us, you see, he was just another one of Mum's mistakes. She couldn't seem to find the things she wanted in life. Mum liked simple things really. It's just that she let people push her around, make her believe she had to do what they wanted, instead of just being herself. Sarah's the opposite. She's like old Max – sort of stubborn.'

'Who are you like?' Tara's heart was aching with love for this boy, so clear-sighted, so loving. 'Are you like your father?'

Dennis laughed unselfconsciously. 'I don't think so! He was husband number two. He was a research scientist, an American. He lives in the States.'

'Do you hear from him?' Tara did not know whether she wanted him to say no or yes.

'Sure. He sent us a sympathy card after the accident!' They laughed together, in perfect harmony and talking and joking wandered on down through the gardens.

By the time they were returning to the house, Tara felt that she had overcome the initial handicap of being Greg's girlfriend enough to establish a real bond with Dennis. They walked together up the wide stairs, and past the door of the master bedroom.

'Is that your mother's bedroom?' Tara asked.

'How did you know?'

She smiled at him. 'Oh, just something about the way you looked when you passed by it before.'

'I'd like to show it you, but we'd better not go in there. Sarah makes it her hideaway when she's home, to hole up and play music on Mum's stereo, and she's in kind of a stinking mood today. She hasn't been seen since she arrived. But she'll come out when she gets hungry.' He gave her a conspiratorial grin. 'Would you like to see my room?'

'Oh, I thought you'd never ask!'

'Well, when people are given the guided tour, they generally give my room a miss . . . because it's such a mess!'

He led her across the landing and threw open a door with a comical flourish to reveal a typical boy's room, colourful and chaotic. Posters of jet aeroplanes covered the walls, and from the ceiling hung models of aircraft of all sizes and vintages. Dennis dashed about making feeble efforts to tidy up. He had worked hard during the past months, Tara thought, as her eye caught a number of new additions to the collection. She remembered to make a proper show of surprise.

'Heavens, did you build all these yourself?'

'Yep.' He was obviously flattered. 'They come in kits, then you put them together.' He showed her a ferocious-looking Focke-Wulf from World War Two. 'This one was really difficult.'

'Yes, I can see it must have been. You've done it well.'

Dennis glowed. 'I want to be a test pilot when I leave school,' he confided.

'Wouldn't that be a bit dangerous?'

'Nah . . . I can handle it.'

'Well . . .' The familiar anxiety of a mother gnawed at her. 'Don't you think there's plenty of time yet to think about your future?'

'That's what my mother always thought. But I'm not going to waste my life, not a single second!'

There was a real firmness in his voice. Oh, if only I'd

known that, she thought. I've wasted so much *time*, sitting around all through my teens and twenties waiting for my handsome prince –

She pulled herself up, frightened by the ferocity of her thoughts. Well, I know better now, she told herself. And I'm doing better too. This is my life, and I'm living it. And I'll live it even better when I've taken care of my . . . unfinished business. I'll live it with you, my son. Soon, soon . . .

As if sensing her unspoken thought, Dennis crossed to his bedside, picked up a photograph and said abruptly, 'That's my mother.' Tara found herself looking into the anxious, kind face of Stephanie, her dead self. She studied it carefully. It really might have been the image of another woman, and no relation to her at all. Tara found the courage to broach the question that had been tormenting her ever since the accident.

'How have you been managing without her?'

'Oh, that hasn't been too bad . . . she was always away quite a lot before, she had to be with the business, you see. Sometimes she took us with her, and once she took us on afterwards to go ski-ing – that was great!' His face flushed with enthusiasm. 'Well, great in one way – I fell, and broke my leg, and had to spend all the rest of the time in bed. I thought it'd be terrible, because Sass and all the others went off every morning and didn't come back until it was dark. But Mum never left me . . . she sat by the bed and read to me . . . and played games. She even had her bed moved into my room and slept there in case I had any pain in the night or wanted her . . .' He was almost in a trance now, looking back on a scene that was still alive for him. 'Before that happened, I never thought she loved me . . . stupid . . .'

Suddenly he came round, and turned to Tara fiercely.

'I don't care what they say! I just don't believe my mother's dead. I know what everyone thinks – but someday, I just know she's going to walk in here and some people – *some people*! – are in for a shock!' He hunched his shoulders, and moved swiftly across to the window, unwilling to let her see that he was crying.

Tara stood paralysed, deathly pale, and not trusting herself to speak. Her sadness was so intense she felt it as a hot pain at the back of her throat. She dug her nails into her palms so that that hurt would distract her from her desperate urge to cry with Dennis. Slowly, slowly, she regained control. Then she moved to where Dennis was standing in the window, laid her arm across his frail bony shoulders and held him tight without speaking. They remained so for a long time.

Like Tara, Phillip Stewart knew what it was to feel like a stranger in his own house. When he had answered Jilly's call at his office in New York, he had been unable to repress the first leap of delight at hearing from her, or the glimmer of hope when she said that she wanted to see him. They had arranged that on his next return trip to Australia he would come straight out to the house, instead of staying at his club, as he invariably had in recent months, and they would have, in Jilly's words, 'a chance to have a proper talk'. During the flight he had allowed himself to fancy that he might get off the aeroplane and find her there to greet him . . . or else welcoming him at the house with a bottle of champagne, and a lovely little dinner for two . . .

But he had arrived at Mascot Airport on a wet chilly night when tempers were frayed and taxis scarce, to find Jilly conspicuous by her absence. Still, he was unprepared for getting home at last to find her already gone to bed, the lights out and not so much as a piece of cheese in the fridge. He tiptoed into the bedroom, but need hardly have bothered – Jilly had passed out and was sleeping heavily, her breathing stertorous and the air thick with the reek of whisky. Cold, sick with disgust and totally alienated, Phillip went to spend the night in one of the guest bedrooms.

The next morning he was up early, showered, shaved and dressed in record time with the firm intention of leaving a house which he now felt was haunted with the ghost of his dead marriage. To his surprise he heard movements as he came down, and found Jilly making coffee and toast for breakfast. She looked grey and puffy in the face, and her eyes were sick-looking, but she had brushed her hair and put on a smart housecoat over her nightdress. Phillip sat down.

'Coffee?'

'Yes, thanks.' He waited for her to speak, but she did not.

'What's on your mind, Jilly?' With a sense of sadness Phillip recognized the rupture of their relationship. He would never have spoken to her so bluntly in the days of their love. Maybe that's where I went wrong, he thought. 'You've got to admit it's pretty rare for us to sit down and eat together these days, more's the pity. I sense a hidden purpose.' Still she did not reply. Irritated almost to breaking point he snapped, 'What do you want?'

Trembling, Jilly reached for a cigarette, but her voice was calm. 'I want a divorce.'

Something inside Phillip answered by reflex, without missing a beat. 'Fine.' What was he feeling? He did not know.

'What took you so long to get round to it?' he resumed. Jilly looked shocked. 'Oh, don't let's play games, Jilly. I've been expecting this.'

'You won't fight me?' Absurdly, Jilly was disappointed at Phillip's easy capitulation.

Phillip gave a wry smile. 'Oh darling, I'm more than a little tired of it all. I've gone along with the situation until now, hoping you'd wake up to Greg Marsden, to the sort of person he is. But frankly, I'm finding it faintly immoral to continue to support my wife's lover.'

'If you knew –' Jilly's voice was hardly more than a whisper '– why didn't you do . . . say something?'

'You got over the others. I still loved you. I was hoping you'd get over Greg as well.'

'Loved – me?'

260

'Yes, loved. Past tense, I'm afraid. It's been over for me for – I don't know how long.'

Jilly's unstable temper was beginning to boil up. 'So you've been quietly indulging me all this time, have you?'

Phillip considered this. 'I suppose I have in a way. For most of our marriage. Not being able to have children was such a terrible thing for you to face. I knew how deeply it hurt you – no one better. So if you could find a brief consolation here and there . . . I recognized that I was not enough for you.'

Jilly laughed, a savage, hurtful laugh.

'Perhaps you have something to reproach me with, Jilly. Perhaps I was to blame for marrying a much younger woman, and then condemning her to this life of uselessness, rattling around a great house all day – God knows I couldn't have stood it. But in the end, I am *not* your father, and it was not for me to run your life. You're an adult woman, and if you choose to roll in the muck, it's not for me to pull you out.'

'How long have you known?' Jilly was blazing with fury.

'Oh, I could probably pinpoint the very day it started.' He looked back with the weariness born of long experience. 'The day we played tennis at Stephanie's with the Rutherfords?'

His accuracy enraged her further. 'Well, you're wrong,' she screeched. 'It happened long before!' Phillip disregarded this foolish show of bravado.

'Did Stephanie know?'

The mention of Stephanie sobered Jilly at once.

'No, of course not,' she muttered.

'Well, let's not drag it out. You'll need a lawyer now of course, and I – I think I'll be able to represent myself. The settlement may need some careful working-out. If I was reluctant to subsidize Marsden when he was the lover of my wife, I'm hardly likely to want to do so when he – and you – are both out of the family, so to speak.'

Jilly glowered at him like a mutinous child. She hasn't even got the sense to think of her financial security, he

261

thought despairingly. Then, aware that this could well be their last real conversation together, he spoke from the heart.

'Jilly – please listen carefully. I don't know what happened when you were at Eden and Stephanie . . . died. But you must look out for yourself. I believe Marsden is capable of almost anything.'

Jilly gathered herself together and spoke with cold venom. 'Don't patronize me, Phillip. Don't talk to me like one of your clients. *I intend to marry Mr Greg Marsden*! And there's nothing you or anyone else in the world can do to stop it!'

Quite unaware of his recent betrothal, Greg Marsden was in fact expending a considerable amount of energy in a totally different direction. He was well pleased with the success of his morning's courtship of Tara and had no doubts of the final overall triumph of his campaign. It had been a brainwave to have the kids home – made him look as if he were a really good bloke, and not just trying to get inside her knickers. Whereas in fact he was a thoroughly good bloke who *was* just trying to get inside her knickers. He grinned to himself. He could forgive her for not going to bed with him on their first dinner date – just about – though it hadn't happened to him before. OK, he respected her for that. But a couple of hours in close proximity to that lovely slender body, fantastic ass, and the tits – fuck it, he wanted her like hell already, and it was only lunchtime! He crossed his legs firmly and looked down the long dining-room table.

Tara was deep in conversation with Dennis, a fact noticed with approval by Matey as he circulated in his usual stately fashion, serving food and pouring drinks.

'You like your tucker, do you?' she was asking.

'Yeah, he sure does,' said Greg, cutting across the boy's reply with his usual insensitivity to others. 'Now then, what do we do after lunch? It's up to you, Tara.'

'Well . . . I'm open to suggestions.'

'OK, there's swimming and sailing, fishing, and –' he laughed teasingly '– tennis?'

'No, not fishing.' Dennis's quiet contribution did not please Greg.

'I'm not asking you!'

Tara turned to Dennis. 'Don't you like fishing?'

He looked down, suddenly childish. 'I don't like killing things.'

Greg's face was a study in contempt. He could be seen mobilizing his forces to crush Dennis with his reply. Oh Greg, why ever did I think you'd make a good father? Tara seethed inwardly to recall those fantasies of the baby she would have with Greg that Stephanie had indulged herself in – and seethed even more as in sarcastic and superior tones he started in on her son.

'Man kills to survive, Dennis. It's nature's law. Survival of the fittest. Don't they teach you anything in that expensive school of yours?'

Tara could not help herself. 'Man – some men – also kill for other reasons, Greg.' She looked straight into his eyes. 'Some men are simply . . . killers.'

She held the pause for what felt like a lifetime. But Greg did not bat an eyelid. He didn't register at all, but went on as if he had not heard.

'It's a part of human nature, that's all. It's always been that way. It's not going to change for you, sport.'

He has not heard, she thought, he just did not hear. In that instant she knew him for what he was – a moral imbecile. *Other* men are killers, *other* men are evil. To himself he's just a regular guy who's making out best as he can, while others . . . others . . . get in his way. Oh, you have to be stopped, Greg Marsden, she thought. You're a runaway train. Somewhere in there you've slipped your controls.

Greg was still harassing Dennis.

'. . . I mean, just look at what you're eating, will you? D'you think that steer died of old age?'

A look of nausea came over Dennis's face, and he pushed his plate away. Greg smiled.

'OK,' he ordered 'Now let's talk about something happy.'

He was interrupted by the arrival of Sarah, who entered the room with her eyes cast down and sullenly slipped to her place at the table.

'I told you she'd come out when she got hungry,' whispered Dennis.

Tara took a long deep look at her daughter. Sarah too had grown, and put on weight. Comfort eating? thought Tara sadly. Her daughter's heavy ungainly body was for all the world hers at the same age. The thick hair fell forward, eclipsing Sarah's face, which wore an ugly expression of resentment. She was the picture of adolescent misery.

'Hello,' said Tara very gently.

'Sarah, this is Miss Welles,' said Greg in the same domineering tone that he used to Dennis. 'She's a famous model. You've seen her on television commercials. Say hello.'

'I know who she is.' Sarah addressed herself coldly to Greg, then turned back to Tara. 'My brother and I,' she said very clearly, 'have been paroled for the weekend in honour of your visit. We assume we are to act as . . . chaperones?'

Tara shot a look at Greg. He was hanging on to his temper with difficulty. 'Matey, I think Sarah is ready for her lunch.'

'Yes, sir.' Matey hastened to comply.

Tara felt a desperate compulsion to make contact with her daughter.

'You're very pretty,' she observed in a low voice.

'No, I'm not!' Sarah's contradiction rang out sharp and clear. 'I look like my mother.'

Greg had had enough. 'Miss Welles,' he began in a frightening voice, 'is a guest in this house, and you ought to know by now that I don't like talking about your mother.

264

Now if you're going to go on behaving like a spoilt brat – you can cut out of here!'

Sarah leaped up. Her voice was shaking but her expression was defiant. 'Don't you order me about! This isn't your house! And you don't frighten me!' She turned and ran out.

Good for you, Sassy, thought Tara. She was burning with pride for her daughter. That's telling him. She felt an unholy childish glee rise up inside her, and knew from his eyes that Dennis felt the same. Greg was lost in his own anger.

'We'll take the boat out,' he announced abruptly.

'Sounds like fun.'

'Yeah, sure,' Dennis added.

Greg directed a frown at him. He had had enough of kids for one day. 'I mean – just the two of us. Me and Tara,' he said dismissively. Dennis looked crushed.

'But Greg –' Tara made herself sound at her most innocent '– I thought you were a family man! And I can't let you sacrifice Dennis's company for *me*. I insist he comes along. Or else I'll stay back quietly while you two boys take the boat out, shall I?'

She looked at Greg wide-eyed. But in the corner of her vision she could see Dennis's delighted face. Soundlessly he was mouthing to her, 'Nice one, Tara!'

Dennis was delighted to have found an ally in Tara. But his young brain could make no sense of support from such an unexpected quarter. On the boat that afternoon he sought some enlightenment.

'Tara, why do you like Greg?'

Good question, she thought. Quickly she dodged it. 'I like lots of people. I like you.' Casually she extended her hand and ruffled his hair.

'Hey, you guys!' Greg was calling from the wheel. 'You swimming today, or what?' With a smile Tara disappeared to the cabin below to change. She laughed out loud as she recalled the last time she had been in there – on her honeymoon with Greg. Or rather, she corrected herself, on

Stephanie's honeymoon. Her sense of her distance from that poor woman gave her an unexpected surge of power. I can do it, she thought. I am doing it. Quickly, she changed, and hurried up on deck where the sun danced on the waters of the harbour. Behind them lay the Harper mansion sleeping in the sunshine, and ahead the reaches of the Pacific Ocean.

'Well, I'm ready,' she called. 'Everyone else should be.'

'Last one in's a nong, right?' cried Dennis as he dived overboard. Greg's eyes raked Tara's body in its bright swimsuit with a blatantly sexual appraisal. She is *good*, he thought, what a great body! She returned his gaze fearlessly, like a woman who knows well that she can stand up to the scrutiny of any man.

'Come on, then.' She spoke lightly, but there was a hint of sexual challenge which his experienced ears did not miss. He pulled off his t-shirt and dropped it on the deck. Then in an unmistakably provocative way he released the button on his jeans and slowly began to unzip his tight jeans, easing the zipper down over his swelling cock. To his surprise Tara did not blush, look away or turn aside as women usually did, but fixed her eyes on him, taking in every detail. He had never had a woman who had really looked at him while he was peacocking it like this before. His excitement flared, he felt the blood pumping into the start of a fantastic erection as he slid his jeans off and stood before her in his brief black swim pants.

Tara studied Greg with care, scanning the broad shoulders, the well-defined muscles of his chest and arms, narrow hips, flat belly and the growing bulge in the front of his briefs. She felt no embarrassment because she felt no emotion of any kind, but a great coldness, a deadness towards him deep within. Yet she felt too a stirring sense of her female power over him – she could see the blood pulsing under the stimulus of her gaze – and her body echoed the call of his at a level far below the workings of the mind or heart. A tiny, hot flame burst into life inside her, her nipples tautened and she grew warm and wet between the legs. What he couldn't do for Stephanie when she loved him, he can do for Tara when she hates him, she thought, entranced by the rich irony of it all.

She knew that in a microsecond he would be reaching for her with the arrogance of a man accustomed to handling women for his own sexual pleasure, not theirs.

'If you're waiting for me, please don't!' she said impudently, and quick as thought whisked to the side and dived into the harbour. The cold water was a shock to the animal warmth which had spread through her body, but it had a tonic, bracing effect. She surfaced with a cry of exultation, rejoicing in her body, its freedom and control.

'Race you, Dennis,' she cried to the boy splashing about round the boat, and the two of them sped off in a fast crawl, laughing all the way.

Left on deck Greg faced the old-as-the-hills problem of a man armed with a mighty erection and not an enemy within reach. Raging, he dived overboard to deal with it in one short sharp shock rather than be stuck on deck presiding over a reluctant detumescence. Once again he had the unfamiliar and disagreeable experience of feeling that he was being played with, fooled and outwitted. He struck out after the others, scowling as he worked his confusions out. He knew she wanted him. He had seen her eyes grow dark and dilated, had almost smelt the sex heat coming off her body when he stripped for her – he couldn't be mistaken. Yet something held her off. Well, not for much longer. He wanted her, he would have her, and when he did he would make her pay for every second of this prick-teasing. And that was how it was going to be. Tara, reading his face as he came powering up in a perfect crawl, could have cried aloud in triumph. She had him! She had got him and there would be no escape!

Chapter Sixteen

Sometimes when you want to be alone it is very comforting to have someone slip along to see how you are doing. So Dennis hoped as he made his way down through the gardens of the mansion to find Sarah in her secret hideaway under the old willow tree. There, where the branches of the tree sweeping down to the ground and the water's edge made a natural shelter, he knew that she was most likely to be found when she had not been in the house after their return from the boat trip. He parted the pale green fronds of the tree like a curtain and entered the cool shade. Sarah sat perched on a rock, like a water nymph, Kaiser stretched out by her side. She gave no sign of Dennis's presence, but he knew better than to expect that. Quietly he sat down on the rock next to hers, and contented himself simply with being there for her.

Sarah was in fact deeply touched to see him, so touched that she immediately braced herself not to show any sign of this weakness. But she was sick to her soul of loneliness and her own company, and though she invariably scorned Dennis as immature and childish, his loyalty and love had often been her only support. Her proud and touchy soul could never let him suspect this, so she sat now and waited for him to open the conversation as she knew he would.

'You do really like her, don't you Sass?' he began presently, without preamble. 'You pretend you don't, but you do.'

'I don't know what you mean.'

'She was jolly nice to you over lunch—'

'What I had of it! And she hardly spoke to me at all.'

'Just because she's a friend of *his*,' Dennis persisted, 'doesn't mean she's the same as he is.'

'Oh Dennis.' Sarah sighed dramatically. 'You're too young to understand these things.'

Tolerantly Dennis decided to let that go, and tried another tack.

'Hey, Sass,' he said frowning, 'does she remind you of anyone?'

'What do you mean?'

'I don't know. But I do know I've seen her before. D'you remember I told you about a woman who turned up at my school once, and took photos of me playing football? Well, it's her! I asked her about it when we were swimming, and she said there must be some mistake. But I know it's her.'

'Really Dennis!' Sarah decided that the time had come for a thorough squelching. 'You must be going *barmy* or something. Why would Tara Welles go all the way out to your wretched school and take photos of a stupid football game? It doesn't make sense!'

'I know I've seen her before,' Dennis argued stubbornly.

'Of course you've seen her before, you idiot! You've seen her on the pages of every magazine that's come into this house in the last however long.' Sarah sighed with exasperation.

'Still . . . Sass . . . you have to admit she's . . . special?'

'No, she isn't,' replied Sarah emphatically. 'She's no different from any of his other female hangers-on. I've seen that look in her eye when she's with him. She wants him to make love to her.'

Dennis's fragile, romantic image of Tara was in danger of being destroyed. Stoutly he defended it. 'I don't believe that. You've got sex on the brain just because you're going through puberty.'

'I have not,' Sarah flared up. 'Anyway, he's got no right bringing *her* into *our* house. I HATE HIM!' She burst into a storm of violent tears. 'And I hate *her*,' she continued on through her weeping. 'I hate them both, they're hateful . . .'

With brotherly resignation Dennis put an arm round

her shoulder as she wept it out. His other hand found Kaiser's smooth furry head and he stroked it. The dog growled softly at the back of its throat. Dennis patted him thoughtfully. 'But you don't hate her, do you boy?' he asked, puzzled. 'You took to her straight away, didn't you?'

Kaiser lolled his pink tongue at Dennis, licked him, and then panted dopily in the heat. But he kept his secret deep in his canine soul and did not tell Dennis the answer to his question.

Up in the house the two adults had retired to their rooms to shower and rest after the strenuous swim. Greg was still in the same state, in equal proportions of growing lust and growing irritation. Another attempt to approach Tara on the boat had met with a scalding rebuff.

'Greg! Think of Dennis, *please!*'

He might have been a teenager trying to get too familiar in the back row of the cinema.

'D'you think he cares?' She's teasing again, he thought.

'*I* care!'

And her eyes warned that she meant it. Balked, he had to content himself with desultory conversation to relieve his tension.

'You seem to care over much about that young man. So what happened between you? You get on?'

'I don't really know.'

'Yeah, they're moody kids,' he said moodily. 'I think it was a mistake to have them home for the weekend.'

'No, it wasn't!' Tara contradicted him rather too vehemently. 'I was pleased to have a chance to meet them,' she continued lamely. 'I can't help feeling sorry for them. The past few months must have been terrible.'

'Ah, they're young. They'll get over it.' Greg was so involved in feeling sorry for himself right now that he failed utterly to notice the special emphasis that Tara gave to her reply.

'I hope so. I surely hope so.'

While Greg brooded on his wrongs, Tara had made use

270

of her time to go in search of Sarah. She had had no more than the brief lunchtime glimpse of her daughter and now the longing to see her had become more than she could bear. She found her back in the master bedroom, her presence revealed by the sound of music issuing from within. Tara knocked on the door, and entered. At once Sarah leapt to attention, switched the stereo off and began to gather up the records lying around on the floor. Her injured silence and ostentatious busyness showed Tara how much she had to do to overcome the girl's deep hurt and resentment. Tentatively she made a start.

'You didn't have to turn the record off,' she said. 'Mozart's one of my favourites – so cheerful, even in sad times.'

'What do you want?' Sarah's aggression was quite undisguised.

'To see how you are. I was sorry you didn't come out on the harbour with us.' She had put her finger straight onto one of the roots of Sarah's hostility.

'No one should have gone! It was my mother's boat! Our lawyers say he's not supposed to touch anything—'

Oh, poor baby, thought Tara, trying to fight him with the weapons of the adult world. Out loud she said, 'I think he was only doing it to please me.'

Sarah flashed her a look of the purest contempt.

'Impress you, you mean. Oh, it's disgusting! Bringing you here, into *my* mother's house, to make love—'

'Sarah!' Tara's head reeled. How could she handle this?

Sarah was totally unabashed and self-possessed.

'He is your lover, isn't he?'

'*No, he is not!*'

Tara's reply came from her with a violence she did not know she was feeling. She could see that Sarah was shaken, and quickly pursued her advantage. 'Greg is not my lover, and nothing will happen in this house that your mother wouldn't approve of, I can *promise* you that!'

'I don't understand. How can someone like you be with – Greg Marsden.'

271

Tara took her hands and looked into her eyes. 'Don't go on surface appearances,' she said slowly. 'Things are not always what they seem.' She could see that Sarah was struggling to absorb this, and her soul turned over. 'Oh Sassy . . . I'd like . . . I'd like to be your friend, if only you'd let me.'

'Why should you bother with me?' Sarah's face was dark with self-dislike. 'You're so beautiful. I wish I was.' In her plaintive words Tara heard the painful echo of her own girlhood, of the ugly duckling she had once been. She had to try to share with this beloved daughter, this child who thought she was a stranger, her own important life discovery – that inside every duckling is a swan awaiting release, if only a woman *dares* to be beautiful. Still holding Sarah's hands, she led her to the bed and they sat down together. With a deep breath, Tara began.

'When I was your age . . . I was scared, very self-conscious, and had braces on my teeth. I was horribly plump, and I felt awful about it. I didn't think I was a bit beautiful then. And above all – I was sure that no one could really like me – ever – unless of course they had an ulterior motive. So—'

She paused, but Sarah was listening intently, eyes fixed on the carpet.

' – so – I pretended I didn't care. I accepted anybody's attention for whatever reason it was given. That way you get to meet a lot of horrible people. I got hurt. A lot. It's taken me a very long time to let go of those fears and insecurities.'

Sarah was thinking hard about all this. 'But now – you know you're beautiful now?'

Tara smiled. 'I have my moments. I'm at my best when I'm not having to think about myself, but concentrating on someone else.'

'My mother was like that.' Sarah's flat statement caught Tara by surprise. 'Because she wasn't beautiful she thought people only liked her because she was Stephanie Harper . . . the one with all the money.'

'But you know sometimes – if you're really lucky – and if you're ready to listen—' Tara hesitated. This was so important that she dared not risk getting it wrong '– someone comes along who shows you that *real* beauty is something that's inside you. It's always been there. And all you have to do is trust it.'

Trust it, my baby, she willed her daughter, believe me – I know.

'That doesn't mean appearances aren't important.' Tara instinctively knew she had made her point, and it was time to lighten the conversation. 'So, for instance, if you drew your hair back, everyone would see how pretty your face is. At the moment you're using it as a curtain to hide behind. And sometimes its fun to dress up – pretty dresses, crazy trousers – instead of wearing the same jeans and sweater all the time, like a uniform.'

Sarah was undoubtedly interested. But again Tara's instincts told her that enough was enough. There was still a reserve in her daughter that had to be respected. Tara sensed this, and did not push too far. There's plenty of time now, she told herself.

'Anyway, Sarah . . . friends?'

Sarah considered this. 'Maybe,' she said at last with a small smile.

Gently closing Sarah's door behind her, Tara came quietly downstairs in a happier frame of mind. She was not inclined to minimize Sarah's difficulties – on the contrary, her own still vivid memories of going through exactly the same things herself quickened her awareness of what Sarah was suffering. But she knew that she had taken the first important step towards building a rapport with Sarah, through which she could help her daughter in the way that she, as a motherless girl in the lost reaches of Eden, had never been helped.

She went now in search of Dennis. She had not seen him since they returned from the boat trip, and she found that she was already longing to be with him again. Crossing the hall, she noticed the door of the study ajar, and went to look in. This little room had been one of her favourite places in the mansion when she lived there – compact and snug, it had been homelier than the great gracious sitting room, and somehow much more Stephanie's style. She looked around the low welcoming sofas, the cheerful prints, the furniture which bore unmistakable traces of Kaiser, and drank in the feeling of peace which it gave her. I'm winning, she thought, I'm winning.

Crouched in the corner of a sofa, Dennis was watching home movies on a small free-standing screen. He waved to Tara, and pointed to her to sit down beside him. Before them on the screen flickered and danced grey, grainy ghosts from way back in the past – Stephanie and Max riding out of Eden, Stephanie on a small fat pony, Stephanie later on King as the huge black stallion thundered up to camera, Stephanie on the launch, with Kaiser, with Sarah and, last of all, with Dennis. There was no soundtrack, but Tara felt she ought to whisper all the same.

'Hope I'm not intruding?'

'Nah. Grab a seat.'

They watched as Stephanie was seen herding the two children into the pool at Eden, watching over them with anxious care as they splashed around and frolicked confidently in the water.

'That's my mother,' said Dennis. 'She couldn't swim. She was always afraid of the water, so she made sure we learned to swim properly, and dive and everything, from the start.

'Now this is her with Grandfather Max.'

Tara's heart contracted as the familiar large frame came into view, the figure still straight and well-muscled even in middle age, the gait swift and determined. She had not seen these films for years. Max walked across the picture, then suddenly turned and swung to the camera. Once again she felt the impact of that harsh, hawk-like face, the arrogant regard cast carelessly on her as if she were a person of no worth, the rather cruel mouth. For a moment

274

she became a frightened child again, shaken, insecure. She felt fat, and clumsy, and knew she could not please. When had she felt like this again in recent years? Of course – with Greg! She had always felt like that with Greg. Her brain reeled under this lightning flash. Max and Greg were in every way so different . . . but was it possible, just possible, that in marrying Greg she had married . . . her father? Married his selfishness, his disdain, his deep devotion to his own ends and his total lack of love?

As she struggled to make sense of this, the scene changed.

'This is a good bit,' said Dennis enthusiastically – 'I'm in this part.'

The film showed Jilly and Phillip Stewart, in much happier days, playing tennis with Sarah and Dennis in the garden of the Harper mansion. Tara remembered the sequence well – it had been one of the tennis parties she had always loved to give for a few chosen people. She was sadly shocked to see how young and bright Jilly looked here, bouncing around the court in obvious enjoyment of this low-level fun and games with the children. Phillip too was laughing, and obviously on great form. Tara's mind went willy-nilly to the tennis party when Greg and Jilly had had their first fateful exchange. Bitterness and gall, never very far away, rose in her heart.

'Matey!'

To her astonishment, Tara suddenly heard the least expected sound in the whole world – Jilly's voice. It came again, louder, from right outside the study in the hall.

'Matey! Where the hell are you?'

'Oh, Mrs Stewart . . .' Matey's voice, restrained, disapproving.

Jilly's manner was exuberant, uncontrolled. 'Sorry to barge in unannounced, like this. Gotta speak to Greg. Where is he?' She laughed, then shouted loudly, 'Where is the master of the house?' She's drunk, thought Tara.

'He's upstairs, madam.' Matey was doing his best to

restore order and decorum. 'I'm afraid he didn't mention that you were coming . . .'

'Oh, Matey, stop waffling, for God's sake!' snapped Jilly viciously. 'Just go tell him I'm here, OK?'

'Very well, I'll let him know.'

'And tell him I've got some news,' Jilly called after Matey's retreating figure. 'Some wonderful news.'

Tara came out of the study in time to see Matey proceeding up the stairs, ramrod stiff with disapproval. Jilly was peering into her handbag mirror, trying to powder her nose and arrange her dishevelled hair. She rocked slightly on her feet.

Tara came up behind her, with Dennis on her heels.

'Hello, Jilly,' she said quietly.

'Hello, Aunty Jilly.'

The effect of their appearance was electric. Jilly gripped her mirror and compact in rigid hands, just trying to take it in. Her eyes bulged, and she looked suddenly grey.

'Ah, Jilly!'

Greg was coming down the stairs at a fast pace. Matey's news had disturbed his afternoon rest with a vengeance, and he was frantic to avert any contact between Jilly and Tara.

'What a pleasant surprise!' he called gaily. 'You should have telephoned to let us know you were coming. Tara Welles, this is Jilly Stewart. Jilly is—' he gave her a warm smile '– an old friend of the family.'

The atmosphere was alive with tension, suspicion and an indefinable menace. Greg hurried on.

'You'll have to excuse us, Tara, but Jilly and I have some very important business to discuss. Dennis'll look after you, won't you, mate?'

And without hesitation he grabbed Jilly by the arm and thrust her across the hall into the dining room.

'That was Auntie Jilly – she drinks,' observed Dennis, in the matter-of-fact way of children. 'Come on, let's get back to the films. There's one of us on that ski-ing holiday I told you about.'

*

Inside the dining room Greg allowed the mask of affability to fall from his face and confronted Jilly with black-eyed anger.

'What the hell do you think you're doing?'

'What am I doing?' Jilly fought back, wobbly but determined not to give way. 'You bastard! You bloody bastard! What the fuck is *she* doing here?'

Greg looked at her with disgust. 'You're drunk.'

'What if I am? Just answer me one thing – you're having an affair with her, aren't you?'

For some reason he could not explain, this undeserved slur hurt Greg. 'I'm warning you, Jilly—' he began.

'AREN'T YOU?' she screamed.

'NO! I AM NOT!' He was angry with himself to let her violence trigger his so easily. Fighting for calm, he resumed. 'I've taken her out a couple of times, that's all.' Don't alienate her, he warned himself. She's a tinder-box, and all it wants is a spark. Keep her sweet.

'Oh, baby,' he sighed softly. 'Baby, come here.' He could see her shoulders drooping now, the fight ebbing out of her.

'Come on.' Slowly, like a lost child, she came up to him. He took her in his arms, folded her to his chest, and stroked her tangled hair. 'Look, try to understand. I'm working it so I'm seen out with a few other women from time to time. You know I've always been careful to take any suspicion off us. And the wild way you've been behaving, I had to do something, didn't I?'

'Is that the truth?'

'Yep, the whole truth.' Jilly was silent, longing to believe yet fearful of being deceived. He kissed the top of her head, caressing her back and the rounded haunches of her hips till she was soothed. 'Come on, babe – do you really think I'd be carrying on with a strange woman under my wife's roof? With my wife's children here? And talking of wives – aren't you forgetting something? I thought we agreed you'd never just turn up here. After all, you do still have a husband.'

'Oh Greg!' Jilly was suddenly excited and happy again. 'Darling, that's what I came to tell you! We needn't hide and slink about any more. Phillip has agreed to a divorce!' She hugged him tightly. 'We can get married. Isn't that great?' Off-key, in a high voice, she began to hum the wedding march. Then she thought to look at his face. 'Well, smile, baby! What's the matter with you – smile for me, please?'

Upstairs in the guest bedroom, Tara was completing her packing. It did not take long. She had brought very little with her. She could only begin to guess what was taking place between the two downstairs in the dining room. But it seemed like a marvellous idea to take the opportunity to extricate herself from this situation, for she was certain that Greg would expect to make love to her that night, and she had not worked out a convincing way of avoiding this. With adults, the foreplay cannot go on for ever. And Greg was hardly a specialist in the old Chinese art of holding off to increase the final gratification. Jilly's drunken arrival gave her a perfect get-out.

It also seemed the perfect poetic justice to leave them alone together to their own devices. It was becoming more and more clear to her that Jilly had been involved in the motive for Stephanie's 'accident', if not in the actual mechanics of it. They were morally partners in crime. They had chosen each other, and they deserved each other. As they became more and more trapped in the toils of their own making, they struck out at one another as wildly and cruelly as they had struck at her. By standing back to let their destructiveness have full rein, Tara was using them as instruments of her own revenge upon each other. It was a sweet thought. It was not even revenge – it was justice.

As she came downstairs with her bag and the faithful Dennis in tow, Greg emerged abruptly from the dining room. He crossed to her with a brusque challenge.

'What's all this?'

'I think I'd better go, don't you?'

'You don't have to.'

'Oh, I think I do.' She looked at him. 'Even if I stayed now it wouldn't be the same.'

She could tell Greg was very angry. 'Well, I'll drive you home.'

'No, no, thanks, it's OK. Dennis has called me a taxi.'

Greg treated Dennis to a nasty look. 'Oh, has he?'

'I asked him to,' Tara said levelly.

'Look—' Greg raised a hand to the back of his head and ruffled his hair. 'Something you should remember. Jilly was a close friend of my wife's. She's also Sarah's god-mother. One of the family.'

'I see.' Tara deliberately made her voice icy.

The taxi horn sounded outside. Tara picked up her bag. 'I'll take that.'

'Well – bye bye, Dennis.' She risked kissing him, then wiped the lipstick from his face. 'See you. And don't forget to say a special goodbye to Sass for me, will you, please?'

They walked out to the taxi and Tara got in.

Greg made one last appeal. 'Are you sure I can't drive you home? It seems awful – you going like this. Tara, I'm really sorry . . .'

'Don't worry about it.' She kept her eyes fixed straight ahead.

'She'd . . . been drinking.'

'I worked that out by myself.'

Greg knew when he had lost. 'I'll – I'll call you later.'

'Fine. Elizabeth Bay, please, driver.' She brushed away Greg's attempt to kiss her hand through the car window, and the taxi drove off.

Greg re-entered the mansion with something very like murder in his heart. As a man totally unused to failure with women he was finding it was becoming more and more important to him to score with Tara Welles. He was constantly being frustrated. He could not blame her for cutting out with this stupid drunken cow showing up, and what a low opinion she must have of him now he couldn't even begin to imagine. He felt an ugly coldness in his heart, and a tension which would have to have relief.

In the dining room Jilly heard the taxi drive off with a thrill of triumph. Exultant, she turned to the sideboard and poured herself a whisky. As she was raising it to her lips, she heard Greg enter the room and close the door behind him. She turned to greet him with a seductive smile on her flushed face. His look of fury came to her as a warning too late for her to defend herself as he slapped her viciously across the face. She stumbled under the blow, aghast, and her glass crashed to the floor and shattered.

'Don't you ever turn up here again unannounced! And drunk. Not ever again. Do you hear me? DO YOU HEAR ME?' Jilly was glazed, reeling, tears in her eyes from the pain of the blow. Greg steadied her carefully with one hand, and then hit her again. His fingers seared the side of her face like a brand. Her head lolled and she made no resistance. But the fury in him was not appeased. He wanted to punish, to humiliate her. In a blind fury he grabbed the buttons at the front of her dress and tore it open. The flimsy fabric ripped right down and he peeled the remainder of it from her shoulders. Underneath she wore very little – ready for being fucked, he thought, she came here wanting it and now she's getting it. Methodically he stripped the wispy undergarments from her body, making sure to rip and ruin them as he did so.

At last she stood naked before him, surrounded by the rags of her clothes. He was breathing hard. She seemed to be in a trance, of drink, of fear, he could not tell. Brutally he shoved two fingers into the silky triangle at the top of her legs and found it warm, moist and receptive. OK, he thought, but not yet. He had not yet sufficiently exorcized his rage. Gripping her wrists tightly he turned her sideways on to him, raised his arm above his shoulder and brought it down in a searing blow across her backside.

Quivering, Jilly let out a howl of pain. Wrenching her wrists free of his grasp she turned on him, punching, scratching, biting. She fought like a cat, and though small, was wiry. She drew blood from a scratch down the side of his neck, and got her teeth to the hand that had struck her, repaying the hurt he had given her with interest. Greg raised the imprint of his hand on her again and again as he struck the soft golden flesh of her unprotected body. But she seemed impervious to these blows, abandoning herself to fighting as she always did to fucking. She was like a warrior goddess. It seemed to be all she lived for. With this realization, Greg abandoned himself to it too. He concentrated on protecting himself rather than striking back, and soon it became a game between them, a game that Greg was finding more exciting than conventional sex play. She hurled herself upon him, knocking him to the ground, rolled him about and played with him like a grizzly bear, clawing and snatching. She released his straining cock from his jeans and went down on him, but he swiftly forestalled her, in a delicious dread of her sharp white teeth which in that mood she might use. He flipped her on her back and drove into her, both of them coming quickly in a raw, bursting, long-drawn-out mutual orgasm. Then both lay bruised, bleeding and sated, like animals on the floor. Above them on the wall, the coming-out portrait of Stephanie Harper looked down on a scene such as her innocent eyes had never encountered before.

Chapter Seventeen

As the cab brought her back into the city from Darling Point, Tara deliberately did not let herself think about Greg or Jilly. Instead she feasted her thoughts upon her children, going over the conversations she had had with them again and again. Then she thought ahead to the evening before her. She would spend it very quietly, reading and relaxing. She would talk to Maxie, tell him all her adventures and boast about Sarah and Dennis. And she would quite definitely switch off her telephone.

Outside her apartment block she paid the taxi driver, then stood for a moment to enjoy the air. Night had descended swiftly, and the sky was alive with a thousand stars. As she prepared to go in, a figure approached her out of the darkness.

'Dan.'

'Hello.'

'I thought – I thought you'd already left Sydney.'

'Well—' he grinned at her amiably. 'Can't a fellow change his mind?'

Tara was at a loss for words. 'Have you been waiting long?'

Dan saw no reason to lie. 'Yeah, most of the day actually. I was beginning to think you must have gone away for the weekend. Still, you're here now and that's what matters.'

'Well . . . would you like to come in for a cup of coffee?'

'No,' he said gruffly. 'Well, maybe. There's something I want to ask you first.' She hesitated, divining his drift, not wanting to hear. 'All it requires is a simple yes or no answer.'

Behind them the harbour lights were looming in the blackness of the night. The air was soft and everything was still. She felt as if she had heard this moment coming from a million years away and could not deflect it from its tragic course.

'Tara – oh my darling – will you marry me?'

She stared at the ground so hard that ever afterwards cracks in a pavement obscurely reminded her of sorrow. Dan's voice was very low. 'Is that my answer?'

'Oh Dan – I . . . can't.'

'Why can't you?'

'Dan . . . please.'

He took her by the arms and turned her to face him. 'Tara, it's a reasonable enough question. I love you, did I tell you that? I want to be with you, spend my life with you – I want to marry you, dammit, is that so ridiculous?'

Tara was trembling. He gripped her forearms painfully hard. 'Now I'm telling you, I've learned to get what I want in life. And I'm warning you, I'm a stubborn devil. I won't give in without a fight.'

Tara closed her eyes. Oh, to be able to soften to him now, to lay her head on his chest, put her arms round him and crawl for shelter under his protection, not to have to fight, and struggle and . . . She straightened her back and set her shoulders and Dan knew her mind before she spoke.

'I thought, on Orpheus, that you and I had reached some . . . understanding—' In spite of her resolution, she felt her eyes beginning to fill with tears. 'Oh, I'm so tired . . .'

'How do you think I feel?'

'I've told you before, Dan – I told you then—'

'You haven't told me anything!' Dan was genuinely angry now, his eyes blazing amber as he glared at her. 'I'm getting very sick of all this mystery-mongering – does it do something for you? Does it give you a thrill? You *wanted* me on that bed the other night – I didn't have to be a doctor to know that. And then – bang! The cut-off point, just like that.' He smiled a grim little smile. 'If you were a doctor you'd know you should treat the human body with more respect.' Still holding her by the arms he gave her a shake to emphasize his words. 'Look, I know something's going on. I know you're involved in some kind of business that's right outside my experience, and yours. I'm getting bad vibes from the whole deal.'

'Dan—'

'Don't try to fob me off again, Tara. This worries me. You worry me.'

'Dan – if you'd let me speak—' She put it as brutally as she could. 'It's not your concern. *I'm* not your concern.'

'Aren't you? So I'm pushy. I'm making it my concern!' Angered, she broke away from his grasp, but he held her with the urgency in his voice. 'Tara – look – I'm not the kind who plays games and you aren't either. What are you up to? What is this thing that's coming between us? I've got no secrets. You know what my life is. You spent months on that island with me. Is that it? You can't see yourself as a doctor's wife? Living on an island doesn't mean you're a prisoner, you know. You can hop backwards and forwards as much as you like.'

Tara had never felt so intensely unhappy. 'That's not it.'

'I know it's not. They all loved you there, the patients, the staff – even the wild turkeys!'

For Tara, the pain of this exchange was mounting unbearably.

'Dan – you don't know the first thing about me.'

'Oh, woman—' he sighed. 'I know every grain of your flesh and every fibre of your bone. I know that you're the other half of my soul. And I know that I want to be with you for the rest of my life.' His tenderness was almost her undoing. She burst out, 'Dan! You're not the only one with responsibilities!'

He laughed in puzzlement. 'Responsibilities? I know I'm not, I never said I was. So that's it, is it? OK, let's pool them, share them. Help each other. That's what marriage is all about, isn't it?' God, he was so loving. No man – no man – had ever offered her this sharing before. She could feel the ground slipping from beneath her feet. She had to get away.

Blindly she headed for the front door, but Dan was there

before her. He grasped her shoulder, and tipped her chin up so that she had to look at him. His face was grim, sardonic.

'Forgive a schoolboy question – but you are behaving like a schoolgirl. Is there someone else?'

How could she answer this? 'In a way.'

'God help us.' Tormented, he fought to contain his anger. His grip tightened on her face, and holding her very close he hissed, 'What kind of an answer is that? Grow up, Tara!'

Stung, she struggled free of his grasp. 'Well, it's the only answer you're going to get!'

'Are you in love with him?'

Now was the moment. Tara said with heavy emphasis, 'Dan, will you please just leave me alone. Go back to your island. And forget I ever existed!'

'Sure! Nothing easier!' He echoed her own heavy emphasis on what he was saying. 'If you can look me in the eyes and tell me you don't love me.' Tara gasped with shock. Oh God—

I don't love you!

Dan's face registered his dying hope. 'I don't believe you!'

'What have I got to do to make you believe me?'

He caught in his breath with pain. 'Tara—'

Her face, her tongue, her heart seemed turned to stone. Hardly breathing she watched the pain of realization tear through him, saw his set face flash past her as he frantically turned away. He took a few steps in to the darkness, then hesitated. If he turned back now . . . But hunching his shoulders he pressed forward and the glimmering night swallowed him up. He was gone. Numb, like an automaton, Tara picked up her bag and trailed up to her apartment. Without bothering to undress she dragged herself into bed and lay there shivering, curled up into a hard ball of misery for hour after hour. As the time crawled by, her mind seemed to be able to accommodate only one thought – I have lost the only true love of my stupid, wasted life!

*

At the Harper mansion, the afternoon's sport took some clearing up to Greg's satisfaction. Awakening from a post-coital doze to find the small but surprisingly compact body of Jilly lying heavily on top of him, his main urge had been to get rid of her as soon as possible – there were not many women Greg ever had any desire to be with once the screwing was over. Gotta get rid of her, he thought. Gotta pack her off straightaway. But one glance had shown him that this would not be easy. After the combined effects of drinking, rowing, fighting and fucking she had passed out, and was breathing thickly, her mouth hanging open in a slack gape. Greg squinted down at her with distaste. Wouldn't it be a great idea if all the women were kept on the other side of the rabbit-proof fence, and only let out for horizontal occasions? Well, time for this little rabbit to be repatriated.

'Come on, Jilly.' He heaved her off him and she slid to the carpet. 'Time to wake up. Rise and shine.'

Jilly came to with a disagreeable thud. Greg was standing above her, tucking his shirt into his jeans, zipping up. He surveyed the ruins of Jilly's clothing with a sadistic satisfaction. She asked for it. That'd teach her. Serve her right if he drove her out of the house as she was, mother-naked, and made her go home to Hunter's Hill like that. Sure would give those snobs up there something to wag their tongues about! It'd be the biggest bloody sensation since we won the Americas Cup. He laughed, tickled at the thought. Nah, he wouldn't do that to the poor cow. Better get her out, though, before he was tempted.

'Up, baby, up,' he said, stirring her ungently with his foot. She groaned, stirred, fell back, one arm thrown across her face to protect her eyes from the light he had suddenly switched on. She rolled over, landing on one of the torn halves of her dress as she did so. Her eyes widened with shock as it all came back to her.

'Greg! My clothes! What am I going to wear?' She relaxed into a sleepy smile. 'I'll just have to stay here till you can send out for some new things for me.'

Oh no, you don't, he thought. I know how to get past you, pussy cat. He left the room and went upstairs. From his wardrobe he selected the smallest of his t-shirts and a shrunken pair of cut-off jeans he only wore to the beach, then grabbing a belt he hastened back to the dining room. He had no fear of being seen or overheard by the staff – he knew that they would be safely tucked away in the staff quarters at the back of the big house – but he was now in a fever for her to go. Pausing in the hall, he called a taxi.

In the dining room, Jilly was still lying on the floor. Roughly Greg pulled her upright, and propped her up against one of the chairs. He pulled the t-shirt over her head and one by one forced her floppy arms through the sleeves, ignoring her mumbled protests. Actually, she looks better like that, he thought coldly, noting the cling of the soft fabric to the outline of her breasts. Then he pulled her to her feet.

'Hey, what's going on?' Jilly peered at him, awakened now and with hostility mounting.

'Gotta get moving, baby,' he said smoothly, planting a passing kiss on the side of her face. 'Gotta go out – big time dinner tonight, mining industrialists' get-together.'

'Can't I come?' she whined plaintively. Greg suppressed a snort of derision that he'd turn up anywhere in public with this drunken tart on his arm. 'Big boys only tonight, I'm afraid.'

He grabbed the jeans and supporting her with difficulty inserted one of her legs, then the other. As he pulled them up the tough denim of the crutch cut harshly into the soft open flesh at the top of her legs. She moaned in protest.

'Greg! You're hurting me.'

'That's because I know you like it, Jilly.'

'I can't go home with no bra and pants on.'

'Y'as good as came with none on, so don't give me that.' Dexterously he threaded the belt through the waist band of the jeans and drew it tight to hold them up. 'There! Latest fashion – cut-off man's look for you.'

Outside in the hall he heard the buzz of the intercom to

the gates. Hurrying out he pressed the release button to allow the taxi to come up the drive, then returned to Jilly. She was still frowning, dazed, where he had left her. Speedily he whisked round the room picking up the flimsy fragments of her underwear and the rags of her dress, stuffing them into her handbag lying on the floor – he wasn't going to have this tell-tale evidence of his afternoon's diversion lying in the Harper garbage bins to tell the tale to all the staff.

Outside the window the taxi hooted. Taking the still unsteady Jilly under the arm, he steered her out through the hall to the front door. Only as they reached the porch, with the taxi there at the foot of the steps, did Jilly seem to realize what was happening.

'Oh, Greg – I don't want to go – I love you . . .' She flung her arms round his neck.

Over her head he caught the eye of the taxi driver, who was watching the scene with interest.

'I'll call you, don't worry.' Reaching behind his neck, he disengaged the clinging arms and turned her to face the cab. Then in full view of the taxi driver, he reached across and taking one of her breasts in his hand he felt the weight of it, and gave it a none-too-gentle squeeze. Then slapping her on the rump like a heifer, he drove her down the steps.

'Hunter's Hill, mate,' he said to the taxi driver, pressing a high denomination bill into the admiring hand, 'and – take care of the lady, OK?'

Some time later, Greg was still occupied with the unfinished business that Jilly's unexpected arrival had forced him to abandon. He had been trying for hours to phone Tara. With Jilly out of the way and his mind free to turn to Tara again, he found that he was thinking of her in terms that he had never thought of a woman before. He wanted to make love to her, badly. But it was more than that. He wanted her company, her quiet presence, her smile. He wanted her love, not just her body. And he wanted her approval, he wanted her to think well of him.

Fucking hell, am I falling in love with her? he asked himself in bewilderment. He didn't know, for although he had mouthed the words of love many, many times, he knew for certain he had never felt that thing that poets sing of and men and women die for. He shelved this conundrum for another time. All he knew was that he wanted to make contact with Tara more strongly than he had wanted anything for a long time, and he couldn't get through to her by hook or crook.

He rang, and rang, and always the phone rang out unanswered. He had had it checked twice by the uncomplaining operator who confirmed that the instrument was in perfect working order. He thought again and again of just jumping into the car and going down to her flat in Elizabeth Bay. But he had no reason to think she would be there – she could very well have gone out somewhere to make up for her ruined weekend, and he could find himself madly driving round Sydney while she could be trying to telephone him here at the mansion. So he stayed put, and with the help of a bottle of whisky, sweated it out on the sofa in the study with the phone right by his hand.

The call came at one thirty in the morning when he had given up any hope of hearing from her or speaking to her that night. He knew it was her as soon as he heard the first ring, and his heart soared.

'Greg?'

'Yep.'

'How are you?'

'Thinking about you. I'm always thinking about you these days.'

'That's . . . nice.'

'Look, Tara – I'm sorry again about today, God! – it really was a farce. A bloody farce.'

'Don't worry about it.'

'When can I see you?' There was a pause, an undefinable sense of – what?

'Greg, I've been thinking . . . I want to go somewhere where there are no people, no . . . interruptions. I wondered how you'd feel—' She paused, and he held his breath '—about going up to Eden?'

Eden. It was the last thing he was expecting. Feverishly he tried to get his mind round it, weigh it up.

'From what you say,' Tara was continuing, 'it sounds like the perfect place for two people to be alone together.'

Or even three, he thought sardonically as the memories of his last time there with Stephanie and Jilly began to crowd in on him.

'Eden? . . . I'd rather not . . .'

From her voice, Tara had been expecting this. 'Well, I do realize it must have some unhappy memories for you.'

'Yeah, it does. Look – why don't we drive out to the Blue Mountains for a week? Now that would be a lot—' Tara cut him off with a sigh.

'We're both too well known. We'd never get away from your fans.'

'Or yours, beautiful,' he said softly.

'Greg . . .' her voice had softened in response. 'I just want to be alone with you . .'

'Really?'

'Really. At Eden.'

He thought it over. It certainly would be alone. There'd be no chance she could tease or evade him there. No taxis to call in the outback. The decision was easy.

'Okay. Let's go. Tomorrow. I'll radio the housekeeper Katie and let her know we're coming.'

'Oh Greg, fantastic!'

'Pack your swim suit. But not too much else.' He paused to let his meaning sink in. 'There's not a lot of cause for dressing up at Eden.'

'Bikini, t-shirt and jeans, I promise. So how will we get there?'

'That's the easy bit. First we fly to Darwin, then we get a light plane. I might even fly you myself.'

'Can you fly?'

'Can I fly?' Just you wait, he thought. I'll fly you higher than you've ever flown before. Aloud he said, 'Got my pilot's licence years ago. I can take you flying round Eden – there's a light plane kept there for emergencies. Just you pack. I'll arrange the transport. It'll be sometime tomorrow. I'll call you.'

'OK, fine.'

'So . . . what ya doing?'

'I'm . . .' Tara paused, seductively '—in bed with my cat.'

'I'll be right over.'

'Oh no you won't.'

He laughed. He knew this was just token resistance, part of the ritual dance, advance, retreat. His moves now were all advances. Black king to take white queen. No contest.

'I could be there – right there where you want me – in five minutes,' he said lazily.

'Oh I'm sure you could.' By her tone, Tara recognized the innuendo and was not put out by it. 'But a girl needs her beauty sleep. I'll call you in the morning.'

'OK. Give that cat a g'night kiss for me.'

'I will. Goodnight Greg.'

'Sleep tight, baby.'

He put the phone down and lay back on the sofa. He had done it – pulled it off. It was all coming together. He felt wonderful. What was it about this woman? Something, undoubtedly, for he felt better than he had done since he couldn't remember when.

If Greg could have known how exactly his own sense of triumph was echoed by Tara across the other side of town in Elizabeth Bay, his complacency would have received a severe jolt. Tara was holding onto herself to avoid jumping up and down with exultation. She had done it – pulled it off. It was all coming together. How easy it had all finally proved to be! After all her plans, schemes, fears, she had suddenly come up with the perfect device to get Greg back to the place where it had all started. And there she could accomplish her revenge. There, he would not get away.

The scheme had proved surprisingly easy to execute. But it had not been born without pain. She had had to send Dan away. She could not forego the drive, the compulsion to bring her plans to fruition after so much time and effort. Nor could she permit herself the luxury of confiding it all to Dan, and letting him take over as he surely would, calling the authorities and getting it all sorted out. She might as well have handed Greg over to the police straight after the accident. No, she had to – she simply had to – go this alone. Even at the cost of Dan's love. The same spirit of frantic independence that had prevented her from simply picking the phone up to reclaim her position and inheritance the moment she arrived in Sydney stood by her now. And during her night of sorrow she had forged her final plan. It had to be good, because it had to be worth the sacrifice of all that she held dear. Brooding on it during the bleak wakeful hours of a long night, Tara felt sure it would be. At Eden she would be on her own ground. This time she, not Greg would have the advantage of surprise. And like Greg – she would use it!

Dawn broke over Eden in a sunburst of golden fire, putting the darkness to swift flight and irradiating the whole station with heat and light. Beside a still-glowing fire out in the bush a figure moved as if awakening from a trance-like sleep. Chris, the station hand, had completed his dreaming. Now he was like a man new-made from his immersion in this mystical, spiritual activity which encompasses the awareness of everything since the dawn of time, reflecting an age-old way of being in which past and present are bound so tightly together that they become the core of consciousness. Chris knew that he could not lose his power of dreaming and live, for his dreaming was his knowledge of nature, of war, and of the cunning of the enemy. This alone teaches an Aboriginal his right course of action and his duties to those whom he must be responsible for. Through his dreaming the ancestral spirits whisper in his ear and guide his footsteps, and to some dreamers – a very few – they impart a sense of impending events so that these individuals are privileged to know the future as clearly as others know the past.

Chris was such a dreamer, and had been since childhood. So when he went missing, as he sometimes did, to light a fire in the night, or spend the day in the bush, his brother Sam would cover for his absence. Today however there was no need, as Chris came back in good time to start the day's work, with a deep spiritual glow and look of renewal, but also with hints and whispers of a kind that no one was expecting.

Which is why none of the Aboriginals showed any surprise when Katie Basklain, Eden's housekeeper for over forty years, communicated to them the news she had just received from Sydney via the radio link.

'Greg Marsden's coming to stay – bringing a woman.' Try as she might Katie couldn't keep the disapproval out of her voice. She was disappointed therefore to receive neither surprise nor shock from the two brothers. You'd have thought they already knew. Katie had lived out at Eden for long enough to know that they probably did – not necessarily details, but certainly the way in which coming events cast their shadows before. The voice of the father of all was in all things, and spoke to them through all things. They listened, and accepted the inevitability of what was decreed.

'Well, we're all ready for him – he needn't think he can catch us out.' Katie's little black eyes narrowed in hatred. She had never forgiven Greg for the accident to Stephanie – she had reared the motherless child like a daughter, the only one Katie had had or was likely to have. For long enough she had clung to a crazy hope that somehow, by some miracle, Stephanie would walk through the door of Eden again. When finally she had been unable to keep that hope alive any longer, a piece of her heart had died with it. And now *he* was coming back here to lord it in Stephanie's house, old Max's house. It was almost more than Katie could bear without reaching for her shotgun. She slaughtered a good number of rabbits when she went out that afternoon, imagining each one of them was Greg and getting a hit every time – though if she could have chosen a way of disposing of the gentleman, she would have had him fed to the crocodiles, piece-meal.

Still, he was coming, and he had to be provided for.

'Sam, you'd better mow the lawns, they don't really need doing, but this way they'll be at their best. Chris, have a good check over all the horses, I should think he may want to ride out – I'll see to the indoors, not much to be done there . . . we'll get by. After all, he won't stay long. Give it a coupla days, and we'll all be back to normal.' In the light of later events, Sam sometimes wondered if Katie had had a dreaming, heard a spirit voice of her own, to bring her such a strangely true word of what was to come.

Neither spirits, dreaming nor sleep had comforted the soul of the man who stood in Sydney's Mascot Airport buying a one-way ticket back to Queensland. Dan looked what he was, tired and sick at heart. He had given it his best shot, and he had failed. He had put his whole soul in trying to woo and win Tara Welles, and he could not even get to first base. He burned with anger to think that he had had her on a bed, in his arms, naked and open to him like a flower – the memory of her beautiful breasts in itself kept him waking – and somehow he had still let her slip through his fingers. What had he done wrong? Why had he failed? *Why? Why?*

But despite his self-punishing retrospective scrutiny, in his heart Dan knew it was not his fault. Tara had not fled his embrace because of her fear, or his incompetence, but because of that shadow, that mysterious something that had been between them from the start. He had made a little progress during this visit in his knowledge of Tara, and in discovering at least that there was another man on the scene. But what little he had gleaned had not helped him a whit, but only served to torment him more. And he could not get past her refusal to let him in on her secret, let him into her world.

Well, he was quitting. He hated to do so, and he hated Tara for it. But he had no choice. Last night's scene outside Tara's apartment in Elizabeth Bay had finally convinced him that he and Tara had no future. So get out while the going's good, he told himself. I've suffered enough and she's done enough damage. I'll just have to learn to think of her as like a fabulous car with a key part missing – beautiful but defective. With this resolution he paid for his ticket, shouldered his bag and checked his bigger case for the flight. By lunchtime he would be back on Orpheus Island, to embark on the life-long task of trying to make himself believe even one of the hurtful things he was thinking about Tara.

Like any major airport Mascot is used to strange scenes, glad or tearful farewells, rushed last-minute phone calls. By these standards the call made by a passenger about to embark for Darwin was neither remarkable nor particularly interesting.

'Hello – Jilly?'

'Yeah – who is this?'

'It's Tara.'

'What do you want?'

'I just want to let you know something . . . I want to tell you – I want to tell you the truth—'

'What truth?' Jilly gasped with fear.

'I'm at the airport. With Greg.'

'No!'

'I'm flying up to Eden with him.'

'You can't—'

'We're at the airport. We leave in a few minutes.'

'What time is it? When—'

'I felt you ought to know.' Tara's voice was concerned, sincere.

'I thought you said there was nothing going on between you and Greg!' Jilly's rising wail drowned the last of her words.

295

'I lied to you. I feared how you'd be about Greg – with me. But it's out in the open now. Goodbye, Jilly.'

'Don't go—' The phone clicked and Tara was gone.

Chapter Eighteen

The light plane spiralled down through the cloudless sky towards the tiny dot that was Eden.

'There it is,' said Greg. He turned to her and took her hand. 'Hope it lives up to your expectations. There's not a lot here, as y'can see.' He smiled at her. 'We'll just have to make our own entertainment.'

Tara smiled back automatically. 'Oh, I'm sure we'll be able to amuse ourselves – somehow.' How strange it felt to be learning how to flirt, she thought – learning how to seduce my own . . . husband? She looked down at Greg's hand lying in her lap. Strong and sinewy, the muscles developed over years of tennis playing, it was as attractive as everything else about him. Lightly she ran her fingers over the golden hairs on the back of it, and quite unbidden the memory of Dan's hands came to her – a darker golden, the fingers longer and thinner than Greg's, the nails short and immaculately kept, the hair dark brown . . . she tightened her grip on Greg.

'Hey, baby!' He was surprised and pleased at this show of interest from her. His ready sexual response quickened, and only the close proximity of the pilot inside the small cabin held him back from kissing her, touching her. Eden was a great idea after all, he thought.

Now the homestead and its surroundings could quite clearly be seen, set out like a doll's house in its surrounding oasis of rich greenery. Before the house the swimming pool shone unnaturally brilliant, like a tiny circle of mirror glass. Beyond stretched the flat, red sun-drenched wilderness without a break from horizon to horizon. Tara's heart ached with love. How could Greg say there was nothing here? Eden was its own world, and for most of her life it had supplied all her wants, and more. Now it would help her to realize the fulfilment of this last, special mission in which Stephanie Harper would be at once liberated and laid to rest. She stole a secret look at Greg, now watching out of the window as the plane began its final descent. She noted the perfect profile, the straight brow and nose, the well-shaped mouth, and felt a pang of grief. God, he was so beautiful. And he had to be destroyed.

Greg knew that Tara was looking at him, and experienced an intense inner satisfaction. He had given up worrying about why this woman was becoming so important to him. He was not a man for introspection, or for questioning any of his own drives or desires. For him the needs of his own demanding ego had always been paramount, had always been followed without check or remorse. So it was with his need for Tara now. But he knew that he was, in his own phrase, 'deeper in' with her than he had ever been with any other woman in the course of a very full sexual life. And he didn't dislike it at all. On the contrary, the feeling of well-being that he had had when she first phoned him to suggest the trip to Eden had stayed with him ever since. He found that it was increasing every minute that he spent with her. If this is love, roll me over, lay me down, and do it again, he thought contentedly. It couldn't happen to a nicer bloke.

'Soon be there now,' the pilot told them. Yeah, soon be there.

On the ground, the various inhabitants of Eden were gathering for the arrival of the plane and its passengers. From the top of the old water tower Chris saw the tiny skybird from very far away, tracing its progress with his habitual unblinking scrutiny until it was almost overhead. He had maintained his vigil here from early dawn, not expecting the plane at that early hour, but needing a high and solitary space for his mystical communion with nature and what was to come. Now on the top platform of the ancient wooden tower he squatted unmoving, a primitive chorus, as forces beyond his control though not beyond his ken brought the protagonists together for the final act of the drama.

In the shade of a clump of gum trees, Katie heard the high whine of the engine of the approaching plane. Hurriedly she completed her task of feeding the chickens and left in haste to prepare to welcome the unwelcome arrivals. Dumping the feed buckets outside the kitchen door, and wiping her hands cursorily on her apron, she set out for the landing strip behind the house. She had deliberately decided not to get changed or to do anything with her hair or appearance – don't want to give the bloody bastard the idea I'm pleased to see him, she reasoned angrily. A tatty, wizened, indomitable little figure, she stomped over the rusty red earth as if at every step she trod on Greg Marsden's face. I would, too, she promised herself grimly. Behind her Sam slipped silently out of the stables where he had been feeding and watering the horses in their early morning routine which Chris normally saw to. He hopped over the cattle grid separating the house and yard area from the grounds, and followed Katie at a distance towards the runway. To his left he saw his brother begin to descend from his eyrie in the water tower as the plane began its final run in to land.

The Cessna touched down in a smooth landing, its wheels sending clouds of dust spiralling along the dirt airstrip. The watchers on the ground saw the plane taxi to a halt, the door open, and the lithe figure of Greg Marsden jump out. Then he turned to help out a tall, slender woman, her face sheltered by a sun hat, who gracefully dismounted without need of his assistance. The three silent watchers moved forward.

'Hi, Katie.' Greg's greeting was restrained and careful. He knew what she must be thinking about him, and was determined not to put her cranky old back up any more than it must be already. 'You don't look a day older. Let me introduce Miss Tara Welles. Chris – Sam, how are yer?'

'Hi.' Katie gave him a stony stare. She hardly looked at

Tara. Tara was heartily relieved to be spared Katie's close examination. This was one of the severest tests of her new identity, with this woman who had known her from child-hood, lived with her for twenty years. She need not have worried. Katie Basklain was not going to dignify the intruder with a moment's notice.

'She's all the way from Sydney,' said Greg expansively, trying to create the feeling of welcome that simply wasn't there. Katie was even less interested in this information. Sydney might as well have been the moon, it was so far away from her world.

'I got your message,' she told Greg flatly. 'I'll show you to your rooms.' She turned and led the way off the airstrip towards the house, as Chris and Sam picked up the bags which the pilot had handed out. Behind her the small procession straggled awkwardly along as the plane took off to return to Darwin.

After the blistering heat of the mid-day sun outside, the cool stone-flagged interiors of the great house were like a blessing. Tara felt a surge of joy as she stepped under the wide verandah and entered the fine old hall. With it came a pride of possession she had not felt for a long time – this is my place! She was on home ground again. Her confidence budded and blossomed like a flower in the dark.

Katie led the way down the long dim corridor from the hall, passing the foot of the stairs.

'We don't use the upstairs any more,' she snapped. 'Not since the – accident.' She bit off the last word as if she found it hard to say.

'It must have been a very difficult time for you.' Tara's voice was gentle. 'I gather that you and Mrs Marsden were very close.'

'Stephanie *Harper*,' returned Katie, making her emphasis on the surname an indication of her resentment, 'was like my own daughter to me.' She turned sharply into a room on her right, and did not catch the expression on Tara's face.

'This'll be yours,' she said to Tara with a brisk wave of her arm round the guest room.

Greg frowned. The moment had come which he had been anticipating. He had to assert himself. He was the master of this house after all.

'Katie,' he said pleasantly, but with an unmistakable threat in his voice, 'I asked you to prepare Miss Stephanie's old room. I'd like our guest to have the best we can offer her.'

'This one's got a good enough view,' Katie mumbled stubbornly. But she knew that her efforts to protect Stephanie's room were unavailing. She moved further down the corridor and brusquely threw open another door. 'This is it,' she said. 'Doesn't need anything doing to it. 'S always kept ready. Just like it was.' She moved down the hall to the next door and opened that. 'You're in Max's room like you said. Lunch in half an hour.' Then she turned abruptly and trudged off.

God, she'd be funny if she weren't such a royal pain in the ass, thought Greg. When I'm in the saddle, my dear, you'll be the first to go. Even out here – in this god-forsaken dump – there's gotta be better service than this. He turned to Tara, anxious that Katie should not be allowed to cast a blight on the proceedings.

'Listen, Tara – y'mustn't mind Katie. She raised Stephanie. Stephanie's mother died when she was born – part and parcel of having a first kid out here in this hole. That was before Max got the little plane for emergencies. He just never thought anything could go wrong for him, I think. Anyway, when his wife died, he blamed the baby for her death – wouldn't have anything to do with it. If Katie hadn't taken her on, Stephanie would've died. So there's all that.' He paused, wanting to get everything out in the open with Tara. 'And – I'm sure she blames me in her way for Stephanie's death. She'll never get over that. So . . . if you want to hit it off with her – and if anyone can, you can – I wouldn't refer to Stephanie as Mrs Marsden again if the subject comes up. OK?'

'I'll remember.' Tara made the effort to sound normal.

'I'm in old Max's room.' He indicated with his eyes the door next to hers. 'Right there. On hand the second you need me.' He grinned, and resisted the temptation to reach for her breast or a handful of ass. Tara wasn't like that – not yet, anyway. Timing, boy, he reminded himself. Pitch, pace and timing. Get that right and you'd crack the Virgin Mary. Out loud he said in a tender, romantic tone, 'I'm glad you're here, Tara.'

He took her hand to raise it to his lips. Tara looked at him, his expression warm and courteous, his eyes full of sexual longing. Behind him through the open door was Max's great bedroom, dominating it the great oak bed on which he had died. And where this nightmare began for me, she thought with obscure longings and resentments raging through her heart. Why didn't you bring me up to fend for myself, she accused Max in her heart, why did you make me so weak that I had to look to a man for that strength I should have in myself, *in my own right?* Greg's mouth was brushing the back of her hand in a series of little sweeps like butterfly kisses. She felt an excitement she could not explain. Suddenly she felt eyes upon them. Chris was approaching down the hall on silent feet, bringing the baggage from the plane. She disengaged her hand. Greg looked up and his expression changed to one of purest irritation.

'I'll leave you to unpack while I just go and check on the preparations for lunch,' he said heavily. Moving away down the corridor he passed Chris. The guy was just a station hand, fuck it, don't let him get to you, Greg scolded himself. Yet at some deep level their naked manhoods called out a challenge to one another – they were natural enemies. Shrugging Chris firmly from his mind, Greg departed.

Standing at the door of her room, Tara turned aside as Chris entered with her bags. She knew she could not look him in the eye and keep up her masquerade. Keeping her voice casual, she said, 'Just put them down anywhere,

302

that'll be fine.' She stood aside to allow him to leave. As he went through the door, Chris stopped, and did not so much look at her as pause and sense her, taking in her presence rather than her appearance. Tara held herself very still, held her breath. Suddenly the illusion that she had created seemed very fragile – a word, a look from this man and it would shatter. But Chris made no sign of any kind, but roused himself, padded off and was gone.

Releasing her tension in a silent sigh of relief, Tara closed the door and leaned against it for a moment to recover. Then she straightened and looked around her. The creamy panelled room with its own bathroom beyond offered her an unselfconscious welcome, as if she had never been away. She moved to the dressing table, where all her girlhood brushes, pots and ornaments were still all in perfect order, the photograph of Max in its heavy antique silver frame dominating the scene as he had done in life. Inspired by an impulse she did not try to understand but simply obeyed, she raised the frame to her lips, bestowed a kiss upon the cold image behind the cold glass, then folded down the stand and put the photograph away in the drawer. Goodbye, Max, she thought. I'm on my own now, my own woman at last. Goodbye, Daddy.

Along the length of one wall was a huge built-in wardrobe. She opened it to reveal all Stephanie's clothes laid out with loving neatness. Her eyes searched along the full racks, noting with surprise and pity how many clothes Stephanie had had that had given her no pleasure, that she had worn simply to cover her body or bought because the saleswomen in the dress shops had assured her that she looked nice, even though she never believed them. Shaking her head, she tracked down some of Stephanie's wedding trousseau that she had brought up from the Harper mansion for the honeymoon here. How could she ever have worn these things? The wedding suit itself, although a beautiful blue, had no style, no glamour. Taking it from the rack she held it against her body and surveyed herself in the long mirror. I wore this the day I married

Greg, she thought in wonderment. Tara's reflection in the mirror told her how much she had changed. The suit was dowdy and far too big for her. Poor Stephanie. Tara firmly replaced it in the wardrobe.

Stephanie had never enjoyed the whole business of clothes, fashion or makeup. Tara crossed the bedroom to what had been her pride and joy, after her black stallion, King – a magnificent stereo which, with his usual determination to have the best of everything, Max had had piped to every room in the house, so that she could listen to her music wherever she was. Opening it, she fondly checked through all the records and cassettes. All Stephanie's old favourites were still there, the Brandenberg concertos, Beethoven's Fifth. But Tara would have liked some uncomplicated, gutsy heavy metal just now, or just possibly Billie Holliday. You came a long way, baby, she told herself with growing delight.

Feeling calm yet exalted, Tara opened the French windows and stepped through them onto the verandah running the length of the house. To her right were the windows giving onto Max's bedroom where Greg would sleep that night. She stood enjoying the cool shade of the elegant sandstone verandah, a halfway house between being cooped up indoors, or outside shrivelling in the baking heat. She gazed out across the lawns, the beloved rose garden and the pool, past the tidy range of outbuildings to the vast sunburned plain beyond, breathing in the thick warm air so heavy with memories. This, this is my place, she thought. This is the country of my heart. I am of it, and it is part of me.

Suddenly the sense of being watched came to her again. She looked round sharply. Away to her left, far beyond the verandah under a clump of gum trees by the kitchen garden stood Christopher. He did not move, but she could see his eyes fixed upon her. Even if he had been nearer, she knew she would not have been able to read the expression in their liquid depths. He watched her with an intensity of concentration quite unattainable by anyone else she had ever known. What was he thinking? Who could tell? But his was not a threatening presence. On the contrary. Tara drew a comfort and encouragement from it she could not express. She looked back at him, a small, still creature beneath the tall trees. Then she went back into the bedroom. Choosing a Mozart cassette from among the collection, she inserted the tape, turned it down softly and lay on the bed. The joyous music poured like a birdsong into the room. Tara lay there at peace. She had come home.

In the cheerful chaos of the Liverpool Lane agency, Joanna Randall was not having a good day. There had been a ritual run-in with today's Bright Young Asshole – as fast as you slap one down another springs up in his place, she reflected – whose radical reworking of the ad agency's script for today's shoot had eliminated one of Joanna's best models to focus entirely on the product. Then there was the strange and unprofessional behaviour of Tara who, quite out of the blue and out of character, had phoned to cancel her shoots for the next few days with no explanation other than the curt message that she would be out of town. Finally – or perhaps not finally, she thought with alarm, as it was still early in the day – Jason was making himself a nuisance, bombarding her with calls about the day's shoot. Joanna had firmly reminded him that it would make no difference to his fee if he shot the car with the girl draped along the bonnet, or without. But he was not pacified. Poor Jason, she thought, he's really grieving for Tara – like all the others around them she had not missed the change in Jason's feelings for Tara and his lack of success with her. He really just wants someone to be nice to him for a while, to make him feel better, poor boy. But poor me, to be elected his and everyone else's mother, expected to do that for them when I can hardly succeed in doing it for myself!

Now Jason had arrived at the agency in person to join in the knock-down, drag-out battle with the ad man, as he cheerfully phrased it. As he entered, Joanna was desperately trying to pull rank.

'Look mate, I've been doing this account since the time when you were still finishing high school!'

Old cow, she's past it, thought the ad man. 'This is a fresh approach,' he said silkily.

'Well, if it's so fresh, why weren't we told about it? I've got my girl here—'

'Why do we need the girl? What we're interested in is the car.' The ad man did not have unlimited patience.

'Y'don't need a girl? What a gay blade!' Jason did not care either way, but could not resist the temptation to make mischief. 'Lemme tell you about the ordinary guy, buster. He *likes* girls! He likes cars too, but he doesn't see why he can't have 'em both – like beer and skittles.'

'Jason's right. The girl is part of the appeal,' argued Joanna.

'Especially *your* girl, Miss Randall, I suppose?'

Outside in the reception area an altercation was beginning.

'I'd like to see Joanna Randall. I don't have an appointment but it's important that I speak with her.'

'Well, I'm afraid she's very busy at the moment. May I ask what it's about?'

'Look, this is desperately urgent. I have to speak with her—'

But, caught up in the ad man's insult that all she was interested in was wangling her model into the shoot to get her fifteen per cent commission, Joanna had seen red.

'Why, you slimy little toad,' she shouted. 'You greasy little turd-burgler! I don't have to take this from you!'

'Don't upset youself, mother,' interposed Jason. 'You'll bring on an attack of your hot flushes. Now do I shoot this or don't I?'

'Yes!'

'No!'

The door opened and a man burst in. Behind him was the harassed receptionist.

'Joanna Randall? I have to see you. It's very important.'

Gratefully the ad man grasped a timely deliverance from the impasse.

'I'll be in touch,' he announced, and swept out before anyone could stop him. Jason and Joanna regarded the intruder agape. Jason was the first to recover, recognizing the newcomer as the man who had disturbed his studio in search of Tara. Feeling the familiar twinges of jealousy, just when he was making some headway in getting over Tara, Jason decided to absent himself too.

'See you, mother,' he warbled, and was gone.

Joanna's face, while not yet of the same improbable red as her hair, was a study in scarlet. She poised herself to release all the vials of her anger on the head of this – *drongo* who just came bursting in when she was working.

'Look, mister—' she began dangerously.

'Before you go any further,' he said levelly, meeting her eye for eye, 'I'm a friend of Tara's, and this is important.' Joanna was checked by his air of authority. His face was severe, and his manner brisk. 'My name's Dan Marshall. May I sit down?' Without waiting for an answer he sat down in front of Joanna's desk and began to speak rapidly.

'Miss Randall, I live up north. I've been in Sydney to visit Tara, and I just flew back to Queensland. I got back to find some information that I'd been hanging on for months for, waiting for me when I arrived.'

'Sorry, what did you say your name was?' Joanna was distracted. What was he on about?

'Marshall, Dan Marshall. What I learned was important enough for me to turn around and catch the next plane back here. It concerns Tara.'

'Look, how do you know her?'

'From Queensland – quite a time back now.' He hesitated. 'Miss Randall, I know that Tara trusts you.'

'Well . . .' It was Joanna's turn to hesitate. 'As much as she trusts anyone.'

'How much has she told you about herself?'

Joanna was not sure where this was going. 'Why?'

Dan coloured, but held her gaze steadily. 'I love Tara,' he said. 'I've asked her to marry me.'

'Really.' Alarm bells were sounding in Joanna's mind. Was this one of those nuts who pursued famous and beautiful women?

'She's been seeing someone else. I want to know who it is.'

Joanna had had enough. Whatever his problem, she was not running an agony aunt service for stray weirdos who wandered in off the street lusting after or pining for her lovely clients. She drew in her breath.

'Is this what this is all about, Mr Marshall?' Ignoring her, he carried on.

'Is it – Greg Marsden?'

'Look . . . you seem like a nice man. Really. But you have to realize I never involve myself in the personal lives of my clients. I'm sure if you—'

'What if I were to tell you that there's no such person as Tara Welles?'

'What?'

'Yeah.'

'D'you mean – you trying to tell me Tara Welles isn't her real name? Lots of models—'

'More than that.'

Joanna's mind reeled. What the hell was this man saying?

'Well, if she isn't Tara Welles, who is she?'

The answer was a long time coming. And when it came, it made even less sense.

'Stephanie Harper.'

Hours seem to pass in seconds as Joanna took this in. Dan's voice flowed on, urgent, authoritative.

'Stephanie Harper did not die in that hunting accident on the East Alligator River. She was neither drowned, nor eaten alive by the crocodile who attacked her, as popularly supposed. Oh, she was badly mauled about, sure. But somehow – and I don't know how – she made her way to a clinic in North Queensland where over a period of

308

months she underwent a series of operations that completely changed her appearance. She then moved back to Sydney, calling herself Tara Welles.'

'Ha! You aren't expecting me to swallow that? It's the craziest thing I ever heard!'

'I can assure you that it is the truth. And apart from myself, and a friend of mine who helps to trace missing people through the Queensland Police Department, you are the only one to know anything about it.'

'But . . . Stephanie Harper was pushing forty.'

'She still is – if she's still alive now!'

Joanna was confused beyond all hope of understanding. She couldn't handle this. She knew what she had to do.

'I'm afraid I'm a very busy lady, Mr Marshall. So if you'd care to—'

'Doctor Marshall,' he corrected angrily. 'I'm the plastic surgeon who performed those operations. You can check me up with the Australian Medical Association. My specialism is cosmetic and reconstructive surgery. I helped to create Tara Welles!'

'You're – a doctor?'

'Yes, God help me! And I've never betrayed a patient's confidence before.' He groaned aloud, dropping the mask of professional distance for a moment. 'But – I've never been in love with a patient before. And I've come to believe that she's in considerable danger.'

'Danger?'

'Yes. It's so obvious, I must have been stupid not to work it out even before I knew who she was.' Swiftly Dan ran through Tara's desire first to change, and then to conceal herself, the important project she could not abandon even for love or life itself, her forced confession that there was someone else even though he knew in every fibre of his being that she did not love the mysterious rival – all these pointed only one way.

'My guess is that she is trying, with a primitive kind of justice, to avenge her own wrongs, not trusting society to do it for her to the full – and how brave, or how stupid, must she be to go in again, against a man who has tried to kill her once and will certainly now *need* to kill her, if he catches her. Miss Randall—' Dan broke off, and with all the force that he could muster, asked, '*now* will you tell me please – who has she been seeing? *Who is he?*'

Joanna could scarcely whisper. 'Greg Marsden.'

Dan's face flamed. 'Where can I find Tara?'

'I don't know.'

'Oh, come on! You'll have to do better than that!'

'I think Greg Marsden's still at the Harper Mansion on Darling Point. Tara could be with him there.'

'Thanks, Miss Randall – you're a pal.' As he dashed out, he threw her a smile which brilliantly illuminated his dark face. My, thought Joanna with a sense of regret, why didn't I notice before how good-looking you were?

So far, so good. Just keep it up and everything will be fine, Tara told herself as she walked down the passageway of Eden to the kitchen. Lunch had passed off very pleasantly, she had to admit, with Greg putting himself out to be charming as he had in the early days of their courtship – but with some subtle special difference. There was more feeling in his expression of caring, more genuine warmth, she now recognized. But poor Stephanie had been very easily deceived. Never having had the real thing, she was so readily fobbed off with the counterfeit.

Tara entered the kitchen in time to catch Katie, flushed and guilty-looking, hastily concealing a bottle of cooking sherry in one of the cupboards. She walked to the side and put down the few dishes that she had brought along from the dining table as her introduction into the kitchen.

'I was just coming to get those,' said Katie suspiciously. 'You just leave them.'

Tara came nearer. 'I wanted to thank you for a lovely lunch. Katie—' They were interrupted by Greg. 'Ah, there you are. I've come to see what you'd like to do this afternoon. Feeling game?'

'That depends what for.'

'Fancy seeing some of the country on horseback?'

Tara laughed. 'Oh, I think I'm game enough for that. I've been riding since childhood.'

'Riding, huh!' Katie began muttering in her head. 'You should have seen Stephanie on King. She could ride like the wind, from the time she was five or six years old. I never seen anything like her on that stallion.' A sudden fear struck her. 'King's her horse, mind. No one's ever ridden him except her!'

'No one's going to ride King, Katie,' said Greg irritably. 'Plentya other horses. I'll see you outside when you're ready, Tara.'

Leaving the kitchen, Greg went to give orders for the horses to be saddled. Chris and Sam were nowhere to be seen. Bloody Abos! Never could find them when you wanted them, yet they were always under your feet when you didn't. By the time he had sorted things out, Tara was ready. They waited under the gently sloping verandah with its delicate fringe of wrought iron for the horses to be brought round to the front of the house.

'I've asked Sam for a nice gentle ride for you,' said Greg. 'Don't want any nasty accidents.' Tara smiled to herself.

'Here they are.'

Sam came into view leading a solid-looking chestnut of over sixteen hands for Greg, and a neat little well-shaped cob for her. She took his bridle and patted his neck.

'Sam,' called Greg irritably as he mounted, 'give the lady a hand to get up.'

'No, it's OK.' Tara stopped Sam with a smile. 'I'm fine.' Gracefully and expertly she mounted the horse and gathered up her reins.

'Whewee.' Greg's eyes expressed his admiration. 'Is there anything you can't do well?'

Tara forced herself to look deep into his eyes with a provocative stare. 'That's something we're just going to have to find out sometime, aren't we?' Then she clapped her heels to the horse's flanks, asked for and got from him a perfect walk-to-canter take-off, and was away down the drive like the wind before Greg was even moving. Behind her she heard his laugh of pure delight, and 'Hey! Wait for me!' as he desperately tried to get some action out of a reluctant nag on a hot afternoon. What Tara did not see was Katie who had given in to her curiosity to see how the fancy woman from Sydney made out on a horse. She emerged from the kitchen only in time to see the flying figure of Tara as heels down, elbows in, she adopted the forward position to urge her horse to greater speed, leaning along his neck to whisper in his furry ears. Disbelief, then shock registered on Katie's walnut countenance. The blood drained from her face and she made a strangled sound in her throat. She leaned against one of the uprights of the verandah for support, then sunk slowly to the ground.

'Effie!' she whispered, 'Effie! You've come back.'

Chapter Nineteen

To those who do not know it, the great outback of Australia seems arid and boring, a level, often threatening, waste land. The deserts and vast plains seem to scream of dullness and monotony – a land to go mad in or die horribly of a lingering thirst. But this is the country of the dreamtime magic, and those who can hear its music, can feel the wonder of its stark and strangely beautiful landscape, can allow the uncluttered simplicity of space to give them freedom, these are the privileged few who can find out there the region's ancient gift of spiritual peace. Stephanie Harper had never failed to find it, once she had learned from Chris how to allow it to find her, and these great spaces, the last true frontier, became for her a cathedral, yet one in which she exercised, played and struggled as well as worshipped and rejoiced. Now she felt once more that exhilaration and sense of liberation that are so hard to come by in any city, and turned her horse's head into the light wind feeling like one new born into glory.

Together Tara and Greg raced across the wide flat sundrenched plain. The horses, fresh and well-tended, willingly stretched their necks in competition, exuberantly leaped over fallen logs, chased herds of kangaroo flying away at forty miles an hour, and sent flocks of parrots squawking noisily to the sky. Despite Greg's best efforts, and he was a harsh and determined rider, the little cob kept ahead and when they drew up to the grove of trees by the river which they had made the finishing post, Tara was the clear winner.

Her blood pulsing in every vein, glowing and breathless, she dismounted and led her horse down to the water's edge. Loosening his nose band and girth, she allowed him to drink, splashing cold water on her face and neck meanwhile, then led him to the shade of a tree.

'Gee, I enjoyed that,' she said. 'It was so good.' She turned to Greg, who had done none of these things for his horse. His face was clouded.

'Don't tell me you're one of those men who can't stand being beaten by a woman!'

This was in fact so perfectly the secret of Greg's annoyance that he felt compelled to deny it completely.

'Certainly not!'

'You were pulling a face like it.'

'I was not.' Hastily he adjusted his scowl into a smile. He didn't mind so much now, when Tara stood before him, laughing, lovely, obviously so full of life and joy after the race. His heart softened towards her.

'You fit this landscape perfectly, don't you? Just like the fashion scene in Sydney. Where'd you learn to ride like that? You are full of surprises.'

Tara laughed. 'You men don't know everything, you know. And we girls have to keep a few tricks up our sleeves.'

'Oh—' Greg was entranced with her. 'I love it when you laugh. You don't do it often enough. You're so lovely.'

Without calculation he pulled her to him, and kissed her. As their lips met, Tara gave herself unreservedly to their embrace, coming into the shelter of his body and returning his kiss with a fiery response that excited him wildly. It was the first time he had kissed her, or taken hold of that slender body he had been thinking of since he met her, and it was even better than he could have dreamed. Tara felt his arms around her and quickened to his touch with instinctive anticipation, tilting her face for his kiss, drinking in his love as if her life depended upon it. She opened her mouth for his tongue, and pressed her body against his, feeling his hardness against her with a woman's triumph. She wanted him. God, how she wanted him!

Suddenly to Greg's amazement he felt her pull roughly away, pushing him off with determined fists.

'What's the matter?' She had no answer, but stared at him with mutinous eyes. He grabbed her again roughly and held her tightly against him. With his face very close to hers he threatened softly, 'Women who play games with me make me very angry.' He thrust his pelvis violently against hers to make his point. 'It was your idea to come to Eden. Don't tell me you came all this way just to ride a horse. Even if you did, I didn't fly all this way just to breathe the country air!'

'You're hurting me, Greg!' Angrily he released her, and ran a hand through his hair.

'Wanting you and not having you is driving me crazy!'

'Greg – you must know how I feel about you.' She hung her head. 'But I—'

'But what?'

'Every time you go to touch me . . . all I can think about is your wife. When you put your arms around me . . . it's as if you were betraying her.'

'So that's it!'

'I'm sorry, Greg, but I just can't get her out of my mind.'

Greg was thinking furiously. How could he convince Tara that she had no unseen rival to fear in the dead Stephanie? He had never told a soul his true feeling for her, but had played the woeful husband, newly-wedded and bereaved, for all the sympathy he could get. But Tara – she had become the most important thing in his life. He had to risk the truth with her – even at the risk of losing her when she found out that he was not the perfect gentleman he had pretended to be. He would tell her the whole situation. He had to prove himself worthy of her love.

'OK, the truth,' he began heavily. 'The truth is I married Stephanie Harper for her money. Things hadn't been going too well for me. The competition was getting tougher. I had a knee injury and guys like McEnroe were coming up through the scene. My game just didn't have the edge it used to have.' He paused. Tara stood as if turned to stone, drinking in his every word.

'I met Stephanie at a charity do she gave at her home, and she seemed to like me. I just thought "why not?" Three months later we were married. But I tell you – even with all her money and position, Stephanie Harper was strictly second-rate! She was old. She was fat. She was boring. And she was frigid! I had to be half drunk before I could make love to her – and even then she needed two weeks' notice and a blow·torch. God, I hated that ugly bitch!'

Tara's head was bowed as if a tempest was howling about her. He could not see her face. With a startling change of tone, Greg reached out for her hand, saying softly. 'You are everything my wife wasn't. Tara, *I love you.*'

Wordlessly she pulled away, ran to her horse, mounted, and was gone at a fierce gallop. Although his first instinct was to pursue, Greg held back and let her make her way unhindered back to the homestead. Give her time, he told himself. It must have come as a shock to her to see his ignoble side like that. But he felt confident that he had, whatever it might look like, played his best card. He had her word for it that she did have some feeling for him. He knew for a certain fact that she wanted him physically, wanted him to make love to her. A man of his experience of women could not be mistaken about that. She would come round to him like a bird to his hand. He loved her. How could that fail? Slowly, to allow her the run of the plain, but still exultantly, he made his way home.

Ahead of him, as if the devil himself were on her heels rode Tara, crying, screaming and cursing his black heart who had deceived her so. Now she had it from his own lips, there could no longer be any doubting either his evil or the rightness of her revenge. She had been disconcerted, frightened even when they kissed to find her body responding to his so strongly. Now she saw the way to use this as part of his punishment. Her body wanted him – her body could have him. Then she would have the pleasure of using him in the way that he had used her, and he would have the pain she had suffered of knowing that his best gift, his body's sweetest love, had been despised and cast aside as of no value. Just a little, little longer to hold him in suspense and ignorance – and then her axe would fall!

When Katie recovered from her swoon on the verandah, she knew exactly what she had to do. Still groggy from the shock she had received, she made her way unsteadily indoors. First stop was the kitchen where she groped eagerly for her secret, as she still fondly believed, her bottle of cooking sherry. Greedily she gulped down a tumbler full of the thick soupy liquor, and its warm roughness steadied her jangling nerves. She poured herself a refill and went down the long corridor to Stephanie's bedroom. Only there would she find any proof or confirmation of the wild hope that had been grabbing at her heart since she had seen Tara Welles riding off hell for leather down the long straight drive of Eden out into the wild country beyond. For there are some things that no surgery could ever change. Katie had taught Stephanie how to ride. A person's style of riding, and the way they sit a horse, are as individual as their handwriting, and no more easily disguised. Tara *was* Stephanie, in Katie's mind. Now to prove it.

Closing the door behind her, Katie put down her sherry glass on the small bedside table and set to work. Opening the drawers of the dressing table, she went methodically through their contents – nothing but a few anonymous pairs of briefs, a couple of bras, t-shirts. In another drawer she found jeans, well-cut shorts and a bikini, along with an elegant Italian one-piece swimsuit. These gave Katie pause. Stephanie couldn't swim, and never went near the water if she could help it, ever since a childhood accident when Skipper, an over-enthusiastic collie who was Katie's gundog at the time, had knocked her into the pool and she had nearly drowned. There was a problem of the sizes, too. Katie fished into the back of the garments and read the labels. Stephanie had never been that slender across the hips, not since she was twelve years of age.

Puzzled, Katie pressed on. Another drawer yielded fistfuls of frothy, foamy lingerie, both white and black. Katie was shocked to her puritan soul. This definitely was not Stephanie, who had never worn anything except good plain cotton to Katie's knowledge from the cradle to the moment of her disappearance. After checking under the frillies to see that nothing else was concealed there, Katie thrust them back with disapproval and closed the drawer on them sharply. She sat down on the bed to think.

Could she be wrong? Maybe it had been just a trick of her old eyesight, a wish-fulfilment fantasy produced by her intense longing to see Effie again? She shook her head. All that now remained was the suitcase. Katie opened it to find some pairs of shoes, low and casual, sandals, a thick sweater in case of chilly nights, and a handful of fashion magazines. Those again were too frivolous for Stephanie. When she wasn't catching up on balance sheets and doing her Harper Mining paperwork, she would have her nose in a good book – none of this rubbish, thought Katie with disdain. Another puzzling item lay hidden under the magazines at the bottom of the suitcase. Katie's ferreting fingers found something soft and springy inside a cloth bag, and to her astonishment she fished out – a wig! The hair was so like Stephanie's, in length and colour, that for a second a wild hope flared in Katie's heart. But if the woman *were* Stephanie, why should she bother with false hair when she could just grow her own? It didn't make sense. Baffled, Katie replaced the articles, and closed the case.

That was it, then. Defeated, Katie turned to go. As she did so, her eye fell on Tara's makeup case in the bathroom beyond the bedroom, resting on the shelf in front of the mirror above the washbasin. It was tightly zipped up. Katie opened it to reveal a clutter of pots and potions, creams and eye colours. Holding it up, she put her hand in and groped around. At the bottom she felt something

318

hard. She pulled out a square parcel, wrapped in a soft silk headscarf. Within were two photographs – of Sarah and Dennis.

'Oh God, the bloody kids,' said Katie with wonder, and sitting down on the side of the bath she threw back her head and wept. Here in her hands was the proof she sought. Oh my God! Praise be! Oh Effie! Foolish phrases of love and joy ran through her mind again and again. Suddenly she was recalled to herself by the unmistakable sound of hooves at the back of the house going across the yard to the stables. The riders had returned. In a panic of haste, Katie rewrapped the photographs and stuffed them back in the makeup case. She zipped it up and replaced it on the shelf, then turned to go. Stopping only to smooth down the bed where she had been sitting on it, Katie ran out of the room. She did not see the small tell-tale glass of sherry still sitting quietly on the corner of Tara's bedside table.

The controller of Mascot airport is a woman, and a very bright woman, and maybe because she was a woman she found herself handling a problem that men junior to her had been unable to deal with. The problem was in fact another woman, who had arrived at the airport in a state of high excitement. She was wildly attempting to charter a plane to take her directly to some station in the outback of the Northern Territories that none of the Sidneysiders had ever heard of. When the booking clerks politely suggested that she would do much better to take a commercial flight to an airport nearer to her final destination she became abusive and like all problems was passed from pillar to post until she landed on the desk of the controller. The controller had not got where she was by being unable to sort things out. She made a few phone calls, worked a little administrative magic, and before much longer Jilly Stewart had been launched on the first stage of the long flight towards the Northern Territories and Eden.

*

In the outback, the night is sweet with a thousand scents and tiny noises. Greg and Tara walked in the rose garden, together, but apart. Greg was watching her attentively, waiting for her to make the first move. When he had got back from riding he found that Tara had gone straight to her room to shower and rest, leaving orders that she did not wish to be disturbed. He had had no option but to wait out the hours until dinner, some of which he occupied in making the most careful preparations himself, much to his own surprise – he couldn't remember when he had last felt that he had to dress up or take care with his appearance for a woman. In his tennis star days, the more dishevelled and sweaty, the more attractive he seemed to be. He grinned at the remembrance as he shaved, showered and dressed with meticulous care. But Tara was so special. He felt that he could not take too much trouble for her. When he came down for dinner, he was still not sure what she was planning to do, or even if she would join him at all that evening. He was enormously relieved when she very soon appeared, rested, refreshed and looking lovely in a shimmering evening gown that he was delighted she had brought with her after his insistence on Eden's informality. They had had an enjoyable dinner – the food was very good and Katie had obviously made a special effort. But the conversation had been restricted to casual topics, and he had very much had a 'hands off' feeling from her. So he was heartily glad when she accepted this suggestion that they take a night-time stroll in the garden for the chance to get close to her again.

They came out of the dining room onto the verandah, and turned down towards the swimming pool. Skirting the pool and the fountain, now gently illuminated by concealed lighting, they came to the rose garden and paused to rest on one of the benches there. All was serene and still, and the odour from the massed blooms hung like intoxication in the air.

Tara was the first to break the silence.

'Eden,' she said dreamily. 'This place was well named.'

'So what would you like to do now?' Greg was fearful of pushing her after the revelations of the afternoon, but wanted her to feel that her wishes were paramount for him. 'The choices for after-dinner entertainment are strictly limited here in the wilderness – I guess Adam and Eve had the same problem.'

'Greg—' she cut through his attempts at banter. 'Thank you for being so straight with me his afternoon.'

'You're the only woman I've ever met I can't lie to.' And that's true, so help me, he thought helplessly. 'I wanted you to know the kind of man I am. Even if it meant that I risk losing you.'

'You haven't lost me,' her voice was firm. 'I respect honesty. Even if the truth is a little hard to take at times.'

Greg was reassured by her words. He had made the right gamble when he told her how he felt about Stephanie. It was all going to be fine.

Behind them Katie emerged from the house onto the verandah, and called through the night, 'Will there be anything else?'

'No that'll be all, thank you, Katie.'

Tara added her voice to Greg's. 'Thank you for a lovely dinner.' Katie went in to bed.

'She's still cooking for Stephanie, you know,' said Greg when she had gone.

'How do you mean?'

'That meal tonight was all Stephanie's favourite dishes.'

'Really?'

'Yes.' Greg laughed. 'You have to hand it to her. She's a stubborn old bird. Nothing'll convince her that Stephanie is dead.'

'It's pretty obvious she still misses her dreadfully. And she is all alone now, isn't she?'

'Yeah. And she's too old to be running a place like this. Time she was pensioned off. She'd be better off in a home in Darwin.'

'Greg! Eden's the only home she's known for forty years.'

321

'Well I'm sorry,' he said easily, 'but time doesn't stand still for any of us.'

Tara fell silent. Greg's callous disregard of Katie had recalled to her his total lack of interest in any human being's welfare other than his own. She felt suddenly very weary and had to get away.

'Forgive me, Greg, but I think I'll turn in. I feel so tired. It must be the ride, or this wonderful smog-free air.'

A flicker of anger passed across his face. Another evasion! How much longer was she going to try to keep him at arm's length? She read his expression.

'D'you mind?'

'Yes!' he said honestly. 'And – no.' Making a joke of it he reminded himself to take his time. It was still only the first evening at Eden after all. And Tara was not a woman to be hustled. Still, he thought as he considerately escorted her to her room and left her at the door, it has to come – and it has to be good when it comes, after all this waiting!

In her room Tara relaxed at last. The dinner had been an enormous strain. Just to look at the man opposite her, so attentive, so kind, so apparently devoted to her and to try to square him up with the man who had destroyed her confidence and done his best to take her life, placed her in a situation of conflict that she just could not resolve. Perhaps there are two Greg Marsdens, she thought, as there have proved to be two Stephanie Harpers. Perhaps with Tara Welles he is all those good things that he wishes to be. He has been more truthful with me than I would have believed possible, in confessing his mercenary motives for marrying Stephanie, she thought. But if this is goodness, it's too little, too late. And it can never wipe out the evil that has been done.

No, there would be no weakening, no matter how brightly his smile flashed, how lovingly his eyes gleamed upon her, nor how stunning he looked in the candle light of the dinner table, or relaxed upon the garden bench under the diamond-studded sky. He was beautiful, but he was damned. She knew now that she must not linger much longer over her plans here. She could not keep up the pretence of never having been to Eden for much longer, or hold up a display of loving behaviour towards a man whom she hated with all the violence of her lacerated soul. Just one more piece to complete the jigsaw, she thought. Tomorrow Jilly would arrive. Then the stage would be set and events could take their course.

There was just one more thing she had to do tonight before she could sleep. Leaving her room by the French windows she slipped along the verandah and round the back of the house until she came to the servants' quarters. Quickly she approached Katie's door and knocked.

'Come in!' By the startled tones, the old lady had few visitors.

Inside the room Katie was sitting at a table with an old tin box in front of her. It lay open to reveal a jumble of old photographs, two or three of which Katie held in her hand. There was a brief electric silence as the two women looked at one another.

'I . . . er . . . I was just going through some snaps.' The old woman was clearly flustered by Tara's unexpected appearance. She suddenly stuck the photographs she was holding out to Tara. Tara took them and saw a picture of herself on King, another of her with Katie taken after Max's death. Did Katie know then? And how much did she know?

'You were in my room this afternoon while I was out riding.' She put the photographs down on the table and looked at Katie.

'No, I wasn't!' Katie fired up defensively. 'I wouldn't do a thing like that.'

'You left your sherry glass on my bedside table.'

Katie coloured. 'Oh yes, that's right,' she said awkwardly, as if she'd only just remembered. 'Yeah, I did just pop in. Wanted to see if I'd left clean towels, that's right, that's what it was.' She looked at Tara. 'I wouldn't want anyone to think I was a liar.'

'No, of course not.' Tara smiled. 'Well, I'll leave you to your photographs.'

She moved to the door. Neither woman spoke, neither quite daring to be the one to tear down the thin veil that hung between them.

'Thank you again, Katie, for a perfect dinner.' The slight emphasis that she placed on 'perfect' brought a smile to Katie's face.

'Y'welcome,' she said. 'G'night.'

'Goodnight, Katie.'

Like a creature of the night Tara slipped back around the verandah making for her own room. Through the window of the library she caught a sudden movement, and froze into the shadows of the wall for fear of discovery. Inside, Greg entered the room and made his way over to the drinks cabinet. He poured himself a nightcap and stood by the fireplace reflectively sipping the mellow golden liquid. Above his head hung the portrait of Max which his friends and colleagues had toasted on the day when Stephanie became head of Harper Mining so many years ago. Now, caught in the half light of the solitary table lamp, Greg lounged at his ease, king now at Eden in place of Max. As she watched from outside, the resemblance between the two men, despite the difference in ages and their physical dissimilarity, was striking – the same glitter about them, the same look of a predatory bird about to stoop to the kill on a defenceless creature of lesser wit and daring. Smiling slightly to himself, relaxed, even charming, he was still very threatening. What was the secret source of his attraction for her?

She could not tell. She stood watching Greg gripped by the fascination that people exert when they do not know they are being observed. He finished his drink, set down the glass and left the room by the door to the corridor. Tara continued her stealthy progress along the verandah, and turned to enter her own room. As she did so, her attention was caught by the tiny flare of a match in the darkness. Behind it she could see the face of Chris as he

324

held the flame. Tara smiled. The simple action recalled the Aboriginal stories she had been reared on, of the birth of fire, its capture by the great wirinun or sorcerer, and the sharing of the great secret with all the world through the sacred burning of the ant-hill from which all could take a brand of their own. Fire was the richest gift that the ancient spirits of the dreamtime gave to human beings. It is the legacy of the All-Father, to spare his creatures from the darkness and the cold. Fire ensures our life and its continuation. In the coldness of her lonely heart Tara received the warmth of the blessing that Chris was invoking upon her and was comforted and strengthened. She was not alone.

Chapter Twenty

The rising run bathed the flatlands around Eden in blood-red splendour. A hot and angry dawn crept over the deserts and vast plains filling the gorges, chasms, and ragged rocky ranges with warmth and light. Only the mournful, insistent lamentation of a bird disturbed the immense stillness. The stark landscape brooded, awaiting the events of the day.

The sad cry of the brolga sounded again. Tara left her room as silently as she could and with great caution slipped past Greg's bedroom door, and out of the house. Outside, the fresh cool of the new day struck her like a benediction, although the sun's rays on her bare arms were already warning of the pitiless heat to come. She breathed deeply, taking in the dry dusty air which still meant home to her, then crossed the yard to the range of stables and outbuildings.

With the highly-developed hearing of their kind, the horses had caught her approach, and as she entered every ear was pricked forward, every great furry head hanging over the door of its box to investigate the newcomer. Tara moved down the line, greeting each one as an old friend. The horses snuffled and whinnied softly, expressing their recognition of her and their pleasure in the reunion. The sweet smell of hay was all around. In the presence of these honest, loving friends Tara felt her parched soul reviving again.

Finally she came to the large loose box at the end of the row. Originally a rearing pen big enough to take a brood mare and her foal, this had been designated as King's as soon as the leggy stallion gave promise of the great height and size he was to attain. Tara approached the door and looked over. King was standing quietly at the back of the box, but his ears were pricked and the whole of his sleek black body was quivering with attention. Tara let herself in, and slid the bolt behind her. Carefully she drew near to him, speaking in a low soothing voice.

'Hello, King. Hello, my beautiful boy. Have you any idea who this is? Do you recognize me still?'

Standing to the side of him she reached up and stroked his warm, smooth neck. A ripple went through him like an electric current and she could feel the massive muscles rock-hard under her hand.

'Did you miss me, darling? Oh God, I've missed you. You know me, don't you?'

The huge beast lowered his head and nuzzled her hand by way of answer. She could feel the smooth as satin muzzle the hot breath as he blew into her fingers, then his heavy sandpaper tongue flicked out and explored her palm. She laughed with joy at the pleasure of the remembered sensation, always part of the ritual of greeting between them. King lifted his great head and bringing his muzzle up to brush against her lips blew gently into her face through his nostrils. Tara stood in silent delight to receive the greeting that King gave her, the salutation that horses reserve for one another and as such the finest compliment a mere human being can hope to receive.

Together they stood lightly blowing on one another and inhaling each other's essence in perfect communion. Then Tara reached up and caressed the long black ears covered in silky fur, knowing of old the special way King liked to be fondled, her fingers finding easily the pleasure spots for him behind his ears and on the tip of the bony poll between them. As she loved him, he brushed her face and nuzzled her neck, whinnying throatily and from time to time letting out little squeals of delight, Overcome with her feeling for him Tara snuggled up to the front of his broad chest, and clasped her arms firmly round his neck. Responding again to the memory of an old ritual, King raised his head, lifting her in the air, and tossed her to and fro, shaking her like a rag doll as she clung on, cooing to him with delight, feeling the power of the mighty stallion within her arms and all through her body.

For Katie, as she entered the stable, this little exchange was the final and ultimate proof that Tara was Stephanie. Of all the station personnel, only Chris could even go into the box with King, or lead him out to the paddock for exercise. No one but Stephanie had ever been able to handle him, let alone in this bold and intimate way. As she watched, the stallion gently lowered Tara to the ground again, standing rock-solid to take her weight without moving forward to tread on her feet. Katie could contain herself no longer.

'Effie!'

Tara was stunned with shock. She kicked herself for not having thought that a sharp pair of eyes might have spotted her early morning flit across the yard from the servants' quarters. She was certainly not ready for revelations now. She forced a bright smile.

'Katie! Good morning. How are you?'

Katie was staring at her as if she had seen a ghost.

'I'm an early riser in the country,' Tara went on determinedly.

'*I* know you are.' Katie's emphasis was plain.

'He's such a lovely horse, aren't you, good feller? I just couldn't resist trying to make friends with him.'

Katie spoke slowly and distinctly, as if addressing a half-wit.

'King belonged to Effie. Never anyone else. He was a present to her from her father. He came to us as a foal, and she broke him, she trained him. No one else could ever get near him, 'cept Chris. He's a one-woman horse. Always has been – and *always will be!*'

'I've always been good with horses,' Tara countered. 'I find I can get on with most of them.'

Katie exploded with impatience. 'Did you think you could fool me, of all people! I knew you weren't dead! I knew you'd come back. I've prayed to God every single night since you went. I knew He'd hear me.'

Tara tried to speak, but Katie rushed on.

'Look, y'can't fool me. No one else I know sits a horse like Stephanie Harper. She had a style all of her own. A man as self-centred as Greg Marsden'd never notice a thing like that. But I'd have to be blind not to notice!'

'You're making a mistake.'

'It's you that's making the mistake, not trusting me. I don't understand all this – any of it – the change in you, or how it happened. How did you survive? Where've you been living? And what's going on? Tell me, Effie. You always used to tell me everything.'

'Tell me, Effie.' Tara heard these words echoing down the long corridor of time. She thought back to her childhood at Eden, with Katie always on hand, always watching over her – but always over-protective, over-anxious. Her love was real, but it was the kind which weakens, not gives strength. 'Leave it to Katie, Katie'll do that for you' – with these and a thousand other phrases Katie had made her dependent, not free, unable to do things for herself but always looking for the person who would do them for her. You mollycoddled me, Katie, she accused her in her heart, and look what it did for me. Instead of feeding my fear of water after the accident with your damn dog, you should have helped me to overcome it. Because when I met a man who threw me in, *I couldn't swim!*

'Tell me, Effie.' Katie's appeal came again. Tara looked at her with the eyes of a stranger.

'I don't know what you mean.'

'Don't talk to me like that! I don't care what you call yourself, you can't hide what you are from me, or from yourself.'

Tara felt again the old pull of the guilt, the inadequacy, that had been Stephanie's bosom companions. That wretched, limiting philosophy of limited people, 'there's no changing what you are', had dogged her childhood. thwarted her full development. But she had proved it wrong. She could not go back to that. With deep feeling she asserted her new self, her new life.

329

'I'm Tara Welles.'

Katie's eyes glittered. She had tried to restore the old relationship, tried to re-establish her former dominance, and she knew she was beaten. Yet her own fierce sense of independence was such that she could not fail to recognize its echo in another human spirit. Grudgingly she made the effort to give it welcome in the one she loved above all.

'All right, all right,' she said emotionally. 'You must have your reasons, so I'll shut my mouth. But whatever you're doing – I'll be here if you need me.'

When Katie was gone, Tara turned in to King and laid her head on the comfort of his neck. She felt drained, distressed. As she rested, she heard behind her the slight metallic clink of a bridle and bit. Chris was padding in through the door with King's saddle and harness in his hands. He came through the stable and down to King's box, opened the door and entered murmuring to the stallion in Aboriginal, 'umbacoora, pichi malla, warrawee', 'Come on then, good boy, here we go'. Hefting the saddle on his thin wiry arm, he handed the bridle to Tara.

Smiling, she felt the familiar unspoken bond between them, and teasingly said, 'Chris, how did you know I wanted to go out riding?' His large expressive eyes glimmered back at her, deep pools of ancient knowing and understanding. His warmth enveloped her. Playfully she continued.

'Shouldn't I take the cob I rode yesterday? This is Miss Stephanie's stallion, isn't it? I'm told no one has ever ridden him except her.'

Impassive as ever, Chris moved past her and placing the saddle high on King's withers he slid it gently but firmly into place. Reaching under the horse's belly for the girth he drew it up, threaded the straps through the buckles and secured it. Taking the bridle from Tara he stood behind the horse's head, drew down the long muzzle and proffered the heavy bit on the palm of his hand, nudging it against the great yellow teeth. With a snap King accepted the bit, and was bridled. Carefully Chris checked him all over, running his blue-black hand over the even blacker skin, the horse shivering now with excitement and the anticipation of the ride. His lean body strained as he lifted the horse's feet one by one to check inside the hooves – King still had his old terrifying trick of leaning all his weight on the handler as his hoof was lifted Tara noticed, but Chris was ready for him. At last the preparations were complete, and Chris led King from the loose box to the yard outside. In the yard King began to show his mettle, jumping around and refusing to stand still. Chris secured the stirrup on one side in his bony fist while Tara mounted from the other, hanging onto the horse's head for dear life to prevent him from charging off into the wide open space he could already see and smell.

'It's OK, Chris, I've got him.' Tara had gathered the reins up tightly in her tough little hands. Chris released his hold on the bridle, and the horse was off like a chaser, covering the ground in long, even strides which Tara knew from long experience he could keep up all day if need be.

'Oh, my beautiful boy, good feller, go for your life,' she whispered in his ear. But King needed no encouragement. With his rider restored to him, a new day as fresh as the first dawning, and all the wide world ahead to gambol in, King put the whole of his noble soul into the gallop.

Never had a ride seemed so important to Tara in her whole life. She needed it first and foremost for the release of the almost intolerable tension that she felt at Eden, a reminder of the basically sound, good and healthy aspects of life here that were threatened and blighted by the presence of Greg, the canker in the rose. She needed too the time and space to think, to be alone to plan – events were reaching their climax now, everything would come up to explosion point in the next twenty-four hours, and she had to be calm, ready, and above all in control. She also had to be off the premises, away, gone – it was essential that she keep Greg uncertain, wrong-footed, guessing. He had thought, in his ignorance, that she could not get away from him at Eden, whereas in that great emptiness a woman could hide an army if she wanted to, let alone herself and a horse. He would never find her out here. She was free.

Yet even as she abandoned herself to the gallop, Tara did not forget another part of her design. She was sure that Jilly would arrive today – her crazy jealous love would not allow her to sit quietly in Sydney while Greg honeymooned with her rival. Tara was determined to be out of the way when Jilly came so that she and Greg, no longer love but hate-birds now, could strike and tear at one another uninterrupted. Still, she needed to know when Jilly arrived. So she kept her ride always within striking distance of the homestead, drawing great loops around it like the petals of a flower, spinning off and then returning again.

By the time she heard the sound of the plane, it was well on into the morning. The countryside had lost its early morning gold and the sun was bleaching the plain with noontide brilliance. The sleepy buzz of the engine sounded at first just like another winged insect. From her shelter on a nearby hill studded with gum trees Tara looked down on the scene below like one of the immortals watching the foolish humans from the heights of Olympus. Almost as the plane taxied to a halt on the airstrip, the door seemed to burst open and Jilly half-stumbled, half fell out of it. The pilot appeared briefly to hand out her bag, saluted her and the door closed again. Jilly stood disconsolate for a moment, then picked up her things and began to trudge towards the house.

Greg came towards her at a run, full pelt. He grabbed her roughly by the arm and hustled her back towards the plane. Shouts and screeches reached Tara distantly through the thin air.

'What the fuck d'you think you're doing here?'

'You bloody bastard, don't you talk to me like that!' Gripping her like a prisoner, Greg was running Jilly alongside the light plane, trying to reach the passenger door. Recklessly, madly, he pushed her right up to it, but the engine had started and unaware of their presence the pilot was preparing for take-off. Just as Greg got his hand to the doorhandle the plane began to move, throwing them both off balance. Together they fell to the ground, in imminent danger both from wings and wheels as the powerful little machine sped by them and took off, bathing them both as they lay there in a cloud of red dust. They lay immobile, looking like corpses caught by petrifying lava in the act of fornication, a jumble of tangled limbs.

Greg was the first to recover, springing up off Jilly as if she were poison. Their shouts were drowned by the sound of the plane's engines, their actions obscured by the still-swirling mist of rust, crimson and orange. Tara saw them as if through a film of blood as jerkily, like marionettes, threatening and striking out at each other, they began to move towards the house. Then turning King's head, she set a course by the sun straight out into the great nothingness before her.

'Away, boy,' she whispered to the quickening ear pricked for her command, 'let me have it now, as hard as you can go!'

'Greg! You bastard! You're hurting me!'

Loudly Jilly raised her voice in protest against Greg's vicious grip on her arm and the way he pushed her into the house careless of knocking her against walls and doorways. He did not reply, but his short breathing and compressed lips told her how angry he was. With fear mounting inside her, as soon as they had reached the sitting room, Jilly began to shout and bluster.

'Right, where is she? And don't tell me she isn't here because I know she is!'

Greg could not bear to discuss Tara with Jilly.

'I don't know what you're talking about.'

'You stinking lousy liar!'

Greg hung onto his temper with extreme effort. 'Who told you where I was?'

'Does it matter?' Suddenly afraid again, Jilly backed off from admitting that she had tackled Tara weeks ago, to accuse her of having an affair with Greg, and had since made a confidante of her. She knew that the information would be calculated to inflame him. Swiftly she returned to the attack.

'Where's Tara? There are a few things I want to say to her. I'm looking forward to giving the lady a piece of my mind.'

'Jilly—' For about the first time in his life, Greg felt an impulse of genuine fear. In a blinding insight he saw Jilly's negative capacity, her power to destroy, to kill his chances with Tara, the thing above all that mattered now like holy hell to him. Surely he couldn't have found what he wanted only to have it torn away again?

'Jilly, for God's sake—'

'God!' Jilly's voice rose to a howl of outrage. 'God! What would you know about God! You who—'

'CUT IT OUT!'

Jilly shifted her ground again. 'How many others have there been, then?'

'Others?'

'Other women,' she sneered. 'Playmates, whores, fucks, whatevers.'

Greg could not bear to have Tara's name linked in this kind of company. But he felt at a loss to deal with Jilly without provoking her further. And his mind was working on the all but insuperable problem of getting her out of here before Tara knew she had come.

'None, Jilly,' he said, trying to take control. 'Look—'

'You're a ROTTEN LIAR!' she screamed.

He stepped up close to her. 'Jilly,' he warned, 'keep your voice down!'

'Why should I? Are you afraid that people may get to know the *real* Greg Marsden?' She laughed in his face, then turned away to the sideboard and poured herself a glass of whisky. She raised it to him in a sarcastic salute, then swigged it down. Looking around her belligerently she demanded, 'Where's Tara – I want to see Tara!'

Greg's fragile control snapped with the ugly repetition of the name.

'She's not here. And I wouldn't let you see her if she were. Get this, Jilly. Get this into your thick head. I'm sick of you. I'm sick of the rows, the scenes, the booze, your stinking whisky breath. It's over for us. Finished. You're washed up.' He paused and scanned her with a withering glance. 'You're disgusting.'

Jilly gasped as if she had been kicked in the stomach.

'Are you in love with her?'

'Yes.'

'No!' Jilly's anguish expressed itself in a desolate wail. 'I don't believe it!'

'You're going to have to,' said Greg heavily. 'Now I want you out of here, Jilly – out of my house, out of my life. There's a plane from Pine Creek in the morning. I'll get one of the boys to drive you down there now. And then I don't want to see you – I don't want to hear from you. If you die I won't send a card to your funeral. I JUST DON'T WANT TO KNOW ANY MORE! Have you got that?'

He stopped to weigh up the effect of his words. One glance told him that she had not accepted a syllable of what he had said. Her face was flushed, her head held high. Jilly was fighting back.

'It's not me you mean, Greg. It's her. Just you get her out of this house and on the fucking plane to Pine Creek!'

The animal in Greg picked up the scent of danger at once.

'And if I don't?'

'If you don't—' She laughed and showed her sharp white teeth. 'Well, I think I'll just go to the police. I think I may find my conscience has become too much for me.' She was enjoying this. 'I'll just have to tell them the full story of the romantic evening's boat ride on the Alligator River. I wonder how they, and all your adoring female fans, will react when they find out that the darling of the

335

centre court pushed his rich wife into a swamp on their honeymoon when he was screwing her best friend!'

'Oh—' Greg was beyond expletives. Jilly threw down another whisky, triumphing.

'You silly, stupid bitch,' he said quietly, 'don't you see that you're in as deep as I am?'

'Oh no you don't!' Jilly's eye had a manic gleam. 'The hell I am! You're in it on your own, buster, right up to your handsome neck. Oho! You should see your face. It was worth coming all the way here just to see that.' She swaggered over to the sideboard, refilled her glass, kept him waiting. She knew she had him. Perching on the edge of the table, she resumed.

'You and I are not the only ones who know what happened out there. I told Phillip.'

'*Phillip?* Why—?'

'Because he still loves me! You may find that hard to believe, but he does. And he's not too fond of you, funnily enough. He's also the best lawyer in Sydney. He'd get me off and incriminate you.' Shoving her face at him she gloated, 'You're stuffed, boy! The worst they could do to me is to find me an accessory after the fact. And then—' she considered '—I'd say that you threatened to kill me too if I said anything. Yeah. So it'd just be your word against mine, baby. And let's face it – *you* had the motive!'

Greg had become very still, like a coiled wire. Oblivious, Jilly railed on, her frustrated love finding its perversion in a sadistic tormenting.

'I remember once watching . . . a stallion being gelded. Made me sick to my stomach. But step out of line, baby – and you'll find yourself worse off than that stallion, OK? So if anyone's leaving here it's Tara. Now – are you going to tell her or am I?'

She never saw the blow that Greg unleashed until it smashed into her face, knocking her sprawling to the ground. She was aware of Greg's presence, smouldering like a live coal, but did not look at him. She sat up carefully

336

amid the broken glass and whisky, and steadied herself on one arm.

'I don't think a church wedding would be quite appropriate for us, do you?' Tenderly she ran her tongue around her mouth, testing her teeth, tasting the blood that ran in a crimson stream from the side of her lip. 'Mmm. We might have to settle for a trip to the register office. But we'll be OK. Phillip's made it plain that when I divorce him and marry you, I blow his income. Well, that's all right.' Heavily she got to her feet, and turned to look at Greg for the first time. 'With Stephanie's money we'll manage very nicely. Life's gonna be good, baybee.'

Greg was standing in front of the gun cabinet with a rifle in his hands. Meticulously he broke it, loaded it, cocked it, and then let it hang by his side. Like the scorpion that he was, he had decided to sting, not smash. He smiled at her.

'Admire your planning, Jilly. But I'm afraid you've overlooked one or two considerations – *bay-bee*.' Savagely he mimicked her endearment. 'I saw Bill McMaster some time ago. Apparently he had Stephanie put a special clause in her will – maybe they were thinking of you, who knows? Simple though – if I remarry I don't get a cent. Not a lettuce leaf. So don't let's hear any more talk of weddings, eh?'

He smiled with the satisfaction of one who has pulled off a copious revenge. 'Just thought you'd like to know.' Jilly's face was a study in desolation. She moved her mouth as if it were dry with dust and ashes. Laughing softly, Greg left the room.

As he did so, his alert senses picked up a flicker of movement as someone whisked out of sight through a doorway across the hall. Had anyone been listening at the door? Furiously Greg ran his mind back over the conversation to try to recall what had been said – enough to hang both of them, he decided grimly. Instantly he went in pursuit. The house was empty except for a voice from the kitchen. He entered to find Katie desperately giving Eden's call sign on the radio set.

'Eden calling Pine Creek, Eden calling Pine Creek. Pine Creek can you hear me? This is Eden. Come in Pine Creek . . .'

Greg came up silently behind her with the rifle.

'Where's Tara?'

Katie's jaw dropped, and she looked at him in obvious dread. She knew something, he decided. Keep it calm and ordinary till I can work it out.

'She's not in her room. I've been looking for her.'

Katie's voice was dry and croaking. 'She . . . she rode out early. Said she had some thinking to do.'

At her elbow the radio crackled, came alive.

'This is Pine Creek, Pine Creek.'

Neither of them moved. Greg held Katie in his gaze, daring her to touch the set.

'Get Sam and Chris round here with the landrover. Ask them if they know where she's headed.'

Again the anonymous voice of the radio crackled between them.

'Eden, this is Pine Creek, Pine Creek calling. Come in, Katie.'

Katie stood transfixed, a rabbit before a stoat.

'Go on!' Greg was suddenly violent. 'Get to it, you old besom! Y'can't stand there all day!'

Like a frightened rabbit, Katie turned and scuttled from the room.

'Eden? Eden? Are you there? This is Pine Creek . . .'

Greg picked up the microphone and ripped it from the set. Then he opened the casing of the radio receiver and removed a component. The radio went dead. Pocketing the component Greg went outside.

In front of the house stood the landrover with Katie, Sam and Chris standing beside it. A heavy tension hung over the awkward trio.

'Did either of you two see Miss Tara leave this morning?'

They looked at each other and shook their heads.

338

'Dammit, what's the matter with you? Y'all asleep or something?'

Act natural, he told himself. No use in putting their backs up.

'OK, we'll go out and look for her. She'll be out there somewhere. We'll find her.' He broke the rifle he was still carrying and handed it to Sam to put into the landrover. 'Do a bit of shooting as well, eh? Bring you back some rabbits, Katie.'

Katie was still looking at him with a kind of paralysed dread. Smiling as amiably as he could, he swung into the vehicle with Chris and Sam and gave the signal for the off.

In the sitting room Jilly was still standing where Greg had left her. Her mind kept flinching away from what he had said. She found it impossible to take it in. A special clause in Stephanie's will? Even from beyond the grave Stephanie seemed to strike at her, to punish and deny her as Max had done to her father in the generation before. She had lost Greg anyway – she could see that plainly. He had told her he loved Tara, when for all the sexual terms he had lavished on her at one time, he had never breathed that word in her ear, no matter how she had abandoned herself to him, served him, pleasured him. And now, this.

She moved unsteadily to the drink bottles and took another whisky. Mournfully cradling the glass between her breasts she tried to look ahead to what would happen for her now. Whichever way she peered into the darkness of her future she could see no glimmer of light. Greg lost – and she had certainly lost Phillip – Phillip who now that he was her only means of support, moral or financial, began to take on the sort of glow she had not felt for him for years. Oh God, whatever was she to do? Panic began to rise up in her and she did what she had learned recently was the one thing she could do – she washed it away with the only comfort she had available.

Chapter Twenty-one

As he sat in the plane bringing him from America, Phillip Stewart was at a loss to explain the motive for this trip. Why the hell was he coming back? He had no call to be here for business reasons – more and more his work was centring on the American market, and with the benefit of telex and telephone it was rare that he had to be physically present in Sydney any longer. He enjoyed life in the States – he'd started to make friends there, and get invited about – so much so that he'd formed the vague idea of moving there for good, when his divorce from Jilly was finalized.

Jilly. There's the rub, he said to himself. When he had left after their last conversation, Phillip had honestly hoped that he might now enjoy some peace of mind after long months of mental distress, even torment. He felt that matters had come to some kind of a head between him and Jilly, without pressure from his side, which he had been most reluctant to apply. And although he could not say that he wanted his marriage to end, he had reached the stage in which any resolution, however unwelcome, was preferable to the continuing limbo of uncertainty and hidden fears. So he had returned to America if not exactly a free man, at least much freer in his mind than when he had arrived in Australia.

But how free is free? How does a man lay down a burden that he has been carrying devotedly for seventeen years? From his early days as a lawyer, before he had specialized in business law, Phillip knew that if you opened the doors of any jail and left them open overnight, three quarters of the inmates would still be there in the morning. Phillip found that he could not so easily break himself of the lifelong habit of worrying about Jilly, taking responsibility for her as he had supposed. In fact, it seemed to be worse now as he had no idea what she would do when she really was cut adrift – and in the company of a reprobate like Marsden . . . Phillip was afraid to imagine. No man can be expected to think well of the individual who has alienated his wife's affections and supplied his place between the sheets. But Phillip was both rational and experienced enough to know that in Greg's case, his strong aversion had other roots too. Marsden was rotten through and through and Phillip became increasingly concerned to think of Jilly in his hands.

That was the real purpose of this trip, which Phillip had had difficulty squaring with his common sense and with his heavy work schedule. He put it to himself that he needed to see that Jilly was sorted out and coping, so that he could dismiss her from his mind and get on with his life. He had made repeated efforts to contact her, but there had been no answer to the telephone. That in itself was not significant, as Jilly had always been out a lot, preferring to be almost anywhere rather than on her own in an empty house. But growing concerned, he had at last arranged for a colleague from the Macquarie Street office to drive out to the house on Hunter's Hill, to leave a message asking Mrs Stewart to telephone her husband in New York – Phillip had even had the phone number included, in case in her scatty way she had lost it. And nothing.

So Phillip had hopped on a plane to investigate, cursing himself for his stupidity in doing so. Perhaps this is like the reverse process of courtship, he thought wryly – just as when people are getting together they take a number of steps to bring them closer, so when marriages are breaking up you have to go through all the stages of letting go. I must let go of her, and I will, he promised himself. It's just that right now . . . it's hard. He was still revolving his troubled thoughts without relief or solution when his plane touched down. And by the time he got out to the house he felt, if possible, even more confused.

There is something so forlorn about an abandoned house. Phillip knew as soon as the taxi turned up the drive that Jilly had not simply gone out, but departed this place. Feeling angry at his fool's errand Phillip let himself in, shivering slightly in the hall at the chill of the disused mansion. He did not have very far to look for the farewell note. It lay on the hall table in the place reserved for outgoing mail. As an outgoing male himself, Phillip recognized the savage irony of her unintended gesture. He opened the letter.

Dear Phillip,

I don't know when you are next coming back from the US, so I don't know when you'll get this, but it doesn't matter. Just to let you know that I've gone to live with Greg, I am going to marry him though you seemed to doubt it when I told you. Don't try to follow me, I won't be at the Harper place and I'll send for my things as soon as we know where we're going to be. I'm sorry for the things I've done, and I hope that as time goes by you'll be able to think kindly of me.

Love,
Jilly.

PS. Wish me luck!

Phillip sat down on the chair in the hall with a heavy heart. Well, he had come from America to try to get Jilly out of his hair, and the visit had done that with a vengeance. She had burned her boats well and truly. He could not help her at all – she did not even want him to know where she was. But marry Greg? He sighed. Phillip had been one of the lawyers of Harper Mining since he first began to practise. His firm, just around the corner from the Harper headquarters in Bent Street in the city, had looked after Harpers since young Max had wandered in from the street over half a century before. He knew of the one good reason in Stephanie's will, inserted by Bill McMaster and made watertight by all the best brains of the entire law practice, why Greg Marsden would never

342

marry Jilly, or anyone. There was nothing to be done. Phillip made a mental note to have someone come in and pack up Jilly's things. He would remove his own personal effects himself, then see if he could not sell the house fully furnished, as it stood, lock stock and barrel. He glanced around. He could not imagine that he would ever want to see any of these objects again. Numbly he picked up the phone to try to get an immediate return flight. The jet lag would be terrible, but not worse than this.

'Hello, British Airways? . . .'

Yes, he would definitely move to America.

Bloody damned heavy awkward thing! Katie cursed her saddle as she struggled under its weight towards the loose boxes in the stables. As soon as Greg was out of sight of the house, the landrover tearing off in a puff-ball of dust, Katie had hurried to her own horse, determined to join the search for Tara, and not leave her to Greg's mercies. Looking for Effie, as she still thought of her, in the vast outback especially when she was riding like the wind on King, was a task which made looking for a needle in a haystack simple by comparison. Still, Katie knew if anyone did Tara's favourite rides and her special places where she would look for her – and anything was better than being idle at home.

'Come on, then, girl.' Katie manoeuvred herself and the horse's tack into the loose box and began to saddle up her amiable and rather elderly mare. As a lifelong country-woman Katie could still ride anything with a leg on each corner, but to pacify Chris who kept a very protective eye upon her as part of his responsibility for honouring the ancients, Katie settled these days for a rather staid old girl. Peggy was an honest mare, not very bright, but guaranteed not to buck, rear, shy, or throw her passenger.

'But y'don't go very fast f'me, either!' said Katie sternly as she cinched the girth with her bony knee rammed in the uncomplaining beast's belly. 'Y'going to have to mend y'paces today, Pegs! We've got to find Effie, that's what.'

Leading her outside, Katie mounted with surprising agility and set off. Ahead of her the afternoon sky was taking on an unhealthy tinge. The brilliant, glistening air was thickening up, darkening, turning a soupy yellow in place of bright gold. Katie's mare smelt the dense atmosphere and reacted uneasily, laying her ears back and moving forward with a plodding and reluctant trot.

'Storm, y'think, Peg?' Katie asked. 'Maybe it won't come this far. 'S a long ways off. Better get going, anyway. Will you git up!'

And heedless of her own safety the indomitable little outbacker set her course and was on her way.

Further out the threat of the storm lay heavier upon the landscape. Overhead the sky was massing with clouds, darkening the whole panorama to a sickly mustard colour. The wind was getting up, tearing through the cluster of gum trees and raising small sandstorms from the dry red earth. As the sun went down it gave an eerie illumination to the heavy bars of cloud that were settling low across the horizon as if the great bowl of the sky were closing in on the helpless land-dwellers beneath. From the north-west came the growling of the rising storm as it rolled on its path towards Eden.

Miles and miles further out than she had ever been before, Tara was streaking along on King, asking the brave horse for a mighty effort to bring them both to shelter before the storm itself or the premature nightfall cut her off from the landmarks she needed to see to be able to find her way home. Darkness was descending fast, bringing the ochre sky through a series of spectacular changes from a clear gold along the skyline to brass, copper, blood-red and finally smoky blue-black where the rain clouds were ominously massing. On and on powered the stallion, still giving and giving, pounding sure-footed over broken ground, scattered rocks and thick scrub. Tara raced forward into the eye of the storm, a dark angel hell-bent on vengeance and calling all the elements to assist her purpose.

In the living room of Eden Jilly had drunk, wept, slept, then wakened to repeat the whole process. Hours of solitude, nursing a badly bruised face, and a ruined life, had reduced her to a state of total and abject despair. On the point of passing out from the amount of whisky she had poured down herself, she was wandering round the room muttering, talking to herself, or laughing crazily from time to time as yet another ironical or ridiculous aspect of her situation struck her. Her attention was caught by a framed photograph of Stephanie on the mantelpiece. With the ferocious concentration of the very drunk she wobbled up to it and carefully peered into the frame, her nose touching the cold glass.

'Ha, Stephanie!' she said thickly, 'still getting your own back on me, aren't you? I once swore I'd get even with the Harpers for what they did to my father. But the same thing's happened to me. And I never wanted it to be as bad as that for you, Steph – I never dreamed it'd be so terrible, oh—' she wept to recall as she had to so often the horror of Stephanie's bleeding face in the swamp. 'I'm so afraid now,' she blubbered, lost in a labyrinth of self-pity, 'Help me, Steph, I don't know what to do . . .'

Darkness had fallen and Jilly was quite alone. Suddenly the silence of the night was broken by the thunder of hooves. King had come flying home in the same style as he had set out, still having enough power in reserve to leap clear over the fence to the stable yard rather than bother to walk through the gate. Foam-flecked and sweating he finally pulled up after the run of his life, and all Tara could do was to hang on his neck in love and gratitude. Then she dismounted, removed his tack, carefully rubbed him down and covered him with his sweat rug to allow him to cool down naturally. Finally she watered and fed him, leaving him an extra reward of the fragrant hay for his services to her today.

As she walked across the yard towards the house, Tara knew that they had only just got in in time. The storm was coming up with a fearsome steadiness of purpose. Yet the storm without may not be more terrifying than the storm within, she thought, bracing herself for the onslaught.

'You . . . you bitch! You rotten stinking cow!'

Jilly was standing shaking in the passageway before her clutching a glass.

'Hello Jilly.'

'Oh, so you knew I'd come then, did you?' Tara's calm greeting triggered Jilly's unstable temper.

'Well, of course.' She walked past Jilly, drawing off her riding gloves matter-of-factly.

Jilly ran behind her and grabbed her arm. 'Who the fucking hell do you think you are?' she demanded wildly. 'Pretend to be my friend while all the time you're having it off with Greg behind my back! Why? It just doesn't make sense?'

Tara ignored her. 'Where's Greg?'

'He went looking for you. He took a gun so he'll probably go shooting – it's the kind of thing he does when he's feeling trapped.'

'I'm going to make a cup of tea.' Tara turned in the direction of the kitchen. 'Want one?' she threw over her shoulder as she walked away.

'Listen to me! You come back here!' ordered Jilly uselessly. 'I want to talk to you. Tara . . .'

In the kitchen, Tara laid down her riding crop and gloves and took up the kettle with a face like stone and a heart to match. It was clear that her plan for allowing Greg and Jilly to punish one another had worked well – dispassionately she noticed Jilly's swollen lip and the ugly blue marking on her cheek and chin. She knew too the kind of murderous frustration that would have driven Greg out with his gun to take the lives of little helpless things that had never harmed him in any way. But she could not feel pity for either of them. They felt nothing for anyone except themselves. Her plan and her purpose were perfect now. There would be no turning back.

Jilly entered the kitchen in haste, staggering towards Tara, spilling her drink.

'Don't you walk away from me,' she blazed. 'You've got some questions to answer, Miss Tara! Why did you tell me you were coming up here with Greg – why?'

You'll know soon enough, my dear, thought Tara. Aloud she said. 'I figured you were entitled to the truth, Jilly. You thought of yourself as my friend, and I didn't want to go behind your back. You thought of Greg as yours, and here he was giving me a great big rush. I told you because Greg would only have lied if you'd asked him.'

'So . . . it's true then – there is something? How long has it been going on?'

'Quite a while.' Tara was deliberately keeping her distance, moving about the kitchen making tea but in reality keeping Jilly on edge.

'How long?'

'I haven't been keeping a score card. It's not that serious for me.'

'Oh, I see!' As Tara had calculated, that really struck home. 'It's only been a game for you then? All a game? You've just felt free to pursue your little fancy when it's my man you're taking, my life you're ruining . . .'

'*Couldn't Stephanie have said the same to you, Jilly?*'

Tara's voice cut to the quick like a surgical scalpel. Jilly gasped.

'Huh? Stephanie? I don't get this, I don't understand. I still don't know why you want to take Greg from me. What have I ever done to you?'

The question hung in the air. Tara fixed Jilly with a grim and accusing stare. Haunted, frightened, Jilly became hysterical and aggressive.

'It's you! It's all you, you're the trouble between me and Greg. We were all right until you came along, he loved me . . .' She turned on Tara, snarling and angry.

'I want you to leave! Now!' She made a drunken swing

347

at Tara, the slack fist missing her face and glancing harmlessly off her shoulder.

'I don't think Greg'd like that very much, if I told him, do you?' Tara asked, her eyes black with disgust.

'Greg!' Alarmed Jilly grasped at once the truth of Tara's words. 'Greg – the bastard – he should be here. Oh, where is he?'

'Well, if you care so much for him—' Tara's voice seemed to be getting colder and colder '—you could always try saddling up one of the horses and go out looking for him.'

The sardonic suggestion reinforced Jilly's feelings of helplessness and mounting terror. Outside, the howling wind heralded the imminent breaking of the storm over Eden.

'You want to be careful though, Jilly,' the cold and distant voice continued, 'Looks like we're in for a storm. You mind you don't get caught out in it.'

With difficulty Jilly focused her eyes on the goading, taunting source of her distress. Before her stood Tara, smiling pleasantly.

'Now, Jilly, how do you like your tea?'

Howling with rage and dread, Jilly hurled the whisky she was holding all over Tara.

'You shove your tea! Shove it! Shove it! Shove it!'

Outside the storm broke with all its frenzy upon Eden. It was travelling at a furious speed, tearing branches from trees and thickening the black air with leaves and dust. Its unholy choir of voices moaned and screamed about the house in every tone from falsetto shrieks to thunderous roars, as if the demons of the air were crazed with fury. Thunder followed lightning so fast that there was not a second between, and torrential rain bore down upon the roofs as if to beat them to the ground.

Hurtling back to Eden on the very lip of the storm came Katie, saved by her old countrywoman's instinct of knowing how and when to run before a hurricane like a ship and get it at your back so that it can bring you in. She had not found Effie. But she had had a real good ride. She was exhausted but relieved of some of the burden of her tension. She was pleased with old Pegs. And she was pleased with herself, to stick a hard ride under bad conditions at her age.

Hurriedly fleeing the first heavy rain, Katie got the little mare under cover, saw to all her needs, and stayed a moment to enjoy the peace of the stable. Re-entering the house she saw the object of her search coming out of one of the spare bedrooms.

'Effie! I thought you were lost! I been out to look for you!'

Tara was touched by the old woman's devotion. 'Oh Katie, you know me better than that,' she said, her voice soft with meaning. 'When did I – would I – ever get lost out there?'

Katie chuckled with delight at the tacit reference to the secret they shared.

'Now listen – did you know we've had an unexpected visitor? Jilly Stewart?'

'Yeah, I seen her arrive – heard her arguing with – *him*.'

'Well, she's in here.' Tara opened the door of the guest room. Inside Katie could see Jilly sprawled on the bed on her back, head tilted up, her breath rattling thickly in her throat. 'I've had to put her to bed – she's seems to have been drinking all afternoon, and she got hysterical in the kitchen, then passed out. Leave her here to sleep it off, OK?'

'Yeah, sure.'

'And Katie – you're pretty well in the picture now about what's going on here. I'm just asking you to trust me. It's all under control. I know what I'm doing, and I have to do it.'

Katie's face lit up. 'Oh, Effie, anything you say! Just as long as you *are* Effie, and y'won't go away again.'

'I won't go away again. But I want you to leave it all to me. You won't need to cook dinner tonight – you can go to

349

your own room now and get an early night. That's what I'm going to do.'

'Right!'

'Goodnight then, Katie.'

'Goodnight Effie.'

Full of joy, Katie bustled off to her quarters, where she fully intended to have another evening with her photographs. But she had no sooner tucked herself up in bed with her box, than the effects of an afternoon's hard riding made themselves felt, and she slept like a baby.

Tara too was feeling throughout her body the joy of her day's sport. She was deliciously languid, every muscle stretched, her whole being fulfilled. Her lower body was suffused with the tingling warmth that only a hard ride can produce – standing there in the hall she thought again of the sensuous feel of the horse between her legs, felt the pleasant ache inside her thighs. Well, she was thoroughly at home inside her own skin tonight, she reflected. Now for the next stage.

Quietly checking again that Jilly was all right, she returned to her own room, and passing through the bathroom beyond began to draw a bath. From her makeup case she produced a Lalique glass bottle, unstoppered it, and allowed a few of the precious drops within to fall into the gently steaming water. Humming to herself she laid out her fine French soap, her softest sponge, her body oils and lotions. The fragrance from the bath drops scented the air with musk and roses. Tara stripped herself of her t-shirt, jodhpurs, bra and briefs, their raw odour of stallion suddenly out of tune with her mood.

The bath was almost ready now, the water churned up to a sweet milky froth by the pouring taps. Tara went through to the bedroom and chose a cassette for the stereo. Without hesitation her hand went to a tape of old French songs of the joy and pain of love. 'Plaisir d'amour,' she sang, 'oh, the sweet bliss of loving . . .' The music filtered softly through to the bathroom. She turned off the taps, swathed her hair in a towel, stepped into the bath and lay in perfect peace. Dreamily the haunting sensual rhythms of the next tune played around her. 'Sous le lilas,' crooned the chanteuse, 'vin d'lilas . . .'

> Lost myself on a cool dark night,
>   Gave myself in that misty light,
> Was hypnotized by a strange delight,
>   Under a lilac tree.
> I made wine from the lilac tree.
>   Lost my heart in its recipe
> Made me see what I want to see,
>   Be what I want to be . . .

Bumping over the rough surface of the plain towards the lights of Eden in the distance, Greg concentrated on trying to hold the landrover on course, half blinded as he was by the sheeting rain. He was riven with anger and fear, a murderous anger against Jilly which was only partially appeased by the slaughter he had made, and a consuming fear that Tara might not have made it back alive if she too had been trapped in the storm. He drove like a madman: careless of stones and potholes, careless also of Sam and Chris in the back being tossed around as if they were as dead as the piles of dingoes and rabbits round their feet. He had no fear of the thunder raging overhead, the lightning forking down constantly to the plain as if pursuing them. He had only one thought – Tara.

Screeching at last into the yard he jumped from the landrover almost before it had stopped moving.

'Get this put away,' he ordered, 'and hang those carcasses up outside the house.' Crossing the yard at a run, he went in prepared for almost anything except what he found, the interior in almost total darkness and silence. Nobody in the kitchen – that suited him, he wasn't hungry and could do without Katie tonight. No one in the sitting room or dining room or library. He finally tracked Jilly down to the spare room where her thick snoring reassured him that she would be out for the night. But where was Tara? Anxiously he pressed on down the corridor to her room. The light was on and from within came the sound of a strange and seductive song.

> Lilac wine
>   Is sweet and heady,
> Where's my love?
> Lilac wine,
>   I feel unsteady,
> Where's my love?
>   Listen to me,
>   Isn't that he,
>   Coming to me?
> Lilac wine,
>   I'm ready,
> For my love . . .

Lapped in the music, luxuriating in the warm water, Tara was for the first time in her life undertaking the sensual and satisfying ritual of preparing herself for love. Her body wanted Greg Marsden – her body should have him. But it must be perfect. For the perfection of her love would be the perfection of her revenge. Lovingly she soaped her body, smoothing out her limbs and caressing every joint and fold of her skin. As Tara she handled her body with pleasure and pride, patting and drying, oiling and creaming until every inch of her from top to toe was tender, moist and fragrant. Her brush with death had given a new value to her flesh and bone and had taught her to love herself and love her body as one of the pleasures of life. But the love of a man – that was another kind of love. And she would be ready, ready for love.

In the room next door, Greg too was following the stages of a similar ritual of his own. First he prepared the bedroom, tidying away the evidence of his occupation, plumping up the cushions and the pillows on the bed. Then he went through to the kitchen, where he found a bottle of champagne in the fridge and brought it through with two glasses. Finally he took off his wet jacket and shirt, jeans and briefs and stepped into the shower.

Sensuously he turned his face up to the water and allowed it to trickle all down his body. He revelled under the spray like a child, splashing and playing, washing away his tensions and giving himself up to anticipation of what was to come. Odd phrases from the tune he had heard outside Tara's door kept coming back to him. 'Lilac wine . . . where's my love?' With arousing interest he rubbed the soap into his arms, his chest, his loins, his appetite quickening every second. 'I'm ready . . . ready for love.'

Up above Eden the storm was reaching its crescendo, in a devastating assault from north, south, east and west upon the isolated homestead. But for Chris in the warm depth of the stables the crash and confusion of that awesome night held no terrors. He knew it was only the antics of the thunder-man, Jambuwul, who travels in the thunderclouds to shed the life-giving rain upon the dry world beneath. Without the thunder-man there would be no life, for his clouds are also the home of the spirit children who travel to earth upon the raindrops to find a human mother. Squatting down on his haunches in King's box, the huge horse quietly attendant upon his meditations, Chris began softly chanting his communion with his sacred voices as his part in the ritual this night would see enacted.

'Bano nato banjeeri, kulpernatoma Baiame, I hear the voice of the ancestor spirit, I call to you, All-Father, let the great spirits charm and bless the woman in her work tonight. You taught us to know the wonder and beauty of woman and a woman's power of love when you made Kunnawarra the Black Swan, and made for her a special companion, for woman is not complete without man, nor man without woman, and without the fire of life kindled in the primal dance when man and woman embrace, all lovely things will vanish and darkness and cold will return to conquer the world. O Julunggul, great Rainbow Serpent, when the first life began in the songs and dances of our ancestor spirits, you were seen to arch your body upwards to the sky in blessing upon them. Rainbow serpent, mother

353

and father of all living creatures, as you are both phallus and womb and the life that is in both, be with this woman, and as you govern both moons and tides may your waters flood her rivers and her rivers run triumphant to the sea!'

Tara was ready. Fresh from the bath, almost sated with the sweetness of the love music and the heavy scent of musk roses in her bath oil, she had smoothed her body into a state of tingling anticipation. From the drawer she took a white negligée, rich with lace at the neck and sleeves, with a wide sash of pink satin, and slipped it on. In her mirror she saw a woman bright-eyed, flushed and undeniably lovely. I am ready at last, she thought.

Crossing the room, she went out by the French windows onto the verandah. There she could see the true magnificence of the storm, the sheets of fire splitting the heavens and the torrential cascades of water that never have the power to quench them. Her pulse quickened in response to the wild rhythms of nature and she laughed aloud in exhilaration. Then she turned and walked along the verandah in the direction of Greg's room.

Wrapped in a soft bath towel, Greg had just finished showering and was checking the room for any last details when he saw through the open French windows a form in white come drifting along the verandah. He caught his breath. She was so beautiful that she might have been created as the original idea of woman. As he watched her, entranced, Tara turned and entered the room. Wordlessly he crossed to greet her, taking her hand and leading her to a chair. That simple action was a sexual one for him, the contact with her warm, curled fingers electric. He moved to open the champagne, but felt himself fumbling it as he could hardly take his eyes off her. Gleaming, scented and fresh, she was also charged with a new and subtle eroticism he had not seen in her before. Somewhat to his embarrassment he felt his cock stirring under the bathtowel. Mustn't rush this, he told himself, what are you, fourteen?

Tara watched Greg as he opened the champagne with

undisguised fascination – the first time she had allowed herself the pleasure of studying a man's body. From his well-set head to the long slender toes of his feet he was wholly gorgeous. His shoulders were broad and bony, the muscles well-developed and strong, and his chest was fretted with golden hairs like the sweepings of a goldsmith's workbench. His belly was lean and flat, and the towel sat low upon his narrow hips, its whiteness showing off his tan. As she looked at him he smiled – he loved to feel her eyes upon him – and pouring the drink he brought a foaming flute across to her.

'To you,' he whispered, raising his glass, 'and your beauty.'

Silently they drank, toasted again, and drank again. Greg would almost have been happy to sit and look at her all night, but his desire to touch her was becoming overwhelming. Setting his glass down on a table at the bedside he crossed to her, relieved her of hers, and drew her to her feet. Then he held her to him and taking her face in his hand he tipped up her mouth for his kiss.

Her kiss was soft and warm like ripe fruit. Gently he explored her mouth, pushing his tongue deeper and deeper as she responded. Eagerly Tara took his tongue, tasting and sucking – she felt as if she were drinking him in. She took his tongue between her teeth and held him, then let him go, and breaking free covered his lips, his chin, and under his throat where she could just reach on tip toe with a score of hot little kisses till he claimed her mouth again.

Standing so, he had dropped his hands to caress her buttocks and press the centres of their bodies together. She could feel the length and strength of his standing cock and felt the excitement of her power over him. She ran her hands lightly over his back, tracing the shape of his shoulder blades and enjoying the smoothness of his skin. Releasing his hold on her he stood back a pace and looked down at her breasts, now longing to be free of the flimsy fabric that bound them. Leading her to the bed, he sat her down tenderly and gently touched her breasts, first one, then the other. Her nipples were full and pink, standing erect through the thin silk of the negligée. He undid the sash and pushed the material aside to let her be free. Never before had Tara experienced the worshipping reverence that a man can give to the body of a woman he loves. With skill and devotion he adored her breasts in a way that made her feel they were fully hers for the first time. Kneeling before her he traced their outlines with his lips, taking each nipple into his mouth by turns to suck it rhythmically. Tara's joy was intense. She felt the excitement burning from the centre of her being. Then holding her breasts in both hands he pushed his face between them and the feeling of the roughness of his chin against the satin-sensitive skin was electrifying.

Now he pushed her back on the bed and parted the negligée along the whole length of her body. Stroking, caressing her belly and her thighs, his lips and fingers discovering nerves and sensations she never before knew she possessed. Her desire growing, she took his hand and hurried it to the triangle at the top of her legs where the silky brown curls of hair were already moist with love dew. His long fingers explored her vulva, felt the warm engorgement of a longing woman, came to the clitoris and felt it quiver to his touch. Delicately he parted the lips and went down on her, expertly tonguing until in an unrecognized rushing sensation and hardly knowing what she was doing or why she was doing it, she grabbed his head to hold herself against the hardness of his chin and in a short stabbing orgasm, came.

Afterwards she threw her forearm across her face as if to hide behind it and murmured, 'I'm sorry.'

Greg laughed lazily. 'What's to be sorry about? If you can come as easily as that, you can come again and again and again. Here, I'll show you.' He slid his fingers in between her thighs and in an instant she felt herself growing hot again there for him, He felt the springing juicies himself. 'There, you see?' He laughed again and his eyes mocked her.

Flaming up, Tara struggled to break his control over her. She reached for him and taking him by the shoulders, she pushed him back on the bed, then twitched away the towel he still had around his waist. Arrogantly he lay back as his cock was exposed, delighting in its strength and in her interest. Fascinatedly she took it between both her hands and felt its smoothness, its wonderful solidity. Gently she drew it between her breasts and running her lips up and down it kissed it tenderly, and buried her face in the dark golden springing hair at its base. Greg felt his excitement accelerating, and knew that as a man he could not afford to be so profligate with his climaxes as women are. So he showed her how to pleasure him without making him come, touched equally by her innocence and by her willingness to learn.

Tara felt as if she were experiencing again all her life in one crash course, and this time getting it right. Her strength, her confidence increased by leaps and bounds. So too did her excitement – that first climax had merely whetted her for more. Her hunger for Greg's hands, on her breasts, on her backside, between her legs, grew. But even more she longed for his cock, which she had had between her hands, between her lips, between her breasts, to come between her legs. Tiring at last of his whispered 'not yet', she finally hopped on top of him and took him by main force, clenching him with the muscles of her cunt so that he could not get out. Taken by surprise, and robbed of controlling the orgasm he had been holding on the brink for so long, he shouted 'you bitch!' in a voice of wild delight, and shot into her like an express train.

Then began the luxury of slow loving, when the immediate desire is satisfied and the deep yearnings still to be fulfilled. Now it was her task to bring him back to life as he put it, and that was her licence to explore every inch of him with her hands and mouth, to stroke the inside of his collarbone and kiss the hollow of his hip. His nipples, she found, were as sensitive as hers, the base of his spine as susceptible to gentle massage. The insides of his thighs were as delicate as tissue paper, and free of the golden-brown hairs which covered the front of his legs. Wonderingly she took the heavy scrotum in her hands and questioned the strange dispensation of nature that had put something so precious in such a fragile packaging. At every discovery her excitement mounted – she was so moist with love juices that she felt as if she was melting from her cunt outwards – and by the time she had finished her voyage of discovery his cock had come back to life with a vengeance.

Tipping her on her back he drove into her and with long, smooth, rhythmic strokes he brought her moaning to a sweet, furious, lengthy climax which racked her body with ecstasy. Only when he was satisfied that she had come and come again did he permit himself release, riding home on the dying waves of her excitement.

They lay like two drowned lovers abandoned by the sea on the shores of eternity, illuminated by the pure clear light now pouring down from the cloudless sky. The storm had spent its passion to rage elsewhere. The sky spirits, the ancestor spirits, and the great Rainbow serpent himself had done their work. She was a woman at last.

Chapter Twenty-two

Dan approached the Harper mansion with care. Having no car in Sydney he had had to take a taxi out to Darling Point, but he paid it off at the bottom of the avenue and covered the last quarter of a mile on foot. But a cautious surveillance suggested that his precautions were unnecessary. There seemed to be no one about. The great white house lay sleeping in the morning sun and there were no cars on the drive or any signs of activity. Dan felt a spurt of anxiety. This was the only lead he had in his search for Tara. What if it proved to be a dead end?

With the patience of his profession Dan set himself to watch and wait. His vigil was not rewarded. Nothing happened. Nothing moved. Nobody came or went. Dan sheltered under the trees overhanging the wall by the gates to the mansion, and gave himself up to his thoughts. When had he first become uneasy about Tara? He didn't know. But it seemed to him now that there had been something about her that had haunted him from the very first – he could still see her as she had been on that initial consultation, ravaged in face and body but with her unique spirit shining in those unusual eyes. And he had known then too that she had lied about the nature of her accident – no car had ever inflicted those injuries. She'd been the original mystery lady all along, hiding her painful secrets in the recesses of her proud spirit, wounded as much in soul as in body.

Time, he knew from experience could be relied upon to heal most wounds. But time is a slow doctor, working without anaesthetic. Dan had come to realize from his recent visit to Tara that her sufferings were still continuing. Whatever had happened to her was not over. He sensed that she had a plan, was pursuing a course of action to deal with whatever was troubling her, and he admired her for that. He also had faith in her courage to bring it to some sort of climax. But as the pieces began to fall into place for him, following the visit of a grave and concerned Sergeant Sam Johnson on Orpheus Island, his fear that her strength could still be defeated by an enemy stronger, bolder and crueller than she was could no longer be contained. Oh Tara, my darling girl, he thought why didn't you trust me? And how can I help you if I don't know where you are?

The slow approach of a delivery van broke the stillness of the avenue. Dan roused himself from his meditations. Time for a frontal assault. He tried the wrought iron gates and as he expected found them locked. But the surrounding walls, built more for ornamentation than as a serious deterrent to invaders presented no problem to an athletic male. Heedless of any damage to his shoes or clothing Dan sprang up, got a purchase on the rough surface, and hoisted himself up. Without pausing on the top for fear of discovery he dropped painlessly into the soft earth on the other side. Brushing the loose soil from his hands and knees he took stock of his surroundings.

Ahead of him the ground rose smoothly in a curve of green lawn. The thickly wooded garden afforded plenty of cover. Dan moved up cautiously towards the house, sheltering behind the clumps of trees and shrubs with which the grassy expanse was studded. He did not allow himself to question the wisdom of what he was doing trespassing on private property, and resolutely pushed from his mind the screaming headlines thrown up by his imagination, 'QUEENSLAND DOCTOR ARRESTED: BREAK-IN AT MANSION'. He worked his way around the side of the house, seeing no movement or evidence of occupation. Towards the back he came as near as he dared to the edge of his protective screen, and peered out through the bushes to the scene beyond.

Behind the house the lush green lawns fell away again in an undulating swell down to the water's edge and the deep mooring where the Harper yacht waited at anchor. The house stood four square on its eminence, all the windows on this side curtained and shuttered against the hot morning sun. Chairs and sun-loungers littered the terrace but no one reclined in them to enjoy the sun's blessing. Only below the patio in the swimming pool a boy could be seen doing a steady crawl to and fro. On the side of the pool, flat out in the heat, lolled an Alsatian, inert and panting.

Suddenly the dog stirred, lifted its head, and scented the air. In a flash it was on its feet and pointed in the direction of Dan's clump of trees. Then with a high yelp of excitement it was off the poolside and haring down the lawn in a dead set for Dan, barking all the way.

Flushed from cover, Dan stepped out from the bushes and walked forward. As the dog came racing up, he stood his ground and dropped to one knee to meet it on its own level.

'Good boy!' he said in as relaxed and friendly a voice as he could muster, 'hey there, feller! You're a good dog, aren't you?' To his intense relief the dog stopped dead before him, watchful but not threatening. ''S all right, boy.' Dan said, more coolly than he felt.

'Who are you?' The shrill, nervous call came from above, where the boy had scrambled out of the pool and was clutching a towel around him as if for protection.

'Friend, I promise you,' Dan called back reassuringly. 'I did ring the bell at the gate, but no one answered.'

'This is private property, you know. People aren't supposed to just walk in.' His voice was guarded, but no longer frightened.

'I must apologize. I don't normally do things like that, but this is an emergency.'

The boy came cautiously over the grass towards him. Dan did not dare to move a muscle for fear of triggering the dog to attack. He glanced at the bright eye, the pointed teeth, the whole body poised to spring and waited as calmly as he could for the boy to come up.

'What do you want? What are you doing here?'

'My name's Dan Marshall! I'm looking for a Greg Marsden.'

'He's not here. Are you a mate of his.'

Hardly, thought Dan grimly. 'No, I'm not,' he said emphatically, and was rewarded with the look of relief on the boy's face. 'I'm a friend of Tara Welles.' And you're her son, with those eyes, he thought.

'Tara!' There was no mistaking the note in the boy's voice. 'Do you know her?'

'She's become a rather special friend of mine. I was hoping that somebody here might be able to tell me where she is. Do you know?'

In his urgency Dan made a small involuntary movement towards the boy, and the dog growled in his throat. The boy smiled.

'It's all right, boy. Off guard.' The dog relaxed. 'His name's Kaiser,' volunteered the boy. 'He's a killer, really.'

'Yes, I could see that he would be.'

'He doesn't usually let anyone get near us.' The boy regarded him with curiosity.

'I hope he could tell that I was a friend. I think he must have done.'

In unspoken agreement they turned and began to walk up the lawn towards the house.

'How long have you known Tara?' The boy was clearly keen to talk about her.

'About a year now.' How much do you know, thought Dan. Anything?

'Where did you meet her?'

'At my clinic in North Queensland.'

'North Queensland!' The boy's face clouded with thought. 'Are you a doctor, then?'

'Yes.'

Above them on the terrace Dan became aware of a silent observer. He looked up to see a girl whose face, like the boy's, he recognized from the photographs that he had seen in Tara's bedroom at her apartment in Elizabeth Bay. Her brooding face was dark and sad.

'That's my sister Sarah. I'm Dennis, by the way.'

They skirted the swimming pool and climbed the stone steps to the terrace. The girl did not move.

'Sarah, this is Doctor Marshall.'

'Hello.' Dan tried to make his greeting warm and easy.

'He's a friend of Tara's,' Dennis went on. Sarah looked at him with some suspicion, but he could see she was softening.

Some instinct told him to say, 'I'm no friend of Greg Marsden, Sarah. I just want to find Tara at the moment.'

She stared at him hard then clearly decided that he could be trusted. 'Won't you come in?' she said.

Indoors the sitting room was deliciously cool and welcoming. Dan's glance took in the luxurious, elegant decor, and was caught by a photograph on a side table.

'That's our mother', said Dennis, following his eyes. 'She's supposed to be dead, but I –'

'Will you shut up!' Sarah's face was contorted with pain. 'Stop it, Dennis! You promised you wouldn't keep going on about it.'

'Dennis –' Dan did not try to keep the urgency out of his voice '– Tara and Greg, where are they?'

'They're at Eden.'

'Eden?'

'Our country home. It's up in the Northern Territory.'

Dan's heart plunged. God – that was miles away, twice as far north and away to the west as he had already flown south to Sydney. His mind raced away trying to think, to plan.

'Doctor Marshall –' Dennis was at his elbow, his upturned face bright with something like hope. 'I saw Tara before.'

'Before?'

'Before she came here for the weekend with Greg.'

'She spent the weekend here with Greg?' A violent spasm of jealousy racked him.

'No, she went away after lunch. But I'd seen her before. At my school. She was there one day taking photos when we were playing football. I saw her right close to. She took a photo of me and I didn't know why. It stuck in my mind.'

In the background Sarah was looking scornful but listening intently.

'When she came here, I knew it was her. I asked her about it, but she denied it. But it wasn't just me. Kaiser knew her too. All day long – the more I was with her – I just had this feeling—'

The room was very still.

'What kind of feeling?' asked Dan, very low.

'That she was our mother!'

Dan saw the tears standing in the boy's bright eyes as Dennis dared to voice his hope against hope. Sarah turned impatiently as if it were all more than she could bear.

'Doctor Marshall, why was she at your clinic in Queensland? What was wrong with her?' Dan hesitated, very afraid of shocking them with premature revelations. But Dennis was ahead of him.

'You said you met her about a year ago.'

'That's right.'

'That was about the time that my mother was supposed to have had her . . . accident.' He paused and flushed up violently.

'I don't want to sound crazy—'

'You're not crazy, son.' The word slipped easily from his lips. Dennis's face was white, the strain around his mouth pitiful in a young child.

'*Is Tara Welles our mother?*'

'Yes.'

Dennis crumpled to a chair and began to cry. Sarah stood rigid, as if in a catatonic state, staring straight ahead of her like an automaton. Then with a cry of pain she burst into tears and threw herself into Dan's arms sobbing convulsively.

'Hey, hey,' he soothed her, stroking her hair. 'It's OK now, it's OK, she's *alive*, remember?' All Sarah's pent-up guilt and grief were released in one dam-burst of emotion. Quietly Dan sat it out, encouraging them by his acceptance to express their conflicting feelings of relief and joy. Only when the tears subsided and they both grew calm did he raise again the subject uppermost in his mind.

'What's the quickest way I can get to Eden, to Tara?'

Sarah considered. 'There's no phone.'

'Eden's completely isolated,' Dennis volunteered.

'How about a plane?'

'The station's got its own airstrip. You can land a light plane.'

Dan was thinking frantically. Flight from Sydney to Darwin, get a charter or air taxi from there . . . He stood up to go.

'Doctor Marshall.' Sarah was completely collected now, and in one of those sudden transitions of adolescence he saw the woman, not the girl any longer. 'Doctor Marshall, we're coming with you.'

'Oh yes please – *please*,' Dennis begged.

Dan looked from one to another. Two pairs of Tara's eyes gazed steadily back at him. He was done for.

'OK.' He smiled. 'Yeah. Come on then.'

'Yeah. Yeah. OK. Thanks for phoning. And – good luck!'

Joanna Randall thoughtfully replaced the receiver. Perched opposite her on the arm of her office sofa, Jason raised his sandy eyebrows.

'The doughty doctor?' he asked satirically.

'Yeah. Apparently Tara's up on some remote station in the outback – place called Eden – with Greg Marsden.'

Jason seemed to have been expecting something like this. His tone was light. 'Well, we won't ask what they're doing out there, will we, mother?'

'I dunno.' Joanna was still recovering from Dan's visit and still had not decided how much of his story, which she had confided to Jason at the first opportunity, she was going to believe. 'If even half what he told me is true . . .'

Jason laughed. 'There you go again – I've told you you

shouldn't go upsetting yourself with fevered speculation at your time of life. I am about to give you a breakthrough in your thinking for which all generations shall call me blessed and you in particular.'

Joanna was not in the mood for this. 'Get to the point, Jason.'

'Sure. It goes like this. *It doesn't matter.*'

'*What* doesn't matter?'

'At the end of the day – or even right now, in the shit where you and I find ourselves, mother – it doesn't matter if Tara is or is not Stephanie Harper.'

'Jason, have you gone crazy?' Joanna was getting angry.

'Listen awhile. Give ear to your favourite camera-clicker. Oh, sure, it matters on some mystical, metaphysical, platonic plane of eternal truth who she is. And right now it matters that if she is in danger, the good doctor is flying off like the cavalry to the rescue – or alternatively, to make himself a right flaming gooseberry and about as popular as the snake in the Garden of Eden, by bursting in on an outback honeymoon. But to you, Joanna, and me, Jason, it doesn't matter a toss.'

'I still don't get it!'

'Because we've lost. You and I. Whoever she is, which-ever of the gallant cavaliers she finishes up with, she won't be modelling again.' Joanna stared at him. This had not occurred to her. 'And me? Well, whoever she chooses, it won't be little Jason. I was on the scene before either of these two stupid mutts and nix, nothing, zilch, zero. Wherever she keeps her love-button, I couldn't push it.' He smiled ruefully. 'So place your bets, mother dear. Which is it to be? Who will win the hand of the lovely lady? On my right, superspunk Marsden, the vagabond cock, the celebrated ripper of knickers from Brisbane to Perth – in the blue corner the challenger Doctor Dan, silent but deadly, the thinking woman's fancy. Who's your money on?' He fell silent.

Joanna was working hard to absorb what Jason said. All her instincts told her that it was true. Besides, she had rarely known Jason to be wrong. He was both sharp and intuitive and had often steered her in the right direction. She looked at him carefully.

'How would you feel about that either way?'

He shrugged. 'I've been making it my business in recent months not to feel too much *any* way – and I'm just beginning to have the odd tiny success. Can't win 'em all, as who knows better than you, me old darling. We shall live, me and my ego.' He turned to her with one of his dazzling smiles. 'And we shall get all the better all the quicker when our old mother finds us another lovely leggy clothes horse for the autumn range.'

'I suppose you're right,' said Joanna slowly.

'I'm always right!' cried Jason, mock-insulted. 'Don't argue with me! Get your head shots out, mother, let's dig into your drawers and find the next face of the future. Or of the next few seasons, anyway. What's the watchword of this business? Repeat after me—'

'Gotta stay ahead,' murmured Joanna, mechanically.

'Atta girl.' He reached over and gave her an affectionate pat. 'And don't you worry about me. With three hundred thousand more girls than boys in Sydney, and most of the men well-adjusted gays, I'm sure to find a girl soon who's not only willing but *grateful*!'

Dawn broke clear over Eden putting the stars to flight from a pure and cloudless sky. The gates of heaven opened to reveal a translucent bowl which seemed to hold no memory of last night's hideous turmoil. The thick livid clouds, torn to rags by the fury of the storm, the alternating streaks of electric fire and drenching water, were gone without trace. The world was clean and gleaming as if newly made, every plant and leaf glistening in the first rays of the morning light. Only the rainbow shimmering in multicoloured splendour as the sun leaped up the sky arched over all as an echo of the last night's events.

Across the plain the laughing kookaburra continued with his ringing call, reminding the sky people to heed the signal of the morning star, and heap more wood upon the great fire that warms the earth, to bring it quickly to its full daylight strength. Emerging from the dark warmth of the stables Chris greeted the light-hearted herald of the morning with a respectful bow, but made no sound to him. He knew that if any offended the kookaburra, or tried to copy his infectious, joyful sound, the bird would no longer rouse the great spirit fire-makers, and impenetrable blackness would enshroud the world again, as it was before the All-Father gave the first light.

Looking up, Chris saw the perfect arch of the rainbow strong and clear across the mother-of-pearl sky. He paused to let his ancestor spirits whisper its meaning to him. Julunggul, the Rainbow Serpent, the ancestral creator had travelled across the sky in the night, blessing the place beneath with his power and might. As Chris watched, the rainbow turned pale and faded, then shimmering and glowing it grew in strength and glistened brighter than before. Then Chris could read its second meaning and the darker significance that it now held. Long ago, when the world was very young and before the warring tribes had learned to live at peace with one another, an enraged hunter threw a boulder to kill one who loved him. He threw it so hard that it flew up into the sky, where it split to reveal all the flashing colours of a huge opal, weeping at the crime which had been done and making the world's first rainbow. To this day a rainbow gives a sign to those who can read such things that somewhere an act of cruelty goes unavenged, and the tears of the opal are falling again in sorrow. But the Rainbow Serpent had been here, in whom all living creatures begin and end, his presence spelling both life and death and the blood tides which ebb and flow for every human being. Silently Chris received the message of the skies and set his soul to prepare for the coming events foreshadowed to him.

As the first fingers of the dawn light found their way into Max's bedroom, Tara was instantly awake. Gliding silently out of the great oak bed she left the man still asleep in it without a backward glance and returned to her own room next door. There she dressed quickly in shirt and jodhpurs and, as soundlessly as she had come, made her way to the kitchen clutching a small bottle that she retrieved from the depths of her makeup case. Opening a cupboard she took Katie's secret bottle of cooking sherry and carefully poured the contents of the small bottle into it. She re-stoppered the sherry bottle, shook it thoroughly, then re-opened it to smell the contents. As she had hoped, the thick sweet consistency of the pungent cheap sherry obliterated any trace of the sedative she had added to it. At last she had found a use for the hitherto unopened sedative that Dan had given her on Orpheus Island. She knew that Katie would be pegging away at her private drink supply from mid-morning at the latest. So when the action she had planned reached its climax, as it must, then Katie would be deeply under, out of harm's way.

Throwing the bottle into the bin, Tara took the largest of the trays in the kitchen and moved across to the sitting room where bottles of whisky, sherry, brandy and port stood on the sideboard. Taking pains not to make a sound clinking the bottles, Tara loaded them all onto a tray and carefully carried it, struggling a little under the weight, back through the kitchen to an outside storeroom, where she placed the tray as it was on the floor, and locking the door, pocketed the key. No one would gain entrance there, she thought with satisfaction – and when Jilly awoke and reached out her hand for the crutch on which she was now limping through her days, it would be gone.

Finally she found a pad and pencil and wrote a note.

As it's such a beautiful morning I've taken King and gone out for a ride to Devil's Rock. Don't wake the sleeping beauties. Back for dinner tonight. See you.

Taking her riding gloves and crop she left the house by the back way and went round to the servant's quarters. There she pushed the note under Katie's door and crossed to the stables. She was not surprised to see Chris waiting patiently for her in King's box, the horse's saddle and bridle ready on the floor outside. Together they groomed and tacked up, and with Tara leading the way and Chris following behind with King, they left the stable. Katie had slept well after her long ride of the day before, and did not really wake when she heard the horse's hooves clattering across the yard on the way out. Must be Effie off for an early morning gallop, she thought – it was a sound she had heard every morning of her life when Stephanie still lived at Eden. No need to get up yet. She lay and listened to the sound of the hooves fading away with deep contentment, and then snuggled down again for as much more shut-eye as she could get before she had to wake up for good.

As always the first conscious thought that came to Greg Marsden in the morning was of himself. You've cracked it, boy, his ego purred like a fat cat, you did it. Revelling in self-delight he ran over the events of the last night, lazily replaying the highlights of his own performance and Tara's. Unhurriedly he called up the memory of her body, her breasts with their proud showy nipples, her white thighs set off by the dark triangle of springy little curls above. Mentally he turned her over and took her from behind and instantly his cock, always something of a problem in the mornings, began to throb insistently for attention or release. He loved sex in the morning, almost better than any other time of the day. Arrogantly he stretched out a hand to pull Tara in to him. And this time, he thought, I'll teach her the words to go with the play.

As soon as his reaching arm encountered a cold space where her warm body should have been, Greg knew he had been cheated. Why should she – how dare she – leave him like this? He knew instantly that she was not in the shower, had not slipped off to prepare a morning surprise, would not presently slip back into the room in her adorable negligée struggling with a tray loaded with orange juice, steaming coffee, croissants and champagne to celebrate their last evening's love rites. A darkness spread through him and he leaped from the bed, coming alive like a great tiger on the day of a kill.

Outside, the sun was high in the sky. Sam, engaged in the task of cutting down a dead tree, was feeling concerned about Katie. As he lopped off the branches from up above she was insisting on pulling them out of the way, then sawing them into logs. It was gruelling work in the midday heat, and Sam came from a race which taught the honouring of the ancients as a sacred duty. Repeatedly he tried in his gentle way to stop her.

'Just leave it to me, Sam,' she told him, breathless with exertion. ' 'Course I can do it. Too old and stringy to have a heart attack . . . and there's too much work to . . . be done . . . will you just let me be, y'bothersome pest?'

Katie in fact as the morning wore on had become a prey to anxiety that she could not relieve in any other way than by some violent physical exertion. Her early pleasure at hearing Tara ride out had received a setback when she read the note. Whyever did Effie want to take herself off to Devil's Rock? There and back, it was a day's ride into the dead heart of the outback. It was the kind of trip normally never made alone. And though Stephanie had always known the way in the old days, had known every path and every track made by the tiniest creature on four legs for miles around, could she still find her way so unerringly after such a long absence? If she or the horse foundered out there, not even her bones would ever be found.

It also dawned on Katie that in the excitement and fatigue of last night, she hadn't told Tara about the conversation she had overheard between Greg and Jilly. She had been so overcome with joy when Tara had as good as owned up to being Effie and had taken her into her confidence, that she had not thought to share with her the revelations she had been an unwitting party to, when passing down the hall she had heard the two voices raised in recrimination and insult. 'Y'stupid old buzzard,' she berated herself, almost weeping with annoyance. But what

371

could she do? Nothing but wait until Effie returned and spill the beans then. For now, it was a question of getting through the hours of the day till nightfall – and making sure that she stuck with Sam while Greg was around. She had not forgotten his face as he came into the kitchen when she was trying to raise Pine Creek on the radio – nor the fact that he had put the radio out of action so they were cut off from the outside world. Trust me, Effie had said. Well, she was sure Effie had some plan. She'll settle your hash, she informed an imaginary Greg in her mind – and y'd have to get up early in the morning to catch Katie Basklain, y'bugger . . .

'Katie!' Greg's voice breaking harshly into her thoughts made Katie afraid in spite of her brave thoughts. 'Where are you? God sakes, I've been looking everywhere for you.'

Even in the hot sun of noon he was white with suppressed feeling, and Katie did not want to meet the blackness in his eyes.

'Where's Miss Welles? Come on, where is she?'

'She went out before breakfast. She told me not to wake you.'

'Where's she gone?'

'She's ridden out to Devil's Rock.'

'Devil's Rock?' His voice was shaking with anger. 'How in Christ's name did she know about Devil's Rock?'

'I . . . I told her,' Katie improvised in a flash of inspiration.

'That was bloody stupid! It's three or four hours just to get there. She could get lost. She could –' His mind recoiled from the fear. He turned on Katie. 'If anything – *anything* – happens to her . . .' He left the threat hanging in the air, ripe with menace. Then he turned and hastened back up through the grounds.

Katie suddenly felt very old and very ill. Sam, gazing with compassion on the little woman below, saw her waver as if she were about to fall. Quickly he clambered down from the tree and took her under the arm to steady her.

Leaning with gratitude on his sinewy arm, she turned her small, shrivelled face up to his.

'Would y'give me a hand up to the house, Sam? I feel real crook.'

Slowly they made their way back into the house, and Sam saw her into the kitchen and sat her down. Out of the intense heat Katie felt a little better. But she did not think she should leave her recovery to nature alone.

'I need a little reviver,' she told Sam, 'just for my nerves. Y'see that cupboard over there? If y'could pass me the bottle in it, and a glass . . .?' And not for the first time that morning, Katie helped herself to a thumping dose of her private remedy.

Chapter Twenty-three

'Chris! Where are you, blast you! Chris!'

Almost beside himself Greg tore up through the grounds of Eden towards the stable block, yelling for Chris to come and help him saddle up one of the horses. He could not bear the idea that Tara had slipped away from him again, and every nerve in his predator's body was tuned up for the hunt. He had to track her down.

'Chris!'

He reached the stables and burst in, but the Aboriginal was nowhere to be found. Cursing obscenely Greg sorted out the fastest of the horses, found the saddle and bridle and tacked it up, frantic with haste. Then he led the horse outside and vaulted into the saddle.

To his supreme annoyance he suddenly spotted Chris ambling across the yard with his usual serene impassivity.

'CHRISTOPHER! Come here!'

Changing direction the Aboriginal walked up without haste till he stood at Greg's stirrup.

'D'you know where Tara went? Which direction?'

Chris shrugged.

'Well, she can't be that far ahead, can she? Which horse did she ask you to get ready for her?'

Without answering Chris fixed his large luminous eyes on Greg.

'Y'don't mean – no, c'mon!' Greg's face changed. Leaping off the horse he threw the reins at Chris and raced back into the stables. At the end of the long block, something he had not noticed in his haste, the door to King's loose box stood empty and the big stallion was gone. Roaring, Greg turned and charged back out into the sunlight of the yard.

Chris was still standing where Greg had left him, holding

the horse's reins loosely in one hand. Swinging his heavy riding crop in a murderous fury Greg made straight for him.

'You bloody idiot! No one rides King!'

As he got near, he raised the whip to slash Chris across the face and body. But Chris's hand shot out and arrested his arm in its downward flight, holding him there, uncowed and fearless. His hand felt like a steel claw on Greg's arm. With a howl of rage Greg shook off Chris's hand, grabbed the reins and mounted the horse. Leaving Chris standing there he clapped his heels to the horse's flanks and rode straight ahead. Leaping out of the yard over the retaining fence to avoid wasting time on the gate, and veering right around the large outbuilding which served as a hangar for Eden's light plane, he raced down the side of the house towards the long drive and the desert wastes beyond.

Suddenly he saw Jilly running from the direction of the house to cut him off.

'I want to talk to you,' she shouted truculently. 'I've been looking for you everywhere.'

Blindly she ran forward as if to throw herself at the moving horse. Cursing, he swerved and reined in.

'What the fucking hell do you want, you lousy bitch?'

'I saw you last night!' Her still badly bruised face was lit with a twisted kind of triumph. He wanted to pound it to a pulp. 'You didn't know that, did you? Never thought to draw the curtains in the throes of passion – never thought anyone might be taking a night-time stroll along the verandah! Well, I saw it all. I watched you making love to her.'

'You're sick, Jilly,' he said, with a calmness he did not feel.

'Sick, am I? Well, *you'll* be sick.' She was working herself into a frenzy. 'You'll be sick when I screw you! I'm going to the police. I just don't care any more. You ought to have the death penalty – I'd love to see you hang, watch you fry. I want to see you suffer like you've made me suffer, burn in hell, OK? And I'm going to make sure they put you away for the rest of your life, and *you'll never see her again!*'

Never see Tara again . . . A blackness rose up in Greg and in a voice not his own he heard himself screaming, 'Get out of here!' At the sudden killing madness in his eyes, Jilly turned and fled. Like a huntsman hard on the trail of a fox he pursued her blindly. She tore down the side of the hangar with the terrifying thunder of the hooves in her ears until she managed to slip down a passage between two buildings too narrow for the horse to enter, and reach the safety of the enclosed yard. But as she paused for breath, to her terror horse and rider came flying over the fence into the yard, the huge shadow like a monstrous centaur darkening the sun. Screaming, Jilly ran for cover, her lungs dry and bursting, her ears filled with the pounding of the great ironclad hooves.

Greg was emitting a high wail, his nostrils already filling with the smell of her blood. Like a hound coursing a hare he hunted her this way and that, till shrieking, sobbing, she could go no more. In her mind she saw herself going down under the flailing horseshoes, felt the heavy iron slice through the thin fabric of her dress, through flesh, through bone and sinew, slashing, crushing. She fell, and screaming with the joy of the kill, Greg rode her down.

To Greg, she was no longer Jilly. He had stopped thinking of her as a human being since her ill-advised threat had woken the darkness in his soul. He did not even hate her with a pure human hatred. She had simply become a worm to him, or vermin to be exterminated, something that was coming between him and his hunt for Tara. Setting the horse's head straight for her, and driving it ruthlessly forward with all the power of his legs, he rode for the crumpled body in the dust and the wide reaches of the outback beyond.

Three strides away . . . two . . . and at the moment when the cruel hooves should have bitten into the soft and defenceless body in their path, Greg's conscious mind recalled something that every rider knows – a horse will never willingly tread on a human being if it can do anything to avoid it. As he felt the horse bunch and gather its forces beneath him, Greg knew what it was going to do, and knew of no way to stop it. At the last possible second the great creature brought its hocks beneath it and sprang like a cat over Jilly, clearing her inert form by several feet. Then bounding away, it leaped the fence and was off for its life, happy to put the blood hunt behind it. Greg too let her go, for in his mind was now only one thought, and that was Tara. Setting a course for Devil's Rock he struck out as fast as he could go.

Crouching forward in the saddle, rhythmically spurring the horse to its ultimate effort, Greg's figure became smaller and smaller and vanished from sight. From the door of the barn Chris watched him unblinking until the moving form had diminished to a scuffle of red dust heading out across the plain. Then he stepped back. Inside the barn, silent and immobile, stood Tara and King. The hours of patient waiting had paid off. Greg was decoyed away on a wild goose chase into nowhere and she was free to begin on her plan here at Eden.

'Thanks, Chris,' she said, handing him the reins of the horse. She stroked King's smooth massy neck as he towered above her, and he lowered his head to have his ears caressed.

'Sorry we didn't get out today, boy,' she whispered. 'Maybe tomorrow.' He snorted, and lifting his front leg struck the ground imperiously with his hoof. 'There'll be other times for us, my darling,' she told him. 'Hang on. Just hang on.' Softly he blew on her face with his warm breath sweet with hay.

'OK, Chris.' She was reluctant to terminate this peaceful moment, but had to tear herself away. 'Could you take King back to his box now?' She watched as Chris, a slight figure scarcely higher than the horse's great sleek shoulders, gently pushed him under the chin as the signal to lead off. Together they set off through the door of the barn across the yard.

377

'Hetra akamarei, alidgea guy pichi, get up, come quickly now.' At Chris's murmur, King picked up his feet and they vanished swiftly into the shelter of the stable block.

Looking out, Tara could no longer see even the puff-ball of dust moving across the plain. From the barn she crossed the yard in the opposite direction from Chris, made for the house and entered the kitchen the back way. Just inside the door stood Sam, on guard. Sitting at the table, Katie was pouring out the final drop of her sherry and holding forth to Sam as she had been for the last half hour.

'Steadies m'nerves, see – tha's the only reason I take it. 'S medicinal. M'doctor told me t'take it once when I'd had a bad fall, horse'd thrown me and I'd got a bit of a kicking. An' it worked. But I can't say –' Katie swilled some of the sweet viscous liquid experimentally round her mouth '– I can't say as I like the taste of it, not really.'

She took another swig to prove her point. ' 'S just when y'bad, when things are bad – 's something to getya through . . .'

From the doorway Tara watched her with a welling love and pity.

'Y'can't be soft out here, Sam, y'know that 's well 's anybody . . . work's gotta get done . . .'

Katie was slurring her words and her eyes were beginning to go. 'Need another rabbit for the pot, gotta get one, 'assa way it is . . . I c'd shoot anything I c'd see . . .'

She waved her arms boastfully, then began to droop over the table.

'Could you give me a hand, Sam?' Tara moved forward and coming up behind Katie she took her weight, leaning her backwards and supporting her under the arms. 'If you could get her feet—'

Together they lifted the wiry little frame and swung her off the chair where she had been sitting.

'What y'doing?' Katie protested dopily. She was going under fast, Tara could see. Her head was rolling on her shoulders and she needed to lie down. Between them Tara and Sam carried her like a child from the kitchen and across to her own room. True to form Katie was arguing and protesting all the way.

'Y'can put me down, Sam, I'm telling yer, I c'n walk by meself . . . willya do's I say . . . let go my feet . . .'

Sam smiled gravely at Tara across the birdlike form between them. They reached Katie's room and laid her gently on her bed. Tara loosened her belt, and Sam drew a light coverlet over her.

'Sleep now, Katie,' Tara whispered, stooping to kiss her dry, weatherbeaten face. 'It's all going to be OK, I promise you. When you wake up, it'll all be over. Sweet dreams!'

Quietly Tara closed the door behind them as they left Katie already away in a heavy doze.

'She'll be all right now. Would you come with me, Sam? There's something I'd like you to do.'

Back in the house, Tara scribbled a few lines on a piece of paper, folded it and gave it to Sam.

'Sam, this is very important. I want you to take the landrover and drive straight to Darwin. Don't stop for anything till you get there, anything, OK?' His large luminous eyes fixed upon her, he nodded. 'When you get to Darwin, give this note to the chief, Jim Gully, at the police station. Nobody else. You must give it to Jim. Jim Gully.' She paused. She had no fear that Sam would misunderstand or fail her. She just did not want to leave anything to chance. 'I'm counting on you, Sam. You mustn't let anybody or anything stop you doing this.'

He gave her a smile of assent, and was gone. As he left, Chris materialized through the open door of the kitchen. Tara felt the sense of calm that he carried within him, and was soothed.

'Oh, Chris – it's all starting to happen . . . will it be OK?'

He made no answer. She looked at him steadily. 'You're with me, aren't you? I shall need your help tonight. When . . .' she could hardly bring herself now to say the name, 'when he returns . . .'

She could see in his eyes that Chris knew, that he had

always known, that he knew too how everything would end. But that was knowledge that he could not impart, for it was his alone. Sighing, she turned to her task with a new determination.

Huddled in the narrow passageway between two of the outbuildings where she had crawled as soon as Greg jumped over her, Jilly shuddered and shuddered with terror. Eventually her frame could bear it no longer and she was violently sick, retching and vomiting till she was bringing up nothing but bitter bile. When the spasms finally left her, she leaned against the wall behind her, racked and exhausted. She was no stranger to Greg's violence, she had often been driven by some answering impulse within herself to awaken it in him and call it forth, even though she would become its target. As their relationship had deteriorated, fighting, biting, hurting had become more and more a feature of it, and had led to some of their intensest love-making even as their hate was also gathering in intensity.

But this was different. For the first time she knew that Greg had felt no urge to find his climax in taking her body, but would only have been satisfied with taking her life.

'I don't want to die!' she moaned aloud. She knew she had to save herself before Greg got back. The only thing that had preserved her now was his obsession with finding Tara. He simply had not wanted to waste his time turning aside to tread on a worm. But he would crush her life out with no compunction if she fell in his way again.

Painfully she hauled herself up. Her knee and leg were damaged where she had fallen and she could not walk properly. She had grazed her elbows and face where she had struck the iron-hard ground, and trickles of blood mingled with the rust-red earth on her face. Traces of vomit clung to the front of her dress and mingled with the taste of terror in her mouth. Got to get out, she told herself, got to get away. Limping badly, she dragged herself through the yard and into the house. In her bedroom she grabbed her overnight bag, which after last night's collapse she had not even unpacked, and made as much speed as she could back outside again. She would take the landrover and drive to Pine Creek. Once away from here she would never risk getting near Greg Marsden again. Oh, if only she had felt like that at the very beginning, when first she smelled that danger and darkness inside him! If only . . .

She reached the vehicle hangar almost spent from the effort of dragging herself to and fro in the intense afternoon heat. Inside the open-fronted building Eden's light plane rested quietly, ready as always for takeoff. But there was no sign of the landrover. Jilly screamed aloud with frustration.

'God, no!' She was trapped here, cut off from hope of escape.

But not done for. Her fighting spirit asserted itself and her mind worked feverishly to find a new plan. There must be somebody who could help her. Katie! She would find Katie, or Chris or Sam, and stick with them. Safety in numbers. Greg could not strike at her in the protection of the company of others. As she tracked back to the house again Jilly had the sense of being like a trapped rat, trailing frantically round a maze from which all the exits were blocked.

'Katie,' she howled, 'Katie! Come and help me, will you?'

There was no answer. No sound at all disturbed the silence of the sleeping house, which had an eerie feeling of being empty and yet guarded by watchful, unfriendly presences.

'Katie! KATIE!'

With mounting hysteria Jilly searched the ground floor of Eden from end to end. There was no sign of Katie. As she came to the sitting room, she dwelt with relief on the prospect of a drink – two or three, quickly, she'd bring the bottle along with her, it would help the pain in her leg. To her horror as she entered, every single bottle was gone. She could not believe it. She pulled open the doors of the sideboard, and that was empty too. God, how was she going to survive? She headed down the passageway back to the kitchen. There she tore open all the cupboard doors hunting down Katie's secret supply. All that remained was an empty bottle. In a fury Jilly sent it smashing to the ground.

Still she would not cry. She would not give in. She was not beaten. She limped back through the house and out through the front door. Systematically she worked her way round the swimming pool, through the rose garden and down to the kitchen garden where Katie might be working. From there she struggled round the side of the house to the buildings and combed those for any signs of human life. At last she tried Katie's room, not previously having imagined that the valiant old woman would be in bed at this time of day. The sight of the frail figure lying there asleep did not move her at all. But when her frantic efforts to rouse Katie from her unnaturally heavy slumber failed, then Jilly knew real despair. There was nothing for it but to return to the house for the final time. As she made her way almost crawling now across the yard, she did not see the figure watching her painful progress from the window of an upstairs room, coldly assessing her deterioration and judging the moment to strike.

There was one thread of hope. Like all who have lived for any time in the outback, Jilly knew how to operate a bush radio. In the kitchen she set herself down before the receiver and began to try to work it. She knew at once that the instrument was dead. Forcing herself to stay calm, she checked it carefully. When she saw the component missing, it was the end of the line. Her fragile control snapped. She began to whimper like a wounded animal, making cries of pain and fear in her throat.

'Where is everybody?' she keened. 'There must be somebody there . . . help me . . . please . . . anybody? . . .'

Suddenly she heard a voice like a reproach from the depths of her buried conscience.

'Was it worth it, Jilly?'

Wide-eyed, she started up and looked around. There was no one there.

'Who is it? Who's there?' she screamed.

'Oh God – don't tell me you've forgotten my voice already?' It was a caressing whisper, wrapping tendrils of fear about Jilly's heart. She knew the voice – but surely . . .?

'You must remember me – haven't we been best friends since we were little girls?'

'No!'

'How could you do it, Jilly?'

'NO!'

'I loved you, always. You were half my life.'

'*Stephanie!*'

Blindly Jilly tried to escape the accusing voice. She hobbled out of the kitchen and struck off up the passage-way. But the voice pursued her, was all around her.

'We were like sisters, you and I. I trusted you . . .'

'Stop it! Stop it!'

Jilly covered her ears with her hands, but the voice went on.

'Was Greg really worth it? Worth all that pain?'

'Oh God!'

'All that guilt . . .!'

'Please . . . please . . .'

Sobbing, Jilly dragged herself into the living room. The accusing voice was there before her.

'Poor Jilly. He betrayed both of us, didn't he?' There was a disembodied sigh. 'First me . . . And now you.'

Jilly could no longer stand. The pain in her leg was like fire, the anguish of her soul agony. She collapsed into a chair and huddled there, beaten.

'Listen, listen,' she pleaded with her unseen tormentor. 'Please listen to me?'

From Stephanie's bedroom nearby, Tara could hear every word. Lightly she nursed the microphone of the stereo through which she had been able to pour her voice into every corner of the house, and prepared herself to listen. Jilly's frantic babble was plainly audible.

'It . . . it was all Greg's idea. I never knew that night –
that night on the river – he meant to kill you, I never knew
that . . .'

Yes, that was credible. Jilly was not a murderess.

'After . . . afterwards, he made me lie to the police – I
was so afraid—'

'Afraid of losing him.'

'Yeah, losing him. I loved him so much.'

'From the very first.' Again the gentle prompting, and
willingly Jilly impaled herself upon the spear of her
accuser.

'From the second I saw him – at the wedding!'

'And he—'

'At the tennis party. He looked at me. He touched me.
And I wanted him.'

'All to yourself.'

'Yeah!' Jilly was shouting, truculent again. 'Yeah, all to
myself. You'd had everything, Steph – money, position –
and now you had the only man in the world I wanted. It
wasn't fair! I always meant to get back at you if I could for
my father, always!' The hate and spite of the put-upon
child were clearly audible. Suddenly her tone changed
again.

'But I didn't want it to happen, Steph. I didn't mean for
it to be . . . so horrible . . . I kept seeing the look on your
face—'

Now the child in Jilly had completely taken over.

'Oh Steph, I'm so scared. So scared. Please help me . . .
please. I don't know what to do . . . I don't want to die . . .
help . . . help . . . *help*! . . .'

On and on rode Greg through the heat of the day, out
across the burning desert, making for Devil's Rock. After
hours of hard riding it was all he could do still to sit the
untiring horse. He had not ridden since his honeymoon
here so many months before, and his body was trembling
with the strain. Worse, though, was the torture of the mind
he had been suffering since the first moment of reaching

out for Tara and finding her gone – this had now come to obsess him to the exclusion of all else. Why had she left him so? Why was she eluding him yet again? What more could a woman want than the love he had given her last night? And above all, the mystery which he divined at the heart of things, and which intuitively he knew threatened him at the very roots of his being – what was her game? Why was she playing with him?

Greg's sense of being at the mercy of something he could not understand struck at the very base of his security, his identity, even. He had always been the one who played, pleased himself, and rejected when it suited him. He had never bothered to imagine how it must feel to be the discarded plaything of a callous lover. Now he was in mortal dread that this was happening to him. Last night had confirmed what he already had felt growing in him, a love for Tara deeper than he had ever felt for any woman before. With Greg it was not a higher feeling, but the quintessence of his monstrous selfishness, so that he felt his love of Tara, entitled him to have her, in the same way that he was entitled to food, warmth and shelter. Nobody – not even she herself – was going to take her away from him.

Madly he spurred on, driving the horse as relentlessly as he was driving himself through these unaccustomed toils of reasoning. Yet even as Devil's Rock appeared on the skyline miles ahead in the distance, he knew that somehow he had missed her. How, he could not imagine. There was no cover, nowhere else for her to be for miles around, nothing but the rolling endless red wastes studded with tiny patches of scrub, against which any horse and rider would stand out clearly visible. If she were anywhere, she could only be around the back of the rock, sheltering there in the shade from the relentless sun.

With a sick sense of failure he drew near to the huge sandstone rock, its upper slopes eroded by wind and weather into the ugly demonic forms which gave it its name. This was the home of Kulpunya, the powerful Spirit

Dingo and creator of evil who even on the hottest day made the air about the rock chill with his presence. In spite of himself Greg shivered as he came within its purple shadow, and avoided the glance of the devil forms above as they leaned down over him. The horse too grew uneasy in this malignant place and drooped beneath him, its ears laid back and eyes rolling from side to side in fear.

Slowly now, since the race to find Tara was over and he had lost, Greg circled the base of the massive monolith, its walls changing colour before him according to its position in relation to the rays of the afternoon sun, from blood red, through flaming orange and curry yellow to brown and black. She was not there. There was one last possibility, but Greg had no hope in his heart as he turned into the cave which lay at the hollow heart of the rock. This had been an ancient sacred place of the Aboriginals, for whom the dreamtime heroes were still sleeping within the folds of sandstone. Here they had daubed the walls with blood in the first initiation rituals, and over the generations the elders had renewed the stains by opening their own veins in sacrifice. Greg stood within this womb of blood and felt as though his heart were bursting – for Tara was not there and the cavern was empty.

'Tara! Tara! TARA!' The screams of a desperate man issued from the heart of the rock to rend the eerie stillness of the air, and continued as the lathered horse and beaten rider rode off through the dusk. And still he searched, lost and alone in the dwarfing landscape, while all the devils of the place laughed and chattered to each other and claimed him for one of their own.

Chapter Twenty-four

No one would deny that Darwin, the capital of the
Northern Territory, is a magnificent town. Devastated by
the fury of Cyclone Tracy in 1974, it has been rebuilt as a
wealthy and cosmopolitan city, and its visitors generally
find much to enjoy. But Dan Marshall, struggling to
contain his anxiety and his impatience, bitterly resented
having to be there at all.

No one would believe that air travel is the world's fastest
form of transport, he mused gloomily as he walked down
Smith Street with Sarah and Dennis. In the complicated
flight from Sydney to Eden, the logistics of the trip, the
number of passengers and the time of day they were
travelling, had all been against them. Add to that the
inevitable delays involved in flying, where the tiniest fault
on one aircraft will not only ground that one, but put all
the others out of their schedule too, and Dan had been
severely frustrated in his hopes of getting speedily to Tara's
side. Now, with evening drawing on, they had reached
Darwin only to discover that an unavoidable delay meant
that the little party would have a couple of hours to kill
before an onward flight would be possible. Rather than
just hang around the airport, Dan had taken the two
children into the city for a brief sight-seeing trip.

Certainly it was better to be on the move than stuck in
an airport lounge, he reflected. Smith Street stretched
before them, a wide, tree-lined avenue, its twinkling lights
already making an impact against the spectacular gold,
pink and bronze twilight thickening every second to
evening darkness. He glanced at the children. Sarah was
looking around her with animation, still wearing the
brightness that had come upon her as soon as he had
confirmed the good news of Tara's identity, despite the

rigours of long travelling. Dennis was similarly contented, his nose buried in a fact sheet he had picked up at the airport.

'Darwin, glittering metropolis of the Northern Territory,' he read stumblingly, 'is home to forty-five different nationalities. In recent years the city has overcome its historical isolation and the mineral wealth of the area has brought it prosperity and sophistication.'

'That means smart people like us,' said Dan lightly. He had not shared with the children his fears for Tara's safety. But it had repeatedly occurred to him that he might have given them the priceless gift of bringing back their mother from the dead, only to have to withdraw it again, if his worst suspicions were realized. This nagging dread he put to one side, as he had trained himself to do in his professional life. But his dark fears, however suppressed, stalked with him like baleful companions who would not be shaken off.

'It's a good place, this,' said Dennis enthusiastically. He read on. 'Darwin has dozens of attractions in its bars and restaurants, and its ultramodern beachfront Diamond Beach Casino. It is also the chief stepping-off spot for the Kakadu National Park. Join the alligator cruise to see salt and freshwater crocodiles in their natural habitat . . .' His voice trailed away uneasily.

'Come on, kids,' said Dan taking their hands and looking round for a taxi, 'let's think about getting back to the airport, shall we?'

They need not have hurried. When they checked in at Darwin in good time for their flight, they learned that once again the fragile chain had broken, this time by an engine failure, and they now had no hope of reaching Eden before the next morning.

Quite unknown to Dan, another of Darwin's visitors on that same day was also failing to appreciate the attractions of the city. Sam had made good time on the long overland journey from Eden, the landrover beating a steady path through the outback for hour after hour without faltering. Once in Darwin he had had no trouble in locating the police station. But his request to see the police chief, Jim Gully, had met a simple but unexpected obstacle.

'The chief? He ain't here. He's off duty.' The desk sergeant was not unsympathetic, just bored and nearing the end of his own shift. 'Won't be back on again till ten o'clock tonight.' He saw the anxiety glimmering in the eyes of the man opposite him, and tried to be constructive. 'Look, can anyone else help you?'

Grasping the note given him by Tara, Sam weighed it up. Then her words came back to him with all their original emphasis. 'You must give it to Jim. No one else.' He knew there had to be a reason. He could not go back on his undertaking. Carefully putting the note back in his shirt pocket and buttoning it up for safety, he shook his head and settled himself down to wait.

Out in the red heartland of the country, way beyond the city, the livid sun set in a blood-red sunset over Eden, seeming to express in its dying all the primitive passions of the universe. The last rays of light threw their final appeal vertically up against the purpling sky and were relentlessly extinguished by the rich velvet blackness. The moist fragrant air was still, but not at peace. A sense of brooding watchfulness hung over Eden as all its creatures waited in anticipation of the coming night's events.

From the high hill behind the house, in the heart of the grove of gum trees, Chris saw the sun down the sky. Only when the last faint glimmer of gold had been lost to the inky dark did he move from his position. Crouching in the clearing at the centre of the grove he began to raise fire. As he did so he chanted in honour of Goodah the wirinun, the clever-man of the ancients who made the dangerous journey to the faraway mountain where the tribes had seen a strange light in darkness. There he bravely captured a piece of the sky-fire when it came down as lightning, and hid it for ever after in dead wood where it still lies sleeping, so that earth people may wake it into flame whenever they wish. As the fire glowed, crackled and roared into life, Chris knew that the ancestor spirit had once again kept his promise with the world.

Feeding the tiny flakes of flame into a red-hearted glow, Chris stood before his fire and stripped off his clothes. Ritually he divested himself of the trappings of the white man's civilization, then free and proud as his spirit ancestors he prepared his body for the sacred dance. With thick white clay he drew a bar across his forehead and down his nose, scarring his cheeks with a broad white slash of the same paste. Using both hands he created a wide band from his navel to the top of his chest, circling each of his breasts in turn. Then one by one he made heavy bars of white on his upper arms, wrists, thighs and knees. With each anointing he shook off the constraints of the new and alien way of living, rejoining a ritual of life so ancient that even Time himself, the dim old magician of all eternity, could not have recalled its origins. Finally he bound up his unruly black curls in a head-dress bright with splinters of dangling bone and the feathers of the white cockatoo. Last of all he donned the bor, his girdle of manhood, and was ready for what he had to do.

At the centre of the grove stood one huge and immemorial ghost gum, towering up eerily in the flickering light of the fire, pallid as a visitor from the land of the dead. At its foot lay the sacred circle of the dancing ground. Taking up his position Chris began his dance, and the words of his chant echoed out through the still night sky.

'Kulpernatoma, Baiame, kungour gar wunalaminju, windana wungiana – I speak and call upon you, All-Father, hear me and let us dance, which way are we going and where are you leading us? Show us the way forward through this wilderness, keep our feet to the path that we must tread, and let us not fail or falter through our weakness or our fear. Tonight, if ever, great spirit, be with the woman in her terrible task, hail down the curse of your anger and destroy this double devil, this man who threatens your creation with his rage to kill.

'Yowi panelgoramata, nurrumbunguttia gunmarl, pornurumi ngende paiale, gwandalan thoomi yant taldumande – Yowi, your messenger of the nearness of doom whispers now to me, and the ancient spirits of darkness, storms and evil hover over this place of death. I feel the blackness of that great cold ahead – I feel its coming. You will choose who you take tonight to set among the stars – but All-Father, bring peace at last to this house!'

Like an avenging demon Greg sped through the night, pitilessly spurring on the flagging horse to renew its failing efforts. Where was Tara? And now another mystery, where was Eden? Normally the whole of the great house was illuminated at night, lit from outside as well as within, so that it stood out on the plain like a beacon for miles around, and could always be relied upon to bring the benighted traveller safe home. But ahead was all blackness. No lights were to be seen, not even a faint glimmer. He did not need it as a landmark to find his way. The horse knew all the paths around and could take him back unaided by its own homing instinct. But what had happened at Eden in his absence to extinguish all its lights?

Coming up Greg found that all he could see was the dim shape of the homestead, a darker shape against the darkness of the night sky. He was sick with an unknown fear. Trembling, he dismounted in the yard and his overstrained muscles almost gave beneath his weight. Willing his body to obey him he hastened into the house. There was no one in the kitchen, and when he switched the light on, it did not work. Cursing, he fumbled for the flashlight kept there for emergencies, and set out to search the house.

In the sitting room nothing moved. But his overstrained senses caught the instant impression of a human presence and he swept the flashlight round in a wide arc. Trapped in the beam he saw the face of Jilly, her eyes glazed and dilated like a rabbit before a snake. She was huddled motionless in her chair, her legs drawn up under her chin and her whole posture speaking of terror and desolation.

'Where's Tara?' he demanded roughly.

Jilly did not speak.

'I said where's Tara?' He leaped for her across the room, raising his heavy riding crop to strike.

'Don't hurt me!' The sudden violent action broke into Jilly's trance of terror. Almost gibbering with fear she raised her forearm to protect her head. 'Greg! Greg! Don't.'

'What have you told her?' All Greg's thought was on Tara, where she could be and how he could hope to save himself with her.

'Nothing, nothing, I swear. I haven't seen her. She's been out all day, all day long. But Greg—' pitifully Jilly reached out a clutching hand and plucked at his jacket. 'Greg, listen—'

'What?' He could hardly hear her, she seemed miles away in the recesses of his throbbing head.

'Stephanie was here!'

'Stephanie!'

'I heard her so clearly. It's her ghost, it's here in this house!'

Stephanie? What could she mean? How –? 'You're drunk,' he said, but without conviction.

In Jilly's eyes flamed a spurt of the old fire. 'You know damn well I'm not, you lousy bastard! You hid it all! I haven't had a drop all day.'

Heedlessly Greg swept all this from his mind.

'Where's Tara. WHERE IS SHE?'

'I don't know – and I don't care.'

'Keep away from her or I'll kill you,' he threatened furiously. In reply, she caught at his arm again.

'Greg . . . I . . . I really did hear Stephanie's voice. She was here. I'm not making it up, I'm not. It's all over. We can't keep killing her a secret any more.'

Despite his overriding obsession with Tara, a pulse of self-preservation beat a warning within Greg's mind. He looked at Jilly properly for the first time, pinned down in the beam of the flashlight like a butterfly on a card. His mind became very clear.

'Who knows you're here? Apart from the pilot?'

'No one!'

'Did you tell anyone else where you were coming before you left?'

'No! Not a soul, I swear it, Greg!' Jilly was gabbling in fear of the threat that she could feel emanating from the blackness beyond the circle of light she was trapped in. But as soon as the words were out she knew she had made a fatal mistake. The beam of light circled away as Greg placed it on the ground. Then a black shape only, like a messenger of death, he came for her.

'NO! NO!' All Jilly's hope of life was expressed in the scream that burst from her. 'DON'T KILL ME, GREG!'

Suddenly all the lights of the house sprang to life. As if frozen in a snapshot of impending death she saw Greg before her, poised for the kill, his hands reaching out for her throat. Paralysed, unnerved, they held the grotesque tableau for what seemed like minutes. Then with a hideous growl Greg threw off the spell of the sudden shock and lunged forward again. Jilly saw him coming almost in slow motion, like movement under water. She could not move her legs but, too terrorized even to scream, she surrendered to her death, recognizing it in those blind black eyes coming for her.

Then as suddenly as they had burst into life, the lights snapped off again, plunging the room into a deeper, more impenetrable blackness. With the impact of the second unexpected shock Jilly's muscles gave way, her limbs crumpled under her and she fell soundlessly to the floor. The soft fall seemed to bring her out of her trance and without conscious thought she rolled her body away towards the wall. As Greg leaped forward to take her by the throat, his fingers closed on emptiness and his arms swept the air in vain.

Too clever a hunter to charge blindly after an unseen

quarry, Greg paused and scented the air. All his being was working now like that of a predatory animal – he was relying on the instincts which had never let him down. Feeling, sniffing the atmosphere which, holding them both in the same thick embrace, would soon yield up the smell of her fear to him, he tracked her presence in the darkness. Jilly was too afraid to move, afraid to draw his attention by the slightest sound – but she had also exhausted her single impulse of self-preservation in that one reflex action. Now she huddled with the resignation of all lost and pitiful creatures in her inadequate hide beneath a table, feeling already the grip of the cruel claws and the teeth sinking into her neck.

'Jilly!' Greg's voice came caressingly through the darkness, low and sweet. 'Jilly, I'm not going to harm you. You don't need to hide from me.' He paused, listening, every nerve strained to catch even a breath. 'Come on, baby.' He was seductive now, charming as of old. 'You know it's you I love – I killed Stephanie to get rid of her so that I could be with you. And I've loved you, haven't I, Jilly? I want you now, I want to make love to you, come to Greg, baby, come on . . .'

Jilly felt his voice like his hands on her body. Even now, coming to her like the angel of death, he still had the power to arouse her body to his will. Quivering, nerveless, Jilly felt her nipples smart and begin to ache, the sweet moisture springing between her legs, and knew that the smell of sex would now be joining the smell of her terror in the airless room. That above all she knew he could not miss. With the high whine of a doomed animal she abandoned herself to him.

But the second before Greg's sharp ears, tuned up now to a peak of intensity, had caught a sound outside the room. All his strained faculties turned towards the French windows leading to the verandah. What was it? A long, slow, crawling sound, heavy, inexorable, like a soul in torment dragging its chain of guilt – Greg's hair rose on his body and he drew blood from his tongue as he bit on it

394

to keep from screaming aloud. His eyes were riveted to the darkness outside the room. It was coming . . . it was coming . . .

A dim light glowed like a coal in the blackness. Dancing, wavering, it came slowly along the verandah towards the French windows. Greg's muscles seemed to turn to steel, he could not move and screamed inwardly under the constraint. On, on danced the tiny flame. At last it paused, waiting outside the window for what seemed like uncounted ages to those inside. From her low vantage point on the floor, Jilly could now see what it was that had stopped Greg in his tracks, and in one surge of hysteria her terror leaped to match his. Neither could move or breathe. The silence in the room weighed on them like the heavy stillness of a tomb.

Slowly the French windows began to buckle, to admit the outside world. Inch by inch they opened to the verandah and the presence out there. Mesmerized, Greg and Jilly could see the little dancing light, and behind it a dark shape ill-defined against the darkness of the night beyond. Motionless, silent, threatening, it dominated their ugly, petty disaster with the magnitude of its accusation. Yet still driven only for herself, Jilly was the first to break the silence.

'Help me! Help me,' she howled, hurling herself from her refuge. 'He's trying to kill me, he wants me dead, please, please—' Sobbing she crawled forward towards the light.

As she watched the light swept upward, broadened and brightened. The figure lifted the lamp, pushing back the windows of the dark lantern to shine out on the scene below. The beam caught Greg immobile, snarling, murderous as a tiger at bay. On the floor Jilly grovelled, looked up, and fell back like a woman kicked in the stomach.

'Steph! Steph! STEPH!' Whimpering, foolish, like a demented child she turned again in her self-defeating bid for human contact to the one who would have struck her dead. 'Greg – I told you – Greg – it's her ghost—'

The voice that cut across her was strong, hard, very much alive.

'Don't delude yourself, Jilly. I assure you I'm no ghost.' It was Stephanie – and yet not Stephanie's shy, tentative utterance. The beam of the lantern swung and captured Greg in its narrow focus.

'What's the matter, Greg? Nothing to say?' The harsh sound echoed tauntingly in his ears. 'Oh, you really thought you'd done it, didn't you. Cracked it, as you would say. Stephanie's cash, the Harper inheritance –' the voice snapped with disdain '– and your whore there. What more could a tennis bum want?'

In a sweeping gesture the figure swung the lantern again and to their horrified eyes showed—

'Yes, Stephanie! I'm alive, Greg. I've come back!'

'How . . . how . . .' The sounds Greg made were not so much questions as the noises of a beast fallen into a pit of spikes.

'You didn't kill me! Nor did that crocodile. I was dragged from that swamp – half dead. But you meant to destroy me. You were Stephanie Harper's murderer as surely as if I had died there.'

The hoarse voice rose, and sank again. 'An old hermit saved me. There are some good men in the world – men of kindness, men of love – not like you! He didn't care that I was grotesque, hideous, my face torn, my body deformed. He loved life! And he saved me!'

Horrified, Jilly threw a glance at Greg. He still stood as he was when the first dread sound caught his attention – savage, desperate, the animal in him poised to spring for the kill, the man's mind struggling with the enormity of a reality too huge to comprehend.

Mercilessly the arraignment continued. 'You wanted me dead. He gave me life! He gave me more – he gave the savings of his whole life to give me a new start. I spent six months being turned into somebody else. It was hard. It was painful. What do you know about pain, Greg. PAIN?'

Nothing stirred.

'It hurt so much. But my God it was worth it!' The woman's voice rose to an ecstatic chant. 'I suffered and I overcame, I thought and I fought, I struggled with myself – and with the ghost of you – and I ate myself up with hatred and rage. Dear God, how I hated you!'

Greg's soul shook in the waves of her passion. Jilly's thin question came like a silly bleat.

'Steph, why – why—?'

'Ha! Why? Oh, it would have been so easy to go to the police, tell them the whole story, who I was, and have you two charged – with my murder!' Cowering, Jilly heard a sigh, followed by a burst of rage.

'But I . . . I wanted to DESTROY YOU! . . . the way you destroyed me!'

The air was thick with hate. Blackly the woman's voice went on.

'I loved you, Greg – no woman more. How could you do it?' Again the lantern swung. 'And you, Jilly. Our friendship – all that we had shared – did that mean nothing to you? Nothing at all?' She heaved a sigh so deep it sounded as if her heart would break. 'The two people I loved most in all the world . . . Oh, I haven't enjoyed watching you both suffer, clawing and tearing at one another. But I have to thank you – *for helping me.*'

Unexpectedly she faltered, then resumed more strongly than before.

'Yes, *helping* me! The magnificent irony of the whole thing is that you two – my greatest enemies – have actually been responsible for my discovering who and what I really am!'

She flashed the lantern round to illuminate her face, Stephanie's face, in full for the first time.

'And for that – at least – I thank you!'

In a violent gesture she reached up and tore the heavy long-haired wig from her head. Throwing it to the floor she angrily fluffed up the short springing curls beneath.

'TARA!'

'Tara! Tara!' she mocked. 'Yes, Tara, the woman you

wanted when she didn't want you – the woman you despised when she was Stephanie, who only needed your true love to release her to her enjoyment of love and beauty.'

'You – you're a fake!' he stuttered. 'A fraud!'

'NO!' she blazed. They quailed before her fury. 'Take that back! Tara Welles is a part of me, not a fiction – that side of me that was always there but never had a chance of life with you. What did you ever do to help me? *Nothing*!'

Her rage was terrible. He had no answer.

'And what can you reproach me with? What have you got to charge against me, compared with what I have against you?' She laughed aloud in bitterness. 'I am a woman who made love to her own husband!'

Her laugh rang in his ears like the cachinnations of demons.

'Tara! Tara!'

'It's finished, Greg.' Her voice was suddenly tired, low. 'The police know everything. I sent a letter with Sam to Jim Gully at the Darwin station. They're on their way.'

The light wavered, dropped, as she let the lamp fall.

'The police will be here soon – any moment.' In the low light she looked full at him for the first time, piercing him with her great eyes full of pain. 'By morning you'll be where you belong, Greg – behind bars.'

Her shoulders drooped and she relaxed. It was over. Her body swayed with the fatigue. As she softened, Greg was released from the bondage which had held him fast. Snarling, raging, he sprang forward.

'Greg, no! NO!' Jilly leaned in to stop him, but her slight weight was no match for his. Brushing her aside, he leaped for Stephanie. He struck her body sideways, knocking the hurricane lantern to the floor. It shattered on the carpet and rolled towards the wall, bursting into flame and scattering a trail of fire as it went. Tongues of flames flickered and caught at the curtains, the carpet, the furniture. Greg was oblivious. He had the dark visitant cornered, cut off by his fury and the fire he had started.

398

She stood before him against the wall, regarding him with fearless eyes. Stephanie? Then where was Tara? His overcharged brain almost burst. Vaulting across the ring of fire where the oil from the lamp had ignited, he pinned her to the wall and took her face in the iron grip of one fist. Now, close up, he could see who she was.

'Stephanie!' he hissed, his face like a lizard's. 'Where's Tara? WHERE'S TARA? WHAT HAVE YOU DONE WITH HER?'

The truth came to him like a starburst in his darkness.

'You killed her!' he mouthed. 'You . . . you . . .'

Half-crazed, his reason gone, he struck her violently on the side of the head. Then his hands found her throat, the thumbs meeting in the hollow at the base of her neck, pumping, pumping . . . Dimly she could hear Jilly's frantic screams of protest.

'Akkai!'

Eyes closed and almost unconscious, Tara felt Greg's muscular frame plucked from her. Choking and gasping she opened her eyes to see Greg grappling with a weird and ghostly figure, naked, daubed, empowered with a strange magic as he pressed Greg hard, pushing him back through the ring of fire into the centre of the room. Together the two men struggled to and fro, the outcome on a knife-edge. The slight body of the Aboriginal was no match for a much bigger, heavier adversary. As Greg prevailed, he drove Chris back until he had him trapped against the gun cabinet where Max had displayed the pride of Eden's armoury. With a violent heave, Greg hurled the slender Chris bodily against the glass doors, then dashed him to the floor, grabbing a rifle through the broken glass as Chris picked himself up. Chris looked at him unafraid. The double demon was armed now. With one last cry he made his peace with the whole of the spirit world.

'Allinger yerra ballama, Baiame, wuna wunaia wuni ingu . . . the sun is setting, All-Father, yet the soul will not die!'

His attacking leap and the retort of the rifle came together and the frail black body dropped like a stone to the ground. Chris lay there motionless, blood pumping from a great wound in his chest.

'No, Chris, no!' Tara made a dash for the still frame, raging, weeping, almost blinded by grief. Suddenly she came up short against Greg, blocking her way with a smoking rifle and a hideous pale killing glint in his eye.

'Stephanie?' he whispered seductively. 'Is it you?'

He stretched out a hand to grasp her. 'Come here, there's a good girl? Y'wanna say hello? Give me a kiss?'

Tara took off like a greyhound from a trap, out of the room before Greg had homed in on where she was. Left alone as Greg gave chase, Jilly raced to the sofa, grabbed a cushion in each hand, and single-handed set herself to fight the fire that had now got a firm purchase on the thick hangings and dried-out woodwork of the old house. Recklessly she ran backward and forward, ripping down the flaming curtains, beating out the greedy flames as they devoured whatever lay in their path. But without water, as she killed fire, she produced smoke. Eventually all the flames were out in the sitting room, but the air was thick with the killing fumes of its aftermath. Possessed by her task, Jilly had no thought for herself until too late. I have to get out of here . . . get out of here, she told herself urgently. But even as she made for the doorway, a fresh gust of smoke overtook her, and breathing it in in her panic, she succumbed to the choking vapour and fell to the floor.

Chapter Twenty-five

Greg moved silently across the grass, a hunter stalking his prey. Hardly human now, he had reverted to the primitive, become the wild, feral thing that had always been part of him and was now released to take its vengeance.

A predator pure and simple, he stalked his quarry with his primeval instincts alert, going joyously with the thrill of the chase. He had no difficulty following the scent – he could smell woman in every breath he breathed.

As he glided forward his feet struck an alien object in the grass. He bent down and his fingers encountered one of Tara's shoes, where she had cast it off in the heat of flight. He picked it up and stuffed it in his pocket like a trophy, smiling a strange slow smile. Then he set off again, tracking her round the far side of the house, where he was swallowed up by the shadows and slid among them silently.

From an angle of the outbuildings within the passageway which had earlier sheltered Jilly, Tara watched and waited for his approach. Her neck still throbbing from Greg's attack, her heart pounding agonizingly and seeming to reverberate through the silence of the night like a town clock, she tried to still herself as she strained every nerve for the stealthy footfall of her killer. She had one small advantage. Before leaving the sitting room, Greg had repossessed himself of the flashlight to assist his search, and she had been able to see the cautious gleam from afar as he turned it on to investigate some corner or other where he thought she might be hiding. If she could have that forewarning, she might just manage to escape him until help arrived from Darwin.

Where was Jim Gully. He should without doubt have been here by now. Tara could not allow herself to believe that Sam had failed her. She knew that like Chris he was faithful unto death. But even the faithful can be overcome, she thought, her heart twisting with grief as she thought of Chris and the way Greg had shot him down. If the police didn't come, she was alone here with her mortal enemy, and Jilly, who was hardly to be counted as anything less. Moreover she would have the safety of Katie to concern herself with, too, as soon as the effects of the sedative wore off. Surely – surely – even Greg would scruple to harm an old lady . . . yet even as she thought of it she knew he would no more pity her than the wolf would spare the lamb.

Methodically Greg worked his way round the outbuildings, checking into every possible hiding place. Already strained, his taut nerves reacted to each sound, each rustle in the darkness. He was careful not to use the flashlight when he did not need it, conscious that his prey, crouched out there in the thick night, could take from it the warning of his approach. He did not use it at all to see by, and coming sharply round a corner into an unlit walkway he collided head on with the hanging carcasses of the animals he had shot the day before in his mad killing spree. Recoiling violently he struck them away from him in disgust, and put them from his mind. But when he went on, his face was smeared in blood like a hunter indeed, its smell was in his nostrils, and blood lust had mounted to his brain like an intoxication.

As he came silently round a corner, Greg caught the sound of the faintest scuffle away to his right. Lightning sharp, he fired from the hip, but there was no reaction. Just an animal of some sort, he decided – a human body would have made a heavy noise as it hit the ground. Working his way round he came to the generator shed and instantly grasped the mystery of Eden's total darkness. A cursory investigation showed that the generator had been switched off. Grinning with triumph, Greg flooded the blackness outside with light.

Still crouched between the outbuildings, Tara sunk her nails into the palms of her hands to stop herself from crying out with despair. She had been hoping against hope that in the compulsion of the chase Greg would not think of the simple device by which she had plunged them all in darkness. Now she and all the homestead were flooded in light as bright as day. Frantically she turned and scurried away before Greg could come out of the generator hut and see her.

But she was not as instinctively quick as hunted creatures need to be. From the corner of his eye Greg caught the whisk of movement and was after her like a retriever. Hearing his feet pounding down the hard dry earth of the passage way she tore out on the garden side and hitting the grass, threw herself to the ground and rolled into the bushes of the nearest rose bed. The well-kept roses, heavier in flower than in leaf, could hardly afford her much cover. But their tall stems gave her a mottled shade and provided a welcome camouflage. Gritting her teeth against the tearing of their thorns, she forced her way through to the inside of the thickly clustering rose bushes, hearing all the time behind her the prowling approach of Greg's feet on the gravel.

'Stephanie!'

Tara's blood ran cold.

'Stephanie!' It was like the howl of an animal at bay. He was close behind her now. She buried her face in the soil, trying to blend into the surface of the earth.

'Where are you, you lousy bitch?' His tone was cajoling, almost reasonable. 'I'm going to have to kill you now – aren't I?' She willed herself not to move. Again he called and again, still in the same blandishing tone so at variance with his words.

'Don't be stupid now, Steph – I know you're there, and you know I'll get you. Why are you hiding from me? You've been a fucking cow to me, Stephanie, and you'll have to pay for it. You're making me very angry . . . very angry . . .'

As she lay there Tara knew that she was hearing the voice of a madman. Terror gripped her like a vice and her guts turned to water. For the first time her brave heart failed her. She could move neither forward nor back and her cover was too flimsy to stand up to a thorough search. Greg paused in the path between the rose beds to call again. Now his voice was belligerent, challenging.

'I never loved Tara – you should know that. I didn't trust her from the start. It was always you, Steph, always you.' He broke off, and she knew that he was scenting each quarter of the garden like a pointer to locate his quarry.

'Remember something, Steph?' He sounded soft, now, and affectionate. 'Remember how we made love? How I used to make you feel? Remember how good it was? I loved you like no other man ever did before. Don't hide from me . . . don't hide from your husband, Steph . . . Come out here, darling. I want you to walk out to me. I've got something for you . . .'

In the dead silence she heard him cock the rifle, the small deadly sound carrying through the still night air. She was terrified that he had her in his sights, but although screaming inside she fought back the temptation to raise her head to look, knowing it could be just an old hunter's trick to get her to show her face and the whites of her dilated eyes.

Suddenly Greg's patience snapped.

'You will walk out to me!' he raged. 'You can't get away. And I'll have you! No mistakes this time!' He turned and ran back to the outbuildings, his feet receding on the gravel. Still fearing a trick, she raised her head with supreme caution to watch him go, but as soon as he vanished between the buildings she could no longer delay in taking advantage of this reprieve. She was on her feet in a second, tearing her way out of the close-packed rose bushes and deeper into the garden away from the floodlit house where at least she could keep on the move and have the cover of the night.

Still she could not understand what Greg's actions or motives were. What did he mean by 'you will walk out to me'? Suddenly she heard his voice again shouting her

404

name. Behind his yelling as it came nearer she could hear a familiar, well-loved rhythmical sound . . . hooves! He was leading a horse – not—?

'D'you hear me, Stephanie? I've got you now,' he crowed. 'My advantage, I think. I've got your stinking horse! I'm going to count to ten, and if you don't show yourself, I'm going to shoot the bastard! Are you listening, my darling? I'm going to shoot the fucking thing!' His maniacal laughter rang around the house as he came into her view, leading King by his head-collar down the side of the house and into the floodlit area at the front. There he took up a central position and began to count.

'ONE . . . TWO . . . THREE . . .'

From the dark depths of the garden beyond the rose bushes Tara tasted the bitterness of defeat. He had not been the cleverer, but was far crueller and more cunning than she could ever be. She could hear King making a high nervous whinnying sound. He had never been handled by anyone except her and Chris, and would hate this forced night-time outing. As she stood up to surrender herself, she could see how uneasy King was, jumping tensely on the spot, the shiny black skin rippling on his neck and flanks.

'FOUR . . . FIVE . . . SIX . . . SEVEN . . .'

She got up and walked towards him out of the darkness, with no hope left in her heart. She had lost. When he sighted her, the smile on Greg's face said that he knew he had won. He stopped counting and smiled horribly as she came up through the rose garden and up the steps by the side of the swimming pool.

'Come here,' he called softly, 'I want you right here.'

Her legs were like leaden stumps. She could hardly drag herself towards him. He watched her like a great cat every step of the way until at last she stood before him, looking into his mad, pale eyes, alight with a terrible flame.

'That's a good girl,' he whispered. 'You should always do what your husband tells you, shouldn't you?'

She was near enough to smell his madness, to see right

405

into the well of darkness and emptiness at this soul's core. The stallion was shivering in the fierce grip of his fist. Yet somehow she was not afraid. For the first time since her accident she felt that she saw him as he truly was, a nothingness, a force for everything evil, but in himself hollow. Reading the contempt in her eyes he was stung to action.

'Gonna kill you, Steph. I mean it. Y'ready to die? Made y'will? Well, this is from your ever-loving husband and grieving widower!'

With sadistic slowness he raised the rifle and pointed it straight at her face, snickering obscenely.

'And y'won't even see it coming!' He cocked the rifle and aimed.

But even as he pulled the trigger, the rifle was spinning out of his hand. The sharp noise of the cocking-piece had been too much for the highly-strung stallion, who reared up on his hocks, knocking the rifle out of Greg's grasp with his flying front legs. As the gun discharged, the shot went wild, losing itself harmlessly somewhere out in the garden. But the retort caused King to rear again, and he struck Greg to the ground. With the fighting instincts of a stallion he plunged once more to trample his enemy into the earth.

'Steph! Call him off! Get him off!' Greg's thin scream could only inflame the horse, Tara knew. She did not hesitate.

'KING!'

Poised in the air, the great beast still heard the voice of command. Effortlessly he pivoted a fraction in the air and dropped his hooves neatly to the side of the man sprawled helpless on the ground. Then in a last gesture of defiance, he reared again, let out an ear-piercing victory squeal, and cantered away round the side of the house.

Almost drained of feeling Tara watched Greg struggle to his knees and slowly pull himself up, dazed with the fall. He staggered to his feet, staring at her, breathing heavily.

'Why did you have to come back, Steph? Why did you

take Tara away from me?' He smiled a crooked smile, pleading with her. 'I've got to kill you, y'got to see that.'

'Greg, please.' Tara fought to stay calm, to overcome the immense weariness inside her. 'Listen to me. The police are on their way. They'll be here any minute. There's nowhere to run, nowhere to hide. Whoever you killed now, it couldn't save you. They know all about you, and wherever you tried to escape they'd track you down. It's over Greg. It's all over.'

She could see from the blind light in his eyes that he could neither hear her nor see her properly – her words were not registering.

'Hafta finish the game,' he said almost to himself. With a sickening spurt of renewed fear she saw him lurch towards her, grabbing for her, and turned to flee. But she had not got more than a few paces before he struck her heavily from behind, knocking her bodily into the swimming pool beside them. As she went down, Tara seemed to be having a nightmare replay of her terrible fall into the Alligator River. The same heavy body was bearing her down, the same vicious grip pulling her under. Down . . . down . . . down . . . Panic overwhelmed her and her lungs were bursting. Water filled her mouth as she opened it in a silent scream.

Suddenly by some miracle the swimming at Orpheus Island came into her head, the lessons with Lizzie and the happy hours of snorkelling with Dan. 'I-can-swim!' she howled silently to herself. Wriggling herself round, she turned on her back in the water and aimed a kick at her attacker. Even though it was slowed down by the water she felt it connect in the softness of the stomach. The clawing hand released its imprisoning clutch on her arm, and she shot from his grasp powering forward with a frantic crawl. Three strokes away from the side . . . two . . . but just as she touched the side and reached out for safety, a vicious grip took her from behind and pulled her back in. Grabbing her head and body he pushed her violently under the water, and she fought back, managing to twist in his arms until she faced him. But as she did so, a terrifying change came over his face, and to her horror the murderous hate in his eyes suddenly gave way to a light of love.

'Tara!' he cried, 'Tara! Oh my darling, I thought I'd lost you!'

He pinned her to the edge of the swimming pool and kissed her hungrily, a desperate, slavering kiss. Almost fainting with the horror of it, she turned her head aside, trying to escape the wet slobbering mouth, the crazy eyes staring at her, mad now with a different passion. But she could not free herself from the weight of his body as he held her rammed against the side of the pool. Now his hands were on her breasts, feeling for her nipples, fumbling with the buttons of her blouse.

'You love me, Tara, don't you, love me darling, I'll give you the kind of loving you want, fuck me good, baby . . .'

The crack of the gun and Greg's scream came almost simultaneously. The impact of the bullet in his back hurled him hard against her, slamming the breath from her body.

'Aaaaaarch!'

Howling with pain, he arched backwards, his arms flailing in the air and plunged beneath the surface of the water, thrashing like a fish on a hook. Tara watched in horrified fascination as the limpid pool began to boil hideously with blood. She raised her eyes and saw a few yards away Jilly standing holding a still smoking rifle. Expressionless, unmoving, she did not seem to know what she had done.

At the opposite side of the pool Greg resurfaced, and struck out for the side, swimming one-armed, the other trailing behind him. As he reached the side and struggled out, Tara saw that one shoulder was useless, streaming with blood from a huge wound at the back. He staggered up, but reeled with pain and shock. Bent almost double he set off on a loping run towards the back of the house.

Clambering out of the pool herself, stiff and bruised, Tara fought for breath, desperately trying to fill her straining lungs with air again. When she was breathing a little more easily, she looked around to see Jilly still standing exactly as she had been when she fired the gun. Moving with difficulty Tara came up to her and gently removed the rifle from her grasp, throwing it in the water to make sure it could not be fired again that night. Then she sat Jilly down on the grass like a child.

'Wait there,' she told her. 'Don't go away, I'll come back for you.'

Then she set off at a painful run after Greg.

He was easy to track even in the dark by the heavy spoor of water and blood he had left in his staggering progress. The trail led round the side of the house to the outbuildings. As she rounded the corner after him, Tara knew in an instant where he was making for. Huge and gaunt ahead of her in the moonlight lay the hangar, within it Eden's plane always kept ready for emergencies. From where she stood she could hear the engine stutter and spring to life, the propellers begin to turn over. In slow motion, like events in a bad dream, she saw the light plane taxi out of the hangar and position itself at the start of the runway.

'NO!'

Impelled by emotions she could not name, Tara raced forward. She could see Greg through the glass of the cockpit, soaked, dazed, and bleeding heavily.

'GREG! GREG! You can't make it!'

The little plane lurched drunkenly out onto the runway, veering from side to side. Tara was running level with it now, begging, pleading above the noise of the engine with the man inside. Could he hear her? She did not know. But just as the plane gathered momentum, he turned his head and seemed to see her for the first and last time. A look of infinite reproach, of heart-tearing agony, passed over his face.

'Tara!' he murmured, and the plane swept on leaving her behind. Still she continued to chase it along the bumpy ground, choking in the dust that it threw up, hoping against hope that something would happen to prevent the takeoff which she knew that Greg could not handle. But helplessly she had to watch as the light craft gathered speed, careering along until at last its nose went up and it lifted unsteadily into the air.

'GREG! You don't have to die. GREG!'

Tara put all her soul into that last hail and farewell. The tiny plane flew up into the bright, star-filled sky. Soon it became as small as one of the stars itself, but the sound of its engine could still clearly be heard. Tara strained her ears to follow it. Then she heard the sound she had dreaded, the note of the engine faltering and changing to a high-pitched whine increasing in velocity as the plane, losing height, plunged to the earth. High up in the sky, Greg had lost his battle, for in losing Tara he had lost his will to live. From where she stood, she heard the dreadful smash as the plane crashed, saw the ball of fire leap up the sky as the plane caught alight. But she never heard the last dying cry of the doomed man as like Icarus he plunged mortally wounded to his doom—

'TARA!'

In his own mind, Chief Jim Gully never forgave himself for being off duty on that particular night – the only time someone had ever really needed rapid and high-powered police action and he had been unable to supply it. He had nothing to reproach himself with in the speed of his response once he had received Tara's message. He knew too that she had been right to insist that no one but he should deal with it, since her story would hardly have been believed by any of his juniors, who in any case would have needed his say-so to mount the rescue operation. Still, he would always regret that he and his men only arrived at Eden as dawn was breaking in time to mop up after the event. And above all, he would have liked to have had the grim satisfaction of arresting Greg Marsden, rather than the dreadful duty of dealing with his burned and twisted body.

But there was police work to be done nevertheless, though he never liked arresting a woman. Uneasily he watched as one of his junior officers brought Jilly from the house and placed her in the police car for transport to Darwin. Just before she got in Jilly turned and almost wonderingly surveyed the great homestead where her most innocent and her darkest hours had been spent. Last of all Jilly looked at Tara, standing beside Jim Gully. Their eyes met, but nothing passed between them. Jilly was still in the same strange trance-like state in which she had shot Greg with a rifle taken from the gun cabinet when she recovered consciousness in the sitting room. And for Tara – what was there to say?

'I still can't believe it,' Gully said heavily. 'When I got your note, I thought somebody was having me on. I'm sorry for the delay, strewth I am.'

'Not to worry, Jim,' said Tara softly. 'It's all . . . worked out . . . in the end.'

As she spoke, the police were gently bringing out on a stretcher Chris, weakened by his injury and loss of blood, but with the little flame of spirit still burning fiercely in the slight body. At his side walked Sam.

'Just a minute.' With a gesture Tara stopped the little procession and coming forward, she took Chris's hand. It was as cold as clay and there was no movement in it.

'He'll be all right, Miss,' the officer reassured her. Tara looked into Chris's eyes and received his own pledge that this was true. Bending down she kissed him tenderly on the forehead, and watched him carefully loaded into the police wagon.

'I'd best get back with them,' Gully said. 'But y'know where y'can find me if y'need me.'

'Bit late for that,' said Katie tartly, issuing from the front door to join in the farewells. 'Where were you when she needed you, Jim Gully?'

Gully knew quite well that Katie's own part in the emergency had been of a horizontal nature only, and was tempted to answer back. But his good nature got the better of him.

'Welcome back to Eden, Miss Harper,' he said simply, and was gone.

'Well, we shall be pretty quiet here now, shan't we?' grumbled Katie when the police cars had beaten their way off along the dirt road out of Eden. 'Y'won't know what to do with yourself after all the excitement.'

Tara smiled, for the first time in what seemed like days. 'Oh, I don't know,' she said. She turned towards the stables where King, easily recaptured after last night's escape, could be heard loudly expressing his displeasure at his present incarceration. 'I think my young man could use some gentle exercise after the excitements he's undergone. Sam, could you—?' But Sam was already on his way.

Quietly Tara rode through the stillness of the outback. At last, after all her struggle and suffering, her soul was at peace. She felt no grief, but an inner calm and sense of relief so deep that it was almost like a blessing. It was as if a terrible illness, a high fever, had left her – left her weakened, she knew, but having turned the corner towards recovery. Where Greg's unquiet soul was doomed to walk in torment she did not know, but his cold rage, his madness and despair had died with him and left her free. She knew now that she would grow strong and straight in the power of her own personality and never again be stunted by the dark shadow of his.

Yet there is no victory without loss, she reflected sadly. The sacrifice of Dan's love had been a cruelly heavy price to have to pay, and one she had not anticipated when she had begun her plan. Could there have been a way to bring her schemes to fruition and yet retain his love, a way that in her frantic desperation she simply could not find? Well, it was too late now. How cruel of fate to bring her such a man and his true faith at a point where she had to throw it away. Heavily she rode on, oblivious to the beauty around her, mourning for Dan every step of the way.

At last she forced herself to put her melancholy thoughts aside and begin to look ahead to the future. Here lay her hope of happiness now – with her children. At last she could enjoy the longed-for luxury of the reunion with Sarah and Dennis. At the mere memory of their names her heart melted and she felt like weeping tears of joy. How and where should this event, so long hoped for and dreamed of, take place? Contentedly she made and re-made mental arrangements, then scrapped them again – it had to be right and she would see that it was perfect in the end.

One thing was clear. Nothing was now preventing her from resuming the reins of her life as Stephanie Harper, and the moment had come to do so. She would be going back all the wiser for what she had learned in her time away, and all the stronger for what she had undergone. For these reasons she knew, she would never go back to being the old Stephanie, anxious, insecure and put-upon. And never again would she, could she become the prey of any man, but would stand on her own feet, run her own life, depend on her own strength and skill to get her through. She would make it. She surveyed the future without doubts or fears. No more dwelling on the past, she thought resolutely – tomorrow belongs to me.

Slowly, slowly a distant sound penetrated her reverie. Startled, she caught the faint but distinctive hum of a light plane approaching. Whoever could it be? Not—? No, she had no right to hope even for one second that a man who had been so badly hurt, his love scorned and rejected, would still be able to forgive – let alone that his love had led him to the dogged feat of detection needed to track her down here. Surely it could not be the press? Although she had vaguely entertained the idea of what a sensational story this would be when it broke, she had not dreamed that the news vultures would be gathering all the way out here. With an angry frown she raced back to the homestead, the horse in a splendid burst of speed staying ahead of the approaching plane over this short distance. As she drew near she could see Sam come out to meet her. Well, he could take King, she decided, and she would greet the invaders with short shrift at the landing strip and send them packing.

From the air Dan could see the tiny figure scudding along ahead, but could not tell if the crouched urgent form was male or female, let alone who it was. His anxiety and impatience were like a physical pain now and he felt that he could hardly hold onto his sanity for much longer. When he saw and recognized her, unmistakably Tara and very much alive, standing by the runway as the plane came down, the relief was so great that momentarily he lost the control of his limbs, and reeled as he tried to stand up to open the cabin door. He knew that she would be beside herself with joy to see and hold her children again. But what of him? Could she now respond with an open heart to his loving demand for her love in return? He was frantic with alternating hope and despair, hardly hearing the excited cries of Dan and Sarah at his side.

Tara watched apprehensively as the plane taxied to a standstill and still no one opened the cabin door. Then as if in a dream she heard a shrill cry from within the plane.

'Mum!'

The door burst open and fighting each other to get out at the same time came Sarah and Dennis. I'm dreaming, dreaming, she thought in wild disbelief. Then galvanized by the joy of mother-love, she leaped forward and gathered them in her arms.

'Oh Mum, I knew you weren't dead—'

'It is you, Mum, isn't it?'

'My darlings – oh, my darlings.'

And they all clung together shedding the tears that always fall to grace the deepest and most joyful occasions.

Dan's heart turned over at this powerful scene of primitive emotion. I'm out of place here, he thought wearily, they don't need me. How could he push himself in between a mother and her children? He stood awkward and abandoned beside the plane, working out definitely and for all time the words of his final farewell. Just as long as you're alive, he would say. Now I know you're safe and everything's OK . . .

But he had reckoned without the woman in Tara. As he watched she raised a radiant face, wet with tears, from between the heads of her two children, and claimed him for her own. Come, she was bidding him with her eyes, come to me now. In a rush of ecstasy she had remembered, almost as if she were rediscovering a rich jewel she had lost, how much she loved this dark and gentle man. Loved him? More, much more than that. Only with Dan would she find the other half of her soul – the true friend who would go through life with her and be hers always in equal and mutual partnership. Now she could give herself to him with no barriers, no secrets, no inhibitions. Her arms ached to hold him, her body to tell him so.

'Oh Dan—'

It was almost a sob. Her tears were rising again under the stress of her feelings.

'Ssshhh, my darling, don't distress yourself – tell me later.' His own joy beginning to soar, Dan could only think of soothing and supporting his beloved. For in the simple look of adoration that Tara gave him from her shining, brimming eyes as she hugged her children to her heart, he knew that he had at last received the answer he had so longed to hear.

All Futura Books are available at your bookshop or
newsagent, or can be ordered from the following address:
Futura Books, Cash Sales Department,
P.O. Box 11, Falmouth, Cornwall.

Please send cheque or postal order (no currency), and
allow 55p for postage and packing for the first book
plus 22p for the second book and 14p for each additional
book ordered up to a maximum charge of £1.75 in U.K.

Customers in Eire and B.F.P.O. please allow 55p for
the first book, 22p for the second book plus 14p per
copy for the next 7 books, thereafter 8p per book.

Overseas customers please allow £1 for postage and
packing for the first book and 25p per copy for each
additional book.